FAMILY

KAREN KINGSBURY

WALKER LARGE PRINT
An imprint of Thomson Gale, a part of The Thomson Corporation

Detroit • New York • San Francisco • New Haven, Conn. • Waterville, Maine • London

LIBRARY OF CONGRESS CATALOGING-IN-PUBLICATION DATA

Kingsbury, Karen.
   Family / by Karen Kingsbury.
      p. cm. — (Firstborn series ; _4) (Thorndike Press large print Christian fiction)
   ISBN-13: 978-0-7862-9611-8 (hardcover : alk. paper)
   ISBN-10: 0-7862-9611-9 (hardcover : alk. paper)
   ISBN-13: 978-1-59415-188-0 (softcover : alk. paper)
   ISBN-10: 1-59415-188-1 (softcover : alk. paper)
   1. Adoptees — Identification — Fiction. 2. Trials — Fiction. 3. Los Angeles (Calif.) — Fiction. 4. Cancun (Mexico) — Fiction. 5. Domestic fiction. 6. Large type books. I. Title.
PS3561.I4873F37 2007
813'.54—dc22   2007012903

Published in 2007 by arrangement with Tyndale House Publishers, Inc.

Printed in the United States of America on permanent paper
10 9 8 7 6 5 4 3 2 1

Donald, my prince charming

In this season of life, with you working as full-time teacher here at home for our boys, I am maybe more proud of you than ever. I am amazed at the way you blend love and laughter, tenderness and tough standards to bring out the best in our boys. A second season of homeschooling? Wow! Don't for a minute think that your role in all this is somehow smaller. You have the greatest responsibility of all. Not only with our children but in praying for me as I write and speak and go about this crazy, fun job God has given me. I couldn't do it without you. Thanks for loving me, for being my best friend, and for finding "date moments" amidst even the most maniacal or mundane times. My favorite times are with you by my side. I love you always, forever.

Kelsey, my precious daughter
You are just newly seventeen, and somehow that sounds more serious than the other ages. As if we jumped four years over the past twelve months. Seventeen brings with it the screeching of brakes on a childhood that has gone along full speed until now. Seventeen? Seventeen years since I held you in the nursery, feeling a love I'd never felt before. Seventeen sounds like bunches of lasts all lined up ready to take the stage and college counselors making plans to take my little girl from home into a brand-new big world. Seventeen tells me it won't be much longer. Sometimes I find myself barely able to exhale. The ride is so fast at this point I can only try not to blink, so I won't miss a minute of it. Like the most beautiful springtime flower, I see you growing and unfolding, becoming interested in current events and formulating godly viewpoints that are yours alone. The same is true in dance, where you are simply breathtaking onstage. I believe in you, honey. Keep your eyes on Jesus and the path will be

easy to follow. Don't ever stop dancing. I love you.

Tyler, my beautiful song

Can it be that you are fourteen and helping me bring down the dishes from the top shelf? Just yesterday people would call and confuse you with Kelsey. Now they confuse you with your dad — in more ways than one. You are on the bridge, dear son, making the transition between Neverland and Tomorrowland and becoming a strong, godly young man in the process. Keep giving Jesus your very best, and always remember that you're in a battle. In today's world, Ty, you need His armor every day, every minute. Don't forget . . . when you're up there onstage, no matter how bright the lights, I'll be watching from the front row, cheering you on. I love you.

Sean, my wonder boy

Your sweet nature continues to be a bright light in our home. It seems a lifetime ago that we first brought you — our precious son — home from Haiti. It's been my great joy to watch you grow and develop this past year, learning more about reading and writing and, of course, animals. You're a walking encyclopedia of animal facts, and that, too, brings a smile to my face. Recently a cold passed through the family, and you handled it better than any of us. Smiling through your fever, eyes shining even when you felt your worst. Sometimes I try to imagine if everyone everywhere had your outlook — what a sunny place the world would be. Your hugs are something I look forward to, Sean. Keep close to Jesus. I love you.

Josh, my tender tough guy

You continue to excel at everything you do, but my favorite time is late at night when I poke my head into your room and see that — once again — your nose is buried in your Bible. You really get it, Josh. I loved hearing you talk about baptism the other day, how you feel ready to make that decision, that commitment to Jesus. At almost twelve, I can only say that every choice you make for Christ will take you closer to the plans He has for your life. That by being strong in the Lord, first and foremost, you'll be strong at everything else. Keep winning for Him, dear son. You make me so proud. I love you.

EJ, my chosen one

You amaze me, Emmanuel Jean! The other day you told me that you pray often, and I asked you what about. "I thank God a lot," you told me. "I thank Him for my health and my life and my home." Your normally dancing eyes grew serious. "And for letting me be adopted into the right family." I still feel the sting of tears when I imagine you praying that way. I'm glad God let you be adopted into the right family too. One of my secret pleasures is watching you and Daddy becoming so close. I'll glance over at the family room during a play-off basketball game on TV, and there you'll be, snuggled up close to him, his arm around your shoulders. As long as Daddy's your hero — you have nothing to worry about. You couldn't have a better role model. I know that Jesus is leading the way and that you are excited to learn the plans He has for you. But for you, this year will always stand out as a turning point. Congratulations, honey! I love you.

Austin, my miracle child

Can my little boy be nine years old? Even when you're twenty-nine you'll be my youngest, my baby. I guess that's how it is with the last child, but there's no denying what my eyes tell me. You're not little anymore. Even so, I love that — once in a while — you wake up and scurry down the hall to our room so you can sleep in the middle. Sound asleep I still see the blond-haired infant who lay in intensive care, barely breathing, awaiting emergency heart surgery. I'm grateful for your health, precious son, grateful God gave you back to us at the end of that long-ago day. Your heart remains the most amazing part of you, not only physically, miraculously, but because you have such kindness and compassion for people. One minute tough boy hunting frogs and snakes out back, pretending you're an Army Ranger, then getting teary-eyed when Horton the Elephant nearly loses his dust speck full of little Who people. Be safe, baby boy. I love you.

And to God Almighty, the Author of life,
who has — for now — blessed me with these.

ACKNOWLEDGMENTS

This book couldn't have come together without the help of many people. First, a special thanks to my friends at Tyndale, who have believed in this series and worked with me to get this fourth book to my readers sooner than any of us dreamed possible. Thank you!

Also thanks to my amazing agent, Rick Christian, president of Alive Communications. I am amazed more as every day passes at your sincere integrity, your brilliant talent, and your commitment to the Lord and to getting my Life-Changing Fiction out to readers all over the world. You are a strong man of God, Rick. You care for my career as if you were personally responsible for the souls God touches through these books. Thank you for looking out for my personal time — the hours I have with my husband and kids most of all. I couldn't do this without you.

As always, this book wouldn't be possible without the help of my husband and kids, who will eat just about anything when I'm on deadline and who understand and love me anyway. I thank God that I'm still able to spend more time with you than with my pretend people — as Austin calls them. Thanks for understanding the sometimes crazy life I lead and for always being my greatest support.

Thanks to my mother and assistant, Anne Kingsbury, for her great sensitivity and love for my readers. You are a reflection of my own heart, Mom, or maybe I'm a reflection of yours. Either way we are a great team, and I appreciate you more than you know. I'm grateful also for my dad, Ted Kingsbury, who is and always has been my greatest encourager. I remember when I was a little girl, Dad, and you would say, "One day, honey, everyone will read your books and know what a wonderful writer you are." Thank you for believing in me long before anyone else ever did. Thanks also to my sisters Tricia and Susan and Lynne, who help out with my business when the workload is too large to see around. I appreciate you!

Thanks to Katie Johnson, who runs a large part of my business life — everything from my accounting to my calendar. God brought you to me, Katie, and I'll be grateful as long as I'm writing for Him. Don't ever leave, okay? And to Olga Kalachik, whose hard work helping me prepare for events allows me to operate a significant part of my business from my home. The personal touch you both bring to my ministry is precious to me, priceless to me. . . . Thank you with all my heart.

And thanks to my friends and family who continue to surround me with love and prayer and support. I could list you by name, but you know who you are. Thank you for believing in me and for seeing who I really am. A true friend stands by through the changing seasons of life and cheers you on not for your successes but for staying true to what matters most. You are the ones who know me that way, and I'm grateful for every one of you.

Of course, the greatest thanks goes to God Almighty, the most wonderful author of all — the Author of life. The gift is Yours. I pray I might have the incredible opportunity and responsibility to use it for You all the days of my life.

CHAPTER ONE

Katy Hart couldn't find her way to daylight, couldn't draw herself from the strange deep sleep that held her in its grip.

She was holding Dayne Matthews' hand, lost in the feel of his skin against hers. But something wasn't right. Dayne felt more like a stranger than a friend, and even though the sun had set, the sand beneath them felt hot. Too hot. Dayne was looking at her, losing himself in her eyes, making her forget how strange it was to be sitting on a private beach in Los Angeles next to one of Hollywood's biggest heartthrobs, and he was saying, "I never planned on being a star."

The air grew colder, and snowflakes mixed in the wind. Snowflakes big enough to hold in her hands, with designs and intricacies that took her breath away. Dayne was saying it was time; they should get going, get her back to the hotel.

When they stood, the snow disappeared

and sand stretched out as far as they could see. Sand and a large clump of dense bushes, and suddenly there was a click. And another. Four more. Dozens at the same time. Cameras. Everywhere she looked there were cameras and lots of people. Thousands of people, all of them whispering, *This is the price for fame . . . the price for fame . . . the price for fame. . . .* And Dayne was leading her toward the bushes, closer . . . closer.

In a rush of motion a yellow-haired woman jumped from the clump of green and grabbed Katy from behind, holding her by the arms.

Katy screamed, loud and shrill, but before Dayne could do anything to help, the woman whipped out a knife. No, not a knife, a sword. A long, curved sword.

"Don't move or I'll kill you," the woman hissed at Katy. She pressed the blade hard against Katy's throat. Harder and harder still, until Katy couldn't swallow or yell for help or utter even the slightest whisper.

Dayne . . . she wanted to shout at him, but she couldn't. *Dayne, help me!* Katy's body trembled and stiffened.

And he was coming closer, closer. He didn't speak, but his expression said he wanted to help Katy, was desperate to help her.

If only Katy could catch her breath. But the blade pressed even tighter against her throat, tight enough that her windpipe was closing off. *Stay back, Dayne! She's going to kill me. . . . I can feel the knife on my throat.* The words built in her mind, her heart, but she couldn't speak them, couldn't squeeze them past the pressure of the shiny blade.

"Hussy!" the hissing voice spat at Katy's cheek. "You'll feel the knife more than that in a few minutes."

Dayne was whispering something, and suddenly a yellow Honda Civic came tearing down the sand straight for them, its engine revving louder, louder as it came.

Behind her, Katy could feel the woman's anger turn to rage, sense her shaking with hatred.

Dayne reached out his hand, but something sliced down the length of her arm and blood began to drip down her fingers. *Dear God, where are You? Help me, please! Dayne . . . she's going to kill me!* Her screams echoed in her soul and clambered for a way out, but there was none.

The people with cameras grew in number, *clicking, clicking, clicking.* Every lens focused directly on Katy. There were so many now that Katy couldn't see past them or around them. They formed a tight circle, and inside the circle the drama continued to escalate.

That's when it happened. The waves grew still. Utterly still. Katy felt the insane woman lower the knife a few inches. Dayne was running toward them in slow motion, but it was as fast as he could go, and Katy knew — she knew with every heartbeat — that he wouldn't reach her in time. The cameras caught every step, every movement. The clicking grew louder . . . louder than her own heartbeat. Dayne kicked the knife with all his strength, and it went flying and became a seagull, squawking and flapping its wings and soaring fast and far over the Pacific Ocean.

Dayne landed hard against the woman, knocking her to the ground and planting himself firmly on her back. The yellow Honda was ten feet away, its engine howling, its presence menacing. Dayne shouted, "Run, Katy . . . run for your life."

But it was too late. The woman's eyes became dark and flinty. The seagull fell from the sky and became a knife once more, and the witch grabbed it and plunged it straight into —

"Ma'am." The voice was calm, kind.

Katy felt something cold against her face, and she jolted back from it. She blinked

18

twice, and everything disappeared — the woman, the knife, even Dayne. She wasn't on a beach, on the hot sand, or being attacked by a witch with a sword. The cold against her cheek was the window of the 757.

"Ma'am, you need to put your seat up." The voice belonged to a flight attendant.

Katy looked past the two businessmen in the seats beside her to the flight attendant. She felt a rush of heat in her cheeks. "I'm sorry. I . . . I was asleep."

"That's fine." The woman gave her a polite smile. "I just need you to put your seat back up."

"Yes . . . okay." She did as she was told, and only then did she realize that she was out of breath, the palms of her hands damp and clammy. She blew the air from her lungs. *Relax, Katy . . . relax.*

The entire ordeal had only been a dream — a dream that, except for the snow and the wild driverless Honda Civic, was exactly what had happened a year earlier.

Katy felt her heart rate slow, felt her breathing even out. Everything was going to be okay. The trial against the insane fan was set for this week, and Dayne had warned her that the media scrutiny would be intense. But she would survive it. Her testimony wouldn't take more than a day or so on the witness stand. Maybe less.

She looked out the window, through the smoggy sunset, and in the time it took her to inhale she was back again. Back to the week when she had actually considered taking a starring role opposite Dayne Matthews. There on the beach, walking hand in hand with Dayne, the ocean breeze stirring her hair and her senses. The reality was as wild a scenario as the nightmare she'd just woken from.

Katy shuddered. She brought her fingers to her throat and lightly massaged the place where the knife had pressed against her all those terrifying minutes. The blade had left lines on her that she had had to cover with makeup for two weeks.

The stalker would've killed her. If Dayne hadn't caught her off guard, Katy wouldn't be on the plane now, wouldn't be on her way to testify. She'd merely be another Los Angeles homicide statistic. Goose bumps rose on her arms. How long had the woman been watching them that night? Using two voices, two personalities, she was both Chloe and Anna during those frightening minutes, but the police had told them her real name since then.

Margie Madden.

The moment Dayne had thrown himself on Margie, Katy pulled herself free. In the seconds after that, Dayne made a mistake that nearly cost him his life. Katy had watched it happen, watched him twist around and find her, shouting for her to call 911, his eyes desperate to know if she was okay. And in the time it took him to do that, Margie had grabbed the knife and reached back. She raised it, intent on sinking the blade into Dayne.

Katy felt sick as she relived the scene. The knife glistened in the moonlight, and she screamed his name. Just in time, Dayne whipped around, and in quick, fluid movements, he kicked the knife out of Margie's hand and wrenched her away from Katy. Only then was Katy sure that they were out of danger.

Even as Dayne held the attacker facedown on the ground, the woman continued to spout death threats. *"I'll have to kill you too, Dayne . . . have to kill you too. . . ."*

Katy inhaled and settled back against the seat. Enough. She'd have to relive the terror on the witness stand in a couple days. No sense making herself sick by replaying it now. She turned toward the window. The setting sun shone a brilliant splash of light against her side of the plane, and the warmth felt good.

Temperatures in the nineties were forecast for LA. Katy wore a white sleeveless blouse and jeans. Absently, she turned her left arm so she could see the fine scar, the single threadlike line that ran three inches along her upper arm. The place where Margie had cut her, proving that she was willing to use the knife, anxious to kill.

The dream was no surprise. It was the same one she'd had three times in the past two weeks. In the daylight, during long conversations with Jenny and Jim Flanigan — the couple whose house she lived in — she was ready to face the trial straight-on. So what if she had to look Margie Madden in the eyes and testify against her? Never mind that she would have to relive the attack in front of a jury and a sea of media members from around the world.

Margie was behind bars, where she most certainly would stay. Nothing about the woman was a threat; at least that's what Katy told herself. But her nightmares betrayed her confidence. And the cameras — there were always cameras — reminded her that another danger lay just ahead. A danger that threatened her privacy, every bit as much as Margie had threatened her life.

The danger of the paparazzi.

Once the trial began tomorrow morning, they would be out for every morsel of story they could find. Most certainly they would learn her identity, and it would be nothing for them to figure out that she — Katy Hart, small-town Christian drama instructor — was the mystery woman who had kissed Dayne Matthews on the beach just moments before the attack.

Katy stared at the city, at the mountains that framed the San Fernando Valley. Back home her theater group was headlong into rehearsals for *Narnia* — the Christian Kids Theater production that would close out their season. Rhonda Sanders, Katy's friend and choreographer, would take over supervising the kids, keeping things on track until she returned. Good thing. The show was set to open the first week of June — in just one month.

A ripple of fear tightened her stomach. What would her reputation be by then?

Dayne had already reminded her two days ago when they last talked that they had to steer clear of the press as much as possible. "We can't be seen together outside court, Katy. Your reputation is on the line."

She had mulled that over. "Wouldn't it be normal for us to be together like that?" The whole media game was still so new to her.

She had tightened her grip on the phone and tried to understand. "As long as they don't think I'm the one you kissed, couldn't we be okay?"

"My new agent's working on that. He's talking to my attorney Joe Morris." Dayne gave a sad chuckle. "The agent's been busy all week coming up with a plausible story to tell the press. Something they might believe so we can keep the spotlight off you."

Not that any story would really work. Once Katy took the witness stand sometime this week, the entire truth was bound to come out. The reason she had been on the beach with Dayne, what they had been discussing, and what they'd been doing prior to the attack. The prosecuting attorney had promised to object any time a question came up that didn't pertain directly to the attack. But still . . .

She narrowed her eyes and stared at the sea of homes and roadways spread out below her. *God, go with me, please. Let me keep my privacy, my reputation. I need Your protection, Lord.*

There was no answer, no soft whispering in her soul. But two verses from the book of Matthew came to mind. "Come to me, all you who are weary and burdened, and I will give you rest. Take my yoke upon you and learn from me, for I am gentle and humble in heart, and you will find rest for your souls."

Katy let the words roll around in her heart, soothing her fears, removing the images of a thousand cameras trained on her. Rest for her soul. Yes, that's exactly what she wanted to take with her as she stepped off the plane in Burbank. If she allowed God to give her rest and peace, then her time in California would go quickly and without incident.

But what about the other part of the passage? "Take my yoke upon you and learn from me." What did that mean? Was it a matter of putting God first, the way she'd tried to do since she met Dayne Matthews? And how would that affect their downtime this week? Especially in light of how she and Dayne had grown closer over the last few weeks.

They had talked on the phone nearly every night lately. He spoke about his newfound faith, his determination that he would live out his days the way his adoptive parents had, the way his biological family apparently still did. He was reading his Bible and growing, sharing bits of discovered truth every time they spoke.

"I read something today," he told her last

time they talked. "The Bible says our bodies are not our own. We were bought with a price." He'd stopped for a moment. "It makes me sick, Katy. All those years when I did whatever I wanted, slept with whoever wound up in my bed. No wonder I felt like something was missing." His tone grew soft, thoughtful. "Sometimes I can't believe God could ever love someone like me."

Katy had refused the strange jealousies his confession stirred in her. Instead she closed her eyes and told him what he needed to hear. "God's forgiven you. Don't ever forget that."

Their conversations were deep and meaningful, bouncing between serious discussions about God and silly, fun talk about the upcoming CKT performance of *Narnia.*

"How do you feel about taking a breather from Hollywood and playing Aslan the lion?" she'd asked him a week ago. "For the life of me, I can't get my lion to roar. He's just a nice big kid, happy to be there. Like Gomer Pyle wandering around the stage yucking it up and aw-shucking it with every other character."

Dayne laughed. "Sounds a lot better than my recent gig."

Something was changing between them, strengthening their friendship and making them both dizzy with possibilities. On the good days, anyway.

On the bad ones, Katy would go to the local market and pick up a tabloid. Always there was something about Dayne — if not on the cover, then inside. Rumors about who he was seeing and who was falling for him, talk about a mystery woman meeting him at the beach or driving with him along Pacific Coast Highway. She wanted to believe that maybe the woman they were referring to was her. But she had her doubts. After all, she hadn't been back to Hollywood since January.

Katy never mentioned what she read. But it made her think. Whatever was happening between them couldn't possibly turn into a normal relationship, the kind that her friends Ashley Baxter Blake and Jenny had with their husbands.

Even so, their recent conversations were wonderful.

"You won't believe what happened," he told her. The emotion in his voice was raw. "I met my birth father. Sat down on a bench beside him and talked with him for an hour." He paused. "You're the only one I've told."

Dayne still didn't mention the man's name, where he was from, or any of the details, but the difference in him after that was undeniable. He seemed stronger, with a confidence that came less from who he was than what he was becoming on the inside. A confidence that grew from somewhere inside his soul. Between the news about his birth father and Dayne's growing faith, Katy considered the changes nothing short of divine, the sort of work only God could've brought about.

She had shared the details with Rhonda and Jenny, and she wanted to share them with Ashley. All three of her friends had been praying and for the most part gently suggesting that Dayne couldn't possibly be the right person for her. But now . . . now even Jenny was beginning to wonder.

There were issues to be resolved, of course. The greatest were the paparazzi and the fact that Dayne needed to stay in LA until he finished his current contract — five more movies with the studio backing him. Katy had no idea how either of them could survive being apart that long, not if their recent conversations were any indication.

The simple fact was this: the longer he talked to her, the more he shared about how God was working in his life and how he was taking walks along the beach every morning praying for her, the more there was no denying her feelings.

She was falling for him harder than ever before.

The plane landed, and Katy gathered her bags and rented a car. She could hardly wait to see Dayne. It had been two months since they'd been together.

She checked into her hotel and waited until the right time. According to Dayne, the paparazzi had been quieter lately. He wasn't hitting the nightclubs, wasn't showing up at the usual restaurants and haunts.

"My old agent told me this would happen," Dayne had told her on the phone last night. "He said photographers stay away from Christians."

"But do they know?"

"I'm not sure." He paused. "Maybe it's something they sense. I'm being too well-behaved. Not that they've lost all interest. They're still taking a hundred pictures of me every day."

"A hundred?" The thought was more than Katy could comprehend.

He chuckled. "Down from a thousand."

Katy had been tempted to say something about the tabloid rumors she'd seen, but she kept her thoughts to herself. He owed her nothing. If it was true about the time he spent with other women, with his leading ladies and supporting actresses, then she prayed that God would show her. That way she could share a friendly week with Dayne and let him go — for good this time.

Until then she had to believe the tabloids didn't know what she knew, that Dayne was becoming someone they wouldn't even recognize. And tonight she would see those changes first-hand.

Dayne had asked her to meet him at the beach. It would be safe, he said, because the photographers hadn't been lurking in the bushes near his Malibu house as often, and he thought they could escape the paparazzi easier tonight than after the trial started. They wouldn't know about her until tomorrow, and they wouldn't know the details until she testified Tuesday or Wednesday. At this point the paparazzi had no idea who she was.

"Besides, we need to talk about that, about how you're going to handle them," Dayne had said. "You need a plan, Katy."

Now that the trial was only twelve hours away she believed him more than ever.

The weather was warm as she headed to the beach in her rental car that evening. She had changed into capris and a form-fitting tank top under a pale blue, long-sleeve blouse, the kind that tapered in at the waist.

Twenty minutes later she found a spot in the parking lot at Malibu Beach, not far from where the paparazzi had tried to catch her last time she was here. She looked around the way Dayne had told her to — in case there were transients or photographers, anyone who appeared suspicious. In that case, she was supposed to drive down the road and pull into his driveway. He would open his garage, and she could park inside. But if the paparazzi saw her, they wouldn't be able to go out on the beach. The photographers would be desperate to know the identity of Dayne's visitor.

Okay, she told herself, *don't be nervous.* They were just a couple of friends getting together to talk. But no matter what she told herself, as she stepped out of her car, the truth was as clear as the hint of perfume she left behind her.

Katy moved quickly, glancing around. People were scattered across the parking lot, loading beach chairs into the backs of cars and packing up for the day. A few surfers washed their boards beneath the outdoor showers along the bathroom building. But no one was watching her. She reached the sand and surveyed the beach. The shoreline wasn't as empty as it had been in January.

A few families played near the surf, and an occasional couple sat together, facing the sea.

The sand felt warm as it pushed over her sandals and between her toes. She wished she could stop and take them off, but Dayne had told her to keep walking. She reached the damp shore where the sand was more compact, and she turned left. She was maybe ten yards into her walk when a guy hurried down the sandy slope toward her.

Just as she was about to pick up her pace, the man spoke in a loud whisper. "Katy . . . it's me." Dayne appeared from the shadows and fell into step beside her. "Keep walking."

The feel of him next to her heightened her awareness, made her notice everything about him, how tall and strong he was beside her and how good it felt when their arms brushed against each other every few steps. "Are they out, the photographers?" She tried to keep her eyes straight ahead, but she couldn't help catching glimpses of him. Strange how being with Dayne in public was like playing a role, like reenacting the scene the two of them had rehearsed for *Dream On* almost a year ago.

"No." He gave her a quick grin. "But I couldn't let you walk the beach by yourself.

The beaches are busier this time of year." He slipped his hands into his shorts pockets and kept moving. "I watched you park, made sure you were okay." He looked over his shoulder. "I'm not taking chances with the paparazzi."

"Oh." She kept her voice low, but she allowed a glance in his direction. "I'm glad."

They kept a steady pace, and after a few minutes Dayne slowed. They came to a stop a few yards from the stairs leading up to his house. He scanned the darkening beach in both directions, then turned and faced the surf. There were no signs of people anywhere near them. He took a deep breath and smiled at her. "I think we're alone."

She kicked off her sandals. "Mmmm. The sand feels so good."

He met her eyes and then looked back at the moonlit surf. "Not as good as seeing you."

He was keeping his distance on purpose; Katy could feel that much. The threat of photographers ruled everything about his public moments.

She breathed in the salty ocean air and worked her toes deeper into the sand. "I can't believe I'm here." She angled her face, finding his eyes again. "Something about you is different."

"Different?" He grinned and kicked a bit of sand at her foot.

"In a nice way." She straightened and let the breeze wash over her. Everything about the ocean felt wonderful, especially after a day in an airplane. "I think it's your eyes." She felt shy telling him this. "It's like I can see Jesus there."

"Really?"

"Yeah." She stared at the surf. Her heart was pounding harder than the waves. Over the phone she had felt things changing for both of them, growing deeper, stronger. But here . . . in person, the force of the attraction between them was enough to knock her to her knees. It was all she could do to hold her ground.

For nearly a minute he said nothing, just stood beside her, the ocean wind washing over them, their elbows touching. Then he groaned. "I can't stand this."

He didn't have to explain what he meant. Katy felt it too. Being together this way and not at least hugging wasn't natural. She breathed out, tried to steady herself; then she lifted her eyes to him.

At the same time, he turned and faced her. "Katy . . ." He reached for her hands, wove his fingers between hers, and once more — very carefully — he looked around.

Then he did what they were both dying to do. He slipped his arms around her waist and drew her into his embrace. "I feel like I've waited forever for this." He brushed his cheek against hers. "I've missed you so much."

Her hands wound around his neck, and she let herself get lost in his eyes. They shone with a love that could only have come from God. Mixed with the hint of moonlight reflecting off the water, the nearness of him was more than she could take. She let herself be pulled in closer, and she rested her head against his chest. "Why is it —" she looked up and let the light from his eyes wash over her — "I never feel complete until I'm in your arms?"

At first he looked as if he might answer her, but in the time it took him to blink, the air between them changed. He brought his hands to her face, and with the most tender care he touched his lips to hers.

But just as the kiss began, just as she was remembering how wonderful it felt to be in his arms, there was a movement in the bushes, a rush of feet, and the clicking of cameras.

Fear and adrenaline mixed and flooded her veins.

In a blur of motion, two men appeared

from behind the bushes beneath Dayne's home — one of them the same as last time she was here, the other one much younger.

Katy held up her hand, but it was too late.

The men blocked their way to Dayne's staircase and began taking rapid-fire pictures.

"Put your hand down," Dayne whispered to her. He used his body to shelter her, pulling her close, wrapping his arm around her, as he hurried her around the photographers to the door that led to his stairs.

The cameras didn't stop clicking until Dayne and Katy were inside the private staircase. Even then the men banged on the seven-foot-high gate. One of them shouted, "Tell us her name! Come on, Matthews. She's not an actress. Just tell us who she is."

The other one chimed in. "She's the mystery woman, right? The one who'll be at the trial tomorrow?"

Only then did Katy fully realize what had happened. The paparazzi had figured it out. All along she really had been the mystery woman. The photographers were desperate for the identity of the woman Dayne had been with back in January, and in the process they'd kept the story alive. They might not know her name — not yet. But the pictures they'd taken tonight would show her entire body — her face and her surprise — and the fact that she had been locked in an embrace with Dayne Matthews.

And that could mean only one thing: Life as she had known it was about to come to an end.

CHAPTER TWO

Dayne thought about going after the photographers. As he and Katy stood there on the steps, hearts racing, hidden by his private fence and gate, he actually considered pushing his way out to the public beach, seizing their cameras, and removing the memory chips from inside. That's all he wanted. The memory chips. Then he and Katy could pretend they hadn't been caught kissing on the beach, and the world would never have proof that the two of them were anything more than associates.

But the thought left him as soon as it came. The cameramen were still banging on the gate, shaking it, threatening to tear it down. He searched Katy's eyes and whispered, "You okay?"

Her face was pale, but she nodded and pointed up the staircase. "Please, Dayne . . . let's get out of here." She kept her voice too quiet for the photographers to hear —

especially above the noise they were making. But as she spoke, her teeth chattered. She was shaken, no question.

How could he have been so careless, meeting her on the beach? So what if the paparazzi had laid low? They knew the trial was about to start, so they'd taken a gamble that maybe — just maybe — the woman who had been on the beach with Dayne at the time of the attack might come around a day early. They'd been right and he'd been wrong. And now Katy would suffer the consequences.

He felt his heart settle somewhere in the pit of his stomach. "Come on." He put his arm around Katy and led her up the private outdoor staircase to his secluded deck and into the house. They moved past the kitchen table and into his living room, and then they dropped onto his leather sofa, breathless.

Anger had its claws around Dayne's throat. "That's so wrong." His teeth were clenched, and he barely squeezed out the words. "How can they live with themselves?"

Katy didn't seem to hear him. She was staring at nothing, her expression frozen in shock. "Do you think —" she turned to him, her eyes big — "they'll figure out who I am?"

He felt his insides melt. If there was a way

he could calm her fears or tell her something different, he would do it. But she deserved the truth. "Yes." He leaned closer and barely touched her face. "I'm sorry, Katy." He thought for a minute. "The pictures, the story . . . all of it will hit early next week." Anger dug in a little deeper. "That's how it works."

She groaned and stared at her lap. "We never should've met outside." There was no accusation in her tone, but her regret was deep. She looked up, her expression tight with fear. "What'll happen, Dayne?"

"They'll learn as much about you as they can between now and the day they go to print." He hated telling her this, but he had to be honest. "Sometimes . . . when a story's bound to wind up in the gossip rags, you're almost better off to provide them with easy information. That way they're less likely to dig."

The details made Katy look dizzy. "How do you mean?"

"Oh, man . . ." Dayne dug his elbows into his knees and hung his head. "I hate this, Katy. I'm so sorry. It's all my fault."

She was still shaking but not as much as before. Anger played in her eyes now as well. "It's not your fault." Her tone told him she was anxious for a way out, a way to discourage the press from digging. "Tell me what you mean, how you provide them with information."

"Simple." Defeat rang in his every word. "My agent or my attorney stages a press conference, puts together the basic details — your name and age, your occupation — something like community theater director, leaving out the part about Christian kids. He also provides a list of people to contact, people you trust."

"Someone like Ashley, maybe? Or Rhonda?"

Dayne felt the air leave his lungs. Ashley Baxter Blake? If the press got hold of her, they would be dangerously close to another truth. A truth he wasn't nearly ready to talk about. He tried to keep his voice even. "Yeah, maybe Rhonda, since she knows you from the theater. Or Jenny Flanigan."

"Dayne . . ." She covered her face with her hands. "I'm scared to death. How can I face the families in Bloomington? The magazines will make me out to be just another one of your conquests. How can I live with that?"

The question stung. He sat back and stared at the ceiling. How come he hadn't thought things through better? *God, why did it happen? What are we supposed to do now?*

My son, lean not on your own understanding; in all your ways acknowledge Me, and I will make your paths straight.

The still small voice blew like a summer wind across his soul. The words were from a verse in Proverbs he'd read this morning.

His own understanding was clear in this case. Pictures of Dayne and the mystery woman had to be worth what the photographers made for ten or twenty typical Hollywood star photos, right? But if he leaned on God, then somehow — someway — his path and Katy's would wind up straight.

He straightened and looked at her, at the way her blonde hair framed her face, at her sweet, guileless blue eyes. This was the girl he thought about and dreamed about, the girl he'd prayed for every day since returning from Mexico. "A conquest, Katy?" The comment hurt more than he first thought. "You don't really think that, do you?"

She stood and paced to the opposite side of the room. From there she faced him. "Not most of the time." She held up her hands and let them fall to her sides. "I mean, I don't know what to believe." She gestured toward the glass door to the deck. "I read the stories too. Every week there's a photo of you and some woman walking through LA or eating together or working on a set." She was shaking again. "The whole world thinks you're a player, Dayne."

The anger was back, stronger than ever. Not at Katy but at the photographers who wouldn't give him a moment's peace, at the stories they were bound to make up in the coming week, and at himself for ever putting her in this situation. He waited, and after a few seconds sadness replaced his anger. He slid to the edge of the sofa and patted the spot beside him. "Please, Katy." His eyes held hers, refusing to let go. "Come here."

Her expression changed, and the look in her eyes softened. She came to him and sat closer this time. "I'm sorry." She searched his face. "That wasn't fair."

"I can't stop them from taking photos." He took her hands, worked his fingers between hers. The feeling filled his heart and soul, and he struggled to remember his point. He swallowed. "But there's been no one."

"You don't have to tell me."

"You deserve the truth." He wanted to kiss her so badly, but he wouldn't. Not now after what had happened on the beach. Especially not after her conquest and player comments. Tonight would be nothing but strategy and friendship, a way to figure out a game plan so they could survive the rest of the week with as little paparazzi and as much time together as possible. He ran his thumb over her hand. "Those women in the pictures, they're friends. Nothing more." His voice fell. "You, Katy. You're the only one I want to be with. Please . . . let's figure out the media thing. Let's make a plan."

She clung to his hands, waiting for him. "Right now?"

"Yes." He eased back a few inches. "Here's what we're going to do. . . ."

For the next hour he helped her imagine a dozen different scenarios involving the trial and how she could best keep the press at bay. At the end of the night, he made good on his silent promise. He held her close and stroked her hair. Then he led her to his Escalade — so no one could take pictures of him walking her back down the beach — and he drove her back to her car.

"Feels like the last time you were here, doesn't it?" He smiled. The conversation between them was lighter now.

"It does." The corners of her lips lifted in a shy smile. "Only now we have a plan."

He gave her a quick hug just as he spotted two guys with cameras running up the beach toward the parking lot. Dayne leaned back. "Go, Katy." He gave her as much advice as he could in a handful of seconds.

She managed to get to her car before the photographers could catch her. As she pulled away, Dayne watched the paparazzi sprint toward their cars. They would follow her, for sure. Something she hadn't had to deal with before.

His frustration seemed to suck the air from the SUV, making it hard for him to breathe. So they had a plan — big deal. The plan might help them feel better about the coming week, but there was no way to undo the damage already done.

Damage that would hit the newsstands in just a few days.

Katy's hands shook as she drove back to her hotel.

Two cars were tailing her, staying as close to her bumper as they could without hitting her. The photographers had spotted her before she climbed into her car, and in what could only be described as dangerously reckless driving, they'd caught up to her in a few stoplights.

Dayne's last words to her were all she was holding on to. "Ignore them, Katy. Don't drive faster; don't try to lose them." He took hold of her shoulders, his expression intense. "They'll find out where you're staying anyway. There's nothing they can do to you that hasn't already been done. So what if they get a picture of you walking into your hotel?"

Still, she could barely focus on the road. Was this really what Dayne dealt with? A constant barrage of scrutiny and camera clicks? *God . . . get me through this, get me back safely. Please, God . . .*

There was no answer, and she thought about the verse from Matthew. The one that had drifted across her soul earlier. Maybe the reason they had been caught on camera was because God didn't want her kissing Dayne on the shore of Malibu Beach. This was a time when Dayne was figuring out his faith, trying to find his way through the maze of distractions that made up his life. What right did she have kissing him when all that could do at this point was confuse him?

Uneasiness rattled her nerves, and she pressed down a little harder on the gas pedal. Suddenly she heard the long wail of a car horn. Then another and another. Her heart pounded. What was happening? She looked in her rearview mirror and saw the three photographers darting in and out of traffic, lobbying for the spot directly behind her.

Impossible, she thought. *Someone's going to get killed, all so a photographer can get the right picture.* It was insanity beyond anything Katy had ever known. She wanted to drive a hundred miles an hour or turn into an alley and take a dozen turns through side streets. Anything to lose them.

But Dayne's words played in her mind again: *"Ignore them, Katy . . . ignore them. . . ."*

She pursed her lips and forced herself to exhale. "Come on, Lord . . . ," she whispered. "Guide my hands."

The minutes passed slowly, the photographers' cars directly behind her the entire way.

When she arrived at the hotel, her heart began to race, slamming against her chest twice as hard as before. *"Ignore them, Katy . . . ignore them."* She clung to Dayne's words like so many life preservers. Valet parking was the best option, no doubt. She pulled in, rolled down her window, and motioned for the nearest person in uniform. "Please . . . I'm in a hurry. Can I have a receipt for my car?"

The man glanced behind her, and at the same time she caught a look in the mirror. Both cars containing paparazzi had screeched to a halt just short of the valet area. They were opening their doors, grabbing their gear, ready to chase her.

The man seemed accustomed to people on the run. He ripped a receipt from his book and handed it to her. "Here you go. I'll get your car moved right away."

"Thanks." She grabbed her purse and opened her car door, her chest heaving. She was halfway to the revolving door when she heard the pounding of feet, the clicking of cameras. She ducked into the hotel and looked over her shoulder.

Two doormen had stopped the photographers on the sidewalk. The diversion gave her time to get into the elevator. As soon as the elevator doors closed, she collapsed against the back wall. What were the paparazzi trying to do? Would they have tackled her to the ground, demanding information and snapping photos until she lay there unconscious?

Katy felt sick to her stomach, and as the elevator doors opened on her floor, she was almost afraid to step out. She glanced both ways. The hallway was clear. She rushed to her room, unlocked the door, and closed it behind her. She leaned against the wall and caught her breath. Good. She had escaped them for now, but tomorrow would be worse.

She headed to the window. The view was breathtaking — the lights from the Hollywood Hills spread out before her like a twinkling blanket. The glitz and glamour of Dayne's life would always seem appealing to people who hadn't been thrust into the limelight. She remembered a conversation from earlier.

Before she left for the airport, Bailey Flanigan had found her. "You're so lucky." Jenny's daughter sighed, her expression dreamy. "Spending the week with Dayne Matthews, running around Hollywood like a celebrity." She giggled. "You have to tell me every detail when you get back."

But the truth was so far removed from the picture most people had in their heads. How had Dayne survived living under such scrutiny? No wonder his photo was in the tabloids every week. If he left his house, no matter who he spoke with or where he ate a meal, the moment would be documented for everyone to see.

She pressed her fist against her middle, staving off the waves of nausea. The terror was fading, but she still felt sick. For the past month or so, Katy had convinced herself that she and Dayne might have a chance, that the friendship they were developing was proof that maybe — just maybe

— something romantic and long-term might come from their time together.

Yes, he had a contract to fulfill, and yes, he was in the public eye. But she had begun to see those obstacles as surmountable. Mountains that could be climbed. Now though . . . she had no control over the photos taken earlier tonight, no idea what the paparazzi might find if they dug far enough. Maybe they'd figure out that she was Tad Thompson's old girlfriend. Tad Thompson, the overnight sensation who died of a drug overdose at a wild Hollywood party.

Or maybe they'd place her as a mistress, someone Dayne was seeing even while he was living with Kelly Parker. Otherwise why would he have chosen Bloomington, Indiana, for his location shoots on *Dream On?*

Her heart began beating faster, her breathing shallow and unsteady. Enough. She turned away from the window. *Please, God, clear my mind.* She couldn't think about Dayne or the stolen moments they might find together or the paparazzi. There was nothing she could do about the pictures or whatever story the photogs might pull together.

She could only focus on the matter at

hand. The trial against a knife-wielding fan set to begin first thing in the morning.

CHAPTER THREE

Ashley Baxter Blake stared at the newspaper. The article was taken from the AP newswire, too brief for many details. But the story made one thing clear — the trial was about to start. Ashley intended to follow the proceedings every day.

"This tells me nothing." She folded the paper and pushed it aside. She was sitting at the kitchen table, baby Devin cradled in her arms. His head was covered with blond peach fuzz. At four weeks old he looked more like Cole every day, though he was definitely an easier baby. He was waking up just once in the middle of the night and nursing every four hours right on schedule. She checked the clock on the microwave. It was nine-thirty. Three and a half hours and he'd be hungry again.

Ashley ran her fingers over Devin's hair and surveyed her husband. Landon was making coffee. He wore shorts and a T-shirt, and he was humming something by Casting Crowns. She would forever be grateful that he had come back from New York, that he had pursued her without ever giving up. "Have I told you lately —" she kept her voice low so she wouldn't wake Devin — "that I'm in love with you?"

He flipped a switch on the coffeemaker and turned to her. "Yes . . ." His eyes were tender, full of a lifetime of emotion. "Every time you look at me." When he reached her, he framed her face with one hand and brought his lips to hers.

The kiss reminded her of everything she felt for him, for the way he'd stayed by her and waited for her, refusing to walk away even when he'd been crazy to stay.

"Hey —" she pulled back and searched his eyes — "I love you."

"I love you back." He ran his finger along the top of Devin's hand. "I'll go lay him down if you want." He gave her one more kiss, tender but quicker than before. Then he straightened and stretched. "You might have time for a nap."

Cole was already off to school, and Landon had a late shift at the fire station.

Ashley looked up at him and smiled. "You like being a daddy, don't you?"

He pointed at the photograph of Cole

hanging on the closest wall. "I've been a daddy for a long time. And, yes —" he touched his finger to Devin's nose — "I love every minute of it."

Ashley adjusted herself so she was facing him. "Luke must be there by now."

"In Los Angeles?"

"Mmm-hmm." She nodded to the folded newspaper. They were both being careful not to wake Devin. "He told Dad he's supposed to be at Dayne Matthews' beck and call. Whatever the guy needs."

"Should be interesting." Landon went to the cupboard and took out two mugs. "Your friend Katy's there too, right?"

"Right." She looked at the paper again. "There was nothing in the article about her. Katy wants to keep it that way."

"You'll probably have to read something other than our local paper to get the real scoop."

"I know." Ashley glanced at Devin. He was proof of God's love for all of them, this tiny boy, their precious son. She watched him take a deep breath and felt him press in more tightly against her chest. She looked up at Landon again. "Are you serious about taking a turn with Devin?"

"Of course." Landon moved back a few steps. "He'll probably sleep in his crib for a few hours, anyway." He crossed the kitchen and checked on the coffeemaker. "You thinking about the nap?"

"Not really." She looked outside. The morning was cloudy, but it was supposed to clear up later. For the past week she'd wanted to get out, spend a few hours at her father's house. She turned to Landon. "I'd sort of like to paint."

A smile lit his face. "That's a great idea. Over at your dad's?"

She nodded. "My easel's still set up there. I have a picture in my head, one that won't leave me alone until I put it on canvas."

"Hmm." The coffee was ready, filling the room with the smell of morning. Landon poured both mugs and added creamer to Ashley's. He brought them to the table and set hers far from their little son. Balancing his own cup, he pulled out the chair and took the seat across from her. "What's the picture?"

She thought for a moment. What would she do without Landon, without his love and concern? He was her best friend, the person she could tell anything to. "My brother."

It took only a second for the realization to show in Landon's expression. "Your *older* brother." His response wasn't a question.

Landon knew, same as he'd always known, what she was thinking.

"Yes." She looked out the window again. "I think about him all the time."

"Any news from your dad?" Landon held his coffee mug with both hands and leaned back in his chair.

"Nothing." She turned to him. "Dad says he'll tell the others next spring at our next reunion." She stopped and pursed her lips. "That's too long. I think everyone should know sooner. Maybe we could . . . I don't know . . . write to him, tell him what he's missing."

Landon was quiet for a moment. He blew at the steam coming off his coffee. Finally he drew a long breath. "Is this about you, Ashley?" He angled his head. "Or about your mother?"

It was a fair question. Her mom had wanted to know her oldest son, wanted to meet him and introduce him to the Baxter family. But she hadn't gotten the chance. She'd died of cancer too young, too soon. Ashley felt the familiar sadness. "A little of both, maybe."

"I thought so."

Ashley stood and carried Devin to his bassinet they'd set up in the living room. She returned to the table and looked deeply into her husband's eyes. "I miss her so much."

"I know." He looked into the next room, to the place where their son was sleeping. "She would've loved Devin."

"Yes." She closed her eyes and took a long drink from her mug. "I like what my dad said that day in the delivery room after he was born." She blinked. " 'Mom's here. She can see little Devin somehow.' " A smile pulled at the corners of her lips. "Some days it's like I can almost feel her near me, hear her voice. Her memory's that strong."

They finished their coffee, and Ashley kissed Landon good-bye. Their home was only seven minutes from the Baxter house, and Ashley called her dad at his office on the way. "Come home for lunch, okay? I'm going to paint for a couple hours."

Her father agreed, and Ashley wasted no time. The moment she was inside her father's house she made her way up to the small bedroom that had once belonged to her. She opened the window and inhaled the cool air that filled the room. It smelled of fresh-cut grass and newborn roses and something sweet and distinct that always marked the Baxter house in late spring.

Ashley studied her old room. Flowered wallpaper still hung on the lower half of the walls, and the corkboard she'd used as a high schooler still spread out across the space above her bed. It was a guest room now, and when family wasn't visiting, it was where she loved to paint. Her father had put her supplies away for the reunion last month, but after everyone left he hauled them out again.

"You need to paint, Ashley," her father had told her the last time he stopped by to visit. "Your easel's up; the paints are ready. When Devin's old enough, come over and get to work."

Her father was right. She needed to paint like some people needed sunshine.

She checked her colors and found a fresh canvas. Some artists sketched first, careful to draw out exactly what they wanted to bring to life. Not Ashley. The picture was so visual, so alive in her head, she had only to dip her brush in the paint and touch the paint to the canvas and suddenly, amazingly, God would help her breathe life into the image.

And this image was stronger than any she'd painted in a year. In her mind, she had a picture of her older brother. He would have Luke's build, Luke's and her father's. He'd have dark blond hair and broad shoulders and eyes that had the ability to see into a person's soul. It was his face she wasn't sure about. Whenever she pictured him she saw him the way she saw him now, with his back to her — a Baxter but a faceless one.

The soft symphony of robins and finches and bluebirds and the rhythmic croak of frogs in the stream behind the house filtered through the open window. The sounds soothed Ashley's soul and provided the perfect background for everything she felt in her heart.

Over the next two hours she put the big strokes down, and when she stepped back the streaky colors and defining borders showed her exactly what had been in her mind all these weeks. The foreground shadowy figure of the back of a man, hands in his pockets, leaning against an old oak tree, staring across a grassy field at a house that could never be anything but the Baxters'.

He could've been Luke or her father in another decade. But Ashley knew him as surely as she knew she would never rest until she had the chance to meet him. The man was her brother, her older brother. The one who had recently rejected the Baxter family in exchange for a life of anonymity.

After she washed her brushes, she inspected the painting again. A few more sessions and it would be complete, a tribute to the feelings she had for a brother she had never known, probably never would know. She ran her finger along the edge of the canvas. *Lord, You know where he is, what he's doing now. Please work on his mind, change his heart. We don't have to be close, don't have to get together with him several times a year.*

A breeze stirred the air in the room and bared her emotions. *You know how much he mattered to my mom, Lord, and You know him — whoever he is. Please . . . I just want the chance to meet him.*

There was a sound downstairs, but before she could walk away, before she could close the door on this moment with God and her imagination, an image came to her mind: Dayne Matthews and along with it the image of Katy Hart. She didn't think long about why they were suddenly on her heart. God must want her to pray for them too. Katy had become a close friend, and before she left on Sunday, Ashley had promised to pray for her.

"My brother will be there," Ashley told her. "Tell him I said hi. Tell him I'll be praying for both of you."

So, as easily as she drew her next breath, Ashley left her prayers about her older brother in the hands of the Lord and silently lifted to Him Katy Hart and the media man

of the hour.
Dayne Matthews.

CHAPTER FOUR

John Baxter was glad for the diversion. Until Ashley's call, all he could think about was the trial on the West Coast. In what could only be a divine appointment, the proceedings would place his two sons together for an entire week, maybe more. Dayne and Luke would work together, sit together, and present a united front to the media and courtroom authorities.

And all the while no one — not even Luke — would know the truth. That Luke Baxter and Dayne Matthews were brothers.

John tossed his keys on the kitchen table. Then he cupped his hands around his mouth and yelled, "Ashley . . . I'm home." She would be down in a few minutes after she had the chance to put away the paints she'd been using. He smiled as he headed for the refrigerator. It was a good sign, Ashley being here, getting back to her painting. Life at home must be good for them if she could allow herself this time.

"Hi, Dad . . ." Her voice traveled down the stairway. "Be right there."

He took a dish of cold salmon from the fridge, separated the filet into two pieces, and put them on separate plates. Ashley loved salmon. He placed one plate in the microwave and set the timer.

The most wonderful thing had happened in the weeks since his meeting with Dayne. The two of them had begun to build a relationship. After their meeting, he had considered calling Dayne but decided against it. The oldest Baxter son had a lot to think about, many decisions to make. Better to let him make the first move if they were to develop more than a passing interest in each other.

Dayne's call came two days later when John was at work between patients.

"Hi . . ." The cool confidence that so clearly marked Dayne's on-screen performances was missing. In its place was an uncertainty, a hesitation. "I wanted to talk about the trial."

John didn't hesitate. "I'm glad you called." His heart thudded against his chest, and his mind raced. What should he say? How should he react? But as the conversation continued, he allowed himself to relax. This wasn't Dayne Matthews the movie star, and it wasn't a man angry because he'd been adopted. It was his son. He could talk to him the same way he might talk to Luke. They didn't have a history, but that didn't matter. Dayne was his son, all the same.

The conversation was the first of several since then. Every few days, without pressure from John, Dayne called. And every time he started the conversation the same way: "Hi." Dayne didn't call him John or Dad; he simply started talking.

Gradually, one conversation at a time, he began seeking John's advice, sharing his feelings about Katy, his position in Hollywood, and his concerns about the paparazzi.

One thing had become clear to John, and this was the part that had John giddy with the possibilities. The more Dayne opened up to him, the more he seemed practically desperate for a relationship with him.

On one phone call, he talked about Katy Hart. "I think I love her." He chuckled. "We couldn't live in more different worlds, but how do I tell my heart that?"

A few days ago, Dayne explained how he hoped to keep Katy out of the media as much as possible. "The weird thing is that I'll probably need Luke's help to do it." A longing sounded over the phone line. "He's my brother, and there we'll be. Working side by side. But if I say anything, if the media finds out, the avalanche will start, and nothing on earth will ever stop it."

Then they talked about God and His plans for their lives. John took a slow breath. "The Lord led you to Luke and to your birth mother and to Katy. I have to believe, Dayne, that when the time is right He'll somehow lead you to make contact with your brother and sisters."

"I don't know." The struggle in Dayne's voice was obvious. "They don't deserve to have their lives turned upside down."

"I know them." John didn't push, but he didn't want there to be any mistake here. "I've prayed about it, and I'm sure about this: they'd gladly give up their privacy for the chance to connect with you."

When Dayne was hesitant, John only prayed longer, harder. He had told Ashley that next spring he would tell the others the truth — that they had an older brother. But how much better, how much happier everyone would be if he could also introduce them, give them the opportunity to get to know Dayne — the real Dayne, the one he was learning more about with every phone call.

He was right about his kids — at least he hoped he was. Brooke and Peter . . . Kari and Ryan . . . Luke and Reagan . . . Ashley and Landon . . . Erin and Sam . . . None of them would mind a little scrutiny, not if it meant fulfilling their mother's dream and getting to know their older brother.

John took out the first plate of hot salmon, popped the second one in, and set the microwave once more. Dayne's words ran through his mind. *"They don't deserve to have their lives turned upside down."*

But would that really happen? John stared at the plate of fish making slow rotations inside the microwave. He broke away and grabbed a bowl of salad from the fridge. What media push would there actually be? The press would be excited at first — Dayne Matthews finds his biological family. And maybe for a little while paparazzi would cloister around Bloomington looking for a better story, a different angle. But eventually they'd have to go home. Hollywood photographers couldn't make a living here.

Okay, so maybe they'd find some dirt on John and his kids. But it wasn't the sort of dirt that would stick. The paparazzi would sniff out the next story, and the Baxters — Dayne's birth family — would be old news.

"Can't you see it going that way?" he'd

asked Dayne.

Dayne was slow to answer. "You can't tell about the gossip rags." He sighed, and the sound of it rattled John's soul. "The Baxters would always be fair game — no matter how much time passed. If you got a speeding ticket or visited the hospital or were caught in a public place in Los Angeles or New York, anytime any of you spent time with me, you'd be subject to the click of the cameras." His voice faded some. "As long as I'm at the top of their list, you would be too."

The view Dayne had presented was sobering, and it made John understand why Dayne had kept his distance. Still, he couldn't help but think it was possible. Once he told his kids, they would be flexible enough to make it work.

Whatever Dayne decided, nothing could take the edge off the joy John was feeling for one single reason — he had found their firstborn son. If Elizabeth could see him now, if God allowed His people a window from heaven, then she had to be rejoicing with him. The boy they had prayed for and longed for and missed with every passing year was found.

The microwave beeped three times. John pulled out the plate and placed a small heap of salad next to it. "Lunch is ready." He raised his voice loud enough for Ashley to hear.

"Coming." There was the sound of feet bouncing down the stairs and Ashley appeared, her face taken up with a sad smile. She hadn't lost all her baby weight yet, but she had never looked more beautiful. She stopped and held out her hands. "I love it."

"Salmon?" John looked at the two steaming plates, then back at his daughter.

She giggled and came to him. A quick hug and a kiss on the cheek and she stepped back. "My painting." She took one of the plates to the kitchen table and sat down.

He joined her at the table with his plate. "Let me guess." John loved this, the easy banter he shared with Ashley. Especially after so many years when she'd kept her distance, years before she let God and Landon into her life. He stroked his chin, teasing her. "It's a painting of the world's most precious baby. This wonderful couple is holding him between them, and the sunlight can't spill enough gold on their faces."

"Hmm." Ashley grinned. "That might be next." She poked her fish with a fork. For a while she looked at him, a knowing look, as if maybe that would be enough to convey the details of her current painting. When she spoke, her voice was softer than before. "It's of him, our older brother."

John felt his jaw go slack, and adrenaline raced through his veins. How could this be happening? How had Ashley once again found out the truth before anyone else? He searched her face. "You . . . you know him?"

Surprise flashed in her eyes, then an understanding. "No, Daddy. Of course not." She sat up straighter in her chair. Her expression slowly took on a faraway look. "But I see him." She touched her finger to the place above her heart. "In here I feel like I know him." Her voice held a familiar longing, familiar tone. She sounded like Elizabeth, the way Elizabeth had talked whenever she spoke about Dayne.

"I understand." Maybe it was time to give her a little more information. He set his fork down and felt his expression grow more serious. "I've been talking to him. Your brother."

The color left Ashley's cheeks. "You have?" She was motionless, probably trying to make sense of this newest detail. "How come you didn't say anything before?"

"He wants to meet you." John rested his forearms on the table. "All of you. He knows your names and ages, who you're married to, the names of your children. He knows everything."

Ashley stood. "Really?" She raised both hands and looked upward. "Thank You, God." She made a sound that was mostly a laugh. Her words came faster than before. "So when's the meeting? When are you going to tell the others? And why did he change his mind?"

John felt his heart sink. Maybe telling her this much wasn't such a good idea. "Sit down, honey. Please."

The smile stayed on her face, but she did as he asked. "I can't believe this, Dad. . . . Tell me."

"It isn't that easy, sweetheart." He leaned closer, willing her to understand. "There are special circumstances. His life . . . his life is very different from ours. He hasn't decided if it'd be good for us if we all met."

Ashley went limp against the back of the chair. "Of course it would be good." She searched his face as if the entire conversation made no sense. "We aren't asking him to move in with us. We want to meet him." Her voice had grown loud, and she made an obvious effort to lower it. "You want to meet him, don't you, Dad?"

He'd told her this much. She might as well know as much truth as he could give her. "I have met him, Ash. I met him last month. He flew here, and we talked at the park downtown."

This time she looked as if she might pass out. "Wow." She pursed her lips and exhaled. "I . . . I don't know what to say."

John picked up his fork and took a bite of salmon. It was colder than he liked it. The whole time he watched his daughter. "I'm telling you this now so you'll see God's working here. There's progress."

Ashley seemed frozen in place. "You're serious. You really met him?" She pushed back from the table. "What's he like? Does he look like us?" She raked her fingers through the roots of her hair. "Dad, I have a hundred questions. Did you tell him about me, that I'm the only one who knows about him?"

"I did."

"Okay . . . so, did you tell him I want to meet him?"

This was harder than John had imagined. How could he keep up the facade when the truth was that Ashley had already met him? Dayne had given her a ride home from drama practice last fall. Both of them had spoken about the incident. *God . . . help her understand. Let it all work out one day soon.* He cleared his throat. "I told him. And he's

71

thinking about it." He lowered his brow, pleading with her. "Keep praying, Ash. Really."

She hesitated. "So what's he like?"

"He's nice." John could see Dayne's face, hear him the way he'd sounded on their recent conversations. "I think you'd like him."

A dozen curiosities danced in Ashley's eyes. "Does he look like me or Brooke or who?"

The question was easy. "He looks like Luke."

"I can't believe this." Ashley stared at him and then out the window. For nearly a minute she was quiet. "Pray, right? That's what you want me to do?"

"Yes, Ash." John's heart hurt. With everything inside him he wanted to tell her the whole truth. "Please understand."

She nodded and ate the rest of her lunch in silence. "I need to get back." She stood and took both their empty plates to the kitchen sink. When they were rinsed and placed in the dishwasher, she turned to him. "Devin'll be hungry." She kissed his cheek. Her lips formed a smile, but her eyes remained flat. "Thanks for lunch."

"Ash, you're mad." He took tender hold of her hand. "Please don't be upset. Things are moving in the right direction."

She looked deeply into his eyes for several seconds. Then the intensity of her expression eased. "Can I ask you one favor?"

"Anything." He hated the pain this was causing them both. How could he have known that his older son would be a top Hollywood movie star?

"Tell the others they have another brother. As soon as possible." Her tone was kinder now, imploring him to see the request as possible. "He could call today and tell you he's ready to meet us." She motioned toward the door. "But Brooke and Kari and Luke and Erin . . . they know nothing about him." She paused. "You can't wait until next spring, Dad. Please . . . tell them now."

John's stomach flip-flopped. He wanted to argue that it was too soon, better to wait until their brother had made up his mind, until a decision had been reached. But in as much time as it took for the argument to flash across his mind, he knew she was right. What would Dayne think if he called and wanted to come for a visit, only to find out that John had dragged his feet in telling the others?

Ashley leaned closer. "They'll be okay, Dad. Nothing's going to change the way they feel about you and Mom." She smiled, and this time her eyes held the familiar glow. "Nothing ever could."

Her words infused a strength into his veins that surged through him and made the answer obvious. He nodded slowly, as if his body were still trying to imagine the possibility. "Okay." He looked beyond her to the window. He felt like a man standing at the open door of an airplane ready to jump. God would have to provide the parachute. That much was sure. He met her eyes. "I'll tell them."

"This week?" She gave him the same look she'd given him as a little girl when she hadn't cleaned her room but wanted to spend the night at a friend's house anyway. "Please . . ."

This week, God? Without any time to get ready . . .

My son, I am with you. . . .

The silent exchange took only a moment, but it brought with it a peace and certainty John couldn't deny. He put his arm around Ashley's shoulders. This time he allowed the hint of a smile. "Yes." He walked her to the door. "This week."

After she was gone, he stayed at the window and stared at the deep blue sky. There would never be an easy way to tell his adult children about their older brother.

But it had to be done. He could write them each a letter, explain the situation the best way he knew how. Then he could ask them to call when they were ready to talk. He pictured Dayne, sitting beside Luke perhaps at this minute, the trial just getting under way. Yes, Ashley was right. He needed to get past this next step.

The sooner the better.

CHAPTER FIVE

All night Dayne tried to think of a way to take the pressure off Katy.

He was still thinking about it that morning when his attorney, Joe Morris, pulled up out front in a rented black Suburban. Dayne wore a dark Armani suit, a crisp white buttoned-down shirt, and a conservative Yves Saint Laurent tie. This wasn't his typical about-town clothing, which meant the cameramen would be all the more anxious to get his picture. Maybe that would mean more attention aimed at him and less on Katy. At least he hoped so.

He stepped out of his house and instantly heard the stir of photographers. Six of them lined his sidewalk, each with a camera aimed at him — the only paparazzi willing to give up a place in line at the courthouse for photos of him leaving his Malibu home. They fired a battery of questions at him.

"Will the woman testify today or tomorrow?"

"Is she staying at your house, Dayne?"

"Dayne, who is she? What's her name? How long have you two been dating?"

He ignored all of them and slipped easily into the waiting SUV.

Joe grinned at him. "Hope you brought your popcorn. The courthouse is a circus from what I hear." He pointed to the cup holder adjacent to the front-passenger seat. "I picked up Starbucks. Got you a venti double-vanilla latte. Your favorite."

Dayne snapped his seat belt in place. "A double?" He looked over his shoulder at the paparazzi, hurrying to their cars, anxious to follow him. "Pretty sure I don't need a double shot to feel wired this morning." He picked up the drink and breathed in the steam. "If I wind up on the ceiling, you get to scrape me off."

"Whatever you need." Joe had one hand on the wheel. He pulled onto Pacific Coast Highway, then glanced in his rearview mirror. "Wow." He clucked his tongue against the roof of his mouth. "They're out for blood today."

There was the sound of screeching tires behind them.

Dayne didn't turn around. "You got that

right." He let the warmth of his drink soak through his hands and into his body. "It's no big deal. I'm used to it. Try to ignore them."

Joe's eyes opened a little wider. He had no funny comeback, almost as if he hadn't thought about that before. This was the life Dayne lived every day — not just when a big trial was about to begin.

The attorney grew quiet and turned his attention entirely to the road. He deftly moved the Suburban through the morning traffic toward the criminal courts building. The crime had taken place outside the jurisdiction of Los Angeles, but early on both attorneys and a judge agreed that the trial would be better off in Los Angeles. If nothing more than for the fact that the LA courthouses could better handle the sheer volume of media interest.

"You nervous?" Joe held his coffee in one hand. He took a quick drink and returned his cup to its place on the console.

"No." Dayne's answer was sure, confident. "Should be an easy conviction."

"Yeah." Joe glanced at him. "I meant about Katy Hart. You seem sort of distracted."

Dayne sighed. Was he that easy to read? He shifted so he could see his attorney better. "I'm worried about her." Dayne hadn't told his attorney about his deeper feelings for Katy, and for another five miles he wondered if he should. Joe was safe — he wouldn't talk to the press. And if he knew, maybe he'd be more determined to help protect Katy. Besides, now that the photographers had photos, there was no point hiding the truth. "Hey, Joe . . . about Katy."

"I know. You want her shielded from the press." He gave a quick nod. "I've got Luke Baxter on it."

His brother. Dayne wanted to laugh. How could any of this actually be happening? "Okay . . . but there's something I need to tell you."

Joe gave him a longer look, one that told him this probably wasn't the time for surprises. "I'm listening."

"Katy and I . . ." Dayne looked straight ahead. He waited a long time, trying to find the right words. Finally he uttered a single laugh. "There's no other way to say it. I'm crazy about her, Joe. I'm in love with her. Seriously." He could hear the amazement in his own voice. He hadn't been this straightforward with anyone but John Baxter. "I've had feelings for her ever since I met her." There was no stopping now. The truth spilled out like water from a dam. "A couple photographers caught us last night on the beach. It was just a quick kiss, but it's on camera."

Joe let out a low whistle. "It'll be in every gossip magazine within a week."

"I know." Dayne made a face intended to show Joe his dilemma. "That's why I need your help. Yours and Luke's — anyone who can keep the spotlight off her."

"But if you're dating, it'll be out soon enough any—"

"We're not." Dayne's answer was quick. "She's the director of a Christian Kids Theater group. We live and work in different worlds."

Joe's brow was twisted, his expression confused. He shot Dayne a look. "I thought you said you love her."

Dayne felt the conflict stronger than he had in a month. "I do." He looked straight ahead again. "It's something we have to work through."

"Sounds like it." Joe thought a moment. "And you want to work it out away from the magnifying glass of the paparazzi, is that it?"

"Exactly."

"All right, no problem. The plan's simple. Between Luke and myself, we'll stage press conferences, do what we can to keep feeding them nonstories." Joe hesitated. "Before lunch I want you to put together a list of things I can tell the press — her name, age, pieces of her background I can mention. That might keep them occupied for a while."

It was exactly what Dayne had been thinking. "I'll get it to you before we break today." The details would be very general, but it was a good strategy. Make the media think they were getting something, even though the information would be less than they'd find on their own. "I think it could work . . . make it easy for them."

"You got it, Dayne." Joe was a fast thinker, a man whose mind was in a dozen places at once. His certainty made the situation with Katy feel a little less complicated.

Dayne leaned back in his seat and felt himself relax. Joe would handle it. He was the attorney after all. He didn't need to understand Dayne's personal life or the decisions he made. He was paid to handle whatever Dayne threw at him.

The rest of the ride Joe went on about a high-profile case in New York City involving a former Hollywood star accused of murdering his wife.

Dayne didn't really listen. With every mile he felt himself growing anxious again. What if feeding the press didn't work? What if the gossip rags still dug, and Katy's entire life was laid bare for the country to examine?

Joe was talking about penalties and prison sentences, the fact that the former Hollywood star could face a life term.

Dayne nodded at the appropriate times, but he couldn't stop thinking about how crazy his life was becoming. He was holding long conversations with John Baxter, sharing his feelings about Katy Hart and the pressure of the paparazzi and his thoughts about getting to know his siblings. When he thought about John now, it was as a son thinks of his father. But was their relationship and the one he shared with Katy all little more than make-believe? Would there ever come a day when he could call John Baxter and say the words that were growing in his soul? "Hey, Dad . . . it's me, Dayne." And that was only a fraction of what was consuming him.

Not only would he need to do everything possible to keep the attention off Katy, but throughout the proceedings he would be sitting next to his brother, Luke Baxter. The people in his attorney's office were right. The resemblance between him and Luke was uncanny. If the media hounds looked hard enough, they were bound to at least joke about the fact that Dayne and his attorney's assistant looked alike.

All of it felt like a twisted movie plot, and combined with the double latte, his heart was pumping hard and fast by the time they arrived in front of the Criminal Courts Building. Spectators stood in large groups on either side of the street, and a swarm of media vans with ten-foot-high antennas was gathered near the courthouse entrance. Police were stationed every twenty feet, keeping the crowd in check and holding the public at bay.

Joe surveyed the situation. "Luke Baxter's bringing Katy in through the back door. They should be inside by now." He looked at Dayne. "You can enter wherever you want, but I've got police clearance to park in front."

"Let's do it." Dayne studied the throng of reporters camped on both sides of the main sidewalk. "Anything to keep the attention on me." He clenched his jaw, ready for whatever they threw at him. "It's my trial, my problem. The psycho would've killed anyone to get to me. None of this is about Katy Hart."

Joe pulled up as close as he could to the curb. An officer came toward them, and Joe rolled down his window. "I've got Dayne

Matthews."

The officer peered into the Suburban and nodded at Dayne. "Sorry about the chaos."

"No problem." Dayne grinned. It was time to be on. "Thanks for holding a spot for us."

"Happy to help." The officer leaned a little closer to the window. He held out a pad of paper and a pen. "I hate to ask . . . but could you sign an autograph for my wife?" A sheepish grin lifted his otherwise serious face. "Her name's Kathy with a *K*."

"Sure thing." Dayne reached across Joe, signed the paper, and handed it back. "Hey —" he flashed his silver-screen smile at the guy — "we might need some help getting one of the witnesses out later on." He nodded at Joe. "Can my attorney be in touch with you after lunch? Maybe make special arrangements?"

"You got it, Mr. Matthews." The officer straightened and took on an authoritative look again. "Whatever you need." He took a few steps back and motioned for Joe to park the Suburban.

Joe winked at Dayne. "Nice work."

The moment Joe killed the engine, they slipped out and headed up the walkway — Joe slightly ahead. Like the depositions in January, Joe straight-armed the crowd, his face grim. He and his famous client took the matter of a knife-bearing fan very seriously.

A CBS newscaster stepped in front of them. "Dayne . . . what's your hope for the outcome of the trial?"

At the same time a woman with a CNN microphone separated herself from the crowd. "Do you think the obsession with celebrity has gotten out of hand, and what should Hollywood do about it?"

Joe waved and shouted, "I have an announcement!"

A hundred cameras were aimed at Dayne, and each of them continued to click. But otherwise a hush fell over the throng.

Joe cupped his mouth so he could be heard. "I'm Dayne Matthews' attorney. He is a witness to this trial, and as such he cannot be interviewed yet. I'll hold a press conference later today on the front steps of the courthouse. When we have a verdict, Dayne will meet with you and answer your questions at that time." He waved off what was an immediate response from the crowd. "Thank you."

Dayne was impressed. As they climbed the steps he leaned in close to Joe. "Nice work yourself."

Joe grinned at him. "That's why you pay

me the big bucks."

Dayne glanced back as they headed through the double doors. The press was packing up, hurrying along behind them. The situation was about to get difficult. It was one thing to walk through a mob of media on a courthouse lawn. Katy hadn't had to face a single one of them. But once they were in the courtroom, the press would fill every available space. Then it would be only a matter of time before Katy and her identity were made known to the world.

He gulped and uttered a silent prayer that Katy would be protected and that even with his biological brother sitting next to him, there would be at least one secret the paparazzi would never find out about.

CHAPTER SIX

Katy was in a small sitting area adjacent to the courtroom. Luke Baxter was sitting at the table, as were a few members of the prosecution team.

Luke was explaining that she had a choice about where to sit during the proceedings. "Oftentimes judges ask all witnesses to leave the courtroom because of the testimony. But in your case there's nothing you don't already know. The police officer is going by the account you and Dayne gave, and —" he smiled — "of course you and Dayne have the same story since you were together."

She nodded. She was trying to listen, but something about Luke was distracting her.

His expression changed. "But you don't have to stay in the courtroom, Katy. You can wait in this room until they call you and leave when you're finished."

"Right." Katy bit her lip. What was it? Luke was Ashley's brother, but she'd never met him until today. So why was he so familiar looking? Not just his eyes and his face but his mannerisms. Katy tried to keep her mind on the matter at hand. "What will Dayne do?"

"He'll be in the courtroom for most of it. His presence is important for the prosecution." Luke kept his tone professional. "Yours is important but not in a high-profile way."

Katy frowned. *Not yet,* she wanted to say. "Do I have to decide now?"

"No." Luke adjusted his tie. He leaned forward. "Are you okay? Ashley said you were pretty nervous about the publicity."

"Yes." She wondered how much to tell him. "There's a lot at stake."

"I'll be meeting with Joe Morris every few hours. We'll do our best to keep the attention off you."

"Thanks."

There was a noise at the door, and they turned.

Joe Morris walked in, his cheeks red. "Intense."

Behind him were Dayne and two police officers. Dayne's eyes met Katy's. For the sweetest second, they weren't in a stuffy room about to be witnesses in an attempted murder case. They weren't ready to take the stand while every major media source took careful note. They were just two people lost in a sea of emotion, a sea neither of them could even begin to navigate.

She allowed the hint of a smile. "Hi."

"Hi." He stepped in and came to her. In a way that couldn't be mistaken for more than a show of support, he put his hand on her shoulder. "You okay?" His voice was meant only for her.

"Fine." His touch was electric, and she wondered at her careless heart. Dayne's world was insane, wilder than anything she could've dreamed. No matter what changes he'd made, she had no right letting herself have feelings for him. Not when they might as well live on different planets. In his world they couldn't hold a single public conversation without it being headline news. "Did you come through the front?"

"We did."

"It's a zoo." Joe wheeled around the table and took a seat next to Luke.

Luke stood and reached out to Dayne. "Good to see you again."

"Thanks for coming." The two shook hands. "We need all the help we can get."

Katy watched them, and again she was struck by something she couldn't quite put her finger on. Whatever it was, the feeling was stronger watching Luke with Dayne. Or maybe it was the look in Dayne's eyes. They held something that hadn't been there before. A sweet shining sadness, as if he were greeting a long-lost friend and not an associate from his law firm.

After a few minutes, Joe motioned to Luke. "I need to talk to you out in the hall for a minute."

The two left, and Dayne took the seat next to Katy. With the prosecution team members talking at the other end of the table, she almost felt as if she were alone with him. He looked incredible, more dressed up than she'd ever seen him. Suddenly her cheeks felt hot. She glanced at her black pants and white lightweight cable-knit sweater. "I'm underdressed."

"No." Dayne shook his head. His expression told her he had a hundred things he wanted to say. "You're perfect."

She wanted to tell him about Luke, about how he seemed so strangely familiar, but the chief prosecutor, Tara Lawson, walked into the room and motioned for everyone to listen up. She was in her late forties, her hair cut short around her face. She looked from Dayne to Katy and then to her fellow prosecuting team members at the far end of the table. "It's time. Katy, I've reserved you a spot in the courtroom. I'd like you there throughout the proceedings, if that's okay."

Katy thought quickly. "Yes. Fine."

"Good." Tara took a quick breath. "Okay, everyone. Follow me."

Katy's heart skipped a beat. She had no choice now. She would be in the courtroom because that's what was expected of her.

Dayne nudged her and leaned in closer. "You'll be fine. Keep praying."

She already was, of course. She'd been praying constantly. Still, his words were like a balm for her soul. He'd changed so much since their first meeting. How incredible that now he was the one reminding her to pray. Peace filtered through her even as they stood and filed out of the small room.

Tara led the way as they headed for the empty row she had reserved directly behind the table where she and her prosecuting team would be stationed. The peace from moments earlier left in a hurry. Katy's heart beat so hard she wondered if the court reporter could hear it.

Tara studied Dayne and Katy. "You'll be fine." Then she and her prosecution team headed toward the front of the courtroom.

Joe Morris directed the rest of them, careful to sit Katy next to Luke Baxter, with Dayne at the opposite end of the row. No sense giving the photographers something to shoot on the first day. At this point, the media could mistake Katy for part of the legal staff, not the woman all of Hollywood wanted to know about.

Not until Katy was seated did she allow herself to look around the courtroom. The crowd amazed her. There were people with cameras packed into every available spot. Tara had already explained that in California each judge had the right to allow or disallow cameras in his or her courtroom. The judge in this case — Henry P. Nguyen — had handled high-profile cases before. He had given select members of the press the okay to attend and to take photos and video footage. But he reserved the right to make them leave if they were disruptive.

Katy shifted her gaze to the left and noticed two rows of six people along the side of the courtroom. The jury, of course. Most of them were looking at Dayne. Tara Lawson had said that one of the defense's strategies was to find a jury that wouldn't be starstruck by Dayne Matthews. The prosecution team had laughed at the idea. Now Katy could see why. At least half of them looked ready to spring from their seats and beg Dayne for an autograph.

She looked to the far right, and what she

saw made her heart skip a beat. Margie Madden was sitting at a table near the front, opposite Tara Lawson and her team. Her hair was shorter and combed straight — not the wild yellow mop she'd had the night of the attack. But her eyes were beady and lifeless and aimed straight at Dayne. She blew him a kiss, and behind her Katy could hear the cameras going off like so many crickets on a summer night in Bloomington.

Next to Margie a gray-haired man in a suit took firm hold of her arm. He whispered something in her ear, and she seemed to snap back at him. Once more she turned her attention to Dayne, but this time she glared at him.

Katy slid down in her seat a few inches. *God, I'm not sure I can do this.*

I am with you. . . . You will not have to fight this battle alone, daughter.

The words — whispered from the most private room in her soul — drowned out everything else. She would be okay because God was with her. It was the single bit of truth that made Katy's heartbeat slow and brought sense to the moment.

For the next hour the judge heard opening remarks from Tara Lawson. "The defense team will tell you that the defendant, Margie Madden, is insane, that by reason of insanity she should not be held accountable for her actions on the night the crime in question occurred." She had complete command of the room, every eye on her. "But we will prove to you that Ms. Madden knew very well what she was doing, and she intended to commit murder that night."

Katy shuddered at the thought.

The gray-haired attorney gave his opening remarks next. "Mental illness is a troubling disease. I intend to prove to you that my client acted out as a symptom of her illness, and she would be best served by being placed in a facility where she can receive medicine and supervision. Not by being treated as a criminal."

Next to Katy, Luke Baxter touched her arm. "How are you doing?"

"I'm fine." Katy remembered to exhale. "It's intense."

"Just wait." Luke frowned. "This is nothing."

The police officer who first responded to the scene took the stand. He told about the mad look in Margie's eyes and how the woman with Dayne Matthews had knife marks on her neck and arm.

"Can you tell us the name of the woman with Dayne Matthews?" Tara Lawson had explained earlier that she had no choice but to get this fact out in the open right off. Katy's testimony was crucial to the case, and her identity needed to be spelled out in order for her place on the witness stand to make sense.

"Yes." The officer faced the prosecuting attorney. "Her name is Katy Hart."

There was a rustling near the back of the courtroom as the members of the media realized what had just happened. The mystery was solved; the woman had a name.

Katy worked hard not to react. They might know her identity, but they didn't have to know she was that person, not yet.

Tara waited for the commotion to die down. "Is it your belief that the defendant, Margie Madden, intended to kill Katy Hart?"

The officer didn't hesitate. "Yes."

"Can you explain to the jury why this is your opinion?"

"From the moment we arrived on the scene —" he looked across the courtroom at Margie — "the defendant was shouting threats at Ms. Hart."

"Can you be specific, please? What was the defendant shouting at Ms. Hart?"

"She was threatening to kill her, telling her that next time she wouldn't wait, that she wouldn't rest until both Ms. Hart and

Mr. Matthews were dead."

Another rustling came from the media.

The judge raised his hand. "Order."

The reporters and photographers responded with immediate silence. Katy could understand why. The information coming from the witness stand was too good. The last thing they wanted was to be kicked out of the courtroom for being unruly.

Luke reached over and discreetly squeezed Katy's arm. "Hang in there."

"I am." Without moving her head, she glanced toward the end of the aisle. Dayne was watching the police officer on the stand, keeping his promise to defer all attention from Katy, to do his part to keep the media from knowing just yet that she was the woman being discussed on the stand.

The testimony grew more technical, and the intensity cooled some. After lunch, the prosecutor finished up with the police officer; then the defense attorney spent an hour on cross-examination.

"Isn't it true," the gray-haired man asked, "that you never, not once, actually saw the defendant with a knife in her hand?"

The policeman looked confused. "Of course I didn't see the knife in her hand. The knife was several feet away where Dayne Matthews —"

"Please —" he held up his hand — "yes or no."

"Okay." He shrugged. "No. I didn't see the knife in her hand."

"So you are relying completely on a report given to you by witnesses. Is that right?"

The questions wore on, and Katy felt herself relax. She had been worked up about nothing — at least for now. Dayne was next on the list of prosecution witnesses, and she was third. They would never have time for all of that today.

Finally Dayne was called to the stand. The photographers snapped into action, though they stayed relatively quiet. Dayne walked slowly, never once looking at Margie Madden.

Katy watched him, the striking figure he made as he moved across the courtroom to the witness stand. No wonder America was crazy about him.

The prosecutor started with the easy questions. His name, occupation, the fact that he was pursued by many people in the course of a day, most of them fans he didn't know.

"Would you say that on occasion there are fans who act a little extreme — following you or asking things of you that make you uncomfortable?" Tara was standing a few feet from the witness stand. Her experience and confidence rang in every word.

"Yes." Dayne nodded. "On occasion a fan can get overzealous."

Tara turned slowly and headed back to the table. One of her team members handed her a document. "Is it true that at some point you were warned by police about a fan who was thought to drive a yellow Honda Civic?"

The gray-haired attorney was on his feet. "Objection, Your Honor." He motioned to Dayne. "The prosecutor is leading the witness."

Tara held up the document. "The warning included the color, make, and model of the car driven by the fan in question."

Judge Nguyen nodded. "Overruled." He looked at Tara. "Show the witness the document, please."

"Very well." Tara was just moving toward the witness stand when it happened.

Margie Madden seemed to realize what was coming, that Dayne was about to describe in detail everything that happened the night of the attack. And in that instant it must have occurred to her that if Dayne was going to share his version of the story, the woman with Dayne that night might be about to testify also.

Whatever was running through her head, Margie spun around and began looking frantically at the crowd of spectators and media members. Her attorney tried to get her attention, but before he could, Margie found her. She locked eyes on Katy. "You!" She stood and pointed at her.

"Order!" Judge Nguyen rapped his gavel on his bench. "Counsel, you will keep the defendant under control."

The defense attorney was trying. He tugged on Margie's sleeve, but she jerked away and took four giant steps toward Katy. Across the back of the courtroom, cameras were clicking as fast as they could. Before two armed bailiffs could grab the woman, she pointed at Katy again. With words that were as chilling as they were loud, she said, "I'm going to kill you! Dayne is my husband!"

Katy wanted to run for her life.

Luke Baxter slipped his arm around her shoulders. "Ignore her, Katy. She can't hurt you."

The bailiffs grabbed Margie's arms and shoved them behind her back. She was cuffed and led back to the defense table, but the entire time she was looking over her shoulder at Katy, snarling something unintelligible.

Before Katy could take her next breath, the cameras shifted. If the reporters had wondered who she was at the beginning of the proceedings, they had no doubt now. She was Katy Hart. How could she be anyone else?

Katy could feel Dayne watching her, feel him praying for her, willing her to be strong, not to bolt. She kept her focus on Luke. "Is she still looking at me?"

"Don't worry about it, Katy." He tightened his hold on her, sheltering her and making it appear that the two of them were lost in an intense conversation.

"Stop the cameras." The judge was rapping his bench, trying desperately to regain control of his courtroom. "I'd like all members of the press to step out while we regain order here."

There was a grumbling from the media horde, but they had no choice. The entire mass of them began shuffling toward the door.

All the while, Margie Madden was shouting at the bailiffs to leave her alone. Katy looked up in time to see her struggling against one of the armed officers. Then Margie's eyes — wild and furtive — made a quick search across the room until they found Katy's again. "You! Stay away from my husband, you tramp! Stay away or I'll kill you!"

From the witness stand, Dayne remained tight-lipped and calm. But Katy knew what he had to be feeling. He probably would've been glad to strangle Margie at this point. Dayne met Katy's eyes and mouthed the word *sorry.*

She couldn't respond, but she tried to tell him with her expression that it wasn't his fault. None of this was his fault.

"Kill you . . . ," Margie spat in Katy's direction. Then she leaned her head back and cackled. By then the room was empty of any cameras or members of the press. Margie seemed to sense something had changed. Without warning, she switched voices. As if two people lived inside her, she began shouting in a high-pitched voice, "Help . . . help me! It's all your fault, Chloe! I'm going down in flames because of you! Help me!"

"Your Honor." The gray-haired attorney stood. He looked and sounded utterly defeated. "I'd like to move to adjourn for the day. Clearly we have some issues with the defendant." He gestured toward the jury. "I'd also like to move for a mistrial, since the jurors cannot possibly remain objective after this display from my client."

Katy looked at the jury. They were gripped by the scene playing out, leaning forward in their seats, eyes wide and unblinking.

Margie Madden was snarling at the bailiffs. The high-pitched voice was gone. "It's none of your business *who* I kill." Her voice was lower than before. "I'll kill her if I *want* to kill her."

"I'll agree to adjourn for the day." Relief filled the judge's expression. He brushed his hand in the direction of the bailiffs. "Get her out of here." He looked at first the defense lawyer and then at Tara and her team of prosecutors. "I'd like to speak to both counsels at the bench."

Katy's stomach hurt, and she realized she'd been holding her breath.

As the bailiffs led Margie from the room, Luke removed his arm from around her and touched her shoulder. "I'm sorry, Katy. That . . . that just doesn't happen."

Frightening questions lined up in her mind, demanding to be addressed. What would become of the trial? Would the judge declare the jury too biased to do their job? The media had figured out who she was, so what exactly was Joe Morris going to tell them at his press conference later today? And what would it take to find a minute alone with Dayne so they could talk?

But with Luke next to her restoring calm to her world, she was consumed by one very intense, very strange realization. The reason Luke had looked and acted familiar was finally clear in her mind. His voice had brought the details together. Not that any of it actually made sense.

Because in that moment Luke Baxter sounded and acted and looked exactly like Dayne.

CHAPTER SEVEN

The situation was worse than anyone had expected for the first day of the trial. Judge Nguyen excused Dayne from the witness stand, then told the jury to go home and wait for further instructions.

Joe Morris led his group into a small room, where they would wait for word from Tara Lawson. When the door closed behind them, Dayne looked at Katy. She was talking with Luke Baxter, but there was no denying the terror on her face.

It was the same terror he'd seen the night of the attack. He could only imagine how badly she wanted to run away, skip the entire trial, and fly back to Indiana. He felt hot frustration rising inside him. Couldn't they share a normal week in his town just once?

Over the next few minutes, Katy looked at him a few times, but before they could talk, Joe pulled him aside. "We need the key points for the press conference."

Dayne motioned for Katy. Again they were forced to keep their conversation nonpersonal. "Can you talk for a minute?"

Katy moved closer, and she and Dayne sat at the table with Joe and figured out what the press would want to know, what information would keep them from looking deeper. In the end they agreed that Joe would share her age and that she lived in Indiana. He would tell them she was in town the night of the attack reading for a part in *Dream On.* He would say that Katy had a history of small on-screen parts, and she and Dayne were friends, that they were still friends.

If anyone asked whether Katy was the reason Dayne had filmed the movie in Bloomington, Joe would remain evasive. Of course, he would tell them, Dayne knew about the town of Bloomington because of his friendship with Katy Hart. Nothing more.

"The goal is to keep the attention on Dayne and Margie Madden and paint Katy as being at the wrong place at the wrong time. We don't want them digging around Bloomington, finding Christian Kids Theater or suspecting that Dayne was carrying on with you while he was living with Kelly

Parker."

"I wasn't!" Dayne's answer was a little too quick. He grabbed at the hair above his forehead and exhaled hard. He didn't owe anyone in the room an explanation about his actions. "Katy and I barely saw each other the whole time I was in Bloomington."

Katy gave him a look, and something about it was sad. It occurred to him that he probably sounded callous, as if the time they did spend together meant nothing to him. He tried to tell her with his eyes that they would talk later, but again everything felt strangely terrible. As if his whole world were spinning off its axis.

Joe held up his hand. "Relax, Dayne. I think we can keep them away from that point." He was cool, his tone assuring. "Either way, it's the best we can do for now. Katy's name is public record at this point. Heading off the press with a conference is the best choice."

They talked a few more minutes, and then Tara Lawson hurried into the room. She wore the first smile Dayne had seen on her all day. "The meeting with the judge was quick," she told them. "We have a plan."

The room fell silent, and Tara continued. "Both sides agree that we can keep the same jury. We'll be allowed to refer to the outbreak — and any future outbreaks — as evidence of the defendant's insanity."

"That means she'll get off." Dayne wanted to yell. Nothing was going the way it was supposed to. "The defense wants her proven not guilty by reason of insanity."

"They can try that, but we'll prove that either way she's dangerous and deserves to be locked up. Besides, we have medical doctors willing to take the stand and declare Margie Madden absolutely aware of her actions, aware of the difference between right and wrong."

That made sense. Dayne relaxed a little. "Fine." He forced himself to lighten up. "As long as you're okay with it."

"I am." She nodded toward the door. "Margie's going to make outbreaks like that often. We'd need a new jury every day if we were going to handle her that way. Whether it hurts her case or not, her attorney agrees. We need to move forward."

They talked strategy until it was time for Joe to meet the media in front of the courthouse for the press conference.

Not long after, Tara excused them, and Katy and Dayne left through the back door. The police officer whom Dayne had signed an autograph for earlier drove them a few blocks to the back section of a city park, where Katy had parked her car. Luke had arranged to meet her there this morning so the media wouldn't see her rental car, and so she could escape their glare after the day's hearing.

The officer chatted the whole time about his wife, how happy she was going to be when he gave her the autograph, and how much they enjoyed Dayne's newest film. Katy stayed quiet the entire ride. When they reached the parking lot, Dayne thanked the man, and he and Katy moved from the police officer's car to hers.

As the officer drove off, Dayne looked around. There were no signs of paparazzi. For the first time since the chaos began early that morning, they were alone.

Dayne released a slow breath. "That was fun." He looked at Katy, sitting behind the wheel. "You okay?"

She leaned against her car door and searched his eyes. "I prayed for this."

Dayne hesitated. The day had gone so badly. "For what?"

"This." She glanced around and leaned her head against the side window. "That we'd have at least a few minutes alone."

This parking lot — smack in the middle of a tree-lined old city park — definitely wasn't a place paparazzi would find them. At the same time it wasn't the safest place. He reached for her hand. The feel of her skin against his breathed new life into him. "Were you scared?"

"Yes." She covered his fingers with her other hand. "I knew she couldn't hurt me. But Dayne . . . the woman is so evil."

"She's insane." He pressed his shoulder into the seat. No matter how difficult the day, this felt wonderful, being alone with Katy, not worrying about cameras and reporters. "Tara will make sure she gets locked up." He wanted to ease her fears so they could do the one thing they hadn't been able to do since she arrived. Talk about their feelings for each other. He kept his tone calm, comforting. "Let's not let the trial consume us, okay? There's nothing to worry about."

"All right." She gazed out the windshield.

He did the same. The park was full of mature oaks and evergreens surrounding a cement basketball court. A group of shady-looking teens — gang members, no doubt — lurked around the edges of the court. There wasn't a basketball among them. The parking lot might be free from photographers, but this wasn't a comfortable place for a conversation.

Her eyes found his again. "How do you live this way?"

The question stung. She didn't have to explain herself. He knew what she meant. The media, the strategizing, the obsessed fans, the scrutiny.

Before he could answer, her face filled with sympathy. "It hurts me to think this is your life." She exhaled, finally relaxing. "It makes me so glad I didn't take the part."

"One part wouldn't make your life as crazy as mine." He brought her right hand to his lips and kissed it. "I still think you should do a film, Katy. You're very good."

A weak laugh came from her. "Not today. I couldn't hide my fear to save my life."

"You weren't expecting her to lash out."

A few of the teens from across the way were looking at them, pointing in their direction. Dayne doubted they had recognized him. Rather, the park was probably their hangout spot, their turf. Newcomers weren't welcome.

Katy started the car, backed out, and headed for the park exit. "Let's get dinner and go back to your house."

They stopped at a Subway, and Katy ran inside. She was still an unknown — at least for a few more days.

Ten minutes later they were a few houses

from his home in Malibu. As Katy slowed down, she gasped. "Dayne . . . look!"

His entire driveway and small front yard were covered with paparazzi. Whatever Joe had told them, it had only made them hungrier — at least for photos of Dayne and Katy together. He waved her on. "Keep going. Don't even slow down."

She did as he asked, but a few of the photographers had been sitting on their cars. They must have spotted him in Katy's passenger seat, because in the side mirror he watched them dart into their cars and pull into traffic. "Great."

"They saw us?"

"A few of them. The others are probably figuring it out by now." Dayne kept his eyes on the side mirror. "Head back to your hotel, Katy. I'll call ahead and arrange for a valet to meet us at the back door."

He made the phone call, and though there were four cars behind them when they pulled into the hotel parking lot, Katy whipped the car around to a door at the back — one Luke had told her about earlier that day. It was a private entrance, meant for celebrities or visiting politicians or dignitaries. A valet hop was waiting when she pulled up.

Dayne grabbed the bag of sandwiches and

followed Katy in a mad dash from the car to the door. The valet ushered them inside. Katy gave him her keys and a ten-dollar bill. "Thank you."

"Here." He handed Dayne a key card. "Use this whenever you come and go. It gives you access to the back door and to the roof."

"Thanks, man." Dayne hurried Katy farther into the hallway, and the valet went back out to move Katy's car. For a moment they stood there, breathing hard. They could hear cars squealing to a stop, hear the voices as the paparazzi shouted at the valet.

"Let's go." Dayne pointed to the elevator. "I've had friends stay here before. I think I know how to get to the roof." They went to the top floor. He took her hand, and they jogged to the end of a hallway. After he opened the door with the key card, the two of them slipped into an outdoor stairwell. A minute later they were on the roof.

The day had been in the high eighties, and now — with the sun about to set — heat still emanated from the roof. Dayne could feel himself unwind. The roof was a great idea. He should've thought about it days ago; they could've had the key ahead of time.

He led the way slowly across the top of

the building. On the far side was a garden, a two-seater glider, a few chairs surrounded by bushes, and a spread of colorful flowers. Dayne moved in that direction. The view never got old, the Hollywood Hills spread out before them in the fading sunlight.

"This is amazing." Katy sat down on the glider and leaned her head back. "I feel like we stumbled into a land of make-believe. A place in LA where the paparazzi can't reach you? Who would've thought?"

Dayne chuckled. "Yeah." He set the bag of sandwiches on an end table and took the spot next to her. A slight breeze washed over them. "It really is that bad, isn't it?"

"Your life?" she asked, her brow twisted. "Yeah, it is."

They were quiet for a moment, and Dayne set the glider in motion. The day's events seemed farther away with each subtle movement. He looked at her. "Hungry?"

"Not yet." She smiled. "I'm waiting for the knots to unwind."

"Katy . . ." Dayne stared straight ahead. "I'm sorry." He looked beyond the wrought-iron fence and railing that surrounded the roof to the silhouette of the nearby mountains. He wanted to take her in his arms, remind her of all the things they'd felt for each other back in Indiana. All the things they had talked about in their recent phone calls.

But even here — on a rooftop with no one to interrupt them — the chasm between them felt wider than the Pacific. He glanced at her, but she had her eyes closed. He sighed, and the sound of it made him feel tired. *Why, God? Why is everything so difficult between us?*

Finally she opened her eyes, reached over, and put her hand on his knee. "It's not your fault." For the first time since her arrival in LA, she sounded at ease, more like the person she'd been the last time they were together. "You can't change what you are. Who you are."

"I wish . . ." He allowed himself to get lost in her eyes. The connection between them gave him a reckless sort of feeling, as if he were being sucked in with no way out. The noises from the street below faded. "I wish we were in the Flanigans' living room, and a storm was raging outside."

"You don't have to wish." Katy smiled. "A storm is definitely raging." She took her hand off his knee. "Tell me the truth, Dayne. Will it be in the paper tomorrow?"

"Definitely." He narrowed his eyes. "I haven't talked to Joe, but I'm sure he handled it brilliantly." He grinned. "He always does."

"Meaning the story will run, and the details about me will probably be secondary?"

"I think so."

She stood and stretched. Then she went to the railing, leaned against it, and stared at the street below. "It's a long way down."

"Yes." He watched her and wondered. Was she talking about the drop from the roof or something else? the life she had lived until this moment and what distance she might fall come morning? A few minutes passed.

She turned and leaned her elbows on the railing. "I don't really know this side of you. I guess . . . I guess that's just a lot clearer now."

Frustration strangled out whatever good he'd been feeling. He pinched his lips together and stared at the rooftop. Why did it always have to come back to this? His public persona, the life he lived because of his fame?

"Dayne . . ." Her voice told him she was sorry, that maybe she'd said the wrong thing. When he didn't respond, she turned her back to him once more. A sigh rattled from her direction.

For several minutes Dayne allowed the silence between them. Her reaction wasn't fair, but it was understandable. How could she see him and not see his public image, his fame? It was part of him, a very real part of being with him. At least in this season of his life. So what were the answers?

He studied the sad picture she made leaning against the railing, gazing at the first stars as if maybe, by magic, an answer would appear the same way.

Or maybe there didn't have to be answers. He stood and took the place next to her. Never mind the difficulties that lay like so many explosive mines on the landscape of whatever they'd started. Right now they were alone together. They were foolish to waste time trying to figure out the impossible. He looked at the same section of the sky where she still had her eyes trained. "The stars are harder to see —" he slipped his arm around her shoulders — "here in the city."

"Mmm." She eased in against his side. "I was thinking that." Her voice was softer, the tension from earlier gone. "The same stars are up there, the millions I can see from the Flanigans' backyard."

Below, a car screeched through the intersection, and two drivers laid on their horns.

Katy glanced at the commotion, and a soft laugh came from her. "Here, there's so much to compete with. The lights and noise and crowds and chaos." She shifted just enough so she could see him. "Something quietly beautiful —" her eyes lifted to the sky again — "is harder to see in your world."

Dayne let her words settle deep in his heart. He eased her around so she was facing him. "Like us." His hand fell to her waist. "Like what's between us."

"Yes." She looked at him the way she had that stormy night back in Bloomington. "Like us." Regret colored her expression. "I'm sorry about what I said, Dayne. Your world, the absurdity of it, it isn't what you want." She touched his cheek. "I know that."

He wanted to kiss her, but he was in no hurry. This — the connection their hearts were finding — was almost better for now. "Ever since I went to Mexico, it's like I live a double life." He took a slow breath. "The one I have at home when I'm praying for you and me, when I'm reading my Bible and asking God what the future holds." His focus shifted to the traffic below. "And the one I lead out there. On the red carpet. Running from the cameras."

She moved her hand to his shoulder. "Remember when we took that walk? the one around Lake Monroe?"

"Do I remember it?" He let his eyes find

hers again. They were grabbing at common ground, working their way back to how things felt in Indiana. He felt the hint of a grin tug at his lips. "Every day."

This time her smile filled her face. It was still cautious and a little shy, but no question, his words had touched her. "Really?"

"Really."

"Well." She seemed to struggle to remember her point. The sky was getting darker, and the few stars that glittered there shone in her eyes. "I told you back then that we were too different, that we lived in separate worlds so this —" she glanced at his hand still on her waist and at hers on his shoulder — "whatever this is could never work."

He wasn't sure where the conversation was going. "I remember."

"But now . . ." Her voice was so soft he could barely hear it. "No matter how strange things seem, we share the most important part."

"Faith."

"Right." She bit the inside of her lip. "The two lives you were talking about?" Noise from the street below seemed to fade, as if the two of them were all that existed. "The one you are at home when you're alone isn't someone far away or different. Not anymore."

Dayne searched her face, his heart suddenly light within him. Was she saying what he thought she was saying? "Meaning . . . ?"

She touched his cheek again. "Meaning . . . I'm here, standing here, because maybe it is possible."

After all the insanity of the day, he could hardly believe this. He framed her face with his free hand, working his fingers into her hair. "You and me, you mean?"

"Yes." Her smile remained, but her eyes grew watery. "We share what matters most, so there has to be a way, right? Maybe we need to ask God."

He had planned to kiss her, longed to take her in his arms and show her how much he felt for her. But her idea was even better. In his life, physical love had always come easy. It was this — a connection of his *soul* with the soul of someone he loved — that had been missing. He swallowed hard, giving his desire a chance to cool. Then he took her hands in his. "Let's do that."

She looked surprised but only for a moment. "Pray?"

He closed his eyes and bowed his head. "Lord, I'm new at this. But Bob tells me it's as easy as talking to You. So here goes."

Katy tightened her hold on his hands.

"We believe You've brought us together

for a reason, God." He exhaled, and it held all the frustration of the reality that still existed once they left the rooftop. "The thing is, my life won't let me have what I want with her. Still, I read in the Bible the other day that nothing is impossible with You. So . . . we come here tonight asking You to show us a way. Please, God. No matter how out of control life seems in the coming days, help us keep our eyes on You. Help us remember this moment, this feeling. This prayer. And please, God, help us believe that somehow — someday — we can act on the feelings we have for each other. In Jesus' name, amen."

When they opened their eyes, he saw tears on her cheeks.

Katy smiled at him. "That was perfect."

He grinned, but he took a step back. If he was going to keep things clean, keep them on an emotional level, he needed distance. Especially now. "You know what we need to do?"

"What?" There was humor in her voice, and it lightened the mood.

"We need to eat."

They both laughed and returned to the glider. They began eating without talking about the trial or Margie Madden or the fact that the rooftop was the only place they could find a moment of sanity. Instead Dayne told her about his conversations with his birth father. Already she knew that the two of them had met — though he'd kept all other details to himself. She knew Ashley after all. There was no reason to make the situation more complicated by letting her know that his family was the Baxters.

She had her sandwich on the open wrapper, spread out on her lap. "Really? So you've been talking?"

"Every few days." He took a bite and realized how hungry he was.

"So tell me about him." She picked up her sandwich. "Do you like him? Are you feeling close to him?"

Dayne nodded. "He's the most amazing guy — strong in his faith. Wiser than anyone I know. His kids adore him — I can tell." He felt the familiar winds of what might have been. "Makes me wish I'd known him all my life."

"He and his wife, they had no choice, right? They had to give you up?"

"Yes. They would've given anything to keep me. But she was young, and her parents wouldn't hear of it."

Katy already knew that his birth mother was dead. Dayne had shared that with her.

They finished their sandwiches, talk between them slow and easy. The conversation shifted from Dayne's birth father to *Narnia,* the play Katy's kids were working on.

"You were right that day." He wadded up his sandwich wrapper and tossed it in the paper sack. "The scene where Aslan comes back to life, it's the most powerful in the story."

"You didn't want to talk about it." Katy eased her knees up onto the glider and tucked her feet beneath her. "I could tell."

"I know." He remembered that afternoon. They had been driving through a terrible storm, heading toward the Flanigans' house when Katy brought it up. But he hadn't wanted to think about Aslan or Narnia. He had been angry at God, still hurting badly over the areas in his life where he felt God deserved the blame. So he'd fallen quiet when she talked about the scene from the play. "I wasn't ready to talk about an allegory about Christ, not back then. Too many questions in my mind, I guess."

She shifted so she was facing him. "I wasn't going to push. I figured God could take care of that part."

"He did." Again Dayne had to fight the urge to reach out to her, hold her close, and give in to the feelings raging in his heart.

What had Bob Asher, his missionary friend, told him last time they talked? *"Take things slow, buddy. Let her know your priorities have shifted."* Yes, that's what tonight was about. Letting Katy see that even though he kissed her on the beach last night, his priorities had indeed shifted. He kept his distance.

Another hour passed with easy talk and laughter, and then Dayne looked at his watch. "You need your sleep. It'll be a long day tomorrow." He patted her knee. "Let's call it a night, okay?"

Disappointment flashed in her eyes, but it lasted only a moment. "Good idea." She stood, pushed her sandwich wrapper into the same paper sack, and smiled at him. "If I can fall asleep at all."

"You will." He pointed up. "God'll take care of that too."

She looked surprised, but her eyes danced. "He will, won't He?"

"Yes." Dayne took her hand and led her slowly across the roof back to the stairwell. Before they walked down, he stopped and turned toward her. "Come here, Katy."

Her expression told him she'd been waiting for him to ask all night. She circled her arms around his neck, and he eased his around her waist. For a long time they held each other that way, swaying slightly in the cooling breeze.

He brushed his cheek against her hair and whispered close to her ear, "Tonight was amazing. Just being with you, alone like this."

"It was." She searched his eyes. Neither of them said anything for half a minute. Then she exhaled and eased back a little. "You're not going to kiss me, are you?"

"No." He angled his head, willing her to understand. "What I feel for you . . ." He drew a slow breath and gathered his senses. He studied her face and spoke to a place he hoped belonged only to him. "I've never felt this way about anyone. Not ever." He let his forehead rest against hers. "I'm trying to listen to God, Katy, trying to let you see it isn't about stealing kisses and letting my body lead."

She was captured, holding on to every word. Her eyes told him that much.

"Tonight we asked God to lead . . . so I am."

Katy didn't blink, didn't seem to want the connection between them to end. But her lips curved into a smile and she nodded. "Good enough."

"So —" he pulled her close once more — "even though I want to stay up here like this all night, I'm going to go." He stepped back and took hold of her hands. "And tomorrow when things get crazy —" he grinned — "and they will . . ."

"For sure."

He chuckled. "Tomorrow when that happens, just know I'll be praying and that somehow . . . someway we'll find ourselves in a sane place like this again. Because God will be leading us."

She looked like she wanted to say something, but the stars in her eyes — far more than the paltry few in the sky overhead — were enough.

Dayne gave her a last look and led her down the stairs. They rode the elevator to her floor. He squeezed her hand just once. "Good-bye, Katy."

She smiled. "Good night."

And then she was gone. The elevator doors shut, and he leaned against the cool back wall. He'd told her the truth; that much was sure. His heart and mind and soul, all of it swirled together in the most amazing feeling he'd ever known. No one had made him feel this way, and suddenly he knew without a doubt that the decision to not kiss her tonight had been more God's than his.

"Keep talking to me, Lord," he whispered as the elevator made its way down to the main level. "I'm listening."

His prayer from earlier came back. The things he'd asked for, a way to make his feelings for Katy real, could happen only through God's intervention. But here, now, with her smile still fresh in his memory, Dayne believed with everything in him that God would make it happen. And that some-how — somewhere down the road — he wouldn't feel caught between two com-pletely different lives. But rather the man he was in the quiet places on the beach and at home would win out. And the public per-sona would have to find a way to fall in line.

So that he could spend forever acting on the deep things he had been allowed to feel for a few hours on a private LA rooftop.

Chapter Eight

The night had been sheer magic. Never for a minute had Katy dreamed that after the horrific events of the day somehow she would wind up alone with Dayne in a rooftop garden overlooking the Hollywood Hills. As she stepped off the elevator, she breathed a dozen thanks to God for allowing them those precious hours, the chance to connect if just for a night — without the glare of the cameras.

She slipped her key into her door and went inside. The most wonderful, unbelievable part was this: Dayne Matthews was a changed man. She could tell herself as much during their phone calls, convince her heart that the meeting he'd had in Mexico with his friend Bob Asher had truly changed him. But only after spending the past few hours with him could she be absolutely sure.

She went to her window and leaned against the sill. When he'd taken her hands and prayed with her, she was sure she'd faint from the shock. She had to work the whole time to focus on what he was saying and not the more obvious fact — Dayne Matthews was praying with her!

The view below was the same one they'd had from the roof, but this time the traffic and confusion didn't feel overwhelming. It felt like a sea that could be bridged, an ocean that could be crossed. Yes, Dayne was living two lives. But at least one of them was like hers — passionate for God and desperate to find a way to work things out. They'd committed their future to God, and now it was up to Him to lead them.

A smile lifted her lips as she thought about what Dayne had said, how he had made a decision not to kiss her so he could show her how much he cared. A part of her had wanted to take over, lean up, and kiss him first, before he could object. But almost as quickly she realized what he was doing. The decision was Dayne's attempt at trying to follow God's will where she was concerned — maybe for the first time.

She hugged herself, warmed by the memory. In that case, she felt wonderful about his decision, safe and protected and more cared for than she could've described. She drew the curtains, turned, and looked at the phone on the table between the two beds. Jenny or Ashley or Rhonda, any of them would've been dying to know the details of her first full day in LA. Any other day she would call them but not tonight. She yawned and headed for the bathroom instead. They would find out in the morning along with the rest of the country.

For now, she wanted only to get ready for bed and turn in, her memory of tonight vivid and consuming. She refused to think about Margie Madden or the outbreak in court or the photos and press conference that might even now be coming together in a front-page story. All that mattered were Dayne's words, his prayer.

Fifteen minutes later she tucked herself beneath the crisp, cool sheets and closed her eyes. But the whole time she was back in Dayne's arms, in a rooftop world of their own, believing that God would lead the way to a future that neither of them could quite see.

No matter what the morning papers held.

Sunlight slipped through the crack in the heavy curtains, and Katy woke with a start. Through bleary eyes she found the digital clock on the table near her bed. Six-fifteen. The paper would be at her door, no doubt, and with it the answers to questions she refused to entertain the night before.

But now in the light of day, there was no running from the facts. She would appear in court today along with Dayne and the rest of the team of lawyers and prosecutors, and whatever today's news held would be common knowledge for everyone in the courtroom. Everyone in the country.

God . . . go with me. Whatever the paper says, help me remember that my identity is in You alone.

I am with you, precious daughter. Peace I give you.

The words washed over her soul, and in the quiet of the hotel room they sounded almost audible. She smiled as she felt the familiar otherworldly peace. No matter what happened today, nothing could take away the safety and certainty she carried within her.

As she swung her feet over the edge of the bed, Dayne's face came to mind, his face and his tender voice, his prayer from the night before.

Lord, help Dayne remember the things he asked You last night. Let him know You're working things out for us, please, God.

There was no answer this time, but Katy smiled anyway. She stared at her hotel door and breathed in. This was it, her hour of reckoning. Dayne had told her that whatever the newspapers said, the story would be tame compared with the articles that were bound to show up early next week in the tabloids.

She stood, opened the door, and picked up the copy of the *Los Angeles Times* lying just outside her room. Even with everything she'd been expecting, with Dayne's warning and the prayer she'd just uttered, nothing could've prepared her for the picture on the front page.

Just beneath the fold, a headline ran across the entire page: "Crazy Fan Lashes Out at Victim." Below that a smaller headline read "Dayne Matthews' Mystery Woman Revealed in First Day of Dramatic Testimony." Three photos accompanied the story. The first two Katy would've expected. A stock headshot of Dayne, next to a close-up photo of Katy sitting in the courtroom during testimony.

It was the third photo that made her start shaking there in the doorway. Somehow the *Times* had gotten hold of the paparazzi photo, the one taken the first night she was in town. The picture was of her and Dayne on the beach, the two of them caught in an embrace that left no doubt about the identity of either of them.

Katy's hands shook as she stepped back into the room and made her way to the edge of the bed. *How in the world?* The photographers must've sold the photo to everyone willing to pay — and the *Times* had clearly been willing. Beneath the photo a caption said "Dayne Matthews embraces Katy Hart near his Malibu home Sunday night."

Katy let the paper fall to her lap. Great. The whole country was waking up to the reality that she and Dayne were involved in what? A tryst? A backstreet affair? Just one more wild night of reveling on the part of playboy Dayne Matthews? How could she ever face her CKT families now? She hugged herself and tried to ward off the pains in her stomach.

She needed to read the story, but she wasn't sure she could. *God, where are You? Where's the peace I felt earlier?*

She heard no words, no reassuring whispers. But the comfort from minutes ago returned. God was with her; she knew His peace was working its way into her soul even if she couldn't feel it. She picked up the paper and tried to still her hands enough so she could make out the words.

The article was fairly straightforward. It began with a recap of the day's testimony.

Katy scanned ahead and held her breath. Nothing, no mention of Christian Kids Theater. She felt her lungs start to work again. For now, anyway, at least that one detail was sacred.

She found her place in the article and continued to read. Once the facts from the case were made clear, including the death threat by Margie Madden and the detail that attorneys for both sides had agreed to continue on with the trial, the article went into greater description about the background of the case.

For months, tabloids have speculated about the identity of the young female victim with Dayne Matthews the night of the attack at Paradise Cove. When court proceedings convened Monday, Dayne Matthews' attorney Joe Morris held a press conference on the steps of the courthouse and confirmed the identity of Katy Hart, an actress and theater director from Bloomington, Indiana.

Katy's stomach hurt more with every sentence. The next paragraph talked about the fact that Katy had been in town reading for the lead role opposite Dayne in his movie *Dream On.*

The part was later given to A-list actress Kelly Parker, who was at the time and for the next several months romantically involved with Matthews.

Next came the part that Katy dreaded most.

Attorney Morris said that Hart was not romantically involved with Matthews at the time of the attack at Paradise Cove. However, tabloid reports show that Matthews was caught on camera kissing a woman who resembled Hart just minutes before the attack.

Lord, what am I going to do?
Be still, and know that I am God.
She closed her eyes and held on to that. It was a verse she'd read the night before her flight to Los Angeles. No matter how out of control things got she needed to remember that God was in control. He was in charge. Even now. She managed the slightest breath and kept reading.

Morris also denied that Hart was the reason Matthews chose to film his location shots for *Dream On* in Bloomington, Indiana. He further said that the two are not currently romantically involved, despite a photo taken of Hart and Matthews Sunday night at Malibu Beach.

"My client and Katy Hart are good friends," Morris said. "Their relationship should be respected as such." He refused to comment on the photo taken Sunday or speculation of a photo taken of the pair the night of the attack. Matthews was living with his costar Kelly Parker at the time of his location filming in Bloomington, Indiana.

There the story came to a merciful end.

The reporter didn't say that Katy and Dayne were involved in a relationship while he was in Bloomington. It didn't have to. The points were as easy to connect as a child's puzzle. There was a picture of them kissing the night of the attack. He was in her hometown during his location filming, and there was a second picture of them embracing just days ago.

The deduction for anyone reading the article was clear — of course they had been in a relationship. Because Katy's identity had been left a mystery, the implications were that she and Dayne were together not only during the attack but ever since. And the conclusion most people would draw was that Katy had been sneaking around with

Dayne even while he was living with Kelly Parker.

She folded the paper and set it on the bed beside her. If there was a way to blink herself back to Bloomington, she would've done it. But before she could imagine how she was supposed to take her next step, her cell phone beside the bed began to vibrate. She grabbed it and glanced at the caller ID. *Dayne.* She opened it and held it to her ear. Only then did she realize that her entire body was shaking. "Hello?"

"Katy, did you see it?" Dayne sounded breathless, more worried than she'd ever heard him.

She closed her eyes and steadied herself. "Yes. I read every word."

"Listen, don't panic." He groaned and muttered something under his breath. "I can't believe they bought the photo from the beach. The whole thing is so much more about me than you, Katy. You have to believe that."

"But they made me look like a tramp." There were tears in her voice, and she gritted her teeth. She couldn't break down, not now. They had an entire day of testimony ahead of them. "Everyone will think we've been together this whole time."

"Katy . . . stop." He breathed out, and his

136

voice grew calmer than before. "Remember my prayer last night?"

"Yes, of course." She couldn't make her ribs expand enough to grab a full breath. Instead she gripped the phone and stared at the slice of light coming from the closed curtains. "I remember."

"So here's what you hold on to." He paused. "It doesn't matter what the *LA Times* says. It doesn't matter if everyone in the world believes that you and I have been in a relationship. God matters; that's all. He knows the truth, and we know the truth. And anyone who knows us will know the truth eventually." His words were clear and measured, without the fear that strained his tone a moment ago. "Can you believe that?"

Her heart was pounding so loud she had to struggle to hear him. But his words made her think. He had a point. So what if the world thought something mistaken about her? They didn't know her. And one day when the dust from the trial settled, she could make things clear with the people who did know her, right? Her body stopped shaking. "I guess so."

"Okay, so you go into court today with your head high. The two of us avoid each other, and Joe Morris handles the media. He'll stick to the same story. You and I are friends. Stories of our romantic involvement are false. We'll get through this, Katy. We will. Just remember the media's only interested in you because of me."

Her heart was still pounding but not as fast as before. "Okay." She ran her tongue along the inside of her mouth. It was so dry she could barely swallow. "I have to get ready."

"Don't panic. Please, Katy. Everything's going to be okay."

She pictured him, the way he'd looked the night before in her arms. "All right." She began to feel the peace she'd had earlier. "I promise."

When the call ended, she took a shower and got ready as fast as she could. Maybe the story had only run in Los Angeles, and if that were the case, then her world in Bloomington might still be intact. Maybe this morning the Flanigans and Rhonda and CKT coordinator Bethany Allen weren't all waking up to the same story spread across the LA paper.

She had ten minutes until Luke Baxter would be at the back door of the hotel to pick her up. She flipped open her phone and called Jenny's cell. It would be hours later in Bloomington. Jenny would be running errands or volunteering at Bailey's high school, the way she often did. Still, it was worth a try.

The phone rang twice, three times, then went to voice mail. She hung up before the end of the message. Whatever the papers in Bloomington said that morning, she'd have to find out later. She gathered her purse, checked her look once more, and begged God to go before her.

She headed down to the lobby and toward the back door. Six photographers were lined up near the door, and edging his way in front of them was Luke, ready to shield her as they moved to his rental car. She thought about running or hiding her face, but what was the point? They knew her name and her role in the trial, and they knew that she was connected with Dayne.

Ignore them. That's what Dayne had advised her before, and it was the only logical course of action now. They couldn't harm her, and the pictures would be useless. Katy Hart leaving her hotel under the protection of a legal assistant? Big deal. Holding her head high, the way Dayne had told her to do, she moved in next to Luke, and the two of them stepped into daylight.

The cameras took aim, and the photographers began making rapid clicks, snapping dozens of photos in a matter of seconds.

Fine. She refused to look at them as they walked to Luke's car. But she wasn't prepared for the questions.

"How long have you and Dayne been lovers?" One of the cameramen stayed a foot in front of her, blocking her path and moving only enough to let her continue on. "Tell us, Katy. How long?"

Luke held out his hand. "Step aside, please."

Katy felt her face grow hot. A memory flashed in her mind, a story in one of the tabloids about a famous pop singer throwing a full cup of pop in the face of a photographer. And another where a well-known, usually levelheaded movie star had knocked a member of the paparazzi to the ground. No wonder. She kept her eyes on Luke's car and let him lead her around the photographer.

"Were you sleeping with Dayne while he was living with Kelly Parker?"

"Where did you and Dayne hook up in Bloomington during the location shoot for *Dream On?*"

The questions blended together and made her nauseous. *Fight, Katy . . . keep walking,* she told herself. Three more seconds, two . . . she reached the passenger door of Luke's car just as he opened it. She climbed inside, and as Luke shut it she hit the lock button. The paparazzi surrounded her half of the car, still snapping pictures even as Luke pulled away.

He made a frustrated sound. "Vultures."

Katy couldn't breathe well enough to respond. Every bit of truth she'd told herself earlier in the hotel room, every sensible word Dayne had spoken to her seemed foreign and unreachable.

"You okay?" Luke was calm. He headed onto the main boulevard, ignoring the revving engines and screeching tires behind him.

"I . . . I don't know." She slumped down in her seat. How was she even here? She hadn't wanted this life, right? Wasn't that why she hadn't taken the part in *Dream On* in the first place? Wasn't this the lifestyle that had led her first love, Tad Thompson, to choose drugs? Maybe he'd taken them because he couldn't see any other way out. The thought sent a shiver down her spine.

Tears stung her eyes, and she glanced at the side mirror. All six cars were following them. She was the hot story of the day, and they weren't about to relent. Not any time soon. And that made her think of something. What if Dayne was wrong? What if their interest lasted after the trial and followed her home to Bloomington? And how, without miraculous intervention, would she and Dayne ever have another moment alone like the one they'd had last night?

"Katy . . . this will pass." Luke pulled up to a stoplight and looked at her. "Dayne warned us it would be like this, but it'll pass. As soon as something else takes their attention."

It was as if he could read her mind. She nodded and turned her gaze straight ahead for the rest of the trip. The whole way she reminded herself that Dayne and Luke were right, that the intense scrutiny couldn't really hurt her, not the person she was inside. But she felt sick and uptight the entire ride and even more so as Luke escorted her through the back door of the courtroom.

Paparazzi had figured out that the back door was a viable entrance, and dozens of cameramen lined the sidewalk.

Katy and Luke were halfway to the door, dodging questions and cameras, when the strangest thing happened. One of the photographers from farther back in the pack yelled, "Dayne, tell us how long you and Katy have been an item."

Luke stopped for a moment, obviously confused. "My name is Luke Baxter. I'm a legal assistant for Dayne Matthews." He shaded his eyes and directed his words to the place from where the question had been fired. "We have no comment at this time."

He put his arm around Katy and ushered her into the building. When they were inside he shook his head. "The guys in my office think the same thing — that I look like Dayne."

In that instant the paparazzi was forgotten. "Yes." Katy caught her breath and studied him. "The other day . . . your voice, the way you moved. Everything about you reminded me of Dayne."

Luke shrugged, and a familiar smile, Dayne's smile, hung on his lips. "They say everyone has a double out there somewhere."

She narrowed her eyes, amazed more than ever at the resemblance. "I guess."

"My wife says I'm better looking." He chuckled. "But she's a little biased." He took a few steps. "Come on, let's get to the courtroom."

The press was back in full force, and they took pictures of her as she walked into the courtroom with Luke. At least they couldn't shout questions at her. She exchanged a look with Dayne but only long enough for her to see that he was confident and collected.

Katy glanced at the defense table. Margie was seated next to the gray-haired attorney. Her hands were cuffed, and she looked more sedate. Maybe they'd drugged her to keep her quiet.

Even so, Katy felt like her stomach was about to drop to her knees. She wasn't sure what would happen next or whether her world was about to crash in on her. Luke sat next to her, and once in a while he patted her arm, but still her stomach remained tight, her breathing shallow.

The proceedings began, and Dayne was called to the witness stand again. Only then did she truly feel that she might survive the day. Not because of anything anyone had said or the atmosphere in the courtroom. But because for the first time she had a reason to look at Dayne, to get lost in his eyes. What she saw there told her he was at peace, and more than that, he was praying.

Strange, really, how he was showing more maturity in his faith than she was. And she'd been a Christian longer. But then, he'd been raised with the same faith. All the truths, all the power of God's Word had been a part of his life since he was a child — same as her. Now that he had claimed that faith as his own, it was stronger than Katy had imagined. Strong enough to give her a sense of protection.

As a little girl she had learned that the eyes were the window to the soul. Since that was true, she could see by looking at Dayne's that his soul was not consumed with fear, the way hers had been. It was consumed with God.

And that was enough to get them both through whatever might come next.

CHAPTER NINE

Dayne was dying to get Katy alone, to hold her and whisper to her the way he had the night before. To assure her that everything really would be okay, no matter how it felt in that moment. But he was helpless to do anything but sit, cool and collected, on the witness stand.

This was the part of the proceedings Dayne was most concerned about. He and Tara Lawson had worked with his attorney Joe Morris making sure the line of questioning would steer clear of the events that led Dayne and Katy to Paradise Cove the night of the attack. Now he could only pray with every breath that the information would remain vague, that he wouldn't be required to admit that he and Katy had held hands or kissed or discussed anything but her possible part in the movie.

Katy had already been traumatized by the publicity, and the scrutiny had only just begun. The tabloids would make the *Times* article look passive. But by then he'd at least have time to talk to Katy. For now he wanted to keep from making things worse.

So far Tara's questions had been perfect. Rather than avoid the subject of why Dayne was at the beach, she tackled it head-on, keeping the details to a professional level. "Mr. Matthews, could you tell the jury who you were with on the night of the attack?"

Dayne leaned close to the microphone. "I was with an actress, Katy Hart."

"Why were you with Katy Hart at Paradise Cove that night?"

"We were discussing the possibility of her taking a leading role in one of my films." He shrugged. "I took her to Paradise Cove because it's a private beach, to avoid the paparazzi."

"Very well." Tara didn't miss a beat. "You and Ms. Hart were at Paradise Cove discussing business. Could you detail what happened as you left the beach and headed for your car?"

And just like that they were past the line of questioning involving the time he and Katy were alone on the beach. He resisted the urge to smile at Katy. Instead he willed her to know that things were going well, and nothing he'd say from the witness stand would cause her any more hurt.

Over the next hour, Tara led Dayne through a vivid description of Margie Madden's attack. For the most part, the defendant remained lethargic, her eyes glued to the table in front of her. Dayne was pretty sure she'd been doped up with Valium or some other drug to keep her quiet.

Tara walked closer to the witness stand. With her tailored suit and note file, she was the picture of self-assurance. "Can you identify the woman who jumped from the bushes and put a knife to Ms. Hart's throat?"

Dayne pointed across the room at Margie. "She's sitting there, at the defendant's table."

For the first time that morning, Margie stirred. She turned her attention to Dayne and glared at him. "You're a lousy husband." The words were out before her attorney could say anything.

Across the back of the courtroom there was a rustle of cameras and reporters flipping notepads as twenty-some people scrambled to capture the colorful quote.

Dayne turned his attention back to Tara. From the corner of his eye he saw the defense attorney talking sternly with Margie.

The prosecutor acted as if she hadn't heard Margie's comment. "Mr. Matthews, did the defendant threaten to kill Ms. Hart?"

"Yes." Dayne worked the muscles in his jaw. He could feel the eyes of the jury on him, feel them anxious to deliver a conviction on his behalf.

"And did the defendant threaten to kill you also, Mr. Matthews?"

"Yes, she did." Dayne kept his attention on Tara, every bit as professional as she was.

"Did you believe, Mr. Matthews, that the defendant indeed intended to kill Ms. Hart?"

"Yes, I believe she intended to kill Ms. Hart. Definitely." Again the media stirred. The story must've felt irresistible.

Tara paced toward the jury and checked her notes. Dayne wanted to cheer her on. She was perfect, allowing the twelve men and women the chance to look from Dayne to Margie and back again, giving them time to process what had happened that night. The defendant had threatened to kill with every intention of carrying it out.

After a long pause, Tara looked at Dayne. "Do you believe the defendant would've killed *you* if she'd had the chance?"

"Yes."

"And why didn't she kill you?"

"Objection." The gray-haired attorney might've looked flustered. He might've been at the helm of a sinking ship, but he wasn't going down without something of a fight. He was on his feet. "The prosecutor is leading the witness, Your Honor."

"Sustained." Judge Nguyen nodded at Tara. "Keep your objectivity, counsel."

"Yes, Your Honor." Tara nodded, stern and remorseful. She checked her notes and tried again. "Mr. Matthews, what happened after the defendant threatened to kill Ms. Hart?"

"I kicked the knife from her hand, grabbed her, and knocked her to the ground."

"Why did you do this?"

Dayne kept his tone grave. "The defendant had the knife pressed against Ms. Hart's throat. If I hadn't done something, I believe she would've killed Ms. Hart."

The questioning continued, all of it one-sided. Tara finished just before lunch, and the judge ordered an hour break.

Dayne returned immediately to his place beside Joe Morris, and the group moved in silence to the private sitting area adjacent to the courtroom. Once they were inside, Dayne found Katy and took her in his arms. He had nothing to hide from his attorney, and Tara couldn't have been surprised.

"Are you okay?" He spoke low near her ear. The others around them fell into various conversations, giving them what little privacy they could possibly have in the cramped quarters.

"I'm fine. Really." She smiled, but he could see the fear in her eyes. "You're doing fantastic up there."

"Thanks."

"Lunch is being brought up," Tara Lawson announced. "I think Joe needs a few minutes with Dayne and Katy before then." She motioned toward the hall. "I want to meet with my team and go over a few details."

Joe shot him a silent apology. "She's right. We need to talk about today's story."

Dayne wasn't finished. He wanted to ask Katy if she felt him praying for her, but clearly this wasn't the time. Instead he gave her hand a single squeeze and led the way to the table where Joe was sitting.

In that moment, even though he'd been praying all morning, he felt drained by the proceedings. Where Katy was concerned, he always felt like they were taking steps backward, falling farther into a hole. When all he wanted to do was move forward, tell her how he really felt, and make plans to do so for the rest of his life. There, in the stuffy windowless room, the idea of ever reaching that place felt utterly impossible.

"I didn't like the article this morning." Joe had a copy of the *LA Times.* He spread it out on the table.

Dayne glanced at Katy. Her face looked a shade paler than before. Sure, she'd already seen it. But seeing it again was bound to send another wave of alarm through her body. He folded his arms on the table in front of him. "None of us liked it."

"I can't believe they ran the picture from the beach." Katy's voice was small but angry.

"They'll run it in every tabloid next week." Joe raised his brow in her direction. "I want you to be ready."

She nodded, her lips pressed tight together.

Until lunch came they talked about the second tier of strategy with the press. They would stay with the story that Katy and Dayne were not romantically involved, no matter what was hinted at or speculated, no matter what story might run in the tabs.

"Remember, you two aren't on trial. You don't owe the press anything."

"But what if they dig up information about Katy's job, her involvement with Christian kids?"

"That's what I want to talk to you about." Joe leaned back in his chair and lowered his brow. "Today I'm going to hold another press conference. I've already alerted the media. They're ravenous, so they'll all be there."

"So . . . ?" Dayne was puzzled. Joe was good, but where was he taking this?

Joe jabbed a finger at the newspaper. "The press has launched an implied attack on the character of Katy Hart." He smiled, and his confidence seemed to ease the tension in the room. "Katy is a private citizen. The test for libeling someone like you, Dayne, is very tough. You're a public figure, pretty much fair game."

Dayne gave a sad chuckle. "You don't have to tell me."

"But, Katy, with you they have to be much more careful. That's why at today's conference I will make a promise to every member of the media. We will file a libel suit against anyone who publishes any material against you that we deem damaging or a violation of privacy in any way."

Dayne sat back and stroked his chin. "Two problems."

"Okay." Joe waited, listening.

Katy sat between them, wide-eyed and watching.

"First, truth is a defense for libel, right? I took a class on this back in college, and I remember that if they could prove validity or truth, a libel case could be thrown out." Dayne didn't hesitate. "And the other's worse. By nature of the fact that Katy's involved in a trial of this magnitude, the fact that she's connected with me elevates her to a public person. Meaning the libel test for her becomes as difficult to prove as it would be if I were the victim."

"I'm impressed." Joe was still smiling. He gave a thoughtful nod. "You know your media law, but you're forgetting one thing."

It was Dayne's turn to wait. Whatever it was, he hoped Joe had something else up his sleeve. He liked the direction this was taking — if the argument held water, anyway.

"The paparazzi may be up on their media law too, but no one — not even slimy tabloid people — wants to be sued. Being sued and winning can still cost a great deal of time, money, and embarrassment. As long as we're feeding the press a few morsels of information, they'd be smarter to leave Katy alone. They have her identity, and they'll certainly try to find out more information this week. But your past is pretty safe. At least it will be once I tell them how

154

serious we are." He shot a pointed look at both of them. "The two of you have to be very, very careful where you go, what you do while you're together in Los Angeles."

"We will be." Dayne turned to Katy. "I've been thinking about that."

She reached for a bottle of water, opened it, and took a sip. "What if it makes them more interested than before, like maybe we're hiding something?"

"It might make them check." Joe crossed one leg over his knee. He didn't look the least bit worried. "But what is there to find, Katy? You teach Christian theater. That isn't worth getting sued over. My bet is they'll back off and try to find out more about you and Dayne this week. Every one of them believes the two of you are romantically involved. They'll be out for blood over who can prove it first."

Katy nodded. Again her face looked pale. She glanced at Dayne, and he could almost hear her thoughts. Joe was right. They had to be careful. They couldn't be caught together in any compromising position. An embrace, a quick kiss, the first night of her return was one thing. Friends could embrace, and in Hollywood they could even let their lips touch. But a tryst or a more involved full-blown kiss, anything of the sort would prove the media's story and elevate her to the roll of Dayne's girlfriend — thus clearly a public figure. Then they could say what they wanted about her and not worry about threats of any lawsuits.

Dayne put his hand over hers. "Don't worry. We'll be careful, Katy. I promise."

She took another drink of water. "My head's spinning."

"I think the press conference today will do a lot to take the pressure off." Joe folded the newspaper and tucked it into his brief-case. "I feel good about it."

"Thanks, Joe." Dayne had to agree. God was looking out for them in the form of their attorney. The threat of a lawsuit was a good idea. "Again, nice work. Let us know any feedback you get after you talk with them."

"I will."

Before Joe could launch into another topic, Luke Baxter returned from a conversation with the prosecution team out in the hall. He joined them at the table and looked at Dayne. "Happened again twice out there just now."

Dayne had been so caught up in the talk with Joe, so involved in testifying and worrying about Katy, that he hadn't had time to look his brother in the face. As he did, a single breath seemed to trap itself deep in his lungs. The guy was so much like him, and in that moment he ached for the chance to tell him, to hug him, and to thank him for watching out for Katy earlier today. Instead he reached for a water bottle and twisted the top open. "What happened?"

Luke laughed. "They think I'm you."

"It happened earlier too." Katy sparked to life for the first time since they'd started talking about the press. "We were walking up the sidewalk, and one of the photographers asked Luke a question as if he were you."

Dayne felt his head start to spin. He was tired and overwhelmed, sick of fighting the battle against the press and desperate for a normal life. He'd asked God to lead him, but he knew as surely as the article on the front page of the paper that it would be a long road, an all but impossible journey. Right here, right now, he wanted to take a swift shortcut and tell Katy the truth, let Luke know there was a reason for the mistaken identity. Of course they were mixing up the two of them.

They were brothers after all.

Instead he held his breath and slowly exhaled through tight lips. He found his familiar smile and managed an easy laugh.

"Maybe it'll take off some of the pressure. We can send you one way and me the other." He grinned at Katy. "Tomorrow's paper can feature Luke, and that'll give us both a break."

Luke laughed, but Katy seemed drawn by the resemblance. Twice during the next few minutes she studied Luke and then Dayne. Finally she shook her head. "You're sure you're not related?"

"Like I said —" Luke shrugged — "everyone has a double out there."

Lunch passed quickly. Soon Dayne was back on the witness stand, and it was the defense attorney's turn to question him. Tara had warned him that the only reason the man would travel down the path of action, of wanting specific details about what Dayne and Katy were doing on the beach, was to raise doubt as to their ability to recount facts regarding Margie.

In other words, if they were involved in a romantic moment, their testimony about the initial aspects of the attack might not be as valid. Joe had explained that Dayne and Katy would've had to have been very involved to miss the details in question. Possibly lying on the beach, maybe without clothes. That sort of thing.

Dayne's stomach turned at the idea that

his own testimony might lead to that kind of impression about someone as true and right and pure as Katy Hart. They had barely kissed that night. He wasn't leaving the stand with a single person believing otherwise.

As soon as the questions began, Dayne steadied himself. Tara was right. The man was definitely heading in that direction. "Mr. Matthews, the beach was dark at the time of the attack; is that right?"

"It was, yes."

"And you were . . . preoccupied with Katy Hart before ever seeing someone come at her; is that right?"

"We were talking, yes." Dayne's stomach tightened.

The gray-haired man held his hand up and paced across the floor. He smiled at Dayne over his shoulder. "You were on a private beach with a beautiful young actress after dark." He chuckled. "It would be fair to say you were doing more than talking. Isn't that correct, Mr. Matthews?"

Tara was on the edge of her seat, ready to object, but Dayne had asked her not to jump in too quickly. If the defense attorney said something that left a damaging impression, he wanted the chance to clear the air. This was exactly that kind of moment.

"Actually we were finished talking, and we were heading back to the parking lot." Dayne worked to keep his tone even. He wanted to look at Katy, tell her with his eyes that he would undo the damage done by the attorney's cavalier attitude. But he didn't dare. "We were not distracted in any way when the defendant jumped from the bushes and grabbed Ms. Hart."

A stir came from the jury and from the media at the back of the room. Dayne was definitely the man of the hour. He wasn't backing down, wasn't allowing himself to be handled by the defense attorney. His story was airtight.

The defense attorney lost his flip attitude. His expression grew serious as he turned and faced Dayne. "Isn't it true that you're not exactly sure about the identity of the defendant, Mr. Matthews, because you were lying on the sand having sex with Katy Hart at the time of the attack? Remember, you are under oath, Mr. Matthews."

A stir came from the press along the back of the courtroom.

Dayne wanted to jump down from the witness stand and punch the old guy, but every eye was on him, every second counting.

Tara slapped the table in front of her and

rose in an angry burst. They had planned this response if the defense attorney dared ask such a question. "Objection, Your Honor, counsel is harassing the witness, taking the line of questioning off the crime and making this a personal attack."

Judge Nguyen lifted his chin and cast a stern look at the gray-haired attorney. "Sustained. Counsel, you will be more careful with your questions." He looked at Dayne. "You may choose not to answer the question if you wish."

"No." Dayne sat a little straighter, indignant. "I definitely wish to answer the question." He looked at the defense attorney. "I am aware that I am under oath. Ms. Hart and I were at the beach that night to discuss a part in my movie. We did not sit or lay on the sand, and we did not have sex." He didn't blink. "As I said, we were finished talking, and we were headed back to the parking lot when the defendant jumped from the bushes and attacked Ms. Hart."

The attorney held his gaze for another moment, but defeat was written across his face. It had been a gamble to attack Dayne in so public a fashion. He was America's hero, its favorite heartthrob. Now, without question, everyone in the courtroom could see that the gamble hadn't paid off. More than likely, it had cost the defense dearly.

Silently, Dayne thanked God. The truth had been allowed to prevail, and at least for this moment Katy's reputation was still intact.

The cross-examination seemed to go more quickly after that. The attorney shifted his questions toward the sanity — or lack thereof — regarding Margie Madden. Ten minutes into the exchange the man seemed to have a change of heart, as if he wanted Dayne off the stand as quickly as possible. Maybe he was only then realizing that anything coming from the mouth of a polished, well-known actor was bound to damage his client.

Afterwards Tara took another turn. She led Dayne through another half hour of questions about the attack. Again it was strategy. She had already covered the ground once. But she had explained earlier that if the defense tried anything funny, she would march the testimony back to the actual attack and away from any signs of insanity on the part of Margie Madden. That way the lasting impression on the minds of the jury and media alike was very clear: Dayne and Katy were nearly killed, and there was no doubt that the defendant was the person behind the attack.

At just before two o'clock, Tara addressed Dayne. "Do you believe, Mr. Matthews, that the defendant, Margie Madden, followed you to Paradise Cove intent on killing you and Ms. Hart?"

The defense attorney lifted his head as if he might object. But instead he turned his attention to a file in front of him.

"Yes, I believe she followed us there. I had seen a similar yellow Honda Civic parked near my studio and also near my home."

Tara raised her brow. "Any other reason, Mr. Matthews?"

"Well —" he studied Margie Madden until he could feel the jury doing the same thing — "the defendant told me she should've killed me while she had the chance."

"She told you?" Tara sounded surprised. "The defendant told you that she should've killed you while she had the chance?"

"Yes."

Tara gave a knowing look to the jury, then to Dayne. "Thank you, Mr. Matthews. No further questions." She checked her file. "The prosecution calls Katy Hart."

Tara had said that she thought Katy's testimony would come Wednesday morning. "But I might change my mind," she'd told them at lunch. "If I feel the pressure's too

163

intense, I'll save my mental-health witnesses for tomorrow and get the two of you out of the courtroom today."

Dayne felt his heart skip a beat. So this was it. They'd finish it all in one day — at least until closing arguments. Dayne exchanged a brief look with Katy as she rose and faced the front of the courtroom, straight and proud. She was shaking but not as badly as the day before when Margie lashed out at her.

As he sat down next to Joe Morris he did the only thing he could do. He prayed with everything in him that Katy would survive the next few hours.

CHAPTER TEN

Katy felt herself being carried. Against a backdrop of constant camera clicks, she crossed the floor, climbed the two steps up to the witness stand, and took her seat.

Dayne was praying for her. She could sense it deep inside her soul. Dayne and somewhere back in Bloomington everyone who cared about her. God was with her; she had no doubt.

Let them see You, Lord, not me. . . . When they take my picture, when they write about me, let them see You.

Peace eased her mind and stilled the trembling in her arms and legs.

Tara wasted no time taking charge. She began with easy questions, Katy's name and the fact that she had indeed worked as an actress. The line of questioning established that Katy was in town at the time of the attack because she was considering a role in the movie *Dream On,* and she was in fact talking with Dayne about that part when the attack took place.

Twice during Tara's early questions, Margie sneered at Katy, mumbling something that Katy couldn't make out. Margie's attorney slid a glass of water to her and whispered something. Margie drank the water and focused on the table in front of her. Whatever had calmed her down this morning was apparently wearing off because she was more combative than before.

"Would you describe what happened the night in question, please, Ms. Hart?"

Katy shuddered. This was the hardest part, going back to those terrifying moments and doing it here, in front of cameras and reporters and a jury. In front of Margie Madden.

She leaned in and adjusted the microphone. "Mr. Matthews and I were finished with our discussion, and we were heading back to the parking lot." Her heart thudded so hard she had trouble thinking. "We approached a section of bushes, and from my left side a woman jumped out and grabbed me." Katy touched her throat. "She held a knife to my neck and told me she was going to kill me."

There was a rustling of notepads and the click of cameras, and Katy understood. The picture of her on the witness stand, her hand on her throat, recounting the attack would be perfect for the front page. She lowered her hand as Tara approached one of her team members. The young lawyer handed her a file, and she held it up. "I'd like to submit this as evidence, Your Honor."

"Describe it for the jury, please." The judge slid his chair closer to the bench and peered over the edge. "Then let me take a look."

"In here —" Tara held the file higher — "are photographs taken by police the night of the attack on Katy Hart and Dayne Matthews. The pictures will show marks on Katy Hart's neck and a cut along the inside of her upper left arm."

The press seemed to jump to action, taking note of this new bit of information. There were police photographs, something new to write about.

Tara handed the file to Judge Nguyen.

After a minute of flipping through the pictures, he nodded. "Yes, this will be admitted as evidence." He handed the file back to Tara. "Show the jurors, please."

Tara seemed more than happy to oblige.

Katy settled back in the witness stand, glad that the attention was off her, at least for the moment.

Ten minutes passed while the jurors looked at the photos and passed them down the row.

After all twelve had studied them, Tara collected the file and turned back to Katy. This time she took out the photos and came closer to the witness stand. "This first picture." She presented a photo of Katy's neck, one where the marks were very clear. "Can you explain how you obtained these marks, please, Ms. Hart?"

Katy steadied herself. "The . . . the defendant pressed the blade of her knife against my throat. She pressed . . . very hard." Again her hand went to her neck. "I couldn't scream or swallow. I could barely breathe."

"So you're telling this courtroom that the defendant, Margie Madden, pressed her knife so hard against your throat that she left these marks?"

"Yes."

Tara sifted through the file to the picture of the cut along the inside of her arm. "And this cut, Ms. Hart? Could you explain for the jury how you received this cut?"

"Yes." Katy felt faint. She folded her arms tight against her middle. "The defendant took the tip of her knife and sliced it down the inside of my left arm. Then she said that pretty girls bleed easy." She was shaking again, shaking and struggling to fill her lungs. "She told me there would be even more blood once she . . . once she sliced my throat."

Again Tara allowed the horror of the moment to sink in before she continued to the next question. She slowly slipped the photographs back into the file and returned them to her assistant. Once she was back in front of Katy, she faced her squarely. "Tell us, Ms. Hart, if Mr. Matthews hadn't intervened on the night of the attack, what do you believe the defendant would've done?"

Katy tried not to look at Margie Madden, but she couldn't help it. She shot her a quick glance, then trained her eyes once more on the prosecutor. "I have no doubt she would have killed me. She told me she would kill me. She said it was . . . it was what she came there to do."

Tara nodded, taking in the information. "Can you identify the person who committed this attack against you, Ms. Hart?"

"Yes." Katy pointed at Margie. "That's her. There at the defense table."

"Thank you, Ms. Hart." Tara turned. "No further questions, Your Honor."

Katy exhaled. She had lasted through this much; now if she could only survive the cross-examination. The cameras were still locked on her, capturing every move, every nuance she might make. But she had to look at Dayne, had to see what he was feeling. Her gaze shifted, and instantly she felt the connection. He was staring at her, probably willing her to feel his support and prayers, his concern for her.

And there, looking at him, she saw what she needed to see. His eyes danced with pride, shouting at her that she had done brilliantly and that very soon they would be finished with this nightmare for good. She drew strength from him, then turned her attention to the gray-haired attorney making his way toward her.

The questions were easier than they'd been for Dayne. The man must've decided there was no point in attacking her character or the reasons why she was on the beach with Dayne Matthews the night of the incident. Instead he tried to imply that Katy might not have had a clear view of his client, since the attack happened from her left side. Finally, he focused on the fact that his client had used two voices that evening. Katy acknowledged that, yes, Margie had indeed spoken in two distinct tones.

"Do you believe, Ms. Hart, that the defendant thought she was two different people as she carried out her attack?"

"Yes." Katy's tone suggested that the issue wasn't relevant. She resisted the urge to shrug.

"In your opinion could someone who believed they were two people possibly be considered sane?"

Tara leaped to her feet. "Objection. The question is beyond the scope of this witness's expertise. We have established that Ms. Hart is an actress, not a psychologist."

"Sustained." The judge adjusted his bifocals. "Ask a different question, please."

"Yes, Your Honor." The defense attorney tried again. "During the attack, did you believe the defendant was insane?"

"Objection." This time the irritation sounded in Tara's tone. "Same thing."

"Sustained." Judge Nguyen gave the defense attorney a wary look. "Please avoid badgering the witness, counsel."

"I'm sorry, Your Honor." The man looked at his notes and then back at Katy. "No further questions."

Tara was on her feet before the gray-haired attorney sat down. "Ms. Hart, once Mr. Matthews physically subdued the defendant, did you get a view of the defendant's face?"

"Yes."

"And she was no longer on your left side

at that point?"

"No, she was in front of me." Katy loved the way Tara worked. Whatever shred of doubt the defense attorney had stirred up in the minds of the jury, it would be eliminated after this.

"And at that time you were able to clearly identify the defendant; is that right?"

"Yes."

"It has been mentioned several times that the attack took place at night. Can you tell the jury why you were able to see the defendant's face so clearly?"

"That's easy." Katy felt more relaxed than she had the whole time she'd been on the stand. The painful part was over. "The attack happened near the parking lot. There were two bright lights nearby, so the area was almost as light as it would be in the daytime."

Tara smiled. "No further questions."

Katy was excused from the witness stand, and again she exchanged a quick look with Dayne. This time in his eyes she saw victory — victory for a dozen different reasons. Because it was over and they'd survived the day in court, because their testimony had been solid and a conviction was all but certain. And because Katy's reputation had come out intact as well.

It was nearly five o'clock. The judge excused the jury and ordered them back at ten the next morning.

The media jockeyed for position trying to capture pictures of Tara talking to Katy and Dayne, but the moment lasted only a few seconds.

Tara pointed to the adjacent room. "Let's get in there." She smiled at them the moment the door was closed. "Great work! I won't need you until Friday most likely. You're on your own until then, but keep your cell phones nearby. Just in case." She looked at Dayne's attorney. "Joe, you've got Luke outside with a different car?"

"I do." He pointed at Dayne. "The media's buzzing with how much you two look alike. I couldn't have planned it better." The attorney chuckled. "Now if I only had a woman who looked like Katy, I think I could send the media on the city's most exciting wild-goose chase."

Katy watched Dayne, watched how he wasn't laughing, how something strange and uneasy flashed in his expression. She would ask him about it later, what he made of the uncanny resemblance between him and Luke.

Joe Morris was going on about how Dayne and Katy could slip out now before the media had a chance to figure out what had happened. "I've got another press conference, so most of them will meet me out front." He smiled at Katy. "Brilliant work, by the way." He shifted to Tara. "Other than the insanity issue, looks like a slam dunk."

"Maybe." Tara was standing at the far end of the table sorting through one of her files. "The technical part will be the toughest. Psychiatrists and experts on insanity." She gave a serious look. "Sometimes the jury gets lulled into forgetting the deliberateness, the horror of the attack."

"You're really worried?" Dayne leaned against the wall. It was the first time all day he'd looked defeated.

"Honestly?" Tara's lips allowed the slightest hint of a smile. "No. But I can't let up until I finish my closing argument. No matter how strong the case looks."

Joe nodded toward the door. "Let's get you two out of here. Luke's waiting."

"Where are we going?" Katy had her purse, but as usual she barely had time to catch her breath.

"Your hotel. You can hang out on the roof for a few hours, and then I've given Dayne instructions for dinner." Joe winked at Dayne. "I think it'll work out for you."

Katy looked at Dayne, but his face gave

away nothing. They followed Joe down the hallway, out into the main passageway, and past a group of milling photographers.

As the cameramen tried to fall in line behind the three of them, Joe held up his hand and addressed the group. "Press conference in an hour. Give us until then. Please!"

The statement worked. The press stopped and set their equipment back on the floor.

Joe led the way down two flights of stairs. "Wish the paparazzi were that easy to handle."

Dayne was last in the line. "Yeah, big difference between newspaper and TV people and the bloodthirsty tabloid guys."

At the main floor, Joe told them he'd be in touch.

Then they slipped out the door and into a car driven by Luke Baxter. He grinned at them. "How did it go?"

Katy and Dayne sat in the back. As soon as they had their seat belts buckled, Dayne slipped his fingers through hers. "Katy was amazing."

"I knew she would be." Luke smiled into the rearview mirror.

For a second, Katy looked from Luke's image to Dayne and back again. No question about the resemblance. It seemed stronger all the time.

"Looks like we got a clean getaway." Luke pulled onto the street and took a turn toward Katy's hotel.

She glanced over her shoulder. He was right. For once there wasn't a single photographer trailing them. She felt herself settle in against the back of the seat. The sensation of Dayne's fingers through hers warmed her and reminded her of the peace that had been there — deep inside her — all along.

The drive to the hotel took fifteen minutes. Dayne spent most of the time talking to Luke, almost as if the two were old friends. Dayne asked about Luke's wife and son. "And Joe says you adopted a little girl from China?"

"We did." Luke's eyes shone as he shook his head. "She's a precious miracle, for sure."

Katy stayed quiet. She knew about Malin from her conversations with Ashley. But why was Dayne so interested? Normally when the two of them had a moment's downtime, his focus would be on her or he would fall quiet, glad for the chance to be out of the spotlight.

"You're staying, right?" Dayne leaned forward, intent on his conversation with

Luke. "You'll be here all week, through closing arguments?"

"Definitely."

"Good." Dayne settled beside her again. "Maybe we can grab lunch somewhere before you go."

"Sure." Luke sounded impressed. Dayne was his boss's client; he was merely the assistant.

"I'd like to hear more about Bloomington. What it was like growing up there, that sort of thing."

Katy glanced at Dayne, trying to figure him out. Maybe that was it. Maybe the conversation had more to do with Bloomington than with some curious interest in Luke and his family. Katy reminded herself to ask him about it later. Then she let the subject go. This was a day of victory, and she wanted only to spend it with Dayne, reveling in the fact that they were finished testifying. Now — someway, somehow — they could spend the next few days together finding their way back to the conversation they'd had on the rooftop last night.

As they pulled into the hotel parking lot, Katy could hardly wait to feel the setting sun on her shoulders, to unwind in a world where the photographers couldn't reach them. Luke stopped the car a few feet from the rear door, and instantly a few camera-men jumped from a nearby van.

"Scavengers," Dayne muttered. "Hey, buddy —" he touched Luke's shoulder — "thanks for the ride."

Katy added her thanks, and they hurried from the car. Photographers snapped a couple dozen pictures of their backs as they rushed for the door. The urgency made Katy more anxious to be alone, to ask him about Luke and about whether he'd been thinking all day about last night the way she had.

Two minutes later they were heading up the stairs onto the roof when Dayne stopped.

Katy was behind him, and she pulled up short, her hand on his waist. "What is it?"

"There." He pointed at the open window of a building adjacent to the hotel. The window was three floors higher than the hotel roof. "A camera." He shaded his eyes. "See it?"

She was still in the stairwell, out of sight. But there was no doubt he was right. Positioned in the window and aimed straight at the garden area of the roof was what looked like a high-powered camera lens. A sick feeling tightened her stomach. "Pa-parazzi?"

"Definitely." He gave her a gentle nudge, urging her down a few steps. As she moved, he followed her. "They rented a room with a view of the roof. I can't believe it."

Disappointment took the place of everything good she'd been feeling. "Now what?"

"I have another plan." He took her hand as they turned and moved quickly down the stairs. "The idea Joe was talking about earlier." A smile played on his lips. "It was going to be a surprise."

Her heart raced. Every minute with Dayne was a surprise, and at times like this the unexpected was almost wearying. "Okay. So what do we do?"

"Go to your room and change into something more casual, and grab a sweatshirt if you brought one. Wear sunglasses and a hat." He checked the time on his cell phone. "I'll stay here in the stairwell. You can meet me back here in ten minutes."

Katy's head was spinning. Whatever he had planned, the idea made her nervous. There was nowhere they could go without the paparazzi following them. Especially now, when the press was bound to understand that Katy and Dayne had been given two days off to spend however they'd like.

Still, the certainty on his face gave her no choice. He knew her, knew her convictions.

He wouldn't lead her into a situation that would harm her; Katy was sure. She nodded and squeezed his hand. Then she left and did as he asked.

Ten minutes later, when she returned to the stairwell dressed in shorts and a sweatshirt, she could see on Dayne's face that the details of the plan he'd been working on were set. "How do we get out of here?" Katy asked.

"The front door." Dayne grinned. "You'll go down the elevator to the main floor. Once you step off, you'll walk quickly, eyes downcast, out the front door to a silver Acura just outside. You'll take the wheel and drive around the block once. Five minutes later, you'll drive through the covered front entrance, and I'll walk out and slip into the passenger seat. Then we'll be off."

Katy doubted it could work. But what choice did they have? She gave him a last look and set off for the elevator. She had a big bag slung over her shoulder and her purse on her other arm. Her sunglasses and hat were in place, and as she stepped off the elevator and started moving through the busy lobby toward the front door, she must've looked like any other tourist. No one seemed to notice her.

The silver Acura was outside just as Dayne

had promised. She walked quickly through the rotating front door, slipped the valet a five-dollar bill, and eased in behind the wheel. She tossed her things in the back and drove off before even a single cameraman could take note. They were probably still camping out at the rear entrance.

As she pulled onto the street, she reminded herself to exhale. It might work, this plan Dayne had made. *Please, God . . . let it work. We need to talk.* She kept her eye on the digital clock over the radio, and exactly five minutes later she zipped the car up to the front door of the hotel.

Dayne looked the way he always did in Bloomington, his face covered with a baseball cap and sunglasses. Things he always carried with him. He slipped out the front door and immediately into the passenger seat. "How does it look?"

"All clear." She wanted to shout for joy, but she didn't have time. She drove through the entrance and out onto the street. Again there wasn't a car following them. She tapped the steering wheel, practically bursting with excitement. "We did it!"

"I knew it was possible. They were looking for a couple, not the two of us by ourselves." He looked up. "Thank You, God!"

After a few miles, Dayne directed her to turn onto a side street and pull over. "I'll drive."

They both hopped out and switched places. The moment she sat in the passenger seat, she felt the tension of the day finally leave. They were back out on the road before she looked at Dayne and smiled. "Do I get to know where we're going?"

"Not yet." An easy grin lifted his mouth. "Soon, though."

Katy's heart soared. Without the paparazzi following them, she almost felt as if they were a normal couple back in Indiana, heading off for one of the surreal afternoons he had given her a handful of other times.

Within minutes they reached Pacific Coast Highway, and Dayne turned north.

She angled herself against the car door. "The beach?" She felt a ripple of doubt. "They'll find us out here, won't they?"

"Not where we're going." He kept his eyes straight ahead, but his smile was brighter than the fading sun. He turned on the radio and relaxed against the headrest. "Have I apologized yet for this week?" There was guilt in his tone but not enough to dampen the mood.

"The trial?"

"No." His eyes sparkled. "The fact that I

haven't taken you on a date. I mean, what sort of gentleman am I, anyway?"

"Dayne —" she giggled — "you can't date." She waved her thumb at the window. "The world out there won't let you."

"Okay, then let's make a deal."

She loved this, loved the teasing and smiling, the fact that they could think about more than whether cameramen were following them and how quick they could get away. Without paparazzi behind them everything felt different. "What?"

He met her eyes briefly, and the feeling turned her heart upside down. "Tonight there is no world out there."

She was breathless for the second time that hour. But this time her head wasn't spinning because they were running or being chased, because the paparazzi had found them or because a dozen cameras were being fired in her direction. It was because for the first time in a very long time she was about to do something that could be more dangerous than all those other things combined.

Spend an evening alone with Dayne Matthews.

CHAPTER ELEVEN

John had the letters written. A single page each with the basic facts. They all said the same thing, but the openings were different. John looked at them, lying in a row on his kitchen table. Elizabeth would've wanted him to gather the kids, tell them in person. The way he should've done during the reunion in April.

But now — based on his conversations with Dayne — he didn't have time to waste. Dayne was coming undone around the edges, his resolve lessening a little more each day. He wanted to know his siblings, wanted to share a life with them — to whatever extent they were comfortable.

Last time they'd talked — late at night after the first day of the trial — Dayne had come out and asked the question John had been dreading. "So —" his tone fell a little — "do they know about me, the others?"

John's hesitation had said more than his

words. "I . . . I wanted to tell them when we were all together. But Ashley's baby . . . and the tornadoes . . ."

"So, they don't know." Dayne tried to hide his disappointment, but it was there.

The sound of it cut John's heart swift and sure. How could he have let it go this far, knowing about Dayne, aware that Ashley knew the truth, and still keeping the entire situation a secret from his other kids? It was wrong, and now the only way he could right the problem was by coming clean.

For a sleepless night he considered calling them and telling them over the phone. But they needed all the details, and they needed time to absorb them before having a conversation with him.

He picked up the first letter — the one to Brooke. Like the others it was straightforward. He read over it one more time, wincing the same way he had when he wrote it.

Dearest Brooke,

I write this letter with a heavy heart, but it's time you know the truth about something. Your mother and I kept a secret all the years we were married, a secret we never expected to share with any of you. The secret is this: you have an older brother, whom your mother and I were forced to give up for adoption the year before we were married.

It's a long story and complicated. I'll be happy to share it with you in person after you read this. The point is, your mother's dying prayer was that she find our firstborn son, and that in finding him she would find peace. Well, God answered that prayer. At just the right time your older brother made a decision to find out about his birth family. He hired a private investigator, and his search led him to your mother. They shared an hour together the day before she died.

As a way of honoring her dying wish, I, too, hired a private investigator. Now our older son and I are in contact. His life is very different from ours, but he longs to know you and your sisters and brother. We are trying to figure out how to move forward from here. But that won't be possible without your forgiveness and grace, without your understanding.

I realize this will come as a shock to you, and again I am sorry. Things were so different back before your mother and I were married. If you made a mistake, people expected you to hide away and . . .

John closed his eyes. What was he doing? He couldn't mail a letter like this to Brooke and Erin, to Kari and Luke. This would be the single most shocking piece of news they ever received. By writing the details in a letter, he was forcing them to make a phone call that was clearly his to make.

He took a deep breath. Then he gathered the pieces of paper on the table and ripped them into shreds. When the pieces were lying in a heap, he picked up the phone and dialed Brooke's number. It was half past seven, so she'd probably be home. All his daughters would be home, and Luke would be available on his cell.

The phone began to ring, and John held his breath. *God, this is a call I never wanted to make, a truth I never wanted to share. Elizabeth should be here with me to help the kids understand. Since she isn't here, I need You . . . now more than ever. Please, God . . .*

"Hello?"

"Brooke?" His heart beat so hard he was sure she could hear it on the other end of the phone line. "It's Dad."

"I know." There was a smile in her voice. "You should see how great Hayley's doing.

She walks by herself all over the house. I don't even hold my breath anymore, and this morning when Maddie —"

"Brooke." He couldn't wait another moment.

She hesitated, taken aback by his interruption. "Dad . . . what is it? You sound funny."

"Honey, I have something to tell you. . . ."

Kari Baxter Taylor hung up the phone and fell into her husband's arms.

Ryan had known something was wrong, same as he always knew. When the call was from her dad, Ryan had only smiled from across the kitchen and told Kari to tell him hello. But he must've seen the color leave her face, must've seen her drop slowly to the sofa, her mouth open.

Whatever gave it away, he had taken care of tucking the kids into bed, and then he'd joined her on the couch while she talked to her dad. He put his hand on her knee, knowing only that whatever the news, it had to be bad. Somehow having him here beside her kept her from falling over as her father went into detail.

They had another brother? An older sibling who her dad said lived in California? And all these years — all the decades of growing up — neither of her parents had ever said anything about him. Her mind reeled, and she steadied herself against her husband. As she held on to Ryan, she replayed part of the conversation in her mind. "Ashley's known for a while. She found a letter your mother had written to him. I've already told Brooke, and I'll be calling Erin next." She could hear tears in her father's voice. He sounded broken and barely able to talk. "I . . . I couldn't wait another day, Kari. I had to tell you."

"So you're serious? You and Mom kept this from us all this time?" She felt a mix of emotions so strong she wasn't sure whether to run or scream or lie on the floor and weep.

"Please, Kari . . . don't blame your mother. Back then the social workers told us to give him up, walk away, and never — not once — look back. They told us it was better to believe we'd never had a firstborn son."

"And you *believed* that?" She'd squeezed her eyes shut. "Even after we were born and you knew we deserved to know about him? Even when you held each of us and you could understand how great the loss really was?"

"We could understand the loss." Her dad

sounded tired but deliberate. Desperate for her to see it his way. "But we couldn't talk about it. We tried to convince ourselves that he was never ours, that we had five kids, not six."

"Dad . . ." Kari felt sick to her stomach. Everything she'd ever known to be true about her family was suddenly not true at all. They had a brother, a brother they'd missed out on far too long. "And Ashley knows about this?"

"She does. I asked her not to say anything." He sighed. "I've been waiting for the right time to tell you."

Her thoughts had spun wildly out of control as her dad talked. How could it be possible? They had an older brother. There weren't five Baxter kids but six. Or maybe this was some sort of dream. Maybe her dad was having a moment of dementia. She would call Brooke as soon as she got off the phone and see what her older sister had made of their father's announcement. If she could make the dizziness stop long enough to dial the number.

"And you've been talking to him, this . . . this brother of ours?"

"Yes. He wants to meet you, but . . . well, it's complicated. You have to trust me on that."

The conversation had run in circles until finally Kari realized what she was doing. She'd asked every question three different ways, and her dad still needed to call Erin and Luke. She breathed deeply. Forgiveness. That's what the moment required. Forgiveness for something her parents had done long before she was born and forgiveness for the way they'd hidden the truth from her and her siblings all these years. "I don't know what to say, Dad."

"I'm sorry, Kari. I wish . . . I wish we would've told you together, your mother and I. We only did what we thought was best."

She had tightened her grip on Ryan's knee. The words were there, stuck in her throat, and finally God loosed them for her. "Dad . . . I don't understand. I guess I'm in shock." She looked at Ryan. His expression had told her he was baffled. "Still, Dad, I can only tell you this. I forgive you. We'll sort through the rest of it tomorrow and, I guess every day from here on out."

"Yes." Her dad's voice had been tight. "Thank you, Kari. I love you, honey."

"I love you too."

Now Kari clung to her husband, trying to believe it was really true. She could think the words over a hundred times, and they would still feel foreign. They had a brother? An older brother their parents had never mentioned all those years? For a while she only rested her head on Ryan's shoulder and let the tears come. Strange tears for a reality that still didn't make sense.

And for a brother she had missed out on for her entire life.

As John called each of his kids, the shock had been there, of course, but after they realized that the news was not some sort of twisted joke, their reactions had been varied.

Brooke, the practical one, had been matter-of-fact. After the round of questions and amazement, the truth had settled in quickly for her. "I'm surprised only because it's you and Mom, only because it's my life this is affecting. But I'm very aware of how things were back then. I've talked with patients who had a similar situation. Adoption forced upon them." She rebounded quickly. "I'm sorry for all you and Mom went through, and yes — I'd love the chance to meet this brother of ours."

John had worried that she would feel cheated somehow, no longer truly the firstborn Baxter. But Brooke was far too level-headed for that. "I'm still the oldest Baxter, Dad." There was an understanding smile in her voice. "He might be our brother, but he grew up in someone else's family. He's an only child, and I'm the oldest." She gave a light laugh. "If he starts coming around and wants to share that role, then I can be big enough to share it."

Brooke's reaction had built strength in John, but it was short-lived after his conversation with Kari. She was wounded, no question. For the first ten minutes of the conversation he was sure she didn't believe him, almost as if she thought he were having a moment of senility. Like Ashley, once she was forced to accept what he was saying, she expressed hurt for the years of loss, for never knowing the truth, and for a brother she had never known. Never had the chance to know.

Erin's reaction had been mixed. She, too, struggled to believe what her father was saying. Over and over she kept saying the same thing: "I can't believe Mom didn't tell me."

And of course that would be Erin's response. She and Elizabeth had been so close, so bonded. They had talked about children incessantly, especially after Erin struggled with not being able to have children. Then when Erin went through the adoption process, when it was foiled at first and Erin's heart was broken, there were countless times when Elizabeth might've shared with Erin about her own adoption experience.

"I just can't believe she never told me." Erin's voice was distant, hurt.

The fallout from these conversations, John knew, would take years to work through. But the process had to start somewhere. Though during the conversation Erin never quite seemed to find peace with the idea that her mother hadn't told her the truth, she didn't sound mad at him. "Obviously the two of you had no choice back then." She sounded teary. "Sam's out of town on business. I guess . . . I just wish someone was here to hug me and make me believe this is really happening."

John hated ending the call with Erin, hated that he wasn't there to give her the hug she wanted. She would be okay; he could hear strength in her tone before he hung up. But she was cut deeply by the truth, definitely more upset over the loss of never discussing the situation with her mother. "I'd like to meet him. Especially since it mattered so much to Mom to meet him before she died. He . . . he carries a piece of her and a piece of you, Dad. A piece of all of us."

"Yes." John pictured Dayne, the look on

his face when they had talked in the park a few weeks back. "He definitely has that."

Luke was the last of his kids to know the truth. He was in a hotel in Los Angeles, watching the Pacers in a televised replay of the game against the Knicks. He had already talked with Reagan, already said good night to Tommy on the telephone. John spent the first part of the phone call listening to Luke spill every detail from the trial, how this was the day Dayne had testified, the day that Katy Hart had also taken the stand.

"And the paparazzi kept thinking I was Dayne." He laughed, the comfortable sort of laugh from someone who had no idea his world was about to be rocked. "Isn't that crazy?"

John couldn't find the strength to comment. He massaged his brow. "Listen, Son, there's something I need to tell you."

The news must've seemed so outlandish to Luke that it took John longer to convince him than any of the others. "You're kidding, right? I mean . . . you're saying this because of the Dayne thing, because I said people are mixing us up?"

"No, Luke. Son, I'm being serious."

They went another round, with Luke asking the same questions and John repeating himself. Elizabeth had gotten pregnant, and her parents had forced her to give the baby up. They'd planned to never tell anyone, to not even remind themselves, but then Elizabeth got sick and it became her dying wish, her final prayer —

"Dad," Luke interrupted. The shock in his voice was undeniable. "Are you feeling okay? Can you hear yourself?" A choked bit of laughter rattled in his throat. "Where's all this coming from?"

And John would have to start again.

They went on that way for nearly fifteen minutes before Luke fell quiet. That was the moment John knew the truth was finally sinking in. "You're . . . you're serious? I really have a brother out there?"

John was afraid Luke might come right out and ask if Dayne was his brother. The paparazzi certainly thought they looked enough alike. But God showed mercy on the moment, and the thought never seemed to occur to Luke. Instead he became resigned. "Well, yeah . . . I mean, I'd like to meet him too. He doesn't belong to our family, but still . . . yeah, we could meet him. Whatever you want, Dad."

It took another exhausting ten minutes before John could get Luke to express himself more, to admit that he'd need time to actually work through his feelings before he could say everything that was clouding up his heart. "So you've . . . you've been talking to him?"

"I have. He wants to know us."

"But he already has a life, right? I mean, he's in his mid-thirties."

John could hear the insecurities between Luke's words. "He does, but he's known about us for a long time. He's held off from making contact because he didn't want to upset any of us."

"Okay, so why the big push now? I mean . . . maybe we would've been better off to just let it go."

"But Ashley knows, and she wants to meet him." John held his breath and exhaled slowly. "I guess the situation just isn't that easy."

"I guess not." He made a sound that suggested he was only barely catching his breath. "How are my sisters handling it?"

They talked about that for a while; then John tried again to explain the timing. "We might have a meeting with him sooner than I'd planned. I needed you to hear everything from me before you found out some other way." John stood and paced across the living room. The phone felt hot against his ear. "I want to tell you everything, but some of this just has to wait." He wanted more than anything to be there with Luke, to put his hand on his shoulder and reassure him.

The others would be okay; they all would. But Luke was harder to read. Until this moment, he had seen himself as the only Baxter son. That much was clear by his almost harsh statement: *"He doesn't belong to our family."* As if maybe Luke needed to remind himself that no one could walk into their lives and overshadow his place, his relationship with John. Especially after the tough year he'd had after 9-11 when he closed off to all of them for so many months. John knew that there were times Luke still felt guilty about his decisions back then, and the last thing John wanted was for the news of an older brother to stir up the insecurities that still plagued Luke. Insecurities that he wasn't good enough to be a Baxter or that he'd let them down in a way that could never really be forgiven.

The news could send Luke into a tailspin, and John could only pray that wouldn't happen. "We'll get through this, Son." John found strength he didn't have as he finished the call with Luke. "Can you agree with me about that?"

"Wow . . . I mean, Dad, I'm still dizzy over here. Pretty sure I won't be sleeping much tonight." Frustration added to the other emotions in his voice. "I need to talk to my sisters."

"That's a good idea."

"Yeah." He hesitated. "But we'll be okay." He sounded like he was trying to convince himself. "We all will." His tone softened. "I love you, Dad."

Relief flooded John's heart. "I love you too, Luke. More now than ever."

The last call was to Ashley. By then John was shaking, his heart a mix of relief and regret, of wretched sorrow and dawning joy, and the strange sensation of a soul clear and clean for the first time since Elizabeth brought him the news that she was pregnant.

She answered on the third ring. "Dad, I talked to Erin and Brooke and Kari."

"So you know."

"Yes." She sounded nervous for him. "Are you okay?"

His eyes welled up. "Are they?"

"Of course." She moaned. "Oh, Dad, I'm so glad you called them. You must need a hug in the worst way."

"I think we all do." He went to the window and stared out. The moon was full, and it splashed light across the field out front. "Tonight . . . those calls. Next to giving him up, next to saying good-bye to your mother, this was the hardest thing I've ever done."

"Kari said that. She said she hoped you believed her when she told you she forgave you." Ashley's words were like a healing balm. "They all forgive you. You have to understand they're still in shock, Dad. Kari even asked me if you were feeling well, if maybe this whole thing wasn't a figment of your imagination."

He would've laughed, but even now there was nothing remotely funny about the situation. "I think she thought I was losing my mind."

"She did." Compassion rang in Ashley's voice. "I told her about the letter. I told all of them, except Luke. I'll call him next." She paused. "Dad . . . I feel so good about this. I think our brother's about to make a decision that it's okay, that meeting us wouldn't be so bad. This way, well . . . we're all ready. There won't be any big surprises from this point on."

John pictured Dayne Matthews, America's golden heartthrob, one of the most famous people across the globe. His son. As he thanked Ashley for pushing him to do what had felt even yesterday too impossible to consider, as he hung up the phone, as he got ready for bed and began an hour-long prayer asking the Lord to protect the hearts of his kids and to help them find peace with the shock they'd just received, as he tried to imagine what each of them might be thinking, he kept being tripped up by one very real thought.

Ashley was wrong. The surprise that still lay ahead was even bigger than any of them could've imagined.

CHAPTER TWELVE

Dayne could feel Katy unwinding next to him.

After a twenty-minute drive north along the coast, he retrieved a slip of paper from his pocket and followed the directions into a private enclave of waterfront homes. Dayne made a series of quick turns, then pulled into the driveway of a small two-story Cape Cod, one that stood off to itself.

"Joe's a genius." Dayne peered out the windshield at the place, then gazed down the beach. The neighborhood was made up of only seven homes, and in the pink light from the sunset he could see no one out or about.

Katy looked at the house and then at him. "This is Joe's?"

"No." He chuckled. "He has a friend who vacations here in the summer." He checked the street in both directions. "I guess most of these houses are only used part time.

Otherwise it's pretty deserted."

"So —" she sounded excited and nervous at the same time — "we can hang out here?"

"I think I'll stay here actually. I have my things in the back of the car. Joe set it all up."

A small laugh came from her throat. "And me?"

He grinned. "Don't worry. I'll take you back whenever you want to go." He rolled down the window and killed the engine. For a few seconds he breathed deep, letting the ocean air fill his lungs. "A beach home with no paparazzi. Maybe we've died and gone to heaven."

This time her giggle sounded more natural. "You have the keys?"

Dayne pulled them from his pocket. "The keys, the security code . . . Joe even had a caterer come in and stock the place. We could avoid the press here for days before anyone would find us."

Katy's expression looked doubtful. But her eyes told him she was too excited to be worried. "Let's take a look."

"Okay." He glanced at the sky. "I want to get down to the beach while there's still a little sunset left."

They took their bags, walked up the steps to the front door and into the house. The place was as quaint inside as it was outside. There was a great room with soft gray leather sofas and an alpaca rug. At one end of the room was a fireplace, and the wall that faced the ocean was all windows. The kitchen was small, with a nook and a table barely big enough for two. Neither of them walked down the hallway toward what must've been bedrooms.

Dayne set the keys and the directions on the kitchen counter and opened the patio door. Fresh air rushed in through the screen.

"This is amazing." Katy stood at one of the floor-to-ceiling windows and stared at the ocean. "I can't imagine having this view every day."

"It's strange." Dayne was a few feet away, his eyes caught by the same sight. "I have this view, but I'm so busy running from photographers, darting in and out of my house that I hardly ever get to do this. Just stand at my window and enjoy it."

She slipped her hands into the pockets of her loose-fitting shorts. "A view like this makes me remember one of my favorite Scriptures."

Dayne liked the feeling of being with her, loved the direction things were headed. No matter what Katy might've thought at first, he didn't bring her here for any reason other than to talk, to share a little more of his heart with her — the only person he wanted to share it with. He leaned his shoulder into the window. "What's the verse?"

"I can't remember exactly." Her eyes narrowed, studying the shoreline. "The point of it is, because of the things God created, people are without excuse when it comes to believing in Him. If we tell ourselves there is no God, we lie to ourselves. His creation is proof that He exists."

"I read that the other day." He felt his heart swell. "It's so true." He held his hand out to her. "Come on. Take a walk with me."

She smiled and there it was again. The shy look that made him want to take her in his arms and protect her, keep her from any worldly harm or trouble all the days of her life.

She put her hand in his, and they went out the patio door and down a short flight of worn, wooden steps. Once they reached the sand, they kicked off their shoes and headed toward the water.

The sun was just dropping below the horizon, but the pinks and pale blues were still slow-dancing across the changing sky. Gentle sounds came from the surf. Dayne surveyed the area. The beach was part of an inlet. The waves were much milder than they were at Malibu Beach. A trio of seagulls rang out in the distance, taking turns diving at the water for fish. Otherwise the beach was empty.

They walked slowly, and Dayne felt his senses being filled by the moment. "Proof of God, for sure."

"Yes." She stayed close to him, and once in a while her shoulder would touch his arm.

He forced himself to focus. The walk, the sunset, the feel of Katy close at his side — all of it was like Christmas morning. But he had more than idle chatter to share with her tonight. They were twenty yards down the beach, still on the warm sand, when he stopped. "Sit by me."

"Here?" She looked around, anxious. Every time they'd been together they'd had to worry about whether they'd be caught on camera. Clearly she was still concerned about who might see them if they sat out in the open. "Are you sure?"

"Yes." He lowered himself. "No one knows we're here, Katy." He patted the spot beside him. "We're safe."

She sat down and faced the water. "I didn't think we'd find this, not after how insane things have been."

"Me either." He looked at the fading

colors in the sky. "But remember?" A cool breeze washed up from the shore. "I asked God that no matter how out of control life seemed this week, He would help us keep our eyes on Him."

She smiled. "And here we are."

"Exactly." He took hold of her hand again. He had something serious to tell her, another step, a way of opening his entire heart, his whole life to the woman who had captured him from the first time he saw her. "Katy —" he turned just enough so he could see her face — "I want to talk about Luke Baxter."

She lowered her brow. "I was going to ask you." She searched his face. "Earlier when the two of you were talking I had the strangest feeling, like you were close friends." She thought a moment. "There were other times too. Your eyes would change when someone brought up Luke's name."

Dayne drew a long breath. He had no doubts about telling her, no concerns. He trusted her completely. "There's something I need to tell you, something I've wanted to tell you for a long time."

Fear toyed with the corners of her eyes but only for a moment. "About Luke Baxter?"

"Yes." Now that he'd started he could

hardly wait to finish. "I told you that I met my birth father a few weeks ago."

"Right." Katy's throat sounded dry. She tucked her feet beneath her and kept her eyes on him.

"So, the part I've never told anyone is this." He tightened his hold on her hand. "My birth father is John Baxter. Bloomington's John Baxter."

Katy's eyes grew wide, and her lips parted. "Ashley's dad?"

"Luke's dad too."

"So Luke's your . . ."

"My brother." Dayne shrugged. "Yes. I've known for almost two years."

Darkness was falling over the beach, but he could still see the shock in her expression. "You haven't told him?"

"Katy . . ." He allowed a single, sad-sounding laugh. "Luke doesn't know his parents gave a baby up for adoption."

She did a quiet gasp and covered her face with her fingers. For a few seconds she only sat that way, but then she lowered her hand. "So, who knows? And how did you find them — the Baxters?"

The story was long and complicated, but they had all night. Dayne squinted as the memories lined up in order. "I guess it all started in New York City when I was on location. I had to stop by my attorney's office. That's where I saw Luke for the first time."

"Out of the blue, you mean? A total coincidence?"

"Right. Luke was clerking there between classes at law school."

"And what . . . you noticed a resemblance?"

"Not exactly." The story began to spill out, and for the next half hour Dayne tried to remember every detail. He told her about the photo on Luke's desk, how strangely familiar it had seemed, and how for the first time in years he'd considered the fact that he'd been adopted.

"I kept a photo of my biological mother in a storage unit." The stars were poking through the dark sky now, but the moon was full enough that they still had light around them. He faced the surf, and the feelings returned, the way they'd been when he first compared the photographs of Elizabeth. "It was the same woman in both pictures, and I knew immediately that Luke was my brother. I hired a private investigator, and in no time I had the details. Including the saddest one of all."

A dawning came over Katy's face. "Ashley's mother."

"Right." He sat up straighter and drew a slow breath. "Elizabeth Baxter was dying. I had to hurry to Bloomington if I was going to have the chance to ever meet her."

Katy slid a little closer to him, caught up in the story.

He explained that he'd arrived at the hospital in time to see the entire Baxter family walking through the parking lot. "There they were — the sort of family I'd longed for all my life. A father and brother and sisters, nieces and nephews. I didn't know if they knew about me, but I was ready to meet them, anyway. I opened the door of my rental car, and that's when I heard it." He let his gaze shift to the crashing surf. "The click of cameras."

A groan came from Katy, and she let her head fall on his shoulder. "Dayne . . . no."

"Yes." He stroked her hair and waited. His throat was thick, the memory sad and vivid.

She lifted her head. "You stayed in your car?"

"I had to." He sniffed hard through his nose, ordering his emotions to even out. "This life —" he gave a sarcastic chuckle — "hiding from the paparazzi, working like a CIA agent just to find a night alone." He shook his head. "I couldn't expose the Baxters to this. Every tabloid in the country would have a field day with them." He drew his hand across the night sky. "Think of the headline: 'Dayne Matthews' Biological Family Found in Bloomington!' "

The reality of the situation was setting in for Katy. She sighed. "Oh, Dayne, I'm so sorry."

"The Baxters are great people, but they've got secrets like anyone else. My investigator found out a lot, and if he could find it, the paparazzi would too."

"So what happened that day at the hospital?"

Sorrow tightened its hold on Dayne's heart once more. "I watched them walk past and drive away. I had no choice. When they were gone, I went in to see Elizabeth."

"So you found her?" Hope sang in Katy's tone. "I couldn't imagine you going all the way there and missing that."

"It was amazing." He let the time fall away, and he was there again, walking into Elizabeth's hospital room and meeting her for the first and only time. "She told me she loved me and that she never wanted to give me up."

Tears shone in Katy's eyes. "It's so sad, that someone would've forced her to let go of you."

"I know." Dayne's voice was quieter,

211

barely audible over the sound of the surf. But the story spilled out, every detail, all the things he and Elizabeth had discussed. "She told me I needed to find God, that faith was the most important thing I could ever have." He smiled. "She said she'd been praying for me my whole life."

"Wow." Katy rubbed her hands over her bare arms. "That gives me chills."

The beach was still completely empty. Dayne lifted his chin and savored how good it felt, sitting here next to Katy, alone without fear of cameramen. If only the night could last forever.

They were quiet for a few minutes, and Dayne slipped his arm around her shoulders. "I guess Elizabeth tried to tell John about meeting me, but he thought she was delusional from the cancer drugs. After she died he decided to find me as a way of fulfilling her dying wish."

"Sounds like one of your movies." There was awe in Katy's voice. "I mean, who could imagine this?"

"I know."

"Wait!" She pulled back and studied him. "That's why you were in Bloomington. The first time I saw you at the theater that night. You told me you were doing research."

"I was." A grin tugged at the corners of

his lips. "Just not for a movie."

She pressed her palm to her forehead. "It's all coming together. I can't believe it."

He took her hand. "There's a little more." The story was almost finished. He told her about John's efforts to reach him and how his agent had spoken for him, telling John that Dayne wasn't interested, and how John made one final attempt to contact him by writing to him at the studio. "I thank God all the time that John's letter finally reached me."

"So where did you meet?"

"At a park in Bloomington. I was in and out of town on the same day."

Again she looked like her mind was spinning. "So what now?"

This was the hard part. "John and I have been talking. He thinks my siblings would want to know me, even if it means being subject to attention from the press."

"I just thought of something."

He stifled a chuckle. The story really was amazing. It took more than once through to understand all the implications. "What?"

Katy stared at him. "You gave Ashley a ride home that night. From the theater."

"Right. The whole time I knew she was my sister."

"Dayne . . ." She closed her eyes for a moment. "That's horrible. I mean, being so close and not being able to say anything."

"Now you know a little of what I've been going through." He stood and dusted the sand off his shorts. "It's getting cool. Let's walk back."

She stood and they took their time walking up the beach. He put his arm around her waist, and she did the same to him. Their steps fell together in a rhythm that made him feel almost a part of her.

"You need to meet them." Katy sounded hopeful, as if the possibilities were just dawning on her. "They're a wonderful family."

"I know." His eyes were watery, more from the images in his heart than from the cool breeze in his face. "But sometimes I still think I'd be better to let it go. I've gone this long without being part of the Baxters, and they've gone this long not knowing about me. Who does it really help if we make the situation public? Once the Baxters lose their privacy, there's no way they'll get it back. Everything they do from that point on will be subject to scrutiny."

They walked in silence the rest of the way, and after a few minutes they were in front of the beach house.

Dayne stopped, the sand damp beneath

his feet, and faced her. "I had to tell you, Katy." He touched her face, her cheekbone. "I don't want any secrets between us."

The shy look was back. "Thank you. For trusting me."

He'd been so busy with his story, he'd avoided the obvious. How badly he wanted to take her in his arms and kiss her, tell her how he was feeling and beg her never to leave. "So —" he smiled — "that's why Luke looks like me."

"Yeah." There was still wonderment in her expression. "It all finally makes sense." She looked out to sea, then back at him. "You know what I was thinking while we were walking?"

"What?" He could smell her perfume. Mixed with the sea air and her closeness it cracked his resolve. His feelings for her filled him, and he drew her a little closer.

But she was distracted, caught up in some sort of realization. Her face told him that much. "If the Baxters hadn't been forced to give you away, you would've grown up in Bloomington." She looked deep into his eyes to the most private part of him. "Maybe we would've met at the theater, and you would've been a regular guy, an insurance salesman or a banker."

"Who painted sets on the weekend for

Christian Kids Theater."

"Exactly." A sudden sadness hung between them. "Maybe by now . . ."

"We would've met and fallen in love." He linked his hands around her waist. "And maybe we'd be married with a houseful of babies."

"Instead of hiding on a beach, stealing a few hours alone." She let her forehead fall against his chest. "It's almost more than I can imagine."

He understood her feelings. He'd let his mind go the same direction dozens of times since realizing the truth about his birth family. What if he'd been raised a Baxter? What if he'd spent his life growing up in Bloomington, running around in the same circles as his brother and sisters, meeting Katy Hart the way any normal guy might've met her?

After a while he crooked his finger and put it beneath her chin. His intention was to tell her how he felt about her, that it didn't matter if they'd met on these terms, and that somehow they'd find a way around his fame so they could have whatever they might've had if things had been different. But the moment his eyes met hers, he was unable to keep from acting on the desires that were all but consuming him. "Katy . . ."

She seemed to know what was coming. Her hand came up alongside his face, and in a pull that was stronger than anything Dayne had ever known, their lips came together. The kiss was sweet and sad and strong enough to set him on fire.

As an actor, Dayne had kissed dozens of women, creating for the big screen an image of love or lust that was intended to enrapture the audience. But kissing Katy was so different. Every other kiss he'd ever done seemed mechanical and make-believe compared with the feelings he had here, now, his toes in the sand and Katy Hart in his arms.

She eased back first, her breathing quick and uneven. "Dayne . . . I need to get back to the hotel."

His heart thudded inside his chest, and her words seemed to take a moment to reach his brain. But then he nodded. "I know." He started to pull away, but he couldn't. Never mind that the day before he hadn't wanted to kiss her. They might not have another chance like this for days or weeks. Months even. The following week he was set to start filming his next picture.

Their next kiss was longer, and the intensity of their emotions was there for both of them, drawing them in, capturing them, and threatening to take over the moment. Dayne's heart felt ready to burst, not because of lust and physical desire — though he felt that too — but because he loved Katy and he wasn't sure how to tell her, wasn't sure what promises he could make that would survive outside the pretend place they'd found tonight on the beach.

She took a step back and then walked a few paces toward the water. She looked up, shook her head, and stared at the sand by her feet. In the moonlight Dayne could see that she was trembling.

He went to her and touched her shoulder. "Don't walk away. Not now."

There were tears in her eyes when she turned to him. "You scare me. I can't . . ." She looked back at the shoreline. "Where can it ever go?"

Katy's words hurt, cut him deep. "I thought the other night on the roof . . . we're so much closer than we were before, Katy." He moved around her, blocking her view so she had to look at him. "Our worlds aren't that different now, are they?"

But the answer was in his heart as quickly as it was in her eyes. "You can't just leave your life here. Even if we share the same faith." She hugged herself. Her teeth started to chatter, and she clenched her jaw. When she had more control she looked at him again. "You have Hollywood and your movies, and I have Bloomington." She lifted one shoulder. "How's that ever supposed to work?"

"People have long-distance relationships all the time." His heart was racing, a quiet desperation replacing the desire from just moments ago. "I can't let you walk away, Katy. I won't."

"I don't know." She raised her hands as if she were out of answers. "I can sit by you on the beach and pretend you're my friend. But when —" her voice was louder than before, and two tears spilled onto her cheeks — "when you kiss me, it makes me know somehow that we're just playing games. We could never have something real, Dayne. Not unless you change your identity."

He felt a calm come over him. She was panicking. He had to hold things together, help her see there was a way out. There had to be. The paparazzi had frightened her this week, and he had to make her believe again. He took gentle hold of her shoulders and lost himself in her anxious eyes. "Then I'll change it."

"Dayne . . ."

"I will, Katy. Whatever it takes to convince you." He pulled her into his arms and kissed her again, a sweet kiss that didn't ask more from her than she could give. "You're forgetting one thing."

"What?" She was still shaking.

He ran his hands along her arms until he felt her breathe out, felt the calm return. "I asked God to show us a way." He kissed her forehead this time. "He brought us here, didn't He?"

Her heart was beating so hard he could feel it. "Yes." She leaned into him. "I want to think so, yes."

"Well, then . . . even though it looks impossible, He'll make a way for us to be together. You have to believe that."

She looked at him, to the places inside him that belonged only to her. "I'm so afraid."

"I know." He touched his finger to her lips. "Let's get you back. We don't have to figure everything out tonight."

They went up the beach and into the house, and she gathered her things. For a single instant he considered asking her to stay. She could have one of the back bedrooms, and he would promise her that nothing would happen between them.

But Bob Asher had told him something that came to him now: *"Moral failure begins with the smallest compromise."*

So instead of even making the suggestion, Dayne drove Katy back to the hotel. Along the way they made a plan that she would take a cab to the beach house in the morning. They could spend the day lying in the sun and sorting through whatever possibilities might exist for them.

He parked by the front lobby door, and again they were able to escape the paparazzi. He loved her; he had no doubt. And before she stepped out of the car, he wanted to tell her so. But the timing was off, and she was in a hurry, the magic from earlier tonight gone.

They couldn't afford to be photographed together, not late at night like this. They were still not sure what direction the tabloids would take when the articles first hit early next week. Speculation about a full-blown affair would only make Katy run farther from him. The more careful they were now, the better.

He let the moment pass and said only, "Believe, Katy. God will make the answers clear." He smiled. "Isn't that what you always told me?"

She nodded and held his gaze a few seconds longer. Then she was gone.

As he drove back to the beach house, he rolled down the windows and let the ocean air fill the rented silver Acura. He knew this for sure. If he lived to be a hundred years old, he would never find another woman who so perfectly fit his heart and body the way Katy Hart did. And something else. No matter how tempted he was, come tomorrow he would be more careful with his feelings, his actions. Yes, he would take Bob Asher's advice.

Because he loved Katy too much to allow anything to ruin their chances. Even the smallest compromise.

CHAPTER THIRTEEN

Katy had no idea how she'd made it into her hotel room. Her body must've found an autopilot mode, because here she was, staring out her window, trying to sort through everything she'd learned tonight. Dayne and Luke were brothers? Dayne and her friend Ashley were brother and sister? Dayne was the oldest son in the Baxter family?

At first the shock had been merely that. But long before Dayne kissed her, another thought had begun to dawn on her. Maybe the only reason Dayne was drawn to her was because of the Baxters, because he longed for a connection to Bloomington and the life he might've had. Why else would he have been attracted to her?

Down below on the streets of LA, a steady river of traffic made its way through the busy intersection. The lights blended into a stream that took her back to Indiana. The real story — the one Dayne only hinted at

— was coming to life in her heart.

She could picture him on a movie set in Los Angeles and getting the news about Elizabeth. His birth mother — a woman he'd never met — was dying. He must've been crushed, desperate to get to Bloomington and meet her before it was too late.

And that's exactly what he'd done, come to her and found a way to her side. But in the process, Katy knew that he'd had to acknowledge something else — that the family he would've been a part of was something he would never know, people he could never connect with. Otherwise he would place them in a peril he couldn't consider, wouldn't consider.

Katy could almost feel the anguish in his heart as he bid Elizabeth good-bye that summer day and set out through the quiet streets of Bloomington. Every street corner, every landmark, every school, every park would've made him think about what he'd never known. The life he'd been denied.

And then he'd stumbled onto the theater. Of course he'd come inside. He was a theater guy, someone who had been drawn to the stage all his life, a graduate of UCLA's drama department. If he'd been raised in Bloomington, he would've certainly been involved in CKT one way or another. So he'd read the marquis outside and realized a play was actually in progress. The last showing of CKT's production of *Charlie Brown.*

Anxious to keep his anonymity, he'd headed into the theater with his baseball cap low on his brow. He must've been looking for a window, a glimpse at what his life might've been like. And there on the stage he'd gotten his first look at her. Katy Hart. Someone without the glitz and glamour of Hollywood, the sort of woman he would've fallen for if he'd lived his life as a Baxter.

Katy blinked and the traffic came into focus again. All of which meant that his feelings for her were little more than a figment of his imagination, a desire intended to bridge the miles between his real life and the one he'd been cheated out of.

A shiver ran down her spine, and she rubbed her arms. She didn't want to be part of his fantasy world, a bridge to a life he could never have. She stepped away from the window and closed her eyes. When Dayne kissed her, the feelings were so real, so strong. Lost in his arms she couldn't imagine life without him, and that's when fear had rushed in and suffocated her.

She'd had no choice but to walk away, separate her heart from his. Otherwise she'd lose herself, and there'd be no way back. She could never fall for another guy when her feelings for Dayne were so strong, when he was filling her mind and soul with whispered prayers and promises about tomorrow.

But what if every word of it was only his personal journey to find himself, to figure out his past? A reason to go to Bloomington where lived the family he was so curious about, the people he longed to be a part of?

Her head hurt from the thoughts warring within her. She needed a sounding board, someone to pray for her that common sense would have its say by the time she met Dayne in the morning. She took her cell phone from her purse, flipped it open, and called the Flanigans.

Jenny answered on the third ring. It was after midnight there, but Jenny and Jim never went to bed before eleven o'clock. "Hello?" Her voice sounded groggy.

"Hi." Katy's voice was strangled with fresh tears. "Did I wake you?"

"Katy? Is it you?" Jenny yawned.

Katy chided herself. It was way too late to be calling the Flanigans. "Sorry . . . go back to bed."

"No, it's okay." Jenny sounded tired but more awake now. "Is everything all right?"

Her concern took precedent over her sleepiness. "I saw you on the news. Your testimony sounded perfect."

"It isn't the trial." She pressed her fingertips to her upper lip and ordered herself to find control. "It's Dayne."

A long sigh sounded over the phone line. "What happened? Tell me."

"Nothing." Katy knew she wasn't making sense. Her heart was in her throat, and her words wouldn't come. She stretched out on the bedspread. "We had the most wonderful night."

Jenny waited.

"But I found out some things tonight." She sniffed. "Dayne's adopted; have I told you that?"

"Umm . . . I think so. You mentioned it after one of your talks when he came here to Bloomington."

"Okay, well . . ." Katy warned herself to be careful. She could only say so much without betraying Dayne's trust. "I found out tonight that his birth family lives in Bloomington." Tears sounded in her voice again. "They've lived there all along."

Jenny hesitated. "Maybe that's a good thing. One more reason why he belongs here instead of there, right?"

"Or maybe that's why he has feelings for

me. Maybe I'm just part of some fantasy he has about living in Bloomington and being part of a normal family."

"Oh." Jenny seemed to sort through the idea, as if she were making sense of it. "You mean maybe the only reason he's interested is because you're from what would've been his home town if he hadn't been given up for adoption?"

"Exactly." Katy drew her knees up and stared at the empty wall. "No matter what he says, he can't find his way back to a family he's never known. And when he realizes that, maybe he'll feel the same way about me. Like I was just part of some dream he could never have anyway."

"Mmm . . ." Jenny's voice had a fresh knowing in it, as if some truth was just hitting her.

"What?" Katy could still feel Dayne's arms around her; her cheeks were still hot from the way he'd kissed her. The way she'd kissed him in return.

"Katy, don't you see? This isn't about whether he fell for you because you were from Bloomington or not." Jenny's tone was softer than before.

"It isn't?" She sat up and propped herself against the headboard.

"No." Jenny's smile came through in her

words. "You're not afraid of that."

She leaned over her knees. "I'm not?"

"No, Katy. You're afraid because this time it's actually happened." Jenny paused. "You've fallen for him. And now that you have, there's no turning back."

Katy sat up straighter and shook her head. She opened her mouth to disagree, but then she pictured herself sitting next to Dayne on the beach earlier. Every moment had felt like something from a dream, hadn't it? The feel of him beside her, his easy conversation, the way he had trusted her with the truth about his past. Jenny was right. She had felt herself falling a little harder with each passing minute. "So . . . you think his feelings for me aren't just a part of the fact that his birth family lives in Bloomington?"

"Does it matter?" Jenny laughed, the lighthearted laugh of someone who believes everything's going to work out. "You're from Bloomington. So what, Katy? All the better that his birth family's here too."

Katy kicked off her shoes. There was still sand between her toes. "But neither I nor his birth family can ever have a future with him." She dusted the sand off the bedspread. "Don't you see? His life won't allow it."

"I used to think that." Jenny's words were

slow, deliberate. "But I've watched the transformation in Dayne through the things you've told me. He's not the same guy he was."

That was the hardest part. "I know." Katy allowed a smile, and the feel of it brought back every good memory from tonight. "He's given his life to God. His faith is as real as yours or mine."

"See?" Again she sounded confident. "God's doing something here."

"So what should I do?" Katy stood and paced across the room toward the window. "I'm supposed to spend the day with him tomorrow. His lawyer found us this beach house no one's using."

"Hmm." Worry crept into Jenny's tone. "Be careful. He's not used to taking things slowly."

"He's slow with me. I'm not worried about that." Katy hugged herself with her free hand. "I guess you were right before. I'm worried about my heart."

They talked about Bloomington and life at the Flanigan house for a few minutes, and then Katy said good night. She hadn't really solved anything, but listening to Jenny had been good for her. Of course Dayne's feelings for her were real, and Jenny was right. There was no separating her from the fact that she was from Bloomington. If it was part of her appeal, she couldn't hold that against Dayne.

There was another fear Katy hadn't wanted to admit either. The dread of what the tabloids would spill across the covers next week and how that would change her life once she returned home.

She dressed for bed and crawled beneath the covers. For the next hour she replayed everything about tonight. Dayne taking her to the beach house, the excitement of being alone without fear of being caught on camera, the sensation of the sand beneath their feet as they walked hand in hand along the shore. His body — taller, stronger — next to hers as they watched the sunset fade to dark. The wonderful way her heart felt as she and Dayne found their way back to the emotional depth that came so easily for them in Bloomington.

And the way she'd so easily allowed herself to be lost in his arms, taken by his kiss. No wonder she was worried. Being with Dayne was magical and amazing. He made her feel the way no other guy had ever made her feel. But his life came with conditions, a visibility she had never wanted, still didn't want.

This week would end and she would go

home, back to directing CKT. Meanwhile Dayne would begin preproduction on a film starring opposite a beautiful, spunky blonde, an Academy Award winner who had been romantically connected with Dayne a long time ago.

How was Katy supposed to compete with that? And how, in the midst of it would they find even a few hours to talk, let alone see each other? Yes, Katy had every reason to be afraid and not nearly so much because of what the tabloids were about to do to her. She was worried about losing her privacy, yes. But far more than that, when it came to Dayne Matthews she was worried about losing something else.

Her heart.

CHAPTER FOURTEEN

Katy made her morning getaway in a taxi without the paparazzi spotting her. She wore a hat and sunglasses and carried her things in a beach bag. Again no one would've taken her for anything more than a tourist heading out for a day at the beach. She spotted a few photographers chatting and sipping coffee from paper cups, but she ducked into the cab before they could see her.

Half an hour later she paid the driver and stepped out in front of the beach house. She was nervous about today, not because she was worried about her self-control but because she didn't see the point of letting herself fall for Dayne a little more. She'd be going home after the verdict, and he'd begin filming another movie. And then what?

Her heart felt heavy as she climbed the steps. The sun was breaking through the fog, but the air was cool and a chill ran down her arms and legs. *God . . . what am I doing? Where can a day like this possibly lead?*

But then the door opened and there he stood, not the Hollywood star but the Dayne she knew, the one the world had never seen.

When his eyes found hers, she stopped, her heart in her throat. "Hi."

"Hi." He smiled, but there was concern in his eyes. "You look like you're ready to run." He came out onto the porch and touched her arm. "Come here."

If she would've looked down, there would've been a hole where her heart belonged. Because it was too late to stop herself. Dayne owned it completely. And that did indeed make her want to run. But not the other direction, like he figured. She closed the distance between them and set her bag down. "I'm not running."

"I know." He wrapped her in his arms and rocked her a little. "Nothing feels right when you're away." He brushed his cheek against hers. "Mmm. I couldn't wait for you to get back."

"Me either." She picked up her bag, her eyes never leaving his. "I'm still afraid."

"Yeah." The emotions in his eyes were deeper than she'd ever seen them. "Me too." He took her free hand and led her toward the door. "Let's have today, and maybe before the clock strikes midnight God will show us how we can make it last. So neither of us has to be afraid anymore."

They went inside, and there on the kitchen table was a breakfast spread. She grinned, feeling the fear leave her, and stared out the window. The Pacific lay spread out in an endless brilliant blue, sparkling with a million diamonds from the morning sun. In this light, the water looked even closer to the beach house than before. "Dayne . . . it's like a dream."

"Yes." He touched her chin. He wasn't taking in any of the scenery outdoors. "Having you here, Katy. That's the dream."

The day unfolded just that way — like something they might've imagined but never thought possible. After breakfast they went outside and set up their towels on a pair of chaise lounges near the shore. The waves came in harder, and the sound was mesmerizing.

Katy didn't have her swimsuit, but her shorts and tank top gave her the chance to soak in the sun, same as Dayne. She tried not to notice his tanned chest or the way the muscles in his arms flexed when he shifted or took a drink of his water. They spent two hours mostly sleeping, enjoying the feel of the sun and the breeze and the occasional spray from the ocean.

At lunchtime Dayne brought out a picnic basket and a blanket. They played backgammon and ate chicken sandwiches and grapes, the whole time avoiding the one topic that absolutely had to be dealt with — what was going to become of them after today?

The afternoon sun was more intense, and they both slathered on sunscreen and played a rousing game of Frisbee in the foamy surf.

"You're pretty good for an Indiana girl," Dayne called to her across the beach. His smile lit up her heart.

Her laugh came easily. "You forget I spend most of my time around kids, and these days —" she flung the Frisbee back at him in a perfect throw — "every time kids get together a game of Ultimate Frisbee breaks out."

"And my little miss Katy Hart is right there at the center of the action, no doubt." He tossed the disk back to her, but it got caught in the wind and headed over knee-deep water.

She ran for it, her bare feet springing through the water. "I'll get it." Before she could snag it from the air, she heard footsteps behind her, loud splashing footsteps.

Dayne bounded over to her, grabbed the Frisbee with his left hand, then with his right, caught her by the waist and fell alongside her into the surf.

"Dayne —" The water hit her in the face. It was so cold it took her breath away, but after an hour of playing Frisbee in the hot sun, the feeling was wonderful.

He had her by the hand and led her farther out. "You can't spend a day at the beach and not get wet!" He laughed and shook his hair at her, spraying water on her face.

A small wave was building ten feet away, and it crashed down on them, knocking them to their knees and leaving them drenched.

Katy worked her way back to her feet. "Okay . . ." She was laughing, winded, but she felt more alive than she had in a long time. "Enough!"

Dayne was on his feet, and he pulled her into his arms. For a moment, she thought he was going to knock her into the water again, but suddenly the waves and the water, the silly game they were playing — all of it was forgotten. His hands encircled her waist, and hers came up around his neck. He was warm against her, and the feeling made her dizzy.

"Katy . . . don't ever leave me." He kissed her, and the salt water mixed with the heat of the kiss sent sensations through her she'd never felt before. He held her closer, kissed her longer this time. When he drew back, there was a desire in his eyes that was unmistakable. "Don't run from me."

She had to lighten the moment, had to do something or she might never come up for air. After one more kiss and then another, she squirmed from his arms. "Like this, you mean?" She took a few light steps parallel to the surf and sprayed him with water. "Come on, Dayne." She could feel her eyes dancing. "You already know I'm going to run." She took another few steps. "The question is, are you willing to chase me?"

She took off, and he came up fast behind her. She could feel herself about to be leveled into the water, but instead of tackling her, he ran past her toward the crashing surf.

"Look." He pointed at the red disk floating farther down the beach. "We forgot the Frisbee." He ran after it, snagged it, and threw it to her — just far enough that she had to run out of the water toward the sand to catch it.

She did, and then she took a few steps and dropped it on the beach. Her body was hot and cold at the same time, and she ached to be in his arms again. She bent over, her hands on her knees.

"You okay?" He jogged back through the surf toward her, intentionally splashing her as he came closer.

She lifted her head and grinned at him. "It's colder than it looks."

"Yeah." He was out of breath, the desire in his eyes replaced with something more lighthearted. "I forgot to tell you that."

She flicked a bit of water at his face as she straightened. "Thanks a lot."

"Come on." He took her hand. "Let's go warm up."

They were walking back to their chairs when Katy heard a helicopter. She stopped and peered toward the southern sky. "What's that?"

"No . . ." Dayne slowed his steps. He squinted in the same direction. "There're two of them." He hesitated. "That isn't good."

"It's not paparazzi, right, not in helicopters?" They reached their chairs. Katy snatched her towel and wrapped it around her arms. The sound of the aircraft was ominous, warlike. As if they'd been caught in the middle of a battlefield without any weapons or form of protection.

"The tabloids do it all the time. Someone tips them off about a wedding or a meeting at the beach, and they grab a chopper. Quickest way to get a picture, and they can cover a lot more ground."

Fear choked out every wonderful thing Katy had been feeling. She shaded her eyes, watching the helicopters. They were approaching faster than before. She squinted at Dayne. "You're serious?"

He grabbed the picnic basket and wrapped his own towel around his shoulders. "Get your things. Come on."

The helicopters were closing in, and suddenly they had no time. Dayne took her hand and began jogging toward the house, and somehow she matched his pace. The pulsating sound of the choppers drowned out every other sound on the beach. Katy looked up in time to see the first one hovering almost directly over their beach chairs. A camera lens poked through the open door, aimed straight at them.

"Don't look," Dayne shouted, his words barely loud enough to be heard.

Her heart pounded, but she turned away and put every bit of effort into following him up the steps of the house and through the back door. They dropped their things, and she fell against the wall, gasping for air.

Dayne ran to the far side of the window and began pulling the cords on the blinds. "From a chopper —" he was out of breath too — "they can see straight into the house." He worked the blinds until they were shut; then he did the same to the kitchen window and the one on the street side of the house.

When every window was covered, he came to her and faced the wall. She leaned her head back, still struggling to draw a normal breath. He only looked at her and shook his head. Then he raised his arm against the wall, resting his forehead in the crook of his elbow. "I can't believe this."

She couldn't either. It had happened so fast. One minute they were enjoying the rarest of chances, a day alone on the beach without anyone bothering them, without any fear of cameras or paparazzi. And the next they were running for what? For their privacy? For their sanity? "How . . . how did they find us?"

"Who knows?" He turned around and rested his back against the wall. "I swear, they're bloodsuckers. It's never . . . ever enough."

She could feel him breathing hard beside her. Her heart was still racing, but at least they'd been close enough to get inside quickly. "Did they get pictures?"

"Definitely." He grabbed at his hair and made a frustrated sound. "How could I be so stupid? I should've been watching for them."

Slowly the reality was hitting Katy. Obviously the helicopters had snuck up on them while they were in the water. The combination of the sounds of the surf and the wind and their laughter was enough to keep them from hearing the helicopters. She didn't want to ask, but she had to. "You . . . think they took pictures of us in the water?"

He sighed and turned toward her, his shoulder pressed to the wall. "I hope not." He winced. "But the cameras they use could've caught us from pretty far out."

"And just now?"

"Absolutely. They'll have a hundred pictures of us running up the beach." He threw his hands in the air. "Sometimes I think it's better to stop and wave at them, rather than give them a picture like that one." He gritted his teeth. "I mean, come on. We have nothing to hide."

She wanted to say he was only half right. *He* had nothing to hide. He was used to seeing his face plastered across the tabloids at every supermarket checkout across the nation. But she was terrified at the idea. They had spent two days telling the world they were only friends, and now . . . now there would be enough photos to convince anyone that they'd been lying. Even so, the news would do nothing to hurt Dayne. No, she was the one with everything to lose.

He touched her shoulder. "I'm sorry. What I said . . . that wasn't fair." He raked his fingers through his wet hair. "Your privacy means the world to me, Katy."

They could hear the helicopters outside, still circling, looking for a crack in the blinds, some way to capture whatever was happening inside the beach house. It was an hour before the sound of them faded entirely. By then she and Dayne had changed into dry clothes and taken up places next to each other on the soft leather sofa.

"Does that mean it's safe?" Katy peeked out of the shades. Two cars were parked across the street, where before there'd been none.

"Of course not." Dayne looked out. "Once one of them sniffs out a story, the rest aren't far behind. They've probably got us circled by now."

"So what do we do?" She was shivering, in part because she was still cold from the dampness. But more because it was a strange feeling, being trapped in a house while rabid strangers lay in wait for them.

Never mind that their weapons were cameras and not knives. They weren't in danger, but the end result was almost as unnerving as if Margie Madden was out there with them.

Dayne had been quiet and edgy since they'd been forced inside. Now he let his head fall back against the sofa, and he looked at her. "We outlast them." A weak smile tugged at his lips. "We eat dinner and watch a movie, and when it's late enough I'll take you home."

The plan worked for a while. They ate and talked about the trial and tried not to think about the people with cameras probably camped around the beach house. Afterwards, Dayne found a VHS tape of *Fletch,* an old Chevy Chase comedy. Once it was on, he took a cozy, thick blanket from the top of a nearby chair. He sat next to her and spread it over their legs.

Somehow being alone with him didn't feel alluring now — knowing that people were gathered outside, watching the house. They held hands and tried to get caught up in the movie. But never did either of them laugh, even at the funny parts.

The movie was half over when there was a loud rap on the door. "Dayne!" a man yelled. He banged the door and shook the knob.

Katy gasped and grabbed hold of Dayne's arm. "He's trying to break in."

"He can't." Dayne slid to the edge of the sofa.

"Come on!" Another several loud bangs on the door. "Let us get our pictures, and we'll get out of your way."

Dayne pointed down the hallway. "Go, Katy. Hide in one of the rooms."

Her heart was pounding. The whole thing felt like a scene from a horror film. "What are you going to do?"

"I'm getting rid of them." He pointed again. "Please, Katy. Go."

She was about to protest when the man outside banged the door again, even harder than before. The sound shot Katy up and off the couch. She hurried down the hall and ducked into a bathroom. The only room without a window. She kept the door open a crack so she could hear what was happening.

It occurred to her that she should've grabbed her cell phone in case Dayne fell into trouble or the man didn't leave easily. She leaned against the counter and closed her eyes. *God . . . protect him. Protect us both, please. . . .*

Daughter, I am with you.

The words echoed in her heart and gave her a reason to hang on. She focused all her energy on listening to what was happening in the next room. First she heard Dayne open the door, and at the same time she heard pounding feet outside. Whoever had been at the door must've run. But then she heard a burst of camera clicks and Dayne shouting, "Get off my property . . . now!"

From the distance someone shouted, "Where is she, Dayne? We want Katy Hart."

"Listen. I'm calling the police." She hadn't heard this much anger in Dayne's voice ever. "Any of you still here when the police pull up, I'll press charges." He slammed the door.

Over the next minute, Katy heard the slamming of car doors and the squealing of tires. She couldn't help but smile at Dayne's good work. Another minute passed, and then she heard him close the front door.

"Katy?"

She stepped out of the bathroom and squinted in the light. "Did they all leave?"

"The nasty ones." He held his hands out to her. "I'm so sorry."

"I know." She came to him, put her arms around him. She was worn out from the feeling of being pursued, a feeling that hadn't left her since she first saw the helicopters. She let herself fall against him. "I'm exhausted. Maybe you should take me back."

"The problem is —" he kissed the top of her head — "I can't be sure they're gone. Not all of them."

She tried to imagine what would happen if they left the house together now. The cameras would catch them, and the story would write itself. Katy Hart and Dayne Matthews, holed up in a beach house together all day. No one would have to ask what they were doing. If Dayne Matthews was involved — the Dayne the public still knew him to be — the answer was obvious.

"Maybe I could slip out first. Or you could," Katy said.

"It wouldn't matter. They'd get the picture of us in the car, pulling away." He frowned and looked over his shoulder at the front door. "I don't want to give them the satisfaction."

Katy didn't either, but she was tired and frazzled, too much to enjoy herself another minute. "So we wait?"

"Awhile." He led her back to the couch. "It's ten o'clock. Let's watch TV, and in an hour I'll go out and see if anyone's stirring."

"Okay." She settled next to him and pulled

the blanket up around their chests. "I'm sorry about all this, the trouble I'm causing."

"It's not you." He put his arm around her and ran his fingers through her hair. "I told you before, this is about me."

"But you're used to them." She snuggled closer and rested her head on his shoulder. "If I didn't care about staying out of the tabloids, we could do what you said earlier. Smile and wave and that would be the end of it."

"No, Katy. Where paparazzi are concerned, there's never an end to it."

He turned on ESPN and they watched Sports Center. She nodded off for part of it, and when she opened her eyes, he was watching country music videos. "I think I fell asleep."

"You did." He kissed the top of her head again. He seemed more interested in protecting her than making a pass at her.

Katy was glad. "We haven't talked about what happens next."

"We don't have to." Dayne held her close, easing her head back to his shoulder. "If you run, I'll follow you." There was a smile in his voice. "Just like earlier."

A mellow song was playing on the television, and she nodded off again. The frenzied feeling from earlier faded. It felt nice, sitting beneath a blanket, her head on Dayne's shoulder. As another hour passed, the last thing she wanted to do was leave. Even if the paparazzi had packed up and gone home.

Eleven became midnight, and sometime later she opened her eyes and realized what had happened. Dayne had turned off the television, and he was asleep, leaning on the arm of the sofa. His hand was around her waist, and her head was still on his shoulder. His breathing came in slow, even measures.

Panic grabbed hold of her. They'd lost track of time, and now what? She was about to wake him up when she realized there was no point. He wasn't going to take advantage of her. They were simply two people who'd been chased from late afternoon on and needed a chance to get beyond their exhaustion. She settled her head back against his shoulder, and within minutes she was asleep again.

The next time she opened her eyes, sunshine was streaming through the cracks in the blinds.

Dayne must've sensed her being awake, because he stirred and opened his eyes. In a rush, his eyes opened wider than before, and he leaned up on his elbow. "Katy! It's morning!"

"I know." She smiled, watching him react to the situation the same way she had. "It's okay." She rubbed her eyes. "I didn't want to go anyway."

The couch was comfortable enough that they'd slept soundly, without ever stretching out. But now she felt his body ease in along hers. "Can I tell you something?"

"Mmm." This was wrong, lying here with him now that they were both awake. It was probably wrong to do so last night when they were only sitting. But she couldn't help herself.

"I didn't want you to leave either." He played with a strand of her hair, and for the sweetest moment he kissed her. But then, as if something had struck him deep inside, he tossed the blanket to the floor, stood, and stretched. "I'm making coffee."

Katy let herself sink into the sofa. She felt humiliated, angry at herself. She never should've allowed herself to fall asleep on his shoulder. In the middle of the night she could've woken him and asked that he take her home. What must he think of her now? That she wasn't the person he thought her to be?

He returned with the coffee before she could berate herself anymore. "Hey . . . sit up." His tone was kind, his eyes filled with a warmth that relieved her guilt.

She did as he asked, and she took one of the cups. "I shouldn't have stayed."

"Nothing happened." He sat beside her and leaned his forearms on his knees. "You're right. I should've taken you home." He cast her a look, and his eyes warmed. "But I've never felt more right in all my life, being there with you sleeping on my shoulder." He blew at the steam coming off his coffee. "I never wanted morning to come."

"Me either." She looked at the front door. "But what sort of trouble are we in now?"

"The paparazzi?" Concern tightened his expression. "I know. I've been trying to figure a way out for both of us."

They talked about the issue for the next few minutes before Dayne came up with a plan. He would call Joe Morris and tell him what happened, that the photographers were so aggressive he didn't feel safe leaving the house with Katy. Only now they would feel they had proof of an affair, because what other reason would there be for Katy to spend the night?

Then he would ask Joe to make an announcement to the press. That Katy Hart was sick of being chased, and she was staying in her hotel room until the pressure let up. They could ask about the woman with Dayne at the beach, and Joe would plead ignorance. He could only speak for Katy, he would tell them. And she hadn't left her hotel room since arriving there Tuesday evening.

The story was a lie, but it was all the paparazzi deserved. Especially after they'd hunted Dayne and her like animals. The two of them had needed a day of privacy, no matter what they had to tell the press.

Dayne made the call, and when he hung up he nodded at Katy. "Joe thinks it'll work."

"But what if the cameramen in the helicopters got a close-up of my face?"

"They didn't." Dayne walked toward the front door. "They may have gotten a picture of two people standing in the surf kissing, but it would be impossible to tell for sure that it was you in my arms." He held his hand up. "I'll be right back." He stepped outside, and after a few seconds he returned. "It looks clear if we go now."

She picked up her bag and followed him toward the door. God couldn't have been thrilled with either of them, falling asleep the way they had done and not making a better attempt to get her back to the hotel. But Dayne was right. Nothing had happened. Now they needed to pray that the press believed Joe's story. Otherwise it wouldn't matter what actually took place last night in the beach house.

The world would never believe for a minute that all they'd done was sleep.

CHAPTER FIFTEEN

Ashley hadn't stopped hearing from her siblings since her father spread the news. She'd spent almost all of Wednesday talking to them, hearing their concerns and anxieties on the topic, listening to them walk through the details as they tried to convince themselves that having an older brother was even possible.

Now it was Thursday morning, and she'd already fed and diapered baby Devin, already laid him back down for his early nap. Cole was off to school, and Landon had a day shift at the fire station. The house was quiet, and she wanted more than anything to take her baby and his bag and head for her father's house.

He would already be at work, but her painting was still standing in her old upstairs bedroom, and after a day of talking about her unknown brother, she could hardly wait to pick up her paintbrush and get back to work. A few more sessions and she'd be finished, the idea in her mind had transferred to canvas in a way that was beyond satisfying.

She made herself a plate of eggs and sat at the kitchen table. Earlier Cole had picked up on her mood. Over his bowl of Cheerios he'd cocked his head and squinted. "You have a lot of thoughts in your head today, don't you, Mommy?"

"I do." She'd sat across from him, her arms folded. "And what about you, Coley? What thoughts are in your head?"

He made a face. "Spelling test. Remember? The words you practiced with me last Friday."

"Well, good. You know those."

"Still . . ." He slurped up a mouthful of cereal. "Spelling tests are never very good for my head."

"I suppose."

His eyes lit up. "Now, frogs . . . and fish! And having an adventure in the backyard with Daddy!" He gave a serious nod. "Those are good thoughts."

Cole made her smile. She missed him when he was gone all day to school, but it was almost summer, and then they'd take day trips to the lake and haul out the old ice chest so he and Landon could find their favorite fishing spot and make more wonderful memories. This time she'd bring Devin and sit nearby, letting summer work its lazy magic on her heart and soul.

But for now there was the issue sending aftershocks through their family, the idea that sometime in the next few months they might meet a man who was their full-blooded brother. She'd had longer to get used to the idea, but she understood the concerns her siblings were having.

Luke had called late last night from Los Angeles. They'd talked a couple times since their dad broke the news. "I guess I still can't believe it, like maybe the whole thing is Dad having a nervous breakdown from missing Mom."

"No, Luke." Ashley had kept calm through phone calls from Kari and Erin and Brooke. She made a point to remain calm for her younger brother too. "I already told you. I saw the letter, the one Mom wrote to him."

"Okay, but how do we go our whole lives and miss something like that? Shouldn't there have been a sign, a clue along the way?"

"You have to understand, back then they convinced people that giving a baby up for adoption was like never having that baby."

Luke hesitated, then exhaled hard. "Still,

they should've told us."

Ashley was quiet for a moment, giving Luke time to think about his statement. "What would it have proved? He belonged to another family. Knowing about him only would've made us wonder and want to meet him."

"The way you and the girls feel now." Resignation filled Luke's voice. "I can't really see him as a brother at this point. He's a stranger who shares our blood, you know?"

"He is." Ashley pictured their father, the way he looked when he talked about his older son. "But Dad's made a connection with him, and pretty soon we'll need to think about whether we want one too."

"What if I want my family the way it was two days ago, before I knew about this?"

"Not knowing wouldn't have changed the truth, Luke." Her tone was even gentler than before. "Mom and Dad had six kids. It's up to us to help each other deal with that."

"You sound like Reagan." His voice lightened some, and he took on his wife's tone. " 'Adoption has many faces. Your parents had no choice in the matter, so thank God someone was willing to open their home to your older brother.' Just like that. All matter-of-fact."

Ashley chuckled. "Sometimes wives know a thing or two."

"I guess." Luke yawned. "I need some sleep. Closing arguments might come tomorrow."

"Okay, little brother. Love you."

"Love you too."

Of course the situation troubled Luke more than the others. Guys were funny that way. Even if their older brother wanted to meet them, Ashley guessed Luke would take a while to warm up to the idea. Today he'd be wrapped up in court proceedings and closing arguments, probably bringing Katy and Dayne back into the courtroom.

Ashley opened the newspaper and searched for the most recent story. The Bloomington reporters were aware that their local sweetheart Katy Hart was at the center of the nation's current big trial. Starting with Tuesday morning's paper, they'd included a box adjacent to the trial coverage with a banner headline that read "Local Angle."

Talking to her siblings about their older brother had made Ashley almost forget her friend suffering through such scrutiny on the West Coast. She scanned the article and felt a rush of relief. So far there wasn't much that would've upset Katy. They had identified her as the mystery woman with Dayne on the beach the night of the attack, and yesterday's paper detailed Katy's testimony.

But the article was clear that Katy and Dayne had been together that night for business reasons and that they were colleagues, nothing more. Today's story said only that Katy and Dayne had spent the day away from the courthouse while medical doctors and psychiatrists testified about the mental abilities of the defendant.

Ashley tapped the open page. "All right, Katy," she whispered, "where did you and Dayne disappear to?" She smiled. Katy wouldn't have let herself get into trouble, not with Dayne and not with all of America watching. Still, she couldn't wait for the chance to catch up with her friend and find out how they'd managed to escape the press for an entire day.

She was cleaning the kitchen when Erin called.

"Do you think Mom tried to give me a sign, and I was too busy with my own situation to see it?" The unrest in Erin's voice was stronger than in all their other siblings combined.

"Erin, no." Ashley dried the frying pan

and slipped it back into the cupboard. "Mom didn't want to admit the truth to herself; she certainly wasn't trying to give you a sign."

"I don't mean an actual sign." Erin sighed, and the heaviness of it stayed between them even over the phone line. "I mean, maybe she hinted at the possibility that she'd given a baby up for adoption. Maybe she wanted me to ask her about it, and I blew it."

"You didn't blow it." Ashley picked up a dirty plate and began to rinse it. "Mom and Dad promised each other to keep their firstborn son a secret. There was nothing any of us could've done to figure it out."

Erin sniffed. "I just keep thinking . . . poor Mom. Her oldest child out there and all those years never knowing where to find him."

Ashley set the rinsed dish aside, opened the dishwasher, and began unloading the top rack. "But at least she got to meet him before she died."

"I guess." Erin's voice held the beginning of hope. "I wish we could've talked with her about it."

"Me too. Dad says they had an hour together, and she told him everything she'd always wanted to say."

A relieved sigh came from Erin. "I have to

hold on to that, I guess. I just wanted to make sure there wasn't something I'd missed. I couldn't . . . I couldn't forgive myself if I'd let Mom down that way."

They talked another few minutes; then Erin had to get two of her young daughters down for morning naps. Ashley silently prayed for her sister as she hung up the phone. If anyone would see it from their mother's viewpoint, it was Erin. Not only because she had four adopted daughters, but because she and their mom had been so close. She was wrestling not only with the truth her mother had hidden from them all but the fact that despite their closeness, Erin hadn't known their mother as well as she had always thought.

Ashley dried her hands on a towel and looked at the clock. The painting was calling to her, while she still had time before lunch. It took her ten minutes to pack up Devin's things and get him buckled into his car seat.

Fifteen minutes later she had him tucked into her parents' old portable crib in a place where she could hear him if he woke up. She was about to head upstairs when she heard a cell phone ring. *Funny,* she thought. She checked the front pocket of Devin's diaper bag where she kept her phone. It wasn't hers. She looked around, and there on the counter was her father's cell. He always had it with him, but he must've forgotten it today.

The phone was only a few feet away, and Ashley didn't want Devin waking up. Besides, maybe it was her dad, calling his own phone to figure out where he'd left it. She darted over to the counter and looked at the small caller ID window. The number had a 310 area code, and the name below it read *Dayne.*

Ashley stared at it, confused. By the time she jolted back into motion, the ringing had stopped. *One missed call,* the window now read. Ashley picked up her father's phone carefully, as if it might bite her. Dayne who? The area code was Los Angeles. Ashley knew because she'd been in touch with a few art galleries there. So what Dayne from Los Angeles would be calling her father?

Dayne Matthews?

There was only one way to find out. She held her breath, flipped open the phone, and pushed the Send button. Instantly the same name and number appeared. Again Ashley hit Send, and in a handful of seconds the phone was ringing.

"Hello?" There was noise in the background, but the voice sounded familiar.

"Hi . . . this is Ashley Blake." She wasn't sure what to say. "I, uh . . . I just missed a call from your number on my father's phone. John Baxter."

"Oh. Right." The man on the other end chuckled. "Hi . . . I was calling for your brother Luke."

Luke? But Luke was in LA at the trial with — "Is this Dayne? Dayne Matthews?"

"Yes." Another easy laugh. "Luke left his phone back at the hotel room. I was . . . he wanted to ask your dad something."

"Wow." Ashley felt her cheeks grow hot. "You're a full-service celebrity. Giving me a ride home from the theater that time and now helping my brother." She was rambling, and she steadied herself against the counter.

"It's the last day of the hearing." He didn't seem fazed by her nervousness. "Luke's been a big help. The prosecutor feels good about the way things are going."

Once she got over the shock of having Dayne Matthews on the phone, she felt her breathing return to normal. "How's Katy doing? I've been praying for her."

"The tabloids will hit the shelves by Monday." His voice was kind, compassionate. "I guess we'll know better then."

"I guess." She sucked in a quick breath. He was too busy to spend another minute chatting with Katy's friend back in Bloomington. "Anyway, my dad forgot his phone at home. I'll leave him a message to call Luke later."

"Good. I'll let Luke know."

The call ended, and Ashley stared at the phone. Dayne Matthews calling her father? doing a favor for her brother? Who would've ever guessed? She was about to set the phone back on the counter when it occurred to her that someday — for some reason — she might need Dayne Matthews' number. Everyone in her family teased her about the size of her phone list and the fact that she felt the need to save every number she ever came across. And how often would she have the chance to capture the number of one of the nation's biggest celebrities?

She snatched her phone from the diaper bag, punched a few buttons on her father's cell, and saw Dayne's number fill the screen once more. On her own phone she popped up her address book, and in a matter of seconds Dayne's number was added to the others in her storage file.

Ashley was still at her dad's house painting — between feeding breaks and a nap with Devin — when he returned home that afternoon. She was downstairs in the rocking chair, Devin in her arms as he walked in. "Hi." She gave him a sheepish grin. "You left your cell phone here."

Her dad hesitated and set his bag down. "Let me guess; you've been answering it all day?"

"Just once actually." She gave him a star-struck grin. "It was Dayne Matthews." She gave a nonchalant shrug. "Calling to say hello."

She expected her father to be curious or at the least to laugh. Instead something very serious came over his expression. "You talked to Dayne?"

"For a little while." She giggled. "I mean, come on, Dad. The two of us go way back to that ride home he gave me from the theater that night. Remember?"

For the first time in half a minute, her father inhaled. He leaned against the entry wall. "So why . . . why'd he call?"

Luke must've used Dayne's phone all the time. Otherwise why wasn't her father acting more impressed? "Dad . . . Dayne Matthews calls on your cell phone and all you can ask is why'd he call?"

Her dad looked away, pretending to busy himself with removing his sweater. "Dayne's working with Luke. I would assume that's why he called."

"It is." She clucked her tongue against the roof of her mouth. "You don't even get excited, Dad. Come on, I'm talking about Dayne Matthews."

This time, when her dad faced her, there was teasing laughter in his eyes. "He puts his pants on same as anyone else."

"I know . . . just having a little fun. It isn't every day that Dayne Matthews and I have a phone chat." She leaned down and kissed Devin's forehead. "And, yes, his message was to call Luke. I guess you both forgot your cell phones today."

"Fine." He came closer and kissed first her cheek, then the baby's. He looked more relaxed. "Was that the highlight of your day?"

"No." She felt a softness fill her voice. "I worked on the painting, the one of our older brother."

A fine layer of sweat beaded on her dad's upper lip. "Good, honey." He nodded toward the kitchen. "I'm making coffee if you want a cup."

"No, thanks." She stood and moved Devin to his car seat. "Landon'll be home in a couple hours. I should get going."

They talked a few more minutes about his day at work and the fact that Dayne thought the trial was going well. Then she was on her way. But even as she left, she had a funny feeling about the day's events. First Dayne's phone call and then her father's reaction.

Maybe Dayne had taken to calling this week with messages from Luke. But the idea seemed sort of strange. After all, Dayne was the celebrity, the person who was supposed to be too busy to make a phone call. Luke was there to run errands for Dayne, not the other way around.

Ashley laughed and forgot about the strange call until later when she made a quick stop at the art gallery where she sold her work. She had Devin in his stroller, and it felt good to be out with him. She hadn't been by the gallery since he was born, and it was time to take stock, see how many pieces had sold and how many new paintings the store owner had room for.

"I'm glad you came by." The owner was an earthy sort, a woman who dressed in layered gauzy skirts and heavy brown sandals. She always had a pair of bifocals balanced on the end of her nose.

"Looks like the pieces I had out front are gone." Ashley felt the familiar rush. The fact that she was pulling in a decent income as an artist was still overwhelming. And every time she brought in a batch of paintings they were gone in a month.

The woman raised her finger in the air. "That's what I wanted to talk to you about." She made a puzzled face. "Some guy came in and bought all three —" she snapped her fingers — "just like that. Didn't even blink at the price."

"Maybe we're not charging enough." She smiled, teasing the woman. There were new candles on display near the register, and Ashley picked one up. The smell was a rich mix of pine and musk. When the store owner didn't laugh, Ashley looked at her. "I'm just kidding."

"No, it wasn't the price, nothing like that." The gallery owner's look lacked any humor whatsoever. "It was something about your paintings. He seemed taken by them. Had them shipped back to some post office box in Los Angeles, California."

Devin stirred in his stroller, and Ashley set the candle down. "Los Angeles?"

"Yes, and here's the strangest thing." She adjusted her bifocals. "I could've sworn the guy was that actor fellow Dayne Matthews. He told me he was in town visiting his kid brother, a student at the university." The woman shook her finger. "But I know a face when I've seen it before, and his belonged to a Hollywood movie star if ever I've seen one."

Ashley was glad she wasn't holding the candle. Otherwise she would've dropped it. "Dayne Matthews?" She moved close to the counter. "Well, how did he pay? Did you see his name?"

"It wasn't Dayne Matthews." She made a suspicious face. "Something similar, though. If you ask me, it was him. I'm convinced."

The conversation shifted. Ashley and the woman talked about what sort of paintings had done the best over the past year. Ashley agreed to bring in another two featuring the Baxter house, one of the old people from Sunset Hills Adult Care Home, and two with a little blond boy as the main subject.

Sometimes she enjoyed painting the same type of scene more than once. It gave her a chance to find ways to make each one unique, even if the subject was similar. But as she pushed Devin's stroller back to her van, she wasn't thinking about which paintings she might bring to the shop in the next few days.

She was thinking about the guy who had walked in and bought everything she had for sale. Could it have been Dayne? And if so, why would he want her paintings? Maybe he'd bought them as a gift for Katy, or because Katy had suggested them. Or maybe the guy only looked like Dayne, and he really was visiting his kid brother at the university.

She mentioned something about it to Landon that night, but he only smiled at her. "Maybe your dad's been giving Dayne advice about decorating his house."

The idea was ludicrous, and Ashley realized Landon was only teasing her. She gave him a playful shove on the arm.

"Come on, Ash. I don't want to talk about Dayne Matthews." He pulled her close and kissed her. "Tell me about my little boys and all I missed while I was waiting for the fire bell to go off."

And just like that, the whole strange day — the call on her father's cell phone, the purchase of her paintings, and every odd mention of Dayne Matthews — was forgotten. Her father was right. The actor put his pants on the same as anyone else, and with the discussions among her siblings about their older brother, she hardly had time to waste thinking about a movie star.

Even one as nice as Dayne Matthews.

Chapter Sixteen

Friday morning Dayne arrived at the courthouse an hour before Katy. From everything Joe had told him, the press conference seemed to have worked. Joe staged it outside on the front steps at nine that morning, just as the media was arriving for what looked like the final day of testimony.

"Katy Hart hasn't left her hotel room since late Tuesday," Joe told them. "I must reiterate that she is not a celebrity. She deserves her space and privacy."

Now as he and Joe Morris sat in the small waiting area adjacent to the courtroom, Joe had to chuckle at the plan. "Brilliant, Matthews." He kicked one leg over the other knee. "Nothing those creeps don't deserve."

Of course, the paparazzi, the people who had hunted them down on the beach and pounded on the door, wouldn't have attended the press conference. But the respectable members of the media — the major networks and newspapers — had all been there. They would report the story, and it would create a reality that would later make the tabloid stories look like nothing more than trashy lies.

Which Dayne was pretty sure they would be. The tabloids would guess that whatever was happening between Katy and him, their relationship was apparently hot and steamy and forbidden. He prayed hourly that whatever they churned out for Monday's editions, the lies wouldn't damage Katy's reputation, at least not for long.

Joe was telling him what to expect this afternoon. "Testimony should wrap up by eleven, and we'd like you and Katy both in the courtroom for closing arguments, all of which should come before lunch." As usual, Joe had an open file in his hands. He was a copious note taker, part of why he was so successful no doubt. "The jury'll take one look at the two of you, and all the boring medical testimony will be forgotten. They'll be right back where you had them Tuesday afternoon, horrified by the details of the attack."

"You think they'll deliver a verdict today?"

"Yes." Joe gave a firm nod. "Tara thinks it'll be an easy decision."

Dayne understood the importance of their

presence in the courtroom, but he had so much to talk to Katy about, so many pieces of their future to work through. He'd meant what he told her yesterday. If she ran he would follow her. He didn't want her to leave, didn't want her running back to Bloomington until he'd told her how he felt. That he loved her and that he was willing to make whatever changes were necessary to be with her.

Instead, the day figured to be another frenzy of drama and media attention. Katy had called him from her hotel room early this morning. Since the case was expected to end today, she'd gotten permission from Tara to book her flight home by Saturday. Katy had sounded distant, anxious to get home.

Great, he wanted to tell her. Where did that leave them? He had felt this way before, trapped by his fame. Every time he longed to meet with the Baxter family. But never mind the trap. Somehow after they were finished at court today, he and Katy would have a last night together. And if the paparazzi got in the way, this time he would call the police.

Whatever it took to find some alone time with her.

She slipped into the private sitting area

adjacent to the courtroom a few minutes before the proceedings. The look they shared told him everything she was feeling. Their time at the beach still shone in her eyes, but she was anxious about what lay ahead, probably terrified about how the paparazzi would play up the fact that she'd stayed all night at the beach house. He wanted to pull her aside and hug her, soothe away her fears.

Instead he only stood and gave her a quick hug. "Joe says the press conference went perfectly."

"Yes." Joe stood and nodded at Katy. "They were happy to have a new angle." An easy laugh slipped from his lips. "The respectable media sees themselves as superior to the paparazzi. They all looked appalled at the idea of you sitting in a hotel room, afraid to leave because of the aggressive tabloid reporters."

Dayne could see by Katy's expression that she wasn't sure. "I don't like lying."

"Look at it this way." Joe sat back down. "You're telling the first lie — an innocent lie — to make their nastier lies look less believable."

The notion was Hollywood logic, for sure. Dayne was about to ask Katy if she had trouble getting inside the courthouse, but

Tara appeared at the door. "Okay, let's go. We begin in five minutes."

As Dayne suspected, the rest of the morning was a blur. In her closing, Tara presented the details of the attack, the way it was plotted and premeditated, the notes Margie Madden had sent to the police warning of her impending attack. The way she had lain in wait for Dayne on more than one occasion.

The gray-haired defense attorney took an entirely different approach. He avoided trying to explain away the details of the attack. Instead he launched into a dissertation on mental illness. "A person with Margie Madden's sick mind could not possibly be capable of premeditating a murder." He gave the jury a sad smile. "She can't even be sure who she is, ladies and gentlemen."

Tara had the final word. She came back strong with a point that Dayne felt was often missed by defense attorneys and prosecutors alike. "Any person capable of killing someone is a person with a sick mind." She looked at Margie. The woman was very subdued, but she was watching the proceedings like everyone else.

"I am not here to convince you that the defendant, Margie Madden, is of sound mind, people." Tara's tone was adamant, self-assured. Every person in the courtroom had to see how convinced she was about this case. She stopped and looked at the face of each juror. "I'm here to convince you that she is a danger to society, that she made a plan to kill, prepared for that plan, and did everything in her power to carry it out. If you agree that the defendant intended to kill Katy Hart and Dayne Matthews, you must — you absolutely must — return a guilty verdict to this court."

The judge gave the jury their instructions for deliberation, and the court was adjourned.

Dayne gave each of the jurors a serious smile as they filed out, nodding his thanks at them for serving. When they were gone, Tara hurried them into the waiting area. A caterer had brought lunch, but Dayne wasn't hungry.

He sat next to Katy and kept his voice low. "If the verdict comes in, Joe wants us to meet with the press later."

Alarm flashed in her eyes. "In person?"
"Yes."

Joe took the seat opposite them. "Katy, it's important. You'll stand on either side of me, and we'll answer as many questions as we can. It'll give the public a professional picture of you. Me between the two of you.

The image you'll want them to remember if the tabloids print a bunch of dirt next week."

"Oh." Katy poked at her club sandwich. "Thanks. That makes sense."

"It's part of the plan." Dayne sighed. "So you can get out of Hollywood in one piece."

She nodded. "I'll do it. Definitely."

Joe was saying something about the closing arguments when Luke pulled away from the team of prosecuting attorneys and sat next to Joe.

Under the table Katy reached over and squeezed Dayne's knee.

He understood. This was the first time they'd been together with Luke since Dayne had told her the truth. The young man sitting across from them was Dayne's brother.

Luke took a drink from a can of pop. "I heard things got a little out of control at the beach?"

"They did." Dayne looked into his brother's eyes. How much they'd missed by being raised in different worlds. Luke was a guy Dayne would've liked to have known better. They might've played pickup basketball games in the summer or gone skiing in the winter. They were more than a decade apart in years, but there was a sameness about them that went beyond their physical resemblance.

Katy fell quiet, eating her lunch and watching the two of them.

Time passed slowly, with Joe and Luke leaving after lunch and holding a meeting in preparation for the press conference at the end of the day.

Dayne studied Katy, and when he was sure Tara and her team were preoccupied, he turned to face her. "You're running."

"I'm not." Her answer was quick. "I just want it to be over, the trial, all of it."

"The Monday morning tabloids too."

"Yes." She crossed her arms, and for the first time today her tone softened. "I wish we were back on the beach."

He smiled. "Me too." An idea hit him. "Hey, let's have dinner at Pepperdine to-night."

She laughed. "We and our hundred clos-est paparazzi friends?"

"No, really." He sat back. "After the press conference, Joe will take you back to your hotel. You'll pack up, and around dinner-time you can take a cab to Pepperdine. I'll find a way there; don't worry. I'm better than you at losing the photographers."

"You're serious?"

"Yes." He paused at a sound by the door. "We can talk about it later."

A clerk stepped into the room and looked at Tara. "The judge would like to see you."

Tara pulled herself away from her team. "Has the jury reached a verdict?"

"It has."

The room went silent. A verdict didn't necessarily mean a victory. Tara left and came back a few minutes later. "We have half an hour."

In that time, Joe and Luke returned and prepped Dayne and Katy on the upcoming press conference. When they found their seats in the courtroom thirty minutes later, the place was packed with reporters and cameramen.

To keep up appearances, Dayne didn't sit by Katy. But he wanted to. He was suddenly more nervous than he'd been throughout the entire proceedings. Margie Madden deserved prison time. If she was released because of her mental illness, then any crazy fan would think it was okay to stalk a celebrity, to make death threats and wield knives — all in the name of insanity.

The jury filed back into the room, and the foreman stood up.

Judge Nguyen peered at the man from his bench. "Has the jury reached a decision?"

"We have, Your Honor."

"Very well." The judge held out his hand.

The foreman gave a slip of paper to the clerk, who then passed the note to the bench.

Judge Nguyen opened it and read it, his expression blank.

Dayne held his breath. *Please, God . . . let there be justice.*

The judge handed the paper back to the clerk, who delivered it once more to the jury foreman.

"Read the verdict for the court, please." Judge Nguyen sat back and waited.

"We, the jury, find the defendant, Margie Madden, guilty as charged in both counts."

They'd done it! They'd won! The judge was asking each juror if the verdict reflected his or her say in the matter, but Dayne was on his feet, hugging Joe Morris and then Luke, and finally he smiled at Katy. Her face was filled with relief, and he could read her thoughts. It was almost over. The trial, the public scrutiny, the hounding press — a few more hours and she could have her life back. At least for now.

"Order, please." The judge's admonition was only halfhearted. He finished questioning the jurors; then he issued a sentencing date. "Until that time, the defendant is to be remanded to the city jail." He rapped his gavel. "Court dismissed." He stood and left the room through a door behind the bench.

The celebration in Dayne's row continued. Joe had told them that this moment — if it came — was one the press needed to capture. It would provide them with a front-page picture and keep the focus on the trial and not the relationship between Katy and Dayne. Dayne hugged Tara Lawson next, lingering near her and shaking her hand in full view of the cameras. Luke did the same with Katy — again making the photo opportunity one they wanted to portray.

Joe addressed the media, explaining that Katy Hart and Dayne Matthews, along with the prosecutor, Tara Lawson, would be available directly outside the courthouse in a few minutes.

The crowd seemed to swell, and Dayne nodded to Luke. "Take care of Katy, okay?"

"Got it." Luke stayed by her side as the group made their way out of the courtroom.

Outside on the steps of the courthouse, the positioning was as deliberate as everything else Joe had put together that week. They stood in a line, Joe, then Dayne, followed by Tara and Katy and Luke.

For an hour Joe fielded questions for the group, acting as an impromptu guest host of some twisted reality show. They asked Dayne to comment on the boldness of fans in seeking access to celebrities.

"It's not only the eccentric fans." Dayne's tone was serious, and he was dressed to fit the part — less the movie star than the successful businessman. "It's the paparazzi. When people are hounded, dangerous situations arise." He spoke like a politician, making eye contact with the press. "I hope the guilty verdict today will make the fanatical fans and the paparazzi take note. A person's fame does not make them fair game for harassment or personal attacks."

The attention turned to Katy. "Was the attack by Margie Madden the reason you turned down the part in *Dream On?*"

Katy stepped up to the sea of microphones. "There were many factors that went into my decision." She smiled, hiding her nervousness. "But, yes. I prefer my private life."

Tara answered the next question, but Dayne was stuck on Katy's words. For some reason, they lodged in his heart like a painful splinter. *"I prefer my private life . . . private life . . ."*

He wasn't sure why her statement hurt. He already knew she felt that way, but still . . . hearing it now at a press conference was like confirmation that she was never — not ever — going to compromise where his fame was concerned. He would have to find a way to love her on her terms, on her turf, or he wouldn't have the chance to love her at all.

When the press conference ended, they hurried off in different directions. Joe took Dayne home, and Luke took Katy back to her hotel.

Three hours later Dayne drove into the parking lot at Pepperdine University and looked around. Three cameramen had followed him, but he'd lost them after driving through Starbucks. He complimented himself as he parked behind some bushes and stepped out of his Escalade with a blanket, two coffees, and a bag of food. Fancy driving and patience. See, it was possible. Living life around the paparazzi. Besides, they could see that Katy wasn't with him, and that made them less motivated, since capturing them together was the hot story of the hour.

Dayne made his way down a path to a plateau that was hidden from the parking lot. He'd been in touch with Katy by cell, and after a few minutes he heard the sound of a car in the parking lot above him. A door opened and shut, and the car drove off.

"Dayne . . ." Her voice was a frightened whisper.

He stood and held up his hand. "Down here."

She took light running steps toward him. "Ugh." She dropped beside him on the blanket. "I can't believe we did it."

A thrill ran through him at the sight of her. She filled his heart like no one ever had. He couldn't believe in just a little while he was going to have to say good-bye.

Nervous laughter danced in her eyes. "I thought I'd find you down here surrounded by cameras."

"No." He chuckled. "I told you, it isn't usually this bad. They have a job to do; that's all." He handed her a cup of coffee and pulled the bag of food closer. He'd brought fruit and cheese and sourdough bread from home. No time to stop at a store and no need rousing the attention of the tabloids that he was planning a picnic.

"Did I hear you right?" She smiled at him. "Telling me the paparazzi aren't that bad when last night they were pounding at the door?"

He shrugged. "I'm just saying you get used to it." He was testing her without coming out and saying so. If she cared for him the way he cared for her, shouldn't she be willing to take a little extra attention? It was something he hadn't considered all week, not until today's press conference. But wasn't that maybe the answer to their problems? That she be willing to give up some of her privacy?

Katy thanked him for the drink, but she set it aside. She seemed to miss the whole talk about paparazzi and getting used to the cameras. The sun was heading toward the shore, and Katy gazed at the ocean. "I talked to Luke." She leaned back on her elbows and stretched out her legs. "I thanked him and told him good-bye."

"He's a nice guy."

"He's more than that." She looked at him. "Dayne, I've been thinking. You have to talk to the Baxters. Hiding from your brother and sisters . . . what does that accomplish?"

"Their privacy." His words were quick and maybe a little too harsh. "The same privacy that matters so much to you."

"But you said yourself this isn't so bad." She turned onto her side and faced him. A smile played on her lips. "If you can convince yourself of that after this week . . ."

"I'm trying." He stretched out on his side a few feet from her and let himself get lost in her eyes. The tensions from the week were getting to him, and he made a conscious effort to let them go. She couldn't know what he was thinking unless he spelled it out. "I have an idea, Katy."

"What?" She reached out and brushed her knuckle against his chin, his cheek. "Run away with you to Mars where no one can bother us?"

He ran his fingers along her bare arm. "No." The moment was tender and light. Trees shaded the grassy area where the blanket was spread out, and an occasional seagull cried in the distance. "Move here. So we can be together and I can finish my contract." He didn't blink, didn't do anything to break the connection he felt with her. "Then who knows . . . in a few years maybe we'll both move to Bloomington."

A fresh hurt dimmed her smile. "Move here? You mean move in with you?" She sat up. "Are you serious?"

"Not move in with me." He pushed himself up and took her hand. Why couldn't anything ever be easy with her? "Come on, Katy. You have to know me better than that."

"Okay, then what? Move here and take an apartment, leave everything I love in Bloomington so we can run around in the shadows together?" Her words were slow, thoughtful, not the least bit sarcastic. She looked at the grass and ran her hand over the tips of the blades. "You'll be busy making movies." Her smile was sadder than before. "It wouldn't work, Dayne."

She was right, and he hated the fact. Hated that he couldn't change his life enough to make it appealing to her and hated the contract that would keep him bound to Los Angeles for several more years.

He groaned and stretched out on his side again. "So you're going to run anyway?"

"I'm not running." She eased back down and onto her side again. "I'm going home." She put her hand on his shoulder. "Where I belong." She hesitated. "Maybe where you belong too." Her voice was gentler than the breeze in the branches above them. "Have you ever thought of that?"

"What . . . I move there and take an apartment?" His teasing felt good, much better than the heaviness from a few moments earlier.

"Yes . . . brat." She gave him a light push. "You buy the whole building if you want. At least you'd have a place to come home to."

"Between films."

"Yes, between films."

"With all of Bloomington watching?"

"Yes." She gave him another shove. "Even the Baxters." She searched his eyes. Despite the easy atmosphere between them, the ultimatum was clear. He would find a way into her world or they wouldn't find a way at all.

He'd thought about the idea, but when would he ever be there? At least for the next few years he needed to be close to the studio, right? Close to the premieres and preproduction publicity and red carpets. Close to his agent and casting directors and costars. He thought about that reality. The list sounded terribly shallow and meaningless compared with Katy Hart.

A sigh filtered through his teeth. "I don't know." He rolled onto his back and looked at her. "You're all I want, Katy." He raised his arm and crooked it over his brow. "It shouldn't be this hard."

She rolled onto her back too and stared up. "I'm serious about wishing you'd move to Bloomington." She glanced at him. "But I'd never ask you to leave your life here for me. Not really."

He inched closer to her. "I'd leave it tomorrow if it made sense." He worked his fingers through her blonde hair, and suddenly he knew he couldn't hold back another moment. She was leaving and this was good-bye. He turned over and touched his lips to hers. His voice was thick with desire when he pulled back. "Katy . . . how can I let you go?"

She angled herself toward him, and this time the kiss came from her. "I'll never forget this . . . no matter what happens after today."

He was about to tell her not to talk that way, that even if they couldn't think of a single sensible scenario, somehow they would find their way back together again. But before he could speak, there was the sound of running feet coming up the hill below them. They sat up at the same time, just as two photographers stopped and began shooting them.

With every click, he could feel Katy panicking. But this time he wasn't letting it happen. "Fold up the blanket, Katy." He stood and glared at the cameramen. "Leave us alone!"

"Dayne . . . please . . . let's get out of here!"

He shot her an angry look. "I'll take care of this." He clenched his jaw. "I've had enough."

She turned her back to the photographers and did as he asked.

Without thinking about his actions, Dayne put himself between her and the paparazzi. They were fifteen feet away, snapping pictures.

Dayne lunged at them and knocked one

of the cameras to the ground. His blow separated the high-powered lens from the camera's body and cracked the casing. Dayne's hand hurt, but his anger was still rising, taking over everything inside him. How dare they hunt him down this way, every time he and Katy tried to find a moment alone?

The photographer nearest him reached for his broken equipment and snarled at Dayne. "You'll hear from my attorney about this."

"And you'll hear from mine." Dayne raised his fist toward them. "Get out of here."

"Come on." The other one elbowed his partner. "Forget about it." He motioned toward the parking lot above them. "You've got nowhere to run, Matthews. The parking lot is full of cars."

"Leave!" Dayne took another step toward them.

The two men jumped back. The one with the broken camera shouted, "You wanted this life, Matthews, so deal with it."

They gathered their gear and stomped off. The angry one hollered over his shoulder, "We got the shot, anyway."

Dayne turned and saw Katy scrambling toward the walkway. Her face was pale.

"What should we do now?"

"Face them." He was fuming, angrier than he could ever remember being. Would they stop at nothing for a single picture, be willing to interrupt any moment so long as it meant a sale to the tabloids? He marched toward her and took the blanket and the bag of food.

Katy carried both coffees as she trailed behind him, struggling to keep up. "They'll see us, won't they?"

"Yes. Stay behind me." His words were tight, drenched in fury. "They won't get anything worth printing."

They came into the open, and just like the photographers had said, the parking lot held half a dozen cars. Some of the waiting cameramen jumped out and began shooting them. Others pointed their lenses through their open car windows and took their pictures that way.

He had the urge to drop the blanket and food and take out each and every one of them, one level punch at a time. Instead he kept his head low. "Stay behind me."

"I am." He could feel her moving along, shaking from the terror of the moment.

They reached his Escalade near the bushes, and he opened the passenger side first. Once Katy was inside he hesitated, staring at each of the photographers. He could take out three of them at least. *God, give me the strength not to kill them. . . .*

Son, man's anger does not bring about God's righteousness.

The words stopped him in his tracks, cut his fury at the knees, and sent him stumbling toward the driver's seat. The quick answer had to be from God, had to be Him speaking truth to his heart. They were words he'd read in his Bible before Katy arrived in town. At the time he hadn't thought much of them. He wasn't an angry person, so why take note of words about anger?

But now he was so furious he could've leveled a full-blown assault at the paparazzi. If it weren't for God's reminder.

He turned the key in the engine and looked at Katy.

She had slid down in her seat, and with one hand she was shielding her face. "What're we doing?"

"We're going to lose them." His anger was back but not like before. He didn't want to lash out at them; he wanted to be rid of them. Whatever the cost. He slammed his foot on the gas pedal and screeched into a U-turn that spit him onto the main road that led off the campus.

In his mirror, he could see the photographers scrambling for their cars and rushing after him. "Not this time," he mumbled under his breath. "Get your seat belt on."

Katy began fumbling with the belt, but her eyes told him she was scared to death. "Don't go too fast, Dayne. It doesn't matter if . . . if they know where we're going."

"It does." He sped up and barely made the light at the bottom of the hill. Screeching his tires, he took the left turn hard and gunned it. "No one's going to dictate what we do."

"Just take me back to the hotel." She was near tears, her words stiff with fear. "Please, Dayne . . ."

"I'll be careful. Don't worry." Behind him he watched every one of the six paparazzi vehicles run the red light. The last one almost broadsided a passenger van. "They're absolutely crazy."

"I know." Katy covered her face. "Dayne, this is stupid. Just get me back to —"

There was the blast of a horn as a car coming the other direction turned left directly in front of him.

"Katy . . . hold on!" He swerved, and his SUV skidded across the intersection and came to rest inches from a pole.

The driver of the car that had turned left honked again, longer this time.

Adrenaline rushed through Dayne's body as he maneuvered his SUV back into the lane and continued southbound.

"Dear God . . ." Katy had her hand over her mouth. "Any faster and we would've wrapped around the pole."

It was true. Dayne felt his heart start beating again. "Katy . . ." He reached for her hand. What was he thinking? Why had it been so important to lose the paparazzi when to do so would only mean having them continue the chase a few hours later or the next day? "Katy, I'm sorry."

"That car . . . it turned right in front of you." In the fading sunlight, he could see tears in her eyes. "We could've been killed."

In his mirror he could see the photographers still on his tail. Katy was right. If he'd been traveling any faster, he would've collided with the other car, causing horrific damage. In that case, the cameramen would've gotten prize photos. Pictures worth a fortune. Never mind that they would've been the cause of the wreck or that injuries and fatalities might've been involved. Car accidents were newsworthy.

The reality made him sick to his stomach. He let up on the gas and settled back to a normal speed. "I'm taking you back."

Back to the hotel, back to the place where

she could make her getaway and return to a normal life. His world wasn't only crazy and unnerving — it was dangerous. He couldn't subject Katy to that type of danger even if she were willing to move to Hollywood.

The six photographers traveled in a row behind them like some sort of bizarre parade. Dayne didn't care anymore. He reached over and eased his fingers between hers. "This was why you got so upset at the beach that night." His tone was quiet, defeated. The adrenaline still had his heart racing, but the fight was over.

The paparazzi had won.

Katy looked at him, as if she were trying to understand his comment. "At the beach?"

"Yes." He held tight to the wheel and kept his eyes straight ahead. He wasn't taking any more chances, not with Katy in the vehicle. "You told me I scared you. You said, 'Where can it ever go?' "

Her eyes grew wet again. She covered her mouth with her fingers, as if she didn't want to remember her own words. But she couldn't deny them either.

"I went to sleep that night so confused," Dayne continued. "You told me I had Hollywood and my movies and you had Bloomington." Every mile took them closer to good-bye, but he was helpless to do anything but keep driving. Driving and convincing himself that letting Katy go was the kindest thing he could do. "You asked me how it was ever supposed to work." Tears blurred his eyes, and he blinked so he could see. "I thought you were just afraid, that you needed time to adjust to all the attention."

"Dayne . . . I don't want to leave."

He brought her hand to his lips and kissed it. "My world doesn't give you any choice." His chin was quivering, anger and sorrow about to break his heart wide open. "Does it?"

She let her head hang, let the tears fall onto her lap. The sobs worked their way to the surface, and she brought his hand to her cheek. "If there was a way . . ."

But there wasn't. Suddenly he knew this was his chance, maybe the only chance he'd ever have to tell her exactly how he felt. How strong his feelings for her really were.

They turned into the hotel parking lot, and behind them the six paparazzi cars followed. He stopped and framed her face with his hands. Before the cameramen could jump out, before they could capture a single picture, he kissed her and looked straight to her heart. To the most beautiful heart he'd ever known.

He could hear them, slamming their car

doors, running along the pavement. "Katy . . . I love you." He kissed her again quickly. "When you leave, you'll take that part with you."

Her lips parted, her eyes wide, as if she couldn't believe what he'd just said.

"Dayne! Katy! Pose for a picture!"

Two doormen were herding the photographers, keeping them back.

"I'm . . . sorry I never said it before." Fresh tears filled Katy's eyes and slid down her cheeks. "I love you, Dayne." She pressed her fingers to her lips, then to his. "Goodbye." She held her bag up to her face, climbed out of the SUV, and hurried through the revolving door. She turned around just once, long enough for him to see that she was crying harder. She mouthed the word *good-bye.*

Then she was gone.

As he drove away, he had no energy to fight the paparazzi or threaten them, no desire to speed through the streets of LA trying to lose them. They were part of his life. They might as well follow him home. What did it matter now?

Katy was gone and not just that. The dream was gone too. He had wanted to think it could work, that she could blend into his lifestyle and come out the same on the other side. But look what had almost happened. They'd nearly been killed just because they were that frantic to find an hour alone.

In the quiet of his Escalade, he let the tears come. Hot and salty and frustrated, they made their way down his cheeks, stinging his eyes and his lips and making him wonder about his new beliefs. He had asked God to make a way for them, to give them a future. But their one week together had come to a sudden, abysmal end. And the tabloids hadn't even hit the stands yet.

Sure, he could make an occasional trip to Bloomington, show up at Katy's CKT practice, and steal a few hours talking to her in the Flanigans' living room. But times like that weren't the stuff relationships were made of. The love he wanted to share with Katy should've meant dinner dates and long walks, cozy conversations and sitting side by side at church.

He dragged his fist across his cheeks and rolled down the window. The ocean air was his friend, washing away the impossibilities of his life and giving him the sense that somehow, someway he would wake up tomorrow and find a reason to live. He had learned from Bob Asher that God had a plan for his life — plans for a wonderful future centered around faith in Christ. Yes, Dayne Matthews would survive, and he would have a reason to live.

But without Katy, without the feel of her in his arms and the light from her smile, there was something he knew he'd never have again. Something he had held tight to every day this week.

A reason to love.

CHAPTER SEVENTEEN

Like every time she said good-bye to Dayne Matthews, Katy couldn't draw a breath without aching because of how much she missed him. She forced herself to get in the shuttle Saturday morning to the airport, and somehow she survived the morning. But just barely.

Paparazzi followed her to the airport, then gave up. If she was going home to Bloomington, there would be no clandestine photographs of her and Dayne to capture. No reason to chase her.

She called him just once — to tell him she'd made it to her gate at the airport.

"Let me know when you reach Indiana." His tone was urgent, as if he wanted more than anything to keep the connection between them.

Her sigh told him what her words could not. "Sure, Dayne." She wanted to believe it was true, even as she felt her heart breaking. "We'll talk later."

But by Monday morning, they still hadn't talked. Rain fell across Bloomington, and Katy wore a hooded coat and her hair pulled back for her trip to the local market.

Her pulse raced as she found an empty checkout stand and stood, horrified. The damage was everything she had feared it would be. Six tabloids shouted the news, each in different ways. For the most part the headlines were the same — big, bold print stating "Dayne Matthews' Mystery Woman Revealed!" The cover of one had the picture of Dayne and her on Malibu Beach. Her face was twisted into a look of shock and fear, and her hand was up, as if trying to stop the picture from happening.

As she looked at it, Dayne's words came back to her: *Put your hand down.* She had wondered how that would help, but now the answer was obvious. By holding her hand up, she looked guiltier than Margie Madden. Guilty and caught — just the way the tabloids preferred their subjects.

The cover of the next tabloid had the shot of Dayne and her kissing, knee-deep in the surf. Katy felt her heart sink as she looked at it. How could she face the CKT families when she was entangled in what must've looked like a national scandal? Each of the magazines had smaller, inset pictures showing Katy and Dayne stretched out opposite each other on the Pepperdine hillside or darting out of the hotel.

The worst one was last in the line, and the photo made Katy feel faint. It showed the two of them running into the beach house that belonged to the friend of Joe Morris. The caption beside it read "The lovers stayed at this romantic getaway."

She brought her fingers to her cheeks and tried to ward off the heat. By reading just the covers of the tabloids, most of America would have to think that Dayne and his mystery woman were definitely sleeping together, caught up in a secret relationship that had obviously been going on since the attack by Margie Madden.

In a rush, Katy grabbed a copy of each magazine and took them to a checkout manned by an older man.

He rang up the sale, bagged the items, and took her money. She was about to thank him and take her bag when he gave her a kind smile. "It'll pass, Ms. Hart. Don't let it get you down."

She thanked him and hurried to the car, her mind swirling with what had just happened. If a sixty-year-old cashier could recognize her from the tabloid covers, then all of Bloomington would know. A person didn't have to buy the magazines or even open them to know her predicament. Everyone who came through the grocery store checkout would see her picture on the covers.

Katy drove home without registering a single street sign. Jenny Flanigan was working at Bailey's school, and at this hour, Jim would be in the back room, homeschooling the boys. Katy was glad. She wasn't ready to face either of them. She raced up the stairs to her apartment and spread the magazines over her small kitchen table. She spent the next two hours reading every word, staring at every photo.

Two of the tabloids had photos of Dayne and Kelly Parker, with captions that suggested Dayne was probably seeing Katy the entire time he was dating Kelly. One of them showed an angry picture of the female star, with a small boxed story that claimed Kelly was furious. "Fighting mad," a source said.

Katy noticed a pattern. Every time substantiation was needed for a story, the tabloids simply claimed "a source" had said the damaging comments. Sources in all six magazines were quoted saying that Dayne had fallen for Katy because of her small-town appeal, while sidebar stories suggested she was nothing more than a lucky fan.

None of the magazines went into great detail about the trial, except for the sensational moments, the times when Margie Madden had lashed out at Katy or Dayne. It wasn't until she reached the last story that she read the line that made her heart skip a beat. The title above the small article read "Score One for the Hypocrites."

Beneath that it said:

Katy Hart, who works with a Christian Kids Theater group in Bloomington, Indiana, isn't proving herself to be so Christian after all. Sources say she spent the night with Dayne at a borrowed beach house, and activities inside the house were so steamy, the couple pulled the shades on every window.

Katy let her head hang. It was the single detail they'd worked so hard to keep from the public, and now it was out in the open.

Dayne phoned an hour later, and she took the call.

"Katy . . . are you okay?"

"They're wretched, Dayne." She carried herself to her bed and stretched out, her head on her pillow. "How can I leave my apartment?"

"You can leave because you know the truth." He sounded strong, sure.

His voice righted her world. Even just a little. She held tight to the phone, wishing it were him beside her instead. She missed him so much it hurt. "How are you?"

"Today? I can't tell what feels worse, seeing your name and face splashed over the tabloids or knowing that the moments they caught were the last . . . the last we'll have."

She wanted to weep for a month or a year. "Why does it have to be this way?" Her question was rhetorical, and they both knew it. But it was how they were feeling. "I miss you so much."

"I miss you too. If there was a way to protect you from all this . . . I'd be there this afternoon." His voice was heavy. "I'm no good for you, Katy. The magazines can tell you that much."

The phone call ended with neither of them any closer to finding an answer, except for the obvious one — the fact that there truly was no answer. The tabloids could capture a kiss or a private moment, but they had done nothing to capture the heart of the man she cared for so much. For all their haunting and chasing and lurking, their stories only skimmed the surface.

That afternoon, Katy called Bethany Allen, Rhonda, and Nancy and Al Helmes for an emergency meeting. There was no point running from the obvious. She brought the magazines with her and spread them out in front of her friends and coworkers.

"You need to hear my side of the story." She looked at each of them.

But before she could launch into her explanation, Al Helmes held up his hand. "I, for one, don't need to hear your story, Katy. You and Dayne Matthews are friends, and you're interested in each other. That's fine." He scowled at the tabloids. "But that bunch of lies wouldn't make me doubt you for a minute."

"Of course not." Bethany took out a pad of paper and a pen. "But let's hear Katy's side of the story, anyway. In case we're approached by any of the CKT parents."

Rhonda was quiet. Her eyes told Katy that she was agonizing over the publicity and that she would stand by Katy regardless of public opinion.

Katy gripped the edge of the table. *Please, God, give me the words.*

No comforting whisper sounded in her heart, and Katy wasn't surprised. So much of what lay spread on the magazine covers was her own fault. If she would've left things with Dayne on a professional level, even on a friendship level, there would've been no pictures to take, no story to guess at.

She took a quick breath. "I'll be honest with you." She looked at Al. "You're right. Dayne and I have feelings for each other."

A dreamy look mixed with the other emotions in Rhonda's eyes. Dreamy and sympathetic at the same time, and Katy understood. The secret they'd kept for so long was finally out.

Katy let her gaze fall to the magazines. "We met a while ago, after he first came to Bloomington. He was researching his film *Dream On,* and he asked me to read for the lead role."

"Katy . . . ," Bethany gasped. "You never said a word."

"Rhonda knew." She looked at her friend, and they shared a pair of weak smiles. "The audition went well, and Dayne offered me the part. We were . . . we were talking about that when the fan attacked us."

"Margie Madden." Nancy Helmes' tone was pure empathy. "You poor dear."

"It was scary." Katy ran her fingers along the inside of her arm, the place where she'd been cut by the woman. "She wanted to kill me. I'm convinced."

All of them had followed the story in the newspaper, so there weren't many questions.

Al reached over and patted Katy's hand. "She got the conviction she deserved."

"She did." Katy nodded. "Anyway, after that . . . I turned down the part. I told Dayne our lives were too different, and I belonged in Bloomington. And there was the issue of faith. Dayne was angry at God for, well, for a lot of reasons. There was no way I could let myself fall for him."

"He called her a few times, but she didn't take his calls." Rhonda's voice was soft, filled with the memory of that time. She gave Katy a sad smile. "He didn't want to give up."

"No, but we didn't have a choice." Katy looked at Bethany. "I love my job here. I felt God calling me to stay and not to be distracted by anyone, even Dayne Matthews. That's when he moved in with Kelly Parker, the actress who took the part."

"Wow." Bethany sat back in her chair, amazed. "I had no idea."

Nancy nudged one of the tabloids. "They say you were involved with him when he came here for the location filming."

"I wasn't." She ran her fingers through her hair. "He had moved on to Kelly. We talked only a few times while he was here."

"He didn't waste much time." Disgust colored Al's tone. "That must've been hard for you, Katy."

"It was." She winced, feeling the ache way down to her soul. "It still is." She sorted through her thoughts. "Things didn't work out with Kelly, and then twice over the next few months he came to Bloomington, surprised me, and took me on walks around Lake Monroe."

"Dayne Matthews?" Bethany's lips parted. "He was here in Bloomington, secretly taking walks with you?" She looked at Rhonda. "I can't believe this."

As she heard herself tell the story, Katy could hardly believe it either. She told them how the feelings between her and Dayne were there every time they were together and how Dayne had given his life to Jesus a few months ago. "But there never seems to be a way to bridge our two worlds."

"So by the time you went to LA for the trial, the two of you had some talking to do." Al made it sound very normal, very sensible. As if Dayne were any other guy she might've been attracted to. "That explains the pictures."

"Yes, well . . ." Katy felt her cheeks getting hot once more. "We should never have kissed, not when we don't have a plan for tomorrow. But even so —" her voice grew stronger — "nothing more than that happened between us. Yes, I stayed the night with him at that beach house but only because we had photographers banging on the door, desperate to take our pictures. We decided to outlast them, but we fell asleep."

She held up her hands. "That's it. Just the two of us asleep on the couch." She pursed her lips. "On our last day we were chased by photographers, and Dayne lost control of his SUV. We could've been killed. And that's when we both realized our situation." She lifted one shoulder. "We can't be together. It won't work for either of us. We said good-bye that night, and truly I don't know if we'll ever see each other again."

Rhonda had tears in her eyes. She looked down, clearly heartbroken over the situation.

"I'm sorry, Katy." Bethany stood and gave Katy a hug around her shoulders. "This must be very hard."

"Yes." She sniffed. With all the tears she'd cried in the past few days, she had none left now. Not because she wasn't sad but because she wasn't finished. She had more to say, more that had caused her to call this meeting. "It was important for me that you know the truth, that Dayne and I haven't done more than kiss." She swallowed. "Even so, what I did this past week wasn't fair to any of you. The Bible says to avoid even a hint of immorality." She closed her eyes for a moment. "Because of that, I'm sorry."

"Katy . . . this isn't necessary." Nancy was quick to speak. "You had no idea what you were getting into in LA."

"Still —" her eyes met Bethany's — "I would understand if you wanted me to step down. If the things people are saying about me are too much for all of you, too much for the reputation of CKT."

Bethany was still standing beside her. She crouched down and put her hand on Katy's shoulder. "They can call you a hypocrite, but we know the truth. You wouldn't be here if your faith wasn't everything to you."

She had expected raised eyebrows and even a scolding. If Bethany would've asked her to take time off, she would've understood that too. No matter what the truth, the rumors would take weeks to settle down. Months, maybe. But this . . . open arms and perfect love, never for a minute had Katy hoped for this response even though it made sense. Of course they would stand by her; they were friends, after all.

A lump settled in her throat, and she put

her arms around Bethany. "I . . . don't know how to face everyone. The Picks and Johnsons, the Reeds, the Shaffers." She felt fear well up inside her. "What will they think of me?"

As she talked, Nancy and Al stood and moved behind her.

Rhonda reached across the table and took her hand. "No one's deserting you, Katy. We know who you are."

"The tabloids don't have any idea what they're talking about." Al's voice was thick, as if even he was choked up watching everyone come to Katy's rescue.

Katy couldn't say another word, couldn't refuse the chance they were giving her. If they were willing to stand by her, then somehow God would pull her through. She'd come out on the other side stronger for every lie told about her. Besides, there was no denying her role in what had happened. She shouldn't have trusted herself in public with Dayne, shouldn't have kissed him at all, not when from the beginning she could see no future for the two of them. And another thing. She shouldn't have allowed lies to be told on her behalf. Lies never amounted to anything good.

Her time with Dayne had been only a dream, a fantasy. He would never be a normal guy. There was no way to undo what fame and celebrity had done to him, no way for him to wake up tomorrow morning and be anyone other than the famous movie star he was.

She and Jenny and Jim had talked about all of it the night she returned from Los Angeles. She'd told them she was wrong, and she'd asked them to forgive her for marring their reputation in any way. Their reaction had been much the same as the one here today. They hurt for her, but they were hardly willing to point a finger at her.

"I think you should go home and get some rest." Bethany stood and gave Katy's shoulder one last tender squeeze. "We have a lot of another sort of drama ahead in the next few weeks."

Narnia. Katy could hardly wait for the distraction. She lifted her head and looked at each of them. "Thank you." She bit her lip to keep from crying out loud. "I couldn't ask for better friends."

The meeting ended with Al praying for her, praying that people who knew her would see the tabloid lies for what they were, and that Katy would feel the love and support of the Flanigans and her CKT family.

"And lastly, Lord, we pray for Dayne and

Katy, these two young people who can't act on their feelings, feelings that may actually be from You." He paused. "Give Dayne wisdom, help the two of them to walk in honesty, and help them keep their faith in You."

Before she left, Bethany assured Katy that she would field any concerns from the CKT families. "I really don't think you have anything to worry about." She gave Katy another quick hug. "But whatever trouble is stirred up, I'll deal with it."

The concerns came, but only one or two each day. For the most part, Katy didn't know more than the fact that Bethany had handled a few phone calls on her behalf. But at Friday's rehearsal, a group of the teenage girls was whispering in a corner, and they stopped when Katy walked over.

"Girls —" Katy kept her tone even — "if you have something to say to me, please . . . just say it."

A brunette stepped forward. She was known for her flirtatious behavior and for being on the fence when it came to faith. Her eyes sparkled. "What's it like kissing Dayne Matthews?" She glanced back at her friends. "Since the rest of us can only dream about it."

They wanted Katy to giggle, and if she

and Dayne had figured out a way to make things work, she might have. But there was nothing funny about what had happened, not when their actions had clearly been a mistake from the beginning. "Dayne's a nice guy." She raised her brow, her expression serious. "Let's leave it at that."

Later that day one of the new mothers approached her and took her aside. "Will this —" she pulled one of the tabloids from her purse — "be a regular thing for you, Ms. Hart?" Her expression was smug, and she kept her voice low. "Because if it is, I'd just like to suggest that maybe you consider another line of work. Where our children wouldn't have to see their . . . Christian drama teacher on the front page of every magazine in the supermarket."

"Yes, ma'am." Katy felt the blood drain from her face. Her arms and legs were suddenly weak. "I'm . . . I'm sorry you had to see that."

"Quite right." She snapped the magazine back into her purse and tossed her head. "Please mind yourself from now on."

Bethany must've seen the confrontation. She was at Katy's side in a hurry. "Mrs. Wilson, did you have a question I could handle?"

"I've handled it." She leveled her look at

Katy. Then she huffed off after her two young daughters.

Katy fell against the wood-paneled wall. "Don't feel sorry for me. It's my fault. I deserve —"

"No, Katy." This time Bethany was angry. "That woman doesn't know the first thing about you." She tightened her lips and stared after the woman. "People like that give Christianity a bad name." Her expression softened. "Far more than anything you've done."

Even so, Dayne had been right that once the tabloids landed on a topic, it wouldn't die out after a week. The tabloids fed off each other. If one found a juicy tidbit or an irresistible detail, it would be in every magazine the following week. And with the revelation in one magazine that she worked with a Christian Kids Theater, Katy fully expected more stories about her.

And there were.

The next Monday, pictures of Katy and Dayne ran on the covers again, and this time each of them was accompanied by a few lines that called Katy a hypocrite. "Mystery Woman Defies Christian Beliefs for Dayne" one cover read.

He called her that afternoon, but she only stared at her phone and watched his name flash in the caller ID window. *Dayne,* she wanted to say, *I'm sorry. I can't do it.* And she couldn't. To answer the phone would be to expose her heart to the same wild roller coaster of emotions. Joy at hearing his voice and then almost at the same time a sorrow that was suffocating.

She loved him — truly she did. But in some ways it was like being in love with a fantasy, an image. Not in the way Dayne's fans were in love with him. They were infatuated with the on-screen image, the handsome playboy, or whatever they'd made him out to be in their minds. Girls like the ones at CKT practice who could giggle and imagine and dream about what a day at the beach with Dayne Matthews might be like.

Katy was in love with a different sort of fantasy. The Dayne Matthews no one but her knew. She didn't dream about the movie star; she dreamed about the man. But there was no separating the two, so the real Dayne was as much make-believe for her as the movie star was for girls across America.

The phone stopped ringing, and she pressed it to her heart. *God . . . why can't there be a way?*

She reminded herself of the "strength" verses in the Bible. "Nothing is impossible with God" and "I can do everything through him who gives me strength." But sometimes it wasn't a matter of willing a thing to happen or believing Jesus would accomplish it. Sometimes it was a matter of accepting His will and letting a closed door be closed, without trying every possible way to pry it open.

And so Katy limped through the next week, laying low mostly and wondering at church and at the library and at the gym whether everyone really was staring at her or whether that was only her imagination.

On Saturday they moved the *Narnia* sets into the Bloomington theater, and Monday began a full week of nightly dress rehearsals. Somehow she kept breathing, kept waking up and putting one foot in front of the other, and in a blur of days it was suddenly Friday, opening night for *Narnia.*

At least Katy could see God in every scene of rehearsals that week, because otherwise she would've felt very far from Him, missing the stolen moments she'd shared with Dayne and wondering why she had been exiled to a life without love. But because of the kids, because of the work they'd done on the C. S. Lewis classic, Katy survived, and as she drove to the theater that night, she stared at the deep blue Bloomington sky and thanked God for His plans.

Even if she couldn't for a single minute understand them.

CHAPTER EIGHTEEN

Dayne had a beautiful blonde on each arm and a hundred cameras in his face.

Also at the party were the heiress daughters of an international shipping magnate and dozens of young starlets, the type who still got a charge out of having their pictures in the tabloids every week. At least it seemed that way.

"Over here, Dayne . . . over here!"

He did a quarter turn with the women and smiled at a new set of cameras. Not a person watching him could've guessed that his mind was two thousand miles away, lost in a bittersweet memory that no Hollywood party could ever match.

The prepublicity party for his next movie was his agent's idea, and by the industry's standards it was a must, the sort of affair that mandated the city's entire A-list to attend. This one was the fourth since the verdict against Margie Madden. Every tabloid was present and welcome, and most of them would include at least a two-page spread detailing who had attended and what they had worn and who they had sat with and what they thought of the idea for Dayne's newest movie.

His new film matched him with Randi Wells, the Oscar Award–winning stunner known for her on-camera attitude. His other costar was Maria Menkens, the talented daughter of Sarah Menkens, a woman who was an icon in Tinseltown. Maria had already starred in half a dozen romantic comedy hits.

With the actresses on either side of him, the image his agent wanted the world to see was clear and intentional. After all, the movie would tell the story of a man in love with two women — one a forgotten high school love and the other the beautiful daughter of a senator — Dayne's fiancée in the movie. The show would appeal to the chick-flick set, but it had enough drama to be taken seriously. Talk around the city was that this could be Dayne's biggest film yet.

"Dayne . . . Randi . . . Maria . . ."

Another quarter turn and the trio waved and smiled some more.

They were halfway up the red carpet, halfway to the door when Randi Wells leaned in close to him. "Jim asked me for a divorce." She waved to a group of cameramen three rows back. "He wants to share custody of the girls."

"Randi, no," Dayne said so quietly that even Maria on the other side couldn't hear. His heart sank. He waved and smiled to three tabloid reporters. "Tell me it's not true."

"It is." She grinned at the same reporters. "I tried everything to keep him. Everything."

"I'm sorry."

They edged their way closer to the door. The tabs had been saying for a year that Randi and her actor husband were on the outs. His career was dying; hers was thriving. Headlines questioned whether he was merely a house dad for their two young girls. Photos showed them together but with scowls on their faces. Body language experts analyzed everything from the opposite directions their feet were pointing to the meaning of a hand in a pocket or the angle of one of their heads.

Dayne felt a rush of anger, even as he made another quarter turn and smiled at a group of fans and media. How often were his Hollywood friends going to let this happen? The tabloids played a diabolical role in all of their relationships. They would lure and tempt and attract, making reference to two people who seemed to have an interest in each other.

Once the pair had been identified as a couple, the photographers couldn't capture enough pictures. Certainly he and Katy Hart were the current tabloid couple of choice — though the frenzy had died down now that he hadn't seen Katy since the trial.

Once the tabs had a couple pegged, once the pair was openly together and had run the course of happy-couple pictures, the headlines would begin to suspect that marriage was on the way. There would be articles about supposed rings and dresses and locations, even if an actual wedding wasn't in the works.

For most of his friends, babies came next. One time he asked an A-lister friend of his why everyone in their circle did things out of order, putting babies before a commitment.

His friend shrugged, his expression cynical. "Are you kidding? Get married and doom the thing to failure?" He had chuckled then. "The longest-lasting couples in Hollywood are the ones who never marry at all. No tabloid can suspect them of breaking a vow they never made."

Sadly, it was true.

Once a couple married, the tabloids could hardly wait to doubt their commitment. "Is He Cheating?" headlines would ask. "Is She Getting Too Cozy with Her Costar?" A few stories would spin into an avalanche of print and photographs designed to give the magazines enough drama to sell copies.

The wake of crumbled Hollywood marriages that paid the price was of no interest to the photographers, reporters, and editors who profited from celebrity pain. Pain like the kind Randi was silently suffering now.

He leaned closer to her. "We'll talk about it later."

She nodded and smiled for a sea of cameras close to the ropes.

Soon they were inside for a private dinner. Invited members of the media — which meant everyone, even the tabs — would join them after that.

When they reached the champagne fountain, Randi took hold of the table and lowered her head.

Dayne put his arm around her and patted her arm. "Hey . . . you okay?"

She slipped her hand around his waist and leaned her head on his shoulder. "He was sleeping with the nanny." She sniffed. "Remember the tabloid story a week ago? It was true."

"I didn't see it." His heart went out to her, and he wondered if she would have the emotional energy to pull off the film if her life at home was a mess. He hoped so. He cared for her more than many of the women he could've starred with. Randi had appeared with him in his first film, and they'd dated seriously for a year afterwards. He moved in with her for a season, and he would've married her, but he was only twenty-three, and everywhere he went another girl was inviting him over for drinks or making passes at him on location. His life had been that wild.

They parted as friends and had stayed so ever since.

Randi stood on her toes and kissed his cheek. "I'm glad we're doing this film together." Her eyes shone with the hint of tears. "You're a good guy, Dayne. One of the last good ones."

Her comment pierced him with guilt. The guy he'd been when he dated her was hardly good. He had been only a handful of years removed from his boarding school, fully aware of what his teachers had taught about right and wrong, but he'd used her the way everyone seemed to use everyone in Hollywood. And the whole time he'd known better. The memory made him suddenly uncomfortable around her, and he made himself a promise. Sometime while they were working together, he'd apologize to her. She deserved that at least — even if she might think him strange for being sorry.

He gave her another pat and took a step back. They'd spent enough time together. Anything more — especially once the press joined them — and speculation was bound to begin. Randi Wells on the outs with her husband, playing the forgotten love of Dayne Matthews. Katy Hart back home in Bloomington. Was there a new love in the works? Dayne took another step away from her. With their history the whole setup was a little too close for comfort. To avoid rumors he'd have to balance being her friend with staying far enough away.

A producer approached him and motioned him over. "Dayne, I have someone you need to meet. . . ."

The night passed in a blur, and before it was over, Randi found her way back to him. "Dayne —" she stood a little too close, her words slightly slurred from the partying she'd done — "let's hang out tomorrow, 'kay? Jim's taking the girls to the beach and I —" her lips curved in a smile that was more suggestive than cutesy — "I don't wanna be alone."

While she was talking to him, a dozen cameramen caught the moment. In a rush, an image filled Dayne's mind. Katy Hart buying milk and eggs at the Bloomington supermarket and seeing a cover story about Dayne Matthews moving on. The idea made his heart race, made his hands clammy. When Randi talked about needing company, he knew exactly what she had in mind.

He backed up and crossed his arms. Let the body language experts analyze that. "Randi, I can't. I've got . . . well, things have changed for me."

"Changed?" She pouted, and the look was exactly the one they'd brought her into the film for. She ran her finger along the side of his face. "You don't like me anymore, Dayne?"

He wanted to run, but he had to deal with her. Otherwise she would feel rejected or more determined with him. He stuck his hands in his pants pockets and raised his shoulders a couple times. "I gave my life to God." He gave a surprised laugh, knowing she would be frightened by the idea unless he kept the moment light. "Went back to my roots, I guess."

"You?" Her eyes got big, and she held her mouth open. "Handsome playboy Dayne Matthews gone and given his life to God?"

A disbelieving chuckle sounded in her throat. "Nah!"

"Hey, I'm serious." He gave her a tender smile. "I'm reading my Bible and everything."

"Wow." As if he'd put a gun to her ribs, she held up both hands. "Well, don't let me get in the way of that." She sidled back, putting distance between them. As she did, she stumbled and pointed at him. "You sure this isn't about that pretty little Indiana girl of yours?"

His heart warmed. He felt the familiar grin tug at the corners of his mouth. "Maybe a little bit of both."

She raised her brow, as if she was concerned for his mental health. "I'll try to look past all that." She closed the distance between them and kissed his cheek. "You'll always be my same old Dayne."

He put his hands on her shoulders to give himself room but also so he could look into her eyes. This was something he wanted her to understand. "I'm not the same old Dayne, Randi. But I'll be your friend." He gave her a hug. "I'm sorry about Jim."

"Thanks." There was a catch in her voice. She pressed her cheek to his. "I'll get through it." She looked over her shoulder at a sea of photographers, then back at him. "I just wish we could lick our wounds in private."

"I know." Dayne flexed the muscles in his jaw. The cameramen weren't ten feet away. The mass of them were shooting Randi and him in rapid-fire mode, capturing every second of the kiss on the cheek, the hug, the closeness — the entire exchange. There wasn't a thing he could do about it. Their agents and the movie execs had invited them intentionally, doing what Hollywood often did — using the tabloids and every other venue of media to their advantage to promote an upcoming film.

Still, at a publicity party like this, even dressed in tuxedoes, the paparazzi felt like a flock of scavengers, representatives from the seedy underground, the voyeuristic side of society.

Randi ran her thumb above his ear and wrinkled her nose. "I think the whole giving-your-life-to-God thing is a little weird." She smiled, and her eyes danced. "But I won't hold it against you."

"Thanks, Randi." His smile let her know that he wasn't going to be baited into letting the conversation turn into a debate on faith. That could come later, and Dayne hoped it would. For now he needed to remember what Bob Asher had told him in a recent phone call.

"Your Hollywood friends are going to think you're a freak, Matthews." Bob had sounded matter-of-fact and at ease. The way he always sounded. "As soon as they find out something's different you'll no longer be one of them."

Instead, Bob had said, Dayne would be strange, a pariah. Especially in the movie crowd where Christians were considered out of touch and insensitive — bigots even. Dayne understood. In his world of celebrity, where thinking seemed to be done corporately, how could any of them understand what he'd done?

"Let your life be your testimony," Bob had told him lastly. "Don't preach at them. Not when they wouldn't understand, anyway."

That was Dayne's plan exactly. But sometimes — when a friend like Randi Wells was making herself available in every possible way — he needed to be very clear where he stood. No matter what she thought.

Before the party was over, the producer caught up with him. "Big things, Dayne. This film is going to do big things for you and Randi and Maria." He made a fist and tapped it over his heart. "I can feel it in here."

Dayne gave a thoughtful nod. "I agree."

Across the room, Randi and Maria were talking and giggling about something. A dozen guys, involved one way or another in the film, hovered around them. Randi would be fine. There would never be a shortage of people willing to keep her company.

Dayne focused on the producer. "Everything the same for the shooting schedule?"

"Definitely." The producer was a black man, fifty years old, highly successful, and serious about his films. He had been an actor in his twenties and thirties, a professional with two Academy Awards on his list of credits. "We'll start the first week of June, and even with reshoots, we should wrap up by the end of August."

"Good." It was a longer schedule than some. They were shooting most of it in Los Angeles, but they would have a week in Maui near the middle of the schedule. The location team had all the details worked out.

The producer took a step closer. He shot a glance at Randi and Maria. "Look, Matthews, I know you and that Indiana woman are over. She's back there and you're here. But I have to tell you —" he smiled — "I wouldn't mind seeing you and Randi together a little more often. Her marriage is a mess, and, well . . . you know the drill. Publicity is everything."

Dayne forced a chuckle. "Tonight should take care of that for a while."

"Right." The man gave him a firm pat on the shoulder. "I'm just saying."

They talked for a few more minutes, and then the producer ambled over to another group.

The break gave Dayne a chance to look at his watch. Almost five-thirty. Eight-thirty in Bloomington. He sighed. The mentions of Katy were getting to him. Not so much because there was anything he could do about the distance between them. But because he had another six hours of party life and plastic smiles ahead of him, a reminder that he wasn't where he desperately wanted to be.

In his favorite seat at the Bloomington Community Theater, watching Katy work her magic for the opening night of *Narnia.*

CHAPTER NINETEEN

John Baxter took his seat in the Blooming-ton Community Theater next to Cole and Maddie and Jessie. The play was set to begin in five minutes, just enough time to send his grandkids to the snack stand. He took a handful of dollar bills from his pocket and handed four of them to Cole. "You and Maddie get popcorn, okay?"

"Really?" Cole's eyes lit up. He grabbed Maddie's hand and took the bills from John. "One each, Papa?"

"Let's see . . ." He looked down the row. Ashley and Landon were here and Kari and Ryan. Brooke and Peter had stayed home with Hayley, who wasn't feeling well. Little Devin was asleep, and Ryan was too young. "Let's get four, Coley. That way we can all share."

Cole gave a serious nod. "Yeah, but more for us kids, right? Since grown-ups don't eat much popcorn."

John chuckled. "We'll see."

"Come on, Jessie." Maddie turned and motioned to her cousin. "Let's help Cole."

They ran off, and Ashley leaned toward John, her eyes shining. "You're the best grandpa ever, Dad. Just thought I'd tell you."

He smiled and patted her hand. "The kids make it easy."

The coordinator for Christian Kids Theater took the stage and explained that the show would start in a few minutes. "Please turn off cell phones and cameras." She smiled. "And let me take this time to tell you a little about the CKT summer schedule. . . ."

Bethany Allen's spiel gave John a chance to turn around and check the balcony, the place where Dayne would be if he'd come. He wanted to be here; he'd told John as much a few days ago when they last talked. "I haven't missed a show in a while." He sounded torn about the situation. "But I'm pretty sure we're having a prepub party that night."

Dayne's tone had reminded John about the strange life his first-born son led, the very public nature of it. If he was attending a prepublicity party, then no doubt the pictures would grace the covers of every tabloid for the next week. Part of the plan certainly. But that hadn't been all that was troubling Dayne. "I'm not sure I can keep up the pace." He had sounded tired, drained. "The new film hasn't even begun, and the paparazzi won't quit."

Then he talked about something he hadn't shared before. He and Katy had been chased by cameramen before Katy returned home. "We were nearly killed." Defeat rang in his tone. "That's when I knew."

"Knew?" John had been outside, checking on the fish in his pond. He waited for Dayne's answer.

"That's when I knew I had to let her go. It's one thing for me to live this crazy life, but Katy . . . she never asked for this." There was heartbreak in his voice.

John hurt for the pain his son was in. "You don't mean you're thinking of letting her go forever . . . do you?"

"Yes." He sighed. "I don't know what else to do. Maybe I'm supposed to love her enough to let her go, let her have the life she's used to living."

The conversation faded, and the kids returned with the popcorn. At the same time, Katy Hart buzzed across the front of the theater and up a set of stairs toward her spot in a box on the left side of the theater balcony, the place she'd sat for every performance John had ever attended. He watched her, tried to imagine what she might be feeling.

He didn't know Katy well, but he couldn't imagine that she was happy with the way things had ended in Los Angeles. Dayne had talked about how close they'd become, how he'd never felt for anyone what he felt for Katy. Every indication suggested she felt the same way for him.

She took her seat, and John was almost certain he saw her turn and look across the theater at the spot where Dayne might've been sitting. Yes, she was dressed nicely for the opening of the play — wearing a stylish summer skirt. But her glances at the empty seat across the theater told a different story.

John exhaled and looked down at his knees. *God, You've made me a perceptive man, able to know my kids' hearts long before they are sometimes willing to share with me. Now, God, Katy Hart isn't my daughter, but I know she must be hurting. So especially tonight, Father, will You put Your arms around her and let her know You love her?* He paused as the houselights dimmed and the stage lights came to life. *And give her answers about Dayne, Lord. He loves her so much. Thanks ahead of time, Lord. Amen.*

John looked at the stage, and a sense of expectation began to build inside him. He loved the old C. S. Lewis classic, the idea of children discovering the fictitious kingdom of Narnia.

The curtain rose and the play started. The CKT kids did a wonderful job telling the early part of the story. With their father fighting in a war and their mother worried about their safety, the four children travel together to a safer house, a place in the country owned by a professor. The point was to establish the characters and the grand old house where they quickly find a mysterious wardrobe.

But John wasn't thinking about the story. The four children of Narnia reminded him of his own kids and how they'd stuck together through the revelation that they had an older brother. They were grounded in faith and in their love for him and their mother. He glanced down the row at Ashley and Landon, holding hands, with Cole now tucked beneath Landon's other arm. A few spots down the row Ryan had his arm around Kari, the two of them cuddled close as they watched the play.

He'd heard from Luke nearly every day, and Erin seemed to be coming to grips with the fact that Elizabeth hadn't been willing to share about Dayne.

Brooke, John's most analytical daughter, had been talking with the others in a straightforward way about the reality of having an older brother. "The important thing is that we figure out what's holding him back and make a connection with him," she'd told John yesterday. "He has his own life, but it would be healthy for all of us to meet."

John leaned back against the padded seat and smiled. Onstage, the four siblings were linking arms and walking slowly toward the wooden wardrobe. The bond between them was emotional and physical, one that nothing could tear apart.

Same as his children.

Yes, the news about Dayne had been difficult for them. But they would be fine even if they'd been thrust into a brand-new world — one they'd never anticipated, one with a brother they hadn't known existed, and one with experiences they had never counted on. They would cope because they were rooted in love, and love would be enough to see them through no matter what lay on the other side of the wardrobe. Same as love was seeing them through this — one of the most trying seasons of their lives. And because of love — God's love — they could all be sure that one day the difficult times would pass.

And like the four children, they'd live together in Narnia forever.

The play was going beautifully, even if every few minutes Katy checked what she could see of the opposite balcony and the empty seat she'd purchased. She had taken a seat a few feet from where she usually sat so she would see if he showed up. Just in case.

It was intermission. Katy sat on the edge of her seat, the way she always did for opening night. Often it was at this point in the play run that she would celebrate God's goodness in bringing their show together, and tonight was no different. By now she knew every line, every word, every voice inflection, and every movement. From the opening scene when the children arrive at the professor's house to the entrance of the White Witch, the kids had pulled off a nearly perfect performance so far.

The child playing Edmund was doing a brilliant job, and now he was onstage stepping precariously over frozen statues of those who had tried to oppose the witch. The scene was a perfect cliff-hanger, and as it ended — with Edmund about to knock on the witch's door — Katy could feel the audience's excitement over what came next.

There was a tug at her elbow, and she turned.

"Katy." It was Audrey Johnson, a precocious girl who had starred in previous CKT plays. This time Audrey's schedule hadn't allowed her to try out, but she was staying involved by ushering. Her eyes were wide, and shock filled her expression. She swallowed. "Alice Stryker's in the lobby. She wants to see you."

Katy stood, confused. "Okay." Audrey was ever the drama queen, but this time she seemed truly troubled. "Why the serious face?"

"Because . . ." Audrey drew out the moment. "She has another family with her, and they have a girl. A girl about Sarah Jo's age." Her eyes grew watery. "I think . . . I think it's the girl."

Understanding came over Katy, and she felt the shock work its way through her. She gave Audrey's hand a quick squeeze. "Tell Mrs. Stryker I'll be there in a few minutes."

Audrey ran off, and Katy dropped slowly to her seat. What had Alice said a while ago? Katy thought hard. She'd been busy, running from one group of kids to another, trying to work out the last-minute kinks in the play. Then she remembered. Alice had told her that the girl who'd received Sarah Jo's eyes and her family would be attending a performance of *Narnia.* This could be the girl.

Katy closed her eyes, and she was there again, sitting in the coffee shop with Rhonda, when Bethany had called.

The news had been terrible. Alice Stryker had taken her two kids and the two Hanover kids out for pizza after auditions for *Annie,* and on their way home they'd been hit head-on by a drunk driver. Everyone in Alice's van had been seriously injured, but little Ben Hanover had been killed, and within a week they had also lost sweet Sarah Jo, Alice's twelve-year-old daughter, the girl who had brilliantly played Becky Thatcher in CKT's *Tom Sawyer* production.

The tragedy had thrust Katy and the drama kids into the most difficult season of their lives, one that culminated in a trip to a lonely jail cell where three van loads of kids each extended forgiveness to the teenage drunk driver. Some of the kids still made trips to the jail to visit the boy.

Katy shuddered at the memory of that difficult time and pressed her fingers to her eyes. She could see it still, the Flanigans' great room filled to overflowing with almost a hundred CKT kids, all of them looking for a place to grieve, for answers to the questions that hurt so badly. Tim Reed, who had starred as Tom Sawyer in the same play, had led the group in a few songs and a prayer for understanding, for something good to come of the terrible loss.

One answer seemed to come that very night. Katy and the CKT staff received news that Sarah Jo's eyes had been donated to a girl about the same age in Indianapolis. A girl with a dream of being onstage but who desperately needed her vision. Over time, Alice Stryker — who prior to the accident had been an intolerable stage mom — began attending Bible studies at the Flanigans' house. On a couple occasions, Katy heard that Alice was in touch with the family of the girl who had received Sarah Jo's eyes.

Katy lowered her hands and looked up at the dusty rafters of the old theater. *God . . . if that little girl is down in the lobby, I need Your help, Your strength. I can't break down and cry, not with all the parents standing around, not on opening night. Please, God . . . help me hide my emotions until later. When it's just You and me.*

A sense of strength filled her. She could do this, even on a night when her emotions were already running high. She drew a long breath, held it, and — moving a little slower than usual — she headed downstairs to the lobby.

Katy surveyed the crowd. People stood in clusters, eating popcorn and candy, smiling and laughing and talking in animated conversations — probably about the first half of the play. Any other opening night and one look at the crowd would've sent happy chills down Katy's spine. The house was sold out; the crowd was upbeat. The show run was bound to be a success.

But now all of that was secondary to finding Alice Stryker and her guests. Katy searched the crowd, looking past the Shaffers and Picks and Reeds and Johnsons, past the Taylors and Kohls and a dozen other familiar faces of kids and families who had been in one CKT show or another.

And then, near the side door, she spotted Alice. She was talking to a couple and a young girl, a girl with long brown hair whose back was turned toward Katy.

Katy exhaled. *Okay . . . strength, God. Please.* On the way across the lobby, she was stopped by several people.

"Amazing show so far!" Bill Shaffer patted her on the back. He had his big Nikon camera around his neck. "I got some great shots in the greenroom during circle-up time."

"Thanks, Bill." Katy smiled big and kept walking. Bill put together a scrapbook after each show, one that was kept at the CKT office. Normally, Katy would've stayed and asked more questions, looked at the shots on his digital camera. But not tonight.

She made it past another few groups before she came alongside Alice Stryker. "Hi!" she kept her tone upbeat, her gaze entirely on Alice. "Audrey said you were looking for me."

"Yes." There was a mix of emotions on Alice's face. Joy and awe and sadness all mingled into a sweetness that seemed to shine from somewhere deep in her soul. She ushered Katy into the group and motioned toward the threesome she'd been talking to. "This is the Bell family. Len, Sue, and their daughter, Cassie."

Katy shook hands with the couple, but when she got to Cassie she felt her heart skip a beat. There was something familiar about the girl's eyes. No doubt this was the girl. Katy kept her smile but looked quickly at the girl's mother. "What'd you think of the first half?"

"Fantastic." She put her arm around her daughter. "In fact —" she grinned at her husband — "we're moving to Bloomington later this summer. Cassie would like to try out for the fall show."

Katy felt like she was hiking through sand in high elevation. Her mind turned somersaults, and she couldn't catch a full breath. She was careful not to look at Cassie. "How . . . how wonderful."

"It is wonderful." Alice couldn't have looked happier. "Sarah Jo would be so glad for Cassie."

Suddenly Katy was certain she would faint there on the weathered wooden floor if she didn't get some air. Tears threatened to fill her eyes, so she blinked fast several times. The girl's parents were talking, and Katy nodded and smiled and made a minute's more of small talk. Finally, when she had no other choice without being rude, she let her eyes find Cassie's. "I guess we'll see you in the fall."

"Yes, ma'am." The girl was petite and somewhat frail looking. But there was no getting past the grin on her face. Whatever her story, the next chapter looked brighter than the sun reflecting off Lake Monroe.

Katy made a quick exit from the group and stopped just once, pretending to check a poster on the wall, before stepping out the side door and collapsing against the cool brick building. It was dark outside, and the street was empty. Katy looked up and savored the feel of the evening breeze against her hot cheeks.

Cassie Bell was going to be a CKT kid? How would that work, when word was bound to get out and everyone in the theater group would know she was the girl, the one who . . .

God, help me. . . . Katy looked down at her feet and steadied herself. She couldn't bring herself to think about it, let alone look at the girl. It felt wrong somehow. Too sad that a part of Sarah Jo lived on when she no longer had the chance. How would it feel seeing Cassie onstage, the place where Sarah Jo had shone so brightly, and knowing that her death had given Cassie the chance to perform?

Her stomach hurt. She thought about Cassie, her pale face and frail frame. Katy hadn't given her much of a welcome, not really. But it had been all she could do to keep from crying in the few minutes they'd had together. Crying and gaping at the girl in shock and running from the lobby as fast as she could. How was she going to spend an entire season working with her?

Katy released a shaky breath and straightened herself. *God, I don't know how to feel about this. . . . Sarah Jo should be here, not . . . not someone with her eyes. So, help me, please. You've brought her here for a reason.* She looked up again. Clouds blocked the stars and moon, and the darkness felt thick around her. *Help me get past whatever it is I'm feeling. Please . . .*

Daughter, My ways are not your ways. I make all things beautiful in My time.

Peace put its warm arms around Katy's shoulders. The words sounded clear and distinct in her heart, almost as if God Himself were standing beside her whispering them. The thought was something she'd read in Ecclesiastes not long ago. In the section about how there was a time for everything. The Lord promised that He would make all things beautiful.

She moved slowly for the door. So what was the message? That no matter how tragic the loss of Sarah Jo, something beautiful would come of it now? Or was it that Alice Stryker's heart had become beautiful through the tragedy?

The second act had already begun as she reentered the theater. She crossed the dark lobby and jogged lightly up the stairs to her box.

A battle was raging onstage. Aslan and his followers were waging war against the White

Witch and the creatures of darkness. Katy settled back into her seat, her eyes wide. She'd watched the kids perform the scene dozens of times, but this was different. The tears she'd held back earlier filled her eyes and spilled onto her cheeks.

The scene was gripping, mesmerizing. The evil forces advancing hard on the side of the light, and then — when it looked like all hope was lost — Aslan's followers moving in strong against the witch's groupies.

Katy let her tears fall. Wasn't it a picture of life? Dayne being lured toward Kabbalah . . . the drunk driver eliminating two lives full of love and promise . . . even her walking away from Dayne, just when he'd found faith and hope in Christ.

Life was a battle, all of it.

Finally and fiercely, the witch raised her hand. Bailey Flanigan was doing such a good job in the role that even Katy no longer saw anything but the character. "Edmund is mine! According to the law of Narnia, the penalty for his crimes is death!"

At that moment — with the help of a voice-changing machine — a loud roar shook the theater. The crowd of fighting parties parted down the middle, and Aslan, the great lion, walked regally and resignedly onto the stage. Up until the last day of dress rehearsals, the boy playing Aslan hadn't seemed adequate for the task. Not passionate enough, not fearsome enough.

But here, now, as he moved slowly from center downstage to center upstage, as he looked from the faces of darkness to the faces of light and back again, he seemed to finally understand. His people would have no hope, no way of escaping the White Witch unless he himself took on the penalty of death — once and for all.

Katy wasn't sure, but it almost looked as if the boy had tears in his eyes as he finally reached the witch, stopped, and faced her squarely. "No." He gave a slow shake of his mane. "No, you may not have Edmund."

"Ha!" Bailey held her chin high, proud. No question this was her finest acting performance yet. "Either Edmund dies —" she narrowed her eyes and leaned closer to the lion — "or someone dies in his place." Her voice boomed as she waved her hand toward her people. "That is the law, and the law must be upheld!"

Aslan steeled himself. "Take me instead."

Katy peered down at the audience. The faces of children and adults alike were frozen, gripped by the drama playing onstage. She saw an older man dabbing at his eyes. Yes, they were struck by the scene. And no doubt by the parallels to their own lives, where a loving King had volunteered to die in each of their places as well.

The killing of Aslan pushed Katy to the edge of her seat. Again, though she'd directed the scene, though she'd blocked it and worked with each line, each word, and each chant, it was striking to see it now. The hissing and name-calling at the lion as he lay strapped to the stone table, the excitement and frenzy over what seemed like the ultimate victory for darkness.

New tears spilled down Katy's cheeks when Susan and Lucy found the lion dead and when he brought about the greatest defeat of evil by coming back to life and destroying forever the White Witch and her hold over the children of Narnia.

As the final act played out, Katy glanced every now and then at the empty seat across the theater, the seat she'd reserved for Dayne. He would've loved the performance, loved everything it stood for and the work the kids had done to bring the salvation story to life.

Katy drew a breath and tried to get ahold of her emotions, but somehow the moment when the children left Narnia was the saddest of all. Because the adventure in Narnia had been magical and mysterious, and when it was all said and done maybe it was only a dream.

The way her time with Dayne was maybe only a dream.

As the show ended and she wiped her tears, Katy was struck by another thought. Maybe her sadness wasn't only about the drama onstage, about the sacrifice of Aslan and the end of an adventure, and even about missing young Sarah Jo Stryker. Maybe saddest of all was the thing she couldn't keep from looking at throughout the performance.

The empty seat where once upon a time Dayne Matthews had sat.

CHAPTER TWENTY

Ashley still hadn't heard about Katy's trip to California or how things had gone with Dayne. CKT's run of *Narnia* had taken up all Katy's time since she'd been home, and something in her demeanor made it clear she wasn't ready to talk yet. Not about the trial or the tabloids or her time with Dayne. None of it.

Midweek Katy had called and said very little. Only that she wanted Ashley to have coffee with her and Rhonda at the coffee shop near the university the day after the play closed. Ashley agreed, and every day since then she'd wondered what the conversation might hold.

Now it was Monday, and she took a last glance in the mirror. She was starting to look like her old self, the way she'd looked before Devin. And her eyes were happier than they'd ever been — even with their little son's early morning wake-ups. Life at home couldn't have been better, and she woke up every day thanking God for that fact.

But Katy was struggling, and with the friendship they'd forged painting sets together, Ashley wanted to be there for her this morning. Whatever the topic of conversation.

With hurried steps, she grabbed her purse, slipped it over her shoulder, and made her way to the family room. What she saw brought her to a halt and made her breath catch.

Landon had Devin cradled in his right arm and his left arm was around Cole, who was snug against his side. Cole had brought the afghan from his bed — the one her mother had made for him when he was Devin's age. It was tucked in around their laps. A John Wayne movie played on the TV, and Cole's eyes lit up as the Duke confronted a trembling bad guy.

Ashley's heart swelled inside her. If she didn't have the coffee with Katy and Rhonda she could've stood there all day, watching Landon and the way he had with their boys. Even Devin seemed to be watching the movie, content with the security of being held by his father.

"That man's strong!" Cole's back was

straight and stiff, his whole being now caught up in the film. He looked at Landon. "Just like you, Daddy."

"And see his partner." Landon pointed at the screen. "He's the tough-looking guy still on his horse."

Cole nodded. "He's John Wayne's friend, right?"

"Right." Landon looked at the TV again. "Well, that guy's like you because he's the perfect partner." Landon kissed Cole on the top of his head. "Same as you and me."

A grin stretched across Cole's face.

Ashley pressed her hand to her heart. What would she have done without Landon, without him in her life? God had known exactly what type of man could've turned her head and her heart at the same time, and even so she'd almost walked away from him. Gratitude welled up within her, and she took a mental picture of the three of them, Landon and their boys. It was a moment she would long remember, one that deserved a place on canvas.

Landon must've spotted her, because he turned and their eyes met. She smiled and let their gazes hold for several seconds. With her eyes she told him everything she'd been feeling, that she adored him and respected him and treasured every moment with him.

And that she could never get enough of watching the way he loved their boys.

"Hi." She came to him.

"Mommy! Shhh! John Wayne and his partner are about to catch the bad guys!" Cole's tone wasn't rude, just excited. His eyes were so wide she could see the whites around his pupils.

Landon paused the movie and gave him a little pat. "Hey, sport. Careful. Mommy's more important than the movie."

Remorse filled Cole's face, and he bit his lip. "Sorry."

"It's okay. John Wayne's exciting. I know that, Coley." She moved behind the sofa where they were sitting and gave the three of them a group hug. "I'm going out for coffee, so when I come back you can tell me all about it."

"Okay." Cole's expression was full of anticipation for the rest of the movie. He turned toward the TV. "Bye, Mom. Have fun."

Landon turned to her. "Hey, you." He took his hand from Cole's shoulder and ran his fingers through her hair. He hit the Play button on the remote, turned up the volume, and whispered in her direction, "You have the most beautiful hair. Has anyone told you that?"

She gave him a tender smile, one made up of all the emotions stirring in her soul. Even sorrow for dear old Irvel, the patient at Sunset Hills Adult Care Home who had asked Ashley about her hair twice an hour every day Ashley worked there. "I have a confession." She brought her lips to his and kissed him. Slow enough to make him aware of her desire and quick enough to escape the notice of Cole.

His eyes danced. In his right arm, little Devin yawned. "Confessions are good."

"I know this girl . . . and she has the biggest crush on you."

"Really." Landon raised his eyebrows. "Does she live nearby?"

"Mmm-hmm." She kissed him once more. "Right down the hall."

"Guys . . ." Cole looked over his shoulder at them. "It's the best part!"

"Okay." Landon chuckled. Then he cast her a look. "Do me a favor."

She nodded as she took a step back. She loved this, the way they could play with each other, the way the laughter between them was sometimes as precious as the love.

"Tell this girl maybe we can meet when I get off work. Late tonight." He winked at her. "If you know what I mean."

She gave him her best flirtatious look. "I

think she'll be very interested." Then she blew him a last kiss and grinned. "Love you, Landon."

"Love you too."

Cole shot up onto his knees and flashed her a smile. "Bye, Mommy. Have fun at coffee."

"Okay, buddy. Have fun with Daddy."

As she walked out the door into the garage she heard Cole's voice ring out. "He got 'em, Daddy! I knew he would get 'em!"

Ashley didn't stop smiling all the way to the Flanigan house. But she spent half the time praying for Katy, that whatever the conversation, she might have some wisdom to add, some way of helping Katy know what to do next. She was in love with Dayne Matthews — no doubt about that.

But could anything good or lasting ever come from someone so famous, so used to living the Hollywood lifestyle? Ashley didn't think so, but she'd have to be gentle with her words. It wasn't long ago when the road was unclear in her own life. Katy needed support more than anything, support and encouragement — no matter what had happened in LA.

She pulled into the Flanigans' driveway a few minutes before ten o'clock. Katy and Jenny Flanigan had taken Katy's car to the shop early this morning for new brakes, so the plan was for Ashley to pick Katy up; then they would meet Rhonda at the coffee shop. She drove slowly up the drive, admiring everything about the Flanigan house. The drive was lined by sunset maples and rhododendrons, and on either side the grass was deep green and well manicured, like sections of the grounds at the local country club.

At the top of the drive, Ashley turned into the circle and parked. She hurried to the front door, admiring the Flanigans' porch, the way it stretched the length of the house, broken up by an occasional white pillar. She knew from Katy that Jenny and Jim Flanigan — as busy as they were with six kids — found time to sit in one of their two porch swings and regularly take stock of just how blessed they were.

Ashley rang the doorbell, and Jenny answered.

"Hi." Jenny smiled and ushered her in. "Katy's not quite ready."

"Hmm." Ashley was surprised. Katy was one of the most punctual people she knew. Almost every time they'd met, Ashley had run a few minutes late. But not Katy. "Everything okay?"

"Our housekeeper got her clothes mixed

up with Bailey's." She laughed. "I knew there was a problem when Katy came zipping down the apartment stairs in her bathrobe and darted up toward Bailey's room. It took a few minutes to get everything sorted out. I heard Katy say something about Bailey's extra long jeans not being an option."

They both laughed, and Jenny led the way through an open hallway into the kitchen. Ashley had been here once before, but she was struck by the size of the place, the size of the kitchen alone. Katy had explained once that the Flanigans had built their house more for other people than themselves.

"It's sort of like a rec center or a ministry center even." Katy's tone had been thoughtful. "And nothing could be truer for that family. They use it all the time — every inch of it."

The island at the center of the kitchen was enormous, and on two sides it was framed by an elevated section of black granite, high enough and long enough for eight barstools.

"I know I've told you before." Ashley stared out the windows along the back of the kitchen before turning to Jenny. "Your home is beautiful."

"Thanks. We'll keep it as long as we can

use it for God." Jenny opened a drawer and took out a tea bag. "Something to drink?"

Ashley looked at her watch. "Actually . . . I think I'll wait. We're supposed to do coffee with Rhonda."

Jenny had instant hot water available from a spigot at the side of her sink. She filled her mug and nodded to the barstools. "Let's sit down."

They sat with a stool between them, and Ashley turned so she could see Jenny. "The show was amazing." There was a chill in the house, and Ashley crossed her arms to stay warm. "Katy outdid herself."

"I know." Jenny took a sip of her tea. "I'm writing an article about it for *Today's Christian Woman.* About Christian Kids Theater in general and how beautifully our local chapter conveyed the story of Narnia."

Ashley had forgotten about Jenny's writing career. Being married to a former NFL star player and coach, it was easy to see her as Mrs. Flanigan. Jim's wife. But Jenny had a purpose all her own, and Ashley liked that. Sort of the way she had her painting, no matter that her family was more important. God had created her to paint, and as long as she lived she'd paint for Him. The way Jenny Flanigan wrote or Katy Hart directed plays.

Ashley looked toward the door that led to the apartment stairs. There was still no sign of Katy. "So —" she shifted her gaze back to Jenny — "how is she? I mean, since she's been back from LA?"

A shadow fell over Jenny's expression. "I worry about her."

"Me too." Ashley kept her tone low. If Jenny was concerned, then the conversation today was bound to be marked by sadness. "I went to the show a few times, once with Landon and Cole and again just Cole and me. Both times I found Katy and told her how wonderful things had turned out."

"Her eyes were distant, right?" Jenny set down her mug.

"Right." Ashley uncrossed her arms. "She was smiling, but she didn't talk long. As if she might start crying if the conversation turned to her California trip."

"Exactly." Jenny tilted her head. "I've talked with her a lot these last few weeks. The situation with Dayne has made us a lot closer."

"That's good." Ashley had a sudden thought. "And how are her parents? I heard her mom was sick?"

"Yes." Sorrow eased the tiny lines near Jenny's eyes. "They live in Chicago, you know. Her mother isn't doing well. She's in her seventies, and I guess she's getting forgetful. Katy feels detached from them; she's trying to convince them to move here."

"Oh." Ashley thought about her mother and the pain involved with watching a parent deteriorate. "No wonder her eyes look the way they do. Between that and the situation with Dayne."

"Yes." Jenny ran her finger absently around the rim of her mug. "I guess their good-bye in LA was pretty final. Still —" she drew a slow breath — "Katy thought he might show up for opening night. The way he has before."

Ashley's heart hurt for Katy. What would it be like to think you'd found the love of your life, but he's one of the most famous men in the country? "That's too bad."

"It is." Jenny frowned. "I sort of thought he'd come too."

"You did?" Ashley was curious. Maybe Jenny had spoken with Dayne, or maybe Dayne had promised Katy he'd be there. "Was he planning to come?"

"No, not that." Jenny took another sip of her tea. "But his birth parents live here in Bloomington. At least that's what Katy told me. It seems like he would've had more than enough reason to come for the play."

Ashley felt her stomach fall to her knees.

"His birth parents?"

"Yes." Jenny shrugged. "Dayne was adopted. A few years ago he hired a private investigator and found out that his birth family lives right here in Bloomington." She smiled. "That's why he was here in the first place, why he met Katy at all."

With a sudden jolt, Ashley's heartbeat slipped into double time. Dayne Matthews was adopted? And his birth parents lived in Bloomington? Dayne, who looked so much like Luke? who had seemed so familiar the night he'd driven her home after drama practice? Dayne, who knew her father's cell-phone number? who called during the trial? Then she realized something else. Dayne's number had been programmed into her father's phone under the name Dayne, right? Otherwise it wouldn't have said so in the caller ID window.

So was it even remotely possible that . . . ?

Before she could ask another question, before she could even order her thoughts to line up so she might even know what that question would be, Katy ran through the doorway. She was red cheeked and breathless. "Sorry . . . I can't believe I made you wait." She gave Jenny a one-armed hug and flashed a smile at Ashley. "Ready?"

Ashley wanted to speak, wanted to turn

back the clock five minutes so she could learn more about Dayne, about his adoption and whatever other information Jenny Flanigan knew. But she couldn't say a word. All she could do was stand, collect her purse, and nod in Katy's direction.

A memory popped into her mind. Years ago when she was six she'd shared a bunk bed with Erin. One night they were telling knock-knock jokes, and Ashley — on the top bunk — leaned too far over the edge. Before she could stop herself, she slipped over the side and landed flat on her back. The fall knocked the wind from her and scared her to death because her lungs seemed to take forever simply to remember how to breathe again, to draw in even the slightest bit of oxygen.

Which was exactly how she was feeling right now.

Katy hated running late.

Her mother had always told her it was a sign of selfishness, that people who were chronically late gave the impression that they didn't care about others and the schedules others kept. But when she opened her closet she knew she was in trouble. The jeans there definitely weren't her own. In a house the size of the Flanigans', there was no telling what mix-up might've happened. One time she'd found four pairs of her jeans neatly folded in Connor's closet.

She moved quickly, leading the way to Ashley's van and breathing apologies. "I'm so sorry, Ash, really."

"It's okay." Ashley took the driver's seat and stared straight ahead.

That's when Katy saw it. Something was wrong with her friend, something she hadn't seen before. Her eyes looked distant and almost terrified. "Ashley? You okay?"

She started the van and gave her a quick glance. "Definitely."

"You look pale." Katy pressed her back against the passenger door and watched her friend. Maybe it was the new baby or sleepless nights. "Are you sure?"

"I'm fine." She uttered an anxious-sounding laugh. "Today's about your life, not mine."

But even as the two of them talked about baby Devin and Landon and Cole's recent love for John Wayne movies, Katy had the feeling that something wasn't right. And that whatever it was, Ashley wasn't going to talk about it. Not now, anyway.

They reached the coffee shop and joined Rhonda at a booth in the back.

"Hey, guys!" Rhonda looked upbeat, the

way she usually did. "Get your drinks and let's get talking. I have a date to talk about, but my story can wait."

Katy didn't want to be a downer, but if she was going to talk about Dayne, the conversation was bound to turn sad. Maybe now wasn't a good time to open up, but she needed to share what was going on in her heart. She missed Dayne more with every breath, and at the very least she needed Ashley and Rhonda to pray for her. Otherwise she might go the rest of her life never finding the right man, always comparing every guy she met with the one she could never have.

They settled in with their drinks. Ashley sat next to Katy, and Rhonda was directly across from them.

Rhonda started in. "Okay, so what gives?" She planted her elbows on the table and gave Katy a sympathetic look. "We've been dying to hear about Los Angeles."

Katy smiled. "I guess I had to leave Narnia first."

Ashley stirred her iced tea with a straw. "Tell us about Dayne." There was a depth in her voice that seemed to cut through the small talk. A depth and a longing, as if she had a deep concern over whatever Katy's answer might be. "What happened during the trial?"

For a moment Katy studied Ashley. Could she know? Could she possibly have found out somehow that Dayne was her brother? Ashley's expression, her voice, everything about her seemed poised to hang on to every word, almost desperate for her answers about Dayne. So did she know?

Katy let her gaze fall to her hands, tightly folded in her lap. No, it was impossible. Dayne hadn't told them, and she hadn't said a word to anyone. Even Jenny knew only that Dayne was adopted and that his birth parents lived in Bloomington, not that they were the Baxters. There's no way the topic had come up in the few minutes while she'd been scrambling to get ready.

Katy lifted her chin and looked from Ashley to Rhonda. "It's over between us." Her voice threatened to give her away, to crack and release the dam of emotion built up behind it. "Dayne and I, we decided it could . . . it could never work."

She spent the next half hour telling them what happened in LA, how she and Dayne had struggled to find a minute alone, and when they did, how it never was long before the photographers found them. She told them about his faith, how sincere it was and how determined Dayne had become to live for God, which led to the details about the trial, the beach house Dayne's attorney had found for them, and how even that hadn't been safe from the tabloids. Finally she told them about the near accident.

Again, Ashley seemed more intense than she'd been before. "Did he say anything about that being a close call or whether he's had near accidents before?"

"He said it could happen anytime. The photographers are always chasing him." Again Katy wondered about her interest in Dayne, in his welfare. Ashley couldn't know; there was no way. Not unless her father told her, and from what Dayne had said, John Baxter was committed to wait until Dayne had made up his mind about the timing and whether it would ever work for the Baxter siblings to know about the identity of their older brother.

"That's terrible." Ashley had finished her tea. She was definitely swept up in the story. "So that's why you ended things?"

"What choice did we have?" Katy stared at the last of her latte. It was too cold to taste good. "I guess that's why I wanted to tell you. So you'd pray for me."

Then Rhonda told her story, how she'd gone out with a guy and how he'd called himself a "believer" and how he'd been a perfect gentleman all night. "Until we drive past a Christian bookstore, and the guy starts laughing."

"About what?" Katy had no idea where Rhonda was headed with this story.

Rhonda raised her hands and let them fall to the table. "About Christians. He says, 'I can't believe anyone really buys all that garbage about faith.' "

Ashley remained quiet, but Katy felt Rhonda's frustration. Were there no good guys left, none that would make the kind of husbands Jenny and Ashley had found? No one committed to faith and family? No one real, anyway? She waited for Rhonda to finish.

"Turns out the guy's a believer all right. A believer in atheism. Studied science all his life, bought every politically correct line of rhetoric any teacher or textbook ever told him." Her eyes grew flat from the irony of it. "The first guy I've met in a month who isn't a regular at some bar, living at home with his mother, or without intimate knowledge of deodorant." She frowned. "And the guy's an atheist."

They laughed, but they did their best to cheer Rhonda up, to convince her there'd be other guys, even if Katy struggled to believe the possibility herself.

When they finished, Ashley drove Katy home. Halfway there, they were at a stoplight and Ashley turned to her. "I think you're making a mistake." Her tone was kind, sympathetic. But there was no mistaking the seriousness in her voice. "You and Dayne both."

"Walking away, you mean?" This was the sort of deeper conversation she'd wanted to have at the coffee shop. But Ashley had been quiet, and the conversation had shifted to Rhonda's dismal date.

The light turned green. Ashley nodded and turned her attention back to the road. "Sometimes life makes love feel next to impossible. It was that way with Landon and me. But Dayne . . . I don't know, he seems very special." She hesitated. "I'll bet you know a side of Dayne that no one else knows, no matter how many times his picture runs in the tabloids."

Katy looked out her window and closed her eyes. She could hear the ocean waves one after another hitting the shore, feel Dayne sitting beside her, sense his pain at knowing the Baxters but not being able to contact his siblings. Her eyes opened, and she leaned her head against the cool glass. She turned to Ashley. How strange it was that here beside her was Dayne's sister. The entire situation was almost more than she could take in. "Yes, I know Dayne very well."

"Okay, then." Ashley's words came faster now, more determined. "You can't let go, Katy. You can't give up just because he's in show business. There has to be a way to make it work."

"That's what I told myself all those months." She felt her throat thicken, felt the sorrow building inside her. "But look where that got me."

"Does he still call you?"

"Once in a while. But both of us know there's no point. He has to live there and make movies, and I have my life here."

Ashley looked as if she were about to say something else, but she stopped herself. As they pulled up in front of the Flanigans', she added only one more thing. "If you love Dayne, you need to beg God for a way." Her tone was kinder, softer than before, and her eyes glistened with empathy. "That's what I did with Landon, and look at us now." She smiled. "Really, Katy, don't give up. With God at the center, you've got to find a way to bridge the distance."

Katy nodded. "Pray for us, okay?"

"I will."

She squeezed Ashley's hand, thanked her,

and climbed out of the van. As Ashley backed down the driveway, Katy couldn't get past the feelings tugging at her subconscious. What if Ashley knew the truth? Could that be why she was so adamant, why she'd brought up Dayne again and made the strong push for Katy to never give up?

Ashley's last words rang in Katy's head as she headed up the steps to the front door: *"With God at the center, you've got to find a way to bridge the distance."*

She looked over her shoulder at Ashley's van as it moved out of sight. Now the question was a simple one, really. Was Ashley referring to Dayne and Katy?

Or Dayne and herself?

CHAPTER
TWENTY-ONE

Ashley was on the cell phone calling her dad as soon as she dropped off Katy. For the past hour she had barely been able to catch her breath. Every time her mind tried to run unbridled toward the wild possibilities, Rhonda or Katy would shoot a question her way, and she'd have to stay in the moment. Yes, it was too bad about the paparazzi; no, she hadn't known about the near accident with the cameramen chasing them; yes, she understood Rhonda's thoughts about the difficulty of finding a good guy.

But all the while she'd wanted to stand up and shout, look Katy in the eyes, and say, "Tell me the truth . . . is Dayne Matthews my brother?"

And he had to be, didn't he? Every piece lined up. Especially his call to her father during the trial. Luke never would've forgotten his cell phone — he was way too detail-oriented for that. What had her father said? That he was talking to their older brother often, right? So Dayne had probably called to catch their dad up on the details of the trial.

Of course Dayne was their brother. It would've been why he was in town when he met Katy, why he had chosen Bloomington for his location shoot, and why he'd given her a ride home. If he was her brother, he would've been anxious to spend time with her, curious about her life, her family.

She'd been dying to ask Katy about it through most of the morning. If Rhonda hadn't been there, she wouldn't have hesitated. But during the ride to the coffee shop, the shock had been too great, and by the time they were headed back to the Flanigans' house, Ashley had changed her mind. If Katy knew the truth, Dayne would've asked her to keep quiet about it, at least until he figured out how to handle the situation. Putting that responsibility on Katy wasn't fair. Besides, if Dayne was her brother, she didn't want to find out from Katy. She had Dayne's number after all. She could call him or her father.

That was the answer. She needed to talk to her dad. All her life, Ashley had never been one to mince words. Never had she tiptoed around an issue when the straightforward method was so much more effective. She could call her father and have the answer in a matter of seconds.

His number was on her speed dial, so it took no time to call his cell. But after three rings, the call went to a message center. The whole time her father's voice was giving instructions about leaving a message, her mind raced. Should she ask on the phone? Should she hang up and try later?

Finally she decided on a cross between the two. When the beep sounded, she cleared her throat. "Dad . . . it's me." She held tight to the steering wheel with her free hand. "I have a question about our older brother. I found out something today, and I think . . . maybe I know who he is. Maybe not, but maybe." She tried to breathe, but her lungs wouldn't fill up. "Call me, Dad. Please."

Only after she hung up did her body find a way to inhale. She called the Baxter house and left the same message there. He must've been in with patients, that or he was meeting with the other doctors. They were forever having meetings. She looked at the clock on the dashboard. Not quite noon.

Landon would understand. He'd help her make sense of the information, for sure. She turned into their driveway, parked the van, and rushed inside. Cole was sitting in front of a half-played game of checkers in the family room, but Landon wasn't around. She dropped her purse on a chair and grinned at him. "Hey, sweetie . . . where's Daddy?"

"Putting Devin down." Cole jumped up and quietly ran to her. "Sorry for shushing you earlier, Mommy. Sometimes us guys get carried away with cowboy movies."

"I know, honey." She stooped to his level and kissed first one cheek, then the other. "That's okay." She stood and looked beyond him. She had to talk to Landon. "I'll be right back."

But before she could get down the hall to meet him, he walked into the room. "Hey! How was coffee?"

She gave Cole a nervous look, then shifted her gaze to her husband. "Can we talk in the kitchen for a minute?"

Landon's smile faded. "Sounds serious."

Cole skipped back to his checkers game. "I'm ahead, whenever you're ready for me to beat you!"

"Okay, buddy." He kept his tone light, but his eyes never left Ashley's.

She hated the look of worry in Landon's eyes. Where the two of them were concerned, a serious conversation could mean just about anything — and usually something that threatened their relationship, their lives, or both. She tried to give a shake of her head, something to ease the fear in his expression, but the concern only grew as he followed her to the small table near the kitchen's bay window. The spot where they'd held many conversations.

"Ash . . . what is it?" He took her hand as they sat in chairs next to each other. "Honey, tell me."

"It's nothing about me or us." She put her free hand on his cheek. "It's about my brother. My older brother." Relief made his shoulders relax, and she watched it work its way through his body. He smiled. "As long as you're all right."

"I am." She winced. "Sorry for worrying you."

"I'm a little fond of you. I can't have anything happen to you, Ash." He kissed her forehead. "Okay, now tell me about your brother."

She had to make him understand it the way she did, so he could see the possibility. "So I'm at the Flanigan house, and I'm talking to Jenny because Katy's laundry got all mixed up with Bailey's and that cost Katy at least ten minutes' time." The story picked up speed. "And Jenny tells me Katy's been sort of down and that she's really surprised Dayne Matthews didn't go to opening night because he's gone before, and it was especially surprising because his birth parents live in Bloomington." She held out her hands. "Landon, can you believe that?"

He looked confused, as if she'd been speaking German. "The Flanigan house? Is that the coffee shop?"

"No." She tried not to sound as exasperated as she felt. "The Flanigans', where Katy Hart lives in their garage apartment."

The concentration on Landon's face was the kind usually reserved for puzzles and brain teasers. "Okay, and something about Katy's laundry, which I think wasn't the point."

"No." She breathed out hard. "Dayne! The point is Dayne Matthews."

"The movie star." Landon sounded pretty sure of himself, but he couldn't see the connection.

"Yes." Ashley hesitated, willing herself to calm down. "Katy told Jenny that Dayne's birth parents live here. In Bloomington."

Slowly, like dawn on a winter day, the light began to shine in Landon's eyes. He pointed at Ashley, his brow slightly raised. "And you think . . . you think Dayne might be your brother because his birth parents live in Bloomington, Indiana?"

"Yes." She broke free from him and stood, her hands on her hips. "Of course I think that. He looks just like Luke, and during the trial I answered my dad's cell phone one time and it was Dayne! Calling for my dad!" She impatiently waved her hand in a circle. "Sure, he had some story about calling to pass on a message from Luke, but that doesn't even make sense." She made an exasperated sound. "Of course I think he's our brother. What else could it be?"

Landon rose, took both her hands this time, and led her back to her chair. "Ashley . . . there're probably thousands of adoptive parents in the Bloomington area. Thousands." He brought her fingers close and kissed them. "A lot of guys look like Dayne Matthews. That's his appeal, sweetie. All-American good looks. And the cell call . . . I don't know. But you have to admit Luke was there at the trial. It makes sense that Dayne might do him a favor." He paused. His eyes were full of empathy, but they held no doubt. "Honey, the idea of Dayne Matthews being your biological brother is just, well . . . it's crazy."

"But he must be *someone's* biological brother, right? If his birth parents had kids, anyway."

"Don't you think if Dayne was your biological brother that someone would've told you by now?" He released her hands and ran his fingers along her arms. "Ash, sweetie, the guy's been in town because of Katy Hart, and okay, because of his family. He's probably been meeting with them. If he were your brother, Katy would know and she would've told you."

Ashley didn't want his kindness. She wanted him to believe in her, to acknowledge that she wasn't crazy, that maybe — just maybe — Dayne really was her brother. "But listen." She searched his eyes, willing him to understand. "Dayne looks just like Luke. Haven't we all said that? And we know that whoever our older brother is, he has some sort of different life, a life where it could be difficult for him to connect with us, right?" She leaned in closer. "Landon, it's possible. I really think it is."

For the first time, Landon had no easy answer. He sat back and blinked a few times, then made a puzzled face. "Hmm. I forgot about the strange-life thing." He pondered for a moment. "I guess . . . I guess you *could* be right." He looked out the window for a moment and then back at her. "It's possible. It just sounds crazy."

Ashley felt the surge of victory. "It sounds crazy to me too. But the pieces line up." She stared at the floor near her feet and thought. Suddenly something else hit her. "His birth date! That would tell us something, wouldn't it?"

"Before you go that route, how 'bout you call your dad? You said he's been talking to your brother, so he'd be the one to know."

"I left him a couple messages." She stood and paced to the kitchen stove. "I can't wait, Landon. I have to know right now."

"Daddy . . . ," Cole called from the next room, "it's your turn."

"Okay, just a minute." Landon rose and headed toward his checker game. He looked at Ashley before he left. "Wait for your father's call, Ash." His smile told her how much he cared, how badly he wanted her to find the answers she was looking for. "You've waited months to find out about this. Another few hours won't hurt."

Landon was right. She breathed out and felt the excitement leave her body. "Okay. I'll wait."

But afternoon slipped into evening, and dinnertime led to baths for the boys and stories for Cole. All the while she could think of just one thing: Dayne Matthews might be their brother! By the time the boys were both down, it was nine o'clock.

Landon pulled her close and kissed her. "I'm going out for milk and bread." He rocked her slightly, swaying with her the way he sometimes did when he held her. "Do we need anything else?"

"Sliced cheese." She drew back and studied him. "Haven't I waited long enough?" Her voice held a subtle whine. "Landon, I need to know. I have Dayne's cell number; shouldn't I just call him?"

"I don't know, Ash." Landon linked his hands at the small of her back. "I think your dad should tell you." He kissed her once more and then pulled away. "Call him again while I'm out. If he doesn't answer —" he angled his head, encouraging her — "I think you can wait until tomorrow."

Ashley sighed. "All right."

As soon as he was gone, she checked for missed calls on their home phone. There were none. Maybe her father hadn't gotten her messages. She tried his cell and the Baxter home number one more time, but he answered neither of them. "Fine," she muttered.

Landon was wrong. She couldn't wait for tomorrow or the next day to find out. She couldn't wait another minute. Whatever had kept her father so busy, she needed to know about Dayne.

She slipped out the kitchen side door, down the hall, and into the small bedroom that doubled as a home office. It was the place where Ashley handled the business associated with her painting.

The house was quiet, so the sound of her tapping fingers on the keys of the computer filled the room. She was online in seconds. In the Google search window she typed, *Dayne Matthews birth date.* Then she hit Enter.

A list of sites popped up, but the first one gave her all the information she needed without even having to click it. Ashley pushed her chair back and stared at the age on the screen. She did the math in a hurry, and any doubts she had dissolved like summer dew. Dayne was born less than a year before her parents were married — which would make the timing perfect.

So why hadn't he wanted to meet them? If Dayne was the first-born Baxter son and if her father was in communication with him, then the reasons had to be noble. Certainly if Dayne had a bad attitude, if he was worried about the Baxter family tarnishing his Hollywood image, then her father wouldn't have wanted a relationship with him.

If their brother was Dayne, if he really was the missing Baxter sibling, then maybe the reason had more to do with them, with their privacy. If that was the case, no wonder he hadn't made contact with his siblings. Not because he was ashamed of them but because if he did, the entire world was bound to find out, and once they did — there wouldn't be a moment's peace for any of the Baxters. They would wind up gobbled and spit out across the tabloids, same as Katy Hart.

Ashley picked up the phone and dialed her father's cell one more time. But again the call went to his voice mail, and this time she didn't leave a message. She didn't want to sound desperate, but she needed to know. The clock on the wall ticked, and the ticking grew louder, louder. As if the second hand was reminding her that every tick, every passing minute and hour were one more bit of lost time where she and her siblings were missing out on knowing their parents' firstborn son.

Should she call Dayne? Landon hadn't exactly asked her *not* to call. He just didn't think it was a good idea. And the thought had never been more than a heartbeat away since Jenny Flanigan mentioned the news. Did she owe it to her father to talk to him first? Would he mind if she simply called Dayne and asked? Her father wouldn't get upset at that, would he?

Her purse was in the kitchen, and she darted back down the hall, scooped it up, and carried it to the office. She rummaged through it, found her cell, flipped it open, and scrolled through the phone book until she found Dayne's number. She stared at it, each digit another hurdle in a small line of hurdles that maybe were all that remained between not knowing and finally having the information she wanted.

No. She exhaled hard and closed her phone. She couldn't call him. She needed to talk to her father first. She sat back in the computer chair, defeated. *Patience, Ashley,* she told herself. *Be patient. God, give me patience, please.*

She looked at the screen. The Google list still displayed the Web sites listing Dayne's birth date. *Get to know Dayne Matthews,* one said. *Dayne Matthews: America's Heartthrob . . . everything for the fanatical Dayne Matthews fan!* boasted another.

Fourth on the list was a site that claimed to be an official gathering place for fans. Ashley clicked it, and the screen filled with a full-size photo of Dayne Matthews, a publicity shot from one of his recent films.

Ashley leaned in and scrutinized the photo, studying the way he rested against an old brick wall, his hands behind his back, one knee up. The pose was strikingly familiar. Hadn't she seen Luke stand that way against the garage door when any of them were outside playing basketball and he was waiting for his turn? She looked at Dayne's eyes, as deeply as she could.

"Are you my brother?" Her whisper hung in the air and blended with the soft whirring of the computer.

She pictured Dayne, the way he'd looked that night when he'd given her a ride home from CKT practice. She'd felt so at ease around him, so aware of how his mannerisms reminded her of Luke. At the time she could only make a mental note, a reminder to herself to talk to Luke about the resemblance. His coworkers were right, she told Luke later. No question, he looked just like Dayne Matthews.

But now . . .

How could she let another day go by without knowing the truth? Did they look like brothers because of an uncanny coincidence? Or because of an uncanny coincidence had she made the discovery of a lifetime?

That they looked like brothers for one reason alone — because they were.

CHAPTER
TWENTY-TWO

John pulled into his driveway at ten that night, tired but with a lighthearted feeling he'd missed over the past two years. The day had been a full one, meetings at the hospital, board reviews, and committee gatherings.

Afterwards, he and several of his colleagues had gone out for what had become a quarterly dinner on the town. Wives were invited, and this time he didn't want to sit alone at the table. He had taken Elaine, and he didn't regret it. Having her beside him made him feel normal again, less lonely. He introduced her the same way to everyone, "This is my friend Elaine. She and Elizabeth did volunteer work together for years."

There was no hand holding or flirtatiousness between them. What he told people was the truth. She was his friend, nothing more. But as such, she was a wonderful companion, adding her thoughtful and sometimes humorous comments at just the right moments in the conversation. The other doctors and their wives had been kind to her, accepting her into a circle where once Elizabeth had fit so well.

Only when he was in his kitchen, when he'd set his keys and his wallet down, did John pull his cell phone from his pocket. He had three missed calls from Ashley and one phone message.

He moved to the living room, sank into his recliner — the one that faced the fireplace and the mantel where the framed graduation photos of five of his kids stared back at him. He kicked the footrest out and crossed his feet. Once he was comfortable, he tapped his code into the phone, put it to his ear, and listened as Ashley's voice filled the line.

"Dad . . . it's me." There was a pause, but her tone told him this wasn't merely another call, not just Ashley fishing for facts about her older brother. "I have a question about our older brother. I found out something today, and I think . . . maybe I know who he is. Maybe not, but maybe." Another pause. "Call me, Dad. Please."

Slowly, John pressed the footrest back into the base of the chair and sat up straighter. Ashley found out something? His heart kicked into a double rhythm. What could she have possibly found out? Unless Dayne had talked to her, how could she know who her older brother was?

He looked at the house phone on the table beside him. The message light was blinking, and this time trepidation made him move faster than before.

Again Ashley's voice sounded in the speaker. "Dad, where are you? I need to talk to you about our brother. Please, Dad . . . call me."

He swallowed hard. Whatever her question, it was serious. If she knew about Dayne, then it was only a matter of time before the others knew also. Which meant change was coming. Either the finality of Dayne's decision to walk away from them or the glare of scrutiny from the paparazzi. He set his cell down next to the home phone and eased back against the headrest. He had no idea what to tell Ashley. He'd have to deal with her in the morning.

Heaviness settled in his chest as he stared at his kids' graduation photographs. The frames had always been there, the picture inside each frame updated by Elizabeth every year until graduation. Countless nights when the kids were growing up, he'd find his way to this spot, this chair, the place where he could look at their faces and pray for them — sometimes one more than the others. More times than John could remember, he'd wake up at one or two in the morning, pad down the stairs, and settle into his chair. Sometimes Elizabeth would find him, and she'd know. One of the kids was on his heart.

He'd sat here praying for Kari when her close friend Ryan, the man who was now her husband, suffered what could've been a life-threatening spinal injury. He'd prayed for Ashley from this chair, monthly, weekly through practically a decade, when she seemed to have lost her way. And after 9-11 he'd prayed for Luke in this spot. Night after night some weeks, begging God for his return to the family.

Always God brought everything together. Not without pain or process, not without consequences and repercussions. But even through great trials and tragedies, they'd survived. The Baxter family. Closer than ever before. Closer to God and closer to each other.

So what about this? If Ashley had found out the truth — that Dayne was their brother — then what would come next? Was he supposed to go against Dayne's wishes and let the others know? Should he call

Dayne and tell him that Ashley might have figured it out?

For a moment, John's tension eased and a slight chuckle echoed in the silent room. Of course Ashley would figure it out. Who else? And what did that mean? That somehow she'd overheard a conversation between him and Dayne? Or that someone had told her? He studied the faces on the mantel. Wouldn't they be fine if they knew the truth, if they had to watch their steps and avoid the press? Photographers might come around for a while, but they'd back off in time, wouldn't they?

Besides, maybe Dayne could make contact with them, and no one would ever find out. It was possible, wasn't it? Dayne had never gone public with the fact that he was adopted, so maybe the press would merely think he'd connected with the Baxter family because of his time in Bloomington. Nice people he'd met at the park or some other such thing.

Either way, the situation was reaching a boiling point. Dayne was their oldest child, and he had no parents, no family. Yes, he was a man in his own right, and he'd be fine without family. But how much better off would he be with them? How much happier and better connected? How much fuller would his life be?

Family was what living was all about, wasn't it? God created families so people would have a place of connection, a haven of rest, a group who would accept and love one another no matter what.

A Scripture flashed in John's mind. Jesus reminding His followers that He had not come to bring peace, not in every situation. Rather, His teachings would in some cases cause divisions between parents and children, brothers and sisters, and even extended family members. John could think of a dozen quick examples where people he knew — because of various issues — were either shunned by their families or busy shunning family members.

He exhaled and tried to rope in his emotions. Maybe that was the hardest part of all. The Baxters weren't that kind of family. They were the kind of family people longed to have, the kind where the members were allowed to mess up or make mistakes, and still the net of love and faith and forgiveness remained intact. The kind of family that would make Dayne's life stronger, richer in every way — no matter what sort of worldly wealth he'd acquired.

God, it was Elizabeth's dream, her hope, that we'd find our first-born and that he might at least know what the Baxter family was all about. You brought about a miracle in letting us find him, especially for Elizabeth. And here we are . . . so close to having him be part of our family. I guess I just don't want to blow it. I don't want Dayne to run and close us out of his life — all so we'll be safe from an enemy that might not even exist. Please, Lord . . . give me wisdom. This battle isn't one I can fight on my own.

And then John heard the answer. *Son, this battle is not yours but God's. Stand firm and see the deliverance the Lord will give you.*

Chills ran down John's spine and his arms. He had barely finished praying when God's words resounded in his heart. How long had it been since he'd thought of those words? He'd relied on these verses as a young man; they had helped him through years of uncertainty. The passage was from chapter 20 of 2 Chronicles, a section about God helping people in times of battle. John had used it when he felt defeated about Elizabeth's first pregnancy, later when he was discouraged and ready to quit med school, and again in their early years of parenting when finding a plan and sticking to it felt all but impossible.

The battle belongs to the Lord. John would tell himself that over and over back then, but he hadn't thought much about the verses in years. And now, just when he needed them, God breathed the words into his soul.

He looked at the cell phone. Elaine would know what to do. They'd shared just about every stage of his search for Dayne, and now he could share this as well. Her number was programmed on speed dial now. He pushed a few buttons, and her phone began to ring.

She answered just when he thought she'd already gone to sleep. "Hello?"

"Elaine, it's me." He sighed. "You still awake?"

She laughed, and the sound eased his loneliness. "Silly . . . you know me. I'm never in bed before eleven."

"I know." He felt himself relax. This was what he needed. A friend, someone to talk to, the friend who at this time in his life knew him better than anyone else except his kids. "So I get a call from Ashley on both phones, home and the cell. She wants to talk, thinks she's found out the identity of her brother."

Elaine's hushed gasp sounded over the phone. "Who would've told her?"

"This is Ashley we're talking about." John looked at the photo of his middle daughter. She had been beautiful even back then —

during her awkward flower-child stage. But she'd always been a challenge. "She finds a way, Elaine. If she thinks she's found out who he is, then she probably has."

"Okay." Elaine's tone became more thoughtful. "I guess that means it's time."

"Time?" He was getting used to the way Elaine communicated. She wasn't nearly as talkative as Elizabeth, but what she said was almost always profound. "To tell them, you mean?"

"Yes." He could almost hear her gentle smile through the phone line. "I've been praying that God would show you. Between you and Dayne, it feels like the truth might never get out. He's afraid, and I understand that. But if Ashley knows the truth . . ."

"It's time for the others to know too?"

"Yes, John. I think so."

He squeezed his eyes shut and tried to imagine Dayne, the life he was living and the insanity of his being chased by cameramen everywhere he went. "What if Dayne's right? What if the paparazzi latch on to us and never let go? We could . . . we could lose what we're about, Elaine."

That was the hardest part, the part that made him almost agree with Dayne at times. If his other kids were so affected by the change that it altered their lifestyles, altered their family dynamic, then it would probably be better for them never to know Dayne at all. Something that could threaten his family, the way they lived? His heart skipped a beat at the thought.

Elaine took her time answering, and when she did, her voice was serene with a practiced peace that marked who she was at the very core, the faith that meant so much to her. "Nothing could make the Baxters stop being the Baxters. Not even if the whole world gets a front-row seat for a season."

There it was. The reason he'd called her. She had a way of setting his world back on its axis, even when it was tilting wildly to one side. Her words echoed in his mind. *"Not even if the whole world gets a front-row seat for a season."* He smiled and opened his eyes. "Elaine . . . I'm glad you're in my life. Have I told you that?"

"Yes, John." A knowing slipped in as she paused. "I'm glad you're in my life too."

Not until the call ended did John wonder if maybe he'd given her the wrong impression. He cared about her, yes. They spent more time together every week, it seemed. A trip to the farmers' market, a dinner out at their favorite Mexican restaurant, a visit on his porch swing. But the idea of anything more than friendship still felt terribly wrong, a betrayal to everything he knew to be good and right with Elizabeth, a stab at her memory. He was grateful for Elaine, but he had to be careful with her heart. With both their hearts. She'd been without her husband for more than a decade, and maybe she was more willing to move forward, to consider him more than a friend.

He chided himself as he set the phone down on the table beside his chair. The situation between them needed to be handled carefully because he truly enjoyed Elaine. Maybe more than he wanted to admit. But there was no way she could ever replace his Elizabeth.

A breeze blew in through the open window and rustled the sheers, the ones Elizabeth had hung just after Cole was born. It was the sort of night in early summer when he and Elizabeth would've taken a walk around their property, checking on her rose garden and what perimeter areas needed weeding or fertilizing or pruning. The sort of night when he could almost hear her in the next room or feel her sitting beside him.

John stood and stretched. She would've found a way to talk Dayne into meeting all of them by now. That was the way Elizabeth had with people, especially her kids. She could make every problem feel small and inconsequential, and she would convince Dayne that nothing would be better for him — for all of them — than to be a family.

Finally.

He wandered up to their bedroom and closed the door behind him. Something about the night made him long for her more than he had in months. If there were a door or a window into heaven, some way to spend an hour with her, he would've found it. Just an hour.

He looked toward his closet. The letters were still there, the ones that had caused such strife between Ashley and him. Elizabeth would be gone two years next month and still he hadn't gone through them, read each one, and made copies of the letters his kids might want. He moved in that direction and avoided looking at the mirrored closet doors.

When Elizabeth was alive, this was the time of night when sometimes he'd look at the mirrored doors and steal a glance at her, admiring the way she brushed her hair or the funny way she wrinkled her nose when she brushed her teeth. Checking the mirror was as good as checking for her, because she was a part of what made up their bedroom. Without her . . . well, it was only a place to sleep each night and get dressed each morning. So now he avoided the mirrored doors. The emptiness was easier that way.

He slipped into the closet and pulled down the box of letters. So many letters from many different periods of her life. That was just one way she'd been different from Elaine. Elizabeth's letters were long and beautifully written. Pages of thoughts and prose and illustrations to the people she loved. If Elaine put pen to paper, she'd wind up with a postcard. A priceless, important postcard.

But still . . .

He sifted through them, and the movement stirred up a familiar smell. Partly the smell of old paper, of treasured letters from years gone by. But partly the smell of Elizabeth's perfume. When she was sent off to have Dayne, she wrote him letters often, and she always did what was common back then — she spritzed the paper with her perfume. Chanel — the same one she wore until the day she died.

The smell fell in around him now like a fine mist, filling his senses and taking him back. As deeply as he could, he inhaled, letting his very being fill with her smell, her words, her memory. *God . . . I miss her. Tell her I miss her.*

There were no words this time. He exhaled and pulled a letter from the mix, a random letter. Then he set the box on the floor. Careful not to damage the envelope, he lifted the flap and removed the letter. The text was shorter than most, only half a page. Based on the date, she'd written this one when she was suffering with her first bout of breast cancer. John steeled himself.

Elizabeth was gone; there was no point in trying to re-create her presence. But even so, he couldn't keep his eyes from running down the page.

Dear John,

I'm not feeling well, but I had some things to tell you. Since you're at work, I thought I'd just write it out. First I want to thank you. I haven't been much good around the house with this little thing I'm fighting. I want you to know I couldn't do it without you. Sure, the kids help when they can, but they're running in and out, off to college and visiting with friends.

The only stability in my life right now is you and God.

And I thank Him for both.

You're an amazing provider, John. So good with the kids and with me, and you never complain about the extra work all this sick stuff has caused you. I'm blessed beyond anything I could ever imagine because I have you.

John blinked back tears, amazed at his wife's wisdom. So many young women struggled with a gift that came naturally to Elizabeth, the gift of building up her husband. She was forever complimenting him, telling him why she was grateful for him, how much she appreciated him. Even for the little things. In turn, he wanted to spend his life pleasing her. Many times he'd heard Elizabeth telling their daughters how important it was to encourage their men.

Now, though, it was only one more layer of loss, one more reason to miss her. A tear fell onto John's cheek, and he steadied his hand. He waited until he could see the words, and then he found his place.

The other thing, John, is thanks for making family such a priority in our lives. If something ever happened to me — and it won't — I have no doubt in my mind that you'd keep the family together, strong and alive and close, the way they are now. You'd make sure they shared Christmas and Easter and

Thanksgiving and birthdays — even if the only way to share them was over the phone. You'd keep up our annual Fourth of July and Labor Day traditions, hauling ice chests and folding chairs and blankets and food down to the shore of Lake Monroe.

Family is everything to me. So you see, I couldn't have married a better man because family is everything to you too. That's why I'm not afraid, no matter what happens. I'm going to beat this cancer. But none of us know the day or hour, and so thanks for being a family man. You define the term, my love.

With all I am,
Elizabeth

John's heart beat hard in his chest. The words from Elaine earlier tonight were wonderful, helpful. But this was nothing short of a miracle, a direct answer to the prayer he'd whispered. The one about the battle. He'd asked for wisdom, and here it was as right and true and beautiful as the words Elizabeth had scribbled so long ago.

She was right. He was a family man, and as such there was nothing he could do now but keep pushing until their family was together. Their entire family.

He held the letter to his chest and then to his cheek. There it was again, the faint smell of her. Once more he read the words, and this time he smiled, even through his tears. *Thank You, God . . . for letting me pick that letter.*

He leaned down and stuck it along one of the sides of the box, so it'd be easier to find if he needed to hear her words of encouragement again sometime. Or if he actually got around to copying a few letters for the kids. Then he lifted the box and put it back on the top shelf. Her memory was as close as this box, as near as the smell of perfume on her letters.

As he brushed his teeth, he made a plan for the next day. He would call Ashley in the morning and hear what she had to say. Maybe she was way off base, and in that case he wouldn't tell her anything. Not until Dayne was ready. But if she'd figured it out, if somehow she'd found out the truth, then he would let her know that she was right.

Then they'd make a decision about the others and how to tell them. Dayne would have to know, of course. And somehow they would all survive — just like every time before. The Bible verse ran through his mind again as he climbed into bed. *"You will not have to fight this battle. . . . Stand firm and see the deliverance the Lord will give you."*

Okay, so his older son was a Hollywood movie star. He was photographed hundreds, sometimes thousands, of times every day. Still there had to be a way to build bridges between him and the rest of the Baxters. In the meantime, John would do as the Bible said. He would stand firm, holding tight to what he knew to be true and right — love, joy, peace, patience, kindness, goodness, faithfulness, gentleness, and self-control. The fruits of living a life connected to God.

And when it came time to battle — whether the media or the mind-sets of his children — God would take care of the rest.

CHAPTER
TWENTY-THREE

Ashley woke three times during the night, and each time she reached for the phone to call her dad. He had to be home by now, she told herself. Then she would look at the alarm clock by her bed, and common sense would interrupt her half-asleep state. "Not yet," she'd whisper. "Wait till morning."

She was restless until dawn, flipping from one side to the other and prompting Landon, sometime around three in the morning, to flip on the light above their bed and study her through tired, squinty eyes. "Everything okay?"

What could she say? She'd already told Landon her suspicion about Dayne Matthews. Clearly the possibility wasn't keeping *him* awake. She patted his hand and kissed his cheek. "Sorry, honey. Go back to sleep."

Morning finally came, and she called her dad's house. Again it only rang. Maybe he was in the shower. But her frustration hit new levels as she hung up the phone. She needed to call Dayne; there was no other choice. Her father wouldn't mind. She thought about making the call and what she would say and how he might react all throughout Cole's breakfast and Devin's half hour of nursing.

Her question for Dayne was on her mind as she saw Cole off to his friend's house and laid Devin down for his first nap. Landon was up by then, even though he had an afternoon shift at the fire station. They sat down to a breakfast of scrambled eggs and wheat toast.

Suddenly Ashley couldn't last another minute. "I have to call him." She planted her elbows on the table and gave Landon her best pleading look. "I called my dad this morning." She held up her empty hands. "Still no answer."

"I hope he's okay." Landon looked unfazed by her question. "That's not like your dad."

Ashley blinked. "He's a doctor. He's had whole weeks where I can't get in touch with him."

"Still . . . wouldn't he normally call you back?"

"Yes, but . . ." She huffed. "That's not the point, honey. I think I should call Dayne."

She evened out her tone, making every attempt to sound rational. "I've thought about it all night, and I don't think my dad would mind." Without waiting for Landon's response, she rushed on. "Our brother's the holdout here, right? I mean, he's the one hesitant about making a connection. So I call Dayne. I tell him that I heard from Jenny Flanigan that he was adopted, that his birth parents live in Bloomington." She shrugged. "I ask him if he's my brother, and that's it. End of story."

Landon caught her hand with one of his and lowered it to the table. "Hardly end of story. What if he says yes?"

The thought brought a surge of hope. "Then we catch up on lost time, and we give my dad the best gift of all."

"And you don't think your dad would be upset?" He sounded hesitant.

"No." She was trying to convince herself, and it was working. "He's obviously at a standstill with the guy, whoever he is. If it's Dayne, then my calling him will make everything work out."

Landon ate a few more bites, thoughtful. "Hmm." The corners of his lips raised just barely. "You know . . . you might be right."

"I think I am." Ashley grinned at him, but her smile faded almost as soon as it began.

"I think I'll go for a drive, clear my head before I call him. You don't work until two, right?"

"Right." He patted her hand and returned to his breakfast. "Do what you think is best, Ash. I'll be here for you."

Twenty minutes later she was in her van. At first she thought maybe she'd make the call from the beach at Lake Monroe, the place where their older brother had missed so many family gatherings. But then, almost as if the van had a mind of its own, she did a U-turn and headed west toward the old two-lane highway, the route that would lead her to the cemetery.

She was making this call in honor of her mother, because of how much having her family together meant to her. She'd wanted to find Dayne with every dying breath, and in the end she'd found him. But she hadn't lived long enough to see him connect with the rest of the Baxters.

The cemetery was cool this morning, the dew still damp on the grass. Overhead, a layer of high fog hung a curtain of gray over Bloomington. Ashley wore tennis shoes, shorts, and a sweatshirt over her tank top. The sun was supposed to come out later in the day, and the afternoon would likely be hot and humid. But for now, even the air around her seemed to hold its breath in anticipation of whatever the phone call would bring.

For a minute, she stood at the entrance to the grassy field, staring at the sea of tombstones. How could her mother be gone when they all needed her so much? Ashley took a slow breath and moved quietly to the place where her mother was buried. A small bench sat just to the side of the stone, a memorial from the doctors at the hospital, her father's friends.

Ashley crouched down near the stone and touched it lightly on the side. "Devin's doing so well, Mom. He's beautiful." Her throat hurt, and with her free hand she massaged it with the tips of her fingers. "I needed a quiet place to make this call."

She hung her head. What was she doing, sitting in a cemetery talking to a stone? Only a few years ago her mother was alive and vibrant. If she were still here she'd know what to do. The situation with their older brother wasn't her father's fault. He was busy at work, and he wanted to be careful with how the matter developed.

But Mom . . . Mom would've found a way by now.

Ashley traced over the letters on the marker. *Elizabeth Baxter . . . devoted wife and mother.* There was so much more to say. Ashley ran her knuckles beneath her eyes and straightened. She needed to make the call. The bench was the perfect spot, so she moved to it and sat down. She pulled her cell from her purse and stared at it. *Okay, God . . . if this is it, if he's our brother, let me know.*

The cemetery seemed to grow utterly still, and even the trees were motionless. She flipped open her cell, called up his number, and hit the Send button. It would be eight in the morning in LA, not too early. One ring . . . she rubbed her damp palm on her bare knee. Two rings. *Please, God, give me the words. Let me know if it's him.*

Just before the third ring, someone answered the phone. There was commotion in the background, but she could make out the voice anyway. "Hello?"

She could feel her heartbeat in her head and neck and hands. Throughout her body. "Hi." Her throat was dry. She ran her tongue along the inside of her lips. "Dayne?"

"Yes?" He hesitated. "Is this Ashley?"

"It is." She couldn't breathe, couldn't think. He must've seen her area code on his phone. She closed her eyes and leaned over her legs. "Hey, Dayne, do you have a minute?"

"Of course." He sounded a little winded, like maybe he was walking as he talked. "We're filming, but it's a break. We started before sunup. Let me get to a quieter place." After several seconds, the background noise faded. "That's better. What's on your mind, Ashley? Everything okay with Katy?"

"She's fine. I mean, she misses you. . . . She's trying to figure it out." Ashley's nerves were so tight they hurt her stomach. "That's not why I called."

"Oh." It was just one word, but in it she heard something change in his voice. "Okay, so what's up?"

"I have a question for you." She gulped. Could he hear her pounding heart over the phone? She opened her mouth to explain, to tell the story of how she went to pick up Katy, but Katy wasn't ready and how Jenny Flanigan had wondered why Dayne wasn't at opening night for *Narnia* and how she'd spilled the truth that Dayne was adopted and how his birth parents lived in Bloomington.

But all that came out was, "Are you my brother?"

His hesitation told her the answer long before he found his words. He cleared his throat, and she heard a low moan come from him. Finally, he exhaled and with it came his response. "Yes. I'm your brother. Did your dad tell you?"

She jumped to her feet, moving in small circles around the grass a few feet from her mother's tombstone. "You really are? You're our brother?" Tears choked her voice and blurred her vision. She'd found him; she truly had. And now all the pieces fit into place. "So that's why . . . that's why you look like Luke."

Dayne chuckled. "Actually, he looks like me, right? Since I came first?"

Ashley dropped slowly back onto the bench as the tears spilled from her eyes. He wasn't mad at her. Whatever came next, he wasn't mad; he was laughing. And the sound of it sent a shot of joy straight to her heart. "I guess." She made a sound, but she wasn't sure if it was more laugh or cry. "Dayne, I can't believe I found you." She took a fast breath and launched into the story, how she'd figured it out. Five minutes later she came up for air. "Does that make sense?"

"It does." He laughed again, and then the sound of it faded. "I wanted to call. Every day I've thought about it." He sounded tired, beat up. "But there's so much at stake. I'm not sure what to do. It's draining me." He hesitated for what felt like a long time.

"Last time Katy was here we were nearly killed running from the paparazzi. I don't want that for you and Brooke, for Kari and Erin and Luke." His words sounded pinched, like he was speaking them through clenched teeth. "And I'm worried about the calls between me and . . . and your dad."

Ashley noticed every word, every nuance. Another wave of elation hit her as she realized something she hadn't really believed before. He knew all their names! He really did care, and he'd probably made a point of knowing not only their names but as many details about their lives as he could know. That's what her father had told her, but she'd always wondered. If he knew so much and cared so much — why not make contact? Now, like every other aspect of the situation, even that question was being answered.

But she also heard his frustration in the area that had kept them apart this long — the public's fascination with and scrutiny of celebrities. And something else, something she couldn't quite figure out. She crossed her ankles and looked up at the branches of a walnut tree not far away. "I guess that's partly why I'm calling. To convince you that none of us cares about all that, Dayne."

His tone lightened. "Your dad says you're

the determined one."

Ashley smiled. "Sort of."

"Do the others know I'm their brother? Have you told them?"

"No." Her answer was quick. "I wanted to talk to you first, to convince you."

He made a sound that expressed his frustration. "It's more complicated than you think, Ashley. The paparazzi — some of them — know I'm adopted. I guess they must've gotten a tip — maybe from the investigator I hired or from my previous agent. They ran records and figured it out. I got a call from *Celebrity Life* magazine the other day. I haven't even told your dad."

"Celebrity Life?" Ashley felt the blood leave her face. Suddenly she imagined her picture in a national magazine, a story with details about her out-of-wedlock pregnancy and all the other private matters that belonged exclusively to the Baxters. Her voice fell. "So . . . they know about us?"

"They're looking." Dayne inhaled sharply. "They asked me to do an interview, talk about my adoption and my search for my birth parents."

"And you said . . ."

"I told them no thanks. I was busy filming a movie." His words were laced with pain, as if it hurt even to speak them. "They told me they were already aware that I'd found my birth family in Bloomington. They thought it would make an interesting story, so they were hiring a private investigator to find the answers. With or without my help."

"Ugh." Ashley dug her elbows into her knees. "How'd they find out?"

"I hid it for a long time, but you can't be in this business without enemies. I fired my last agent — he could've leaked it. Just to appear important. I may never know." Resignation made his tone lifeless. "That's what I tried to tell your dad. If there's a secret, they'll find out."

"And your coming to Bloomington would've made a tip from your old agent seem plausible?"

"Maybe." He grew pensive sounding. "Maybe it's coincidence, or maybe it's all part of God's plan. Sometimes I can't tell one from the other."

Ashley's mind raced. "Okay, but if someone's onto the story, then does it really matter? We might as well meet, right?"

"Or maybe the other way around. Maybe since they're onto the story, I'd be better off to distance myself. That way they're less likely to go public with your names and identities. There are laws protecting private citizens from their type of scrutiny. But once you connect yourselves to me, you'll be placing yourselves in the public eye. Willingly." His tone faded. "Anything's possible then."

Ashley thought about Katy, about the accident he'd referred to. "What about Katy? Have you talked to her?"

"Not lately." Emotion layered his words. "I keep telling myself if I love her . . . if I really love her, then it's my duty to let her go. She doesn't want this . . . this crazy life I lead."

For the first time since the call had gone through, Ashley felt anger join in the mix of feelings tugging at her heart. "Katy's crazy about you, Dayne. You can't let strangers determine how you'll care for a person. She's miserable without you."

"I don't know." Dayne's sigh sounded like a huge weight was on his shoulders. "I have a lot of thinking to do."

She felt him close the door on the subject, so she moved on. "Katy tells me you've gotten back to God."

"I have. I feel Him in everything I'm doing these days." His voice lightened again. "That's why I wonder about the magazine article. Maybe it is God's plan, His way of letting me know there's no way to avoid the publicity. Like you said, I might as well get to know my brother and sisters."

"And your nieces and nephews." New tears nipped at the corners of her eyes. "There won't be a Baxter gathering from here on out where you're not missed." She struggled to maintain her voice. "All of us know we have an older brother." An idea hit her. "They give you a break for Fourth of July, right?"

"Usually. A long weekend at least." He hesitated. "Why?"

"We have a family picnic every year." Ashley closed her eyes. *God . . . don't let him be scared off.* "You should come."

"Hmm." He was silent for a while. "What was it like? Growing up in the Baxter family?"

His question released a flood of emotion in her. The guy on the other end of the phone was the baby her mother had held, the son she had never wanted to give up. He was the big brother who had never been given the chance to give her a ride to school or scrutinize her boyfriends, the one they'd never had at the dinner table or at Christmas morning, the one whose graduation and milestones had been missed.

All because her grandparents had refused to let her mother keep him.

"Dayne . . ." Ashley's chin quivered, and

she opened her eyes. A hole in the clouds had opened, and through it she could see the blue sky beyond. That's what this was. A hole in the clouds that had kept Dayne from knowing them all these years. A hole that she prayed Dayne would climb through before things changed and the chance disappeared forever. She swallowed a sob, but when she spoke her voice was strained. "It was . . . wonderful. Mom and Dad, they're the best people I know. The best parents."

"I figured." She couldn't tell if Dayne was moved, but his tone spoke volumes. "My parents were nice too. They've been dead a long time."

Ashley's cheeks were wet. She brushed her hand across them and wiped her tears on her legs. "I'm sorry." This was the part she knew nothing about. "Tell me about them."

"They were missionaries. I grew up in a boarding school in Indonesia." He let loose a soft chuckle. "Until recently I hated them for it. Thought they chose God over me."

A boarding school? "Oh, Dayne . . ." He'd grown up in a boarding school and missed out on the Baxters? "I'm sorry."

"Yeah. I get it better now." His voice told her he was pulling back, distancing himself. "Hey, Ashley, I have to go." The background commotion level rose a little. "Break's over."

She looked at her mother's tombstone. "I'm glad you met her."

Dayne hesitated but only for a moment. "Our . . . Elizabeth?"

"Yes." She stood and moved closer to the marker. "She wanted to know you more than anything."

"Me too."

Panic swirled in Ashley's veins. He was going to hang up, and the moment would be over. She needed permission to move ahead, to tell the others. "Please, Dayne . . . can I tell Kari and Brooke and Erin and Luke about you? Can they . . . I don't know, can they call you? Maybe introduce themselves that way?"

"I'm not sure. I've missed so much. Maybe it's better if I just move on. That way no one'll get hurt by my crazy life."

She wanted to reach through the phone line and hug him. "No matter what happened on the pathway to this moment, you're part of our family, Dayne. Please . . . let us have a place in your life. Join us on the Fourth." She blinked the wetness from her eyes. "Come just once. Then you'll see."

"I want to." He waited, and when he spoke again there was agony in his voice. "You have no idea how much I want to."

A carload of people was entering the

cemetery, their voices breaking the serenity of the moment. Ashley concentrated on the conversation. She didn't want to push him, but she had to make him understand how important this was — to her, to her siblings, to her father. She stared at the marker. How important it was to their mother. She held her breath. "So . . . will you come?"

"I'll get back to you, okay?" The background noise grew louder. "I need time."

"Okay. Thanks, Dayne. I'm glad . . . I'm glad I called."

"Me too."

As they hung up, Ashley returned to the bench. Not once during the call had she remembered exactly who she was talking to. Dayne Matthews. *The* Dayne Matthews. She hadn't remembered because his fame, his celebrity, his public persona no longer mattered. Dayne Matthews might've looked like he had it all. Huge blockbuster films, the most recognizable face in Hollywood, and the millions of dollars that must've come with that.

His adoptive parents had been loving people, no doubt. But Dayne had been lonely as a child, and now, from what the tone of his voice told her, he was even lonelier as an adult. Ashley tried to picture him, hiring the private investigator and figuring out not only that his birth parents were still together but that they'd raised an entire family. That he had full-blooded siblings he'd lost a lifetime with.

Ashley felt the sadness of it heavy in her soul. She stood and looked one last time at her mother's tombstone. She wouldn't give up on Dayne Matthews. Her mother would've spent another ten years trying to help him find a place in their family. Ashley took a few steps back. If that's what it took, she would do the same.

As she turned around, as she made her way through the cemetery to the parking lot, she did something she'd never knowingly done before. She prayed for Dayne Matthews — Hollywood movie star, America's heartthrob, her parents' firstborn son.

Her brother.

CHAPTER
TWENTY-FOUR

Streaky pinks and pale blues lined the Los Angeles sky in the waning twilight that Thursday of the following week. Dressed in rugged hiking boots, khaki shorts, and a white T-shirt, Dayne climbed a few steps, then anchored himself on the narrow dirt path that wound its way up from the San Fernando Valley floor along the craggy edges of the Santa Monica Mountains.

He wiped a fine layer of sweat and trail dust off his forehead. "Ellie —" he held out his hand to the pretty blonde a few steps behind him — "I can't do this."

She was dressed much like him, the boots and shorts and T-shirt. But she wore a straw hat and carried a backpack. "I know." Her eyes grew teary, and she hesitated. Tentatively, she slid her fingers between his, and together they stared at the panoramic view. Her voice was faint, heavy with sorrow. "Me either."

Dayne searched the valley floor below him, the city spread out like a vibrant tapestry, alive and in motion, a sharp contrast to the quiet of the mountains. He gritted his teeth. "The pretending is killing me." He turned to her, and slowly — with the subtleness of the whistling evening breeze through the canyon — he drew her close against his chest.

He searched her eyes, and his breathing grew faster. "When all I want to do is . . ." The air between them changed, and he lost sight of everything but her eyes.

"But . . ." She eased one hand around his waist, the other up alongside his face. Her tone held a hint of panic, the sense that no matter what she said she was too far gone to stop herself. "It's impossible . . . you're in love with her. Everyone thinks so."

"No, Ellie." He put his hands on her shoulders, then moved one to the small of her back. He brought his lips to hers and kissed her, the sort of kiss that was intended to unlock the door to her heart. He pulled back just enough to get lost in her eyes once more. "I'm in love with you."

A small cry came from her, but it was a cry of passion and longing and fading resolve.

Before she could speak, he kissed her

again. This time the kiss was long and involved, the passion between them building and growing until, from fifty yards below, from the place where the road met the trailhead, there came the sudden piercing sound of squealing tires.

The noise made them jerk apart. Dayne stared, lips parted, down the trail. "What in the — ?"

"It's her." Ellie took three steps back, her chest heaving. "Where can we go?"

A booming voice came from a few feet behind them. "Cut! Got it!" The director clapped. "That was perfect! Beautiful!" He stomped down the hillside to a spot between Dayne and Randi Wells. He patted both their backs at the same time, his entire face taken up with a grin. "The lighting, the passion, the kiss. People are going to talk about that scene for years."

Dayne's cheeks felt hot. There was a time when doing scenes like this one meant nothing to him. Another day at the office. But now he had to wonder. What would his missionary friend Bob Asher think about the love scenes he had to perform in this movie? No, there was nothing over the top. Nothing on a bed or in a shower. But still . . .

"Ah, really?" Randi gave the director a mock disappointed look. "You mean we don't get to do another ten takes?" She brushed her knuckles against Dayne's cheek. "I was sorta hoping one of us would mess up."

"I like your attitude, Randi." The director winked at her. "Don't worry. We have lots more of this still to come." He shook his head. "I mean, the two of you are red-hot together." He gave Dayne another pat as he walked off. "It's working, folks," he announced to the twenty-plus cameramen and crew gathered around the hillside. His voice was more cheerful than it had been since filming began. He rubbed his palms together as he headed back to his assistant. "We've got ourselves a hit here. I can feel it."

When he was out of earshot, Randi closed the distance between them. She lowered her chin and looked up, giving Dayne the flirty, cutesy look America loved. "You know what?"

He crossed his arms, protecting his space, and found a brotherly smile for her. Randi was easy to work with. She wasn't seductive like other actresses. They'd been filming for several days now, and so far she'd respected his wishes about keeping things on a friendship basis. But still she could be blunt. He had a feeling this was one of those times. "What?"

She tilted her head, her gaze as direct as it had been a minute earlier when the cameras were rolling. "You're still the best kisser in Hollywood, Dayne." She gave his cheek a light pinch. "With or without your Bible." She shrugged. "Makes my job easy."

Before he could respond, she flashed him a grin, turned, and headed toward the director. Her spunky walk and the way she flipped her hair showed all the attitude she was famous for.

He watched her go, then faced the valley floor again. The compliment settled like wet cement in his gut. The old Dayne would've felt smug about the reputation, glad that an A-list actress thought of him that way. Instead he felt dirty and cheap, unable to find the real thing and left only to act out love on the silver screen.

The director stood a little higher on the hill and waved for everyone's attention. "Listen, we have one more scene to shoot before the sun sets. Let's get moving, people. Places!" He motioned to a few of the assistants, and they immediately sprang into action. "Let's go. Let's get it done."

The next hour passed quickly, and just about everything met the director's high standards on only a handful of takes. "Amazing." He took his glasses off and waved them at the group. "You people are amazing."

It was a zone, Dayne figured. One of those times when everything about his acting culminated in a mix of professionalism and intensity. He understood why it was happening this way. He had to put his energy somewhere after all.

His intensity came from his bottled-up feelings. He longed for Katy Hart, and there was nothing he could do about it. As long as he kept making films — and he was obligated to do so — his fame would increase, and the things about his life that made their relationship impossible would only get worse.

And that wasn't all. The phone conversation with Ashley Baxter Blake was on his mind also — every day, every hour. A week had passed since they talked, and still he was no closer to a decision. Fourth of July in Bloomington sounded better than the Bahamas, but what would be the point? With the paparazzi already sniffing out information about his adoption, he'd only be giving them license to delve into the Baxters' lives.

He walked to the food table and downed a paper cup full of water.

"Hey." Randi came up alongside him and

did the same. Her eyes held a teasing look as she jabbed him in the ribs with her elbow. "Don't hold the kissing comment against me, okay?" She gave him a side hug and leaned her head on his shoulder. "It's meant the world being around you these last two weeks." Sincerity replaced the flirtatiousness in her expression. "I mean it."

"Thanks." He returned the hug and moved to get more water. "No harm taken."

"Good." She sipped her water and gave him a side glance. "Heard from Miss Indiana lately?"

"No." He wadded his cup into a ball and tossed it in a nearby trash can. Missing her was almost a physical hurt. "We have a lot to figure out."

Randi nodded, thoughtful. She gestured toward the camera crew and the handful of tabloid photographers that had been granted permission to attend the shoot. "All this, you mean?"

His short laugh was almost bitter. "Yeah. She struggles with it."

"We all do." Randi leaned against the table. "The tabloids drove the first wedges between my husband and me, and they'll keep driving until we wave the white flag and announce our divorce. It's like they're driving all of us wherever they want to take us." She tilted her face, and the wind played in her hair. "We're just along for the ride."

Before Dayne could respond, the director broke free from a group of crew members and came to them. "Good news." He had a pencil behind his ear, his trademark. "We'll be shooting some technical shots, working on some of the background stuff for the next few days." He grinned. "The two of you are off until Tuesday."

"Bummer." She elbowed Dayne again and grinned at him. "I was looking forward to another day of on-screen kisses."

"You're a bad girl, Randi." The director waved a finger at her, his eyes dancing. "That's why I love working with you." He winked at Dayne. "Maybe you two can get together and practice."

"Exactly." Randi raised her eyebrows at Dayne, but the suggestive look in her eyes didn't last long. "Just kidding." She glanced at the director. "Dayne's a good boy these days." She leaned up and kissed his cheek. She seemed more sincere than she'd been all day. "Nothing wrong with that."

"Making up for lost time." Dayne kept his tone light. Randi was doing her best to understand him, his newfound faith, his lack of interest in anything intimate with her. He could cut her some slack here.

The break ended, and half an hour later they wrapped up for the evening. Dayne had driven his Escalade, wanting to avoid the caravan of trailers and studio vehicles. He took a shortcut near Calabasas and out to the Ventura Freeway and finally through Malibu Canyon.

Every mile he found himself asking the same questions. Where was Katy tonight, and what was she doing? What was she feeling? Was she making plans to move on, or was she miserable without him? The way he was without her. And what about the Baxters? He'd talked to his dad the other day, and neither of them had mentioned Dayne's conversation with Ashley. Did that mean Ashley hadn't told him? Or that the family was going to let the matter go, let Dayne keep his distance if that was really what he wanted?

He pushed a button on his dashboard, and the sunroof on his SUV slid open. A gust of fresh air filled the vehicle. He leaned back in his seat and stared at the winding road ahead of him. He knew Malibu Canyon better than any other road around Los Angeles, every straightaway and curve, every rocky outcropping where each time it rained the hillside would spill onto the pavement and close the road for a day or two. The canyon was deep and narrow, and on the other side the mountains were untouched by developers.

This stretch of roadway was one of his favorites, a great place to think, a place where paparazzi didn't bother to chase, what with the two narrow lanes and the sharp curves. Always it was a great place for sorting through and prioritizing, for thinking over life's choices.

But tonight . . . tonight Dayne had only questions. He grabbed a piece of mint gum from the console, unwrapped it, and popped it between his lips. There was no one in the canyon, so he moved faster than usual. *God . . . what are the answers? Every day I'm tempted to get on a plane and leave all this behind. So, tell me . . . if I'm supposed to let go of Katy and the Baxters, how do I convince my heart?*

He paused, wanting the gentle voice, the quiet stirring in his soul, the assurance that God would help him figure things out. At that moment his cell phone sprang to life, vibrating from where it was plugged in to the cigarette lighter. With practiced ease, he unhooked it from the cord, flipped it open, and pressed it to his ear. "Hello?"

"Dayne . . . it's Bob." The connection was clear, unusual for Malibu Canyon. "How're you doing?"

Bob Asher, his missionary friend. The one who had known him longer than anyone. The one who had led him to Christ during a street service in Mexico City a few months back. "Your timing's amazing, friend."

"Good." Bob chuckled. "I couldn't stop thinking about you. It was either call or lose a perfectly good night of sleep." His tone was relaxed. "What's going on?"

Dayne groaned. "My heart and body, man. They're living in different time zones."

"Hmm." The line remained clear, even in the heart of the canyon. "I wondered about that. I went online and saw some of the tabloids. Katy Hart, she's back in Bloomington, right?"

"Right." Dayne pressed his lips together. He came up behind a slow delivery truck and eased off the gas. "We've got four days off, and all I want to do is get on the next plane to Indiana." He made a sound that was more frustration than laugh. "But then what? All the things that have taken us in different directions would still be in place."

"True." The lightheartedness in Bob's voice faded. "I had a feeling about this, once you told me about the near accident. She doesn't want to be at the center of a tabloid spread, right?"

"No." Dayne heard anger creep into his tone. "*I* don't want her there either. It's not her."

"And the Baxters?"

Dayne was at the part of the canyon where cell calls were almost impossible, but still the connection was clear. "I've been talking to my dad, and then one of my sisters calls. She wants me to come to Bloomington on the Fourth of July. Only all I can picture is that the lives they're living will never be the same again if I do. All because of some curiosity we have about meeting each other."

For a while, Bob said nothing. When he spoke, his words were slow and measured. "It's more than a curiosity, Dayne."

"I don't know." He worked his gum a few times. "Why do you say that?"

"Because —" Bob paused — "last time we talked you called him John."

Dayne frowned. What was Bob talking about? He rounded a corner and saw the familiar straightaway ahead and Pacific Coast Highway beyond that. "What did I call him this time?"

"You called him Dad."

An awareness dawned in Dayne's heart. His friend was right. He'd been thinking that way lately. A conversation with John

Baxter would play in his head, and he'd think of him as a father, not merely a man who had a part in bringing him into the world. His throat tightened. "See?" He forced a laugh, but only so he wouldn't cry. "I'm more confused than even *I* know. More questions than answers, no matter how much I pray."

"Okay, listen." Bob exhaled hard. "Your director gave you four days off, right?"

"Right." Dayne eased his foot onto the brake and took the left turn at PCH. His house was only a mile or so south of the busy intersection.

"Matthews, you've got all the money in the world. Ditch the paparazzi and get on a plane to some beautiful remote beach. Do it tomorrow. Spend two days staring at the water and making a list."

"A list?" Dayne shifted in his seat, open to the possibility.

"Yes. A list of what matters most in your life."

"Okay." He pictured himself taking two days on a beach to think things through. The idea was sounding better with every heartbeat. "So I figure out what matters most and then what?"

There was a smile in Bob's voice. "Then you spend the rest of your life going after it."

■ ■ ■ ■

The plans came together quickly, and Dayne was still tempted to switch gates and board a plane for the Midwest, instead of one to Mexico. But he'd found a rental house south of Cancun, a luxury three-bedroom far from the touristy areas.

He pulled out one of his disguises for the travel day — a baseball cap with straggly blond hair sticking out along the back. Kelly Parker had given it to him as a prank gift, and he'd never worn it. What was the point? It would buy him only a day or two of sanity. But if he wanted to be alone, there was no time like today to wear it.

Between that, his worn backpack, brown earthy sandals, and his oversized sunglasses, he managed to maneuver Los Angeles International Airport without being recognized. He slept most of the way to Cancun and hired a taxi to take him to a grocery store and then to his rental house.

He put away his food, and the moment he stepped out onto the beach he knew. Bob Asher was right. This was where he needed to be. No cell phone, no connection to the world back in Hollywood. Just God and him and his own private stretch of paradise.

He wore a loose tank top and a pair of

shorts, and for the first evening — until sunset — he found a chair on the beach and read his Bible. Psalm 119 and the importance of God's word, His truth. Then he read Matthew chapters five through seven, the entire Sermon on the Mount. With the gentle lull of the surf in the background, he suddenly felt like he was there, watching Jesus, listening to His powerful words.

Finally he read Ecclesiastes. Again he felt himself connecting. King Solomon was one of the wisest men of his day. Maybe ever. And still he pondered the fact that wealth and success and the trappings of life were meaningless.

Dayne returned to the house, ate halibut and salad, and slept hard that night. When morning dawned — the sky the bluest ever — he woke with a purpose.

It was time to make the list.

He found his spot on the sand and set his Bible, notebook, pen, and a bottle of water on a towel beside him. For an hour he stared at the open sea. *God, bring me into Your presence, fill me with Your Holy Spirit so I can know my priorities. My career, my commitments? Or the woman I love? My visibility as an actor or a relationship with the Baxters?*

The longer he prayed, the more he felt God stirring his heart, changing his soul.

What was fame, anyway?

A string of situations paraded across his mind, aspects of being a celebrity that he didn't want to dwell on. A month ago, one of his actor buddies spent an evening with a well-known millionaire heiress. They went to a movie premiere and were just leaving, just making their way to a waiting limousine when five hooded figures ran up and threw sacks of flour at them.

Tabloid photographers — always on hand — caught the entire incident on film and ran the pictures in all the tabloids later that week. Police at the event caught the perpetrators and later announced that they were members of an activist group determined to make a statement about Hollywood's use of animal fur for coats and clothing.

The heiress hadn't been wearing anything with fur, and certainly Dayne's actor friend hadn't killed an animal for its coat. Still, they'd been the brunt of the attack. Together with Dayne's stalker incident, the truth was chilling: celebrities were always potentially in danger, the same way their friends and spouses were in danger.

It was the reason so many of his friends were hiring bodyguards. One very visible couple — neighbors of Dayne's — had two kids and another on the way. As the woman's due date neared, the couple had hired additional bodyguards. Dayne had asked the guy about it once. "Looks like you've got the Raiders' offensive line following you around."

"You know why?"

Dayne was pretty sure he did. "You don't want flour thrown in your face?"

"No." His friend's voice sounded strained. "I could take that. It's the kids I'm worried about."

"The kids?"

"We've been getting threats. From different people." The actor sighed. "Kidnappers figure we'd pay millions to get one of our kids back."

A team of bodyguards so their kids wouldn't get taken? The thought made Dayne sick. "I had no idea."

"Yeah, well, it's reality. We'll spend way over seven figures on bodyguards this year."

Reality? Dayne shuddered. Living in Malibu, working in Hollywood, having cameras forever clicking, and spending more than a million dollars to live life from inside a circle of bodyguards?

For the next several hours, through lunch and into the afternoon, Dayne thought about the life he'd been living since his first big movie. His agents and the studio, the directors he worked for — all of them would say that being a movie star was important, that it belonged somewhere high on his list of what mattered.

But then he pictured himself sitting next to Katy that long ago afternoon high in the stadium at Indiana University, golden sunlight shining in her hair. He could win an Oscar, but it wouldn't compare to the way he felt with her that day, the way he felt with her every time they were together.

Even so, he could never, ever put her life in danger because of his job.

Dayne scanned the sea and saw a pair of dolphins break through the surface, push high into the air, and dive back down. The sun was slipping behind the house, and shade covered most of the beach, making the ocean sparkle brilliantly in contrast.

Suddenly God's presence around him felt more real than the sugary white sand beneath his feet. This was what Jesus did, wasn't it? He drew away and found a quiet place to pray, to think.

Dayne grabbed the notebook, opened it, and reached for the pen. Then, as if a floodgate of common sense had been released in him, as if God Himself were moving his fingers, he began to write. Peace filled him, sharpening his thoughts and clearing his vision. The list wasn't that hard really. Here in the solitude, what mattered most was obvious. In fact, it was as clear as the blue-green Cancun waters.

As he finished his list, a deep resolve came over him, and he made a decision. He didn't need another full day alone in Cancun. The list he'd made required action and phone calls, finality and determination. In the days to come he'd need to have conversations that would change his life, no matter how difficult they might be. He stood and tucked the notebook under his arm. He'd made the list Bob had asked him to make.

Now it was time to spend the rest of his life going after it.

CHAPTER
TWENTY-FIVE

Ashley was quiet on the ride to her father's house. Landon seemed to sense her feelings, and without saying a word he covered her hand with his and gave her a concerned smile.

In the backseat, Cole was talking to baby Devin. "I'll catch extra frogs for you, Devin." His voice wasn't as singsong as it had been a year ago. Being an older brother had changed him, made him take a giant step toward growing up.

Ashley listened, filled with a combination of pride and sadness. She was awed at how well he'd taken to his new role, but watching Cole grow up would never be easy.

Devin cooed from his car seat.

"I know." Cole's tone was earnest. "I like frogs too. But wait till your legs work and you can see the fish in Papa's pond! They're amazing!"

Next to her, Landon smiled. "I love listening to him."

A soft laugh played on her lips. "Me too."

Landon turned onto her father's street. "You're quiet today."

"Yes." She narrowed her eyes and stared at the farmland that stretched on either side of the two-lane highway. "Dayne hasn't called."

"Mmm." He patted her hand. "I thought it was that."

Ashley spotted the old Baxter house. She shook her head. "He doesn't know what he's missing. We don't care if he's a movie star. Big deal. He was a Baxter long before he was a celebrity."

Landon looked like he wanted to say something, but he held back.

"What?" She kept her voice down, but she heard the cry in it. "He was a Baxter. Don't you think so?"

"In some ways." Landon drove up the driveway and parked in his usual spot. He turned off the engine and looked at her. "If you're talking bloodlines, yes, he's a Baxter." There was empathy in his eyes, empathy and a caring that came from the core of who he was. "But, honey, Dayne Matthews isn't a Baxter the way you're thinking. He's had . . . well, a completely different life from any of the rest of you."

Ashley remained quiet. She loved this about Landon, that he could see deep inside her and kindly call her way of thinking into question.

He glanced at the boys. Cole was talking about how to bait a fishing pole. His eyes met hers again. "He's concerned about all of us losing our privacy, right?"

"Yes." Ashley wanted to add her thoughts that Dayne was wrong to worry about privacy and that she doubted they'd even have issues with the tabloids, but she wanted Landon to finish.

"Okay, so maybe he's decided the trade-off isn't worth it. Risking our privacy all so he can meet up with us a few times a year and realizing every hour he's with us that he has none of our shared memories, no understanding of the trials and tragedies and triumphs this family has been through." Landon brought his fingers to her face and gently touched her cheekbone. "All so maybe he can come to the tougher realization. In every way that matters, he's not really a Baxter at all."

"Landon . . ." Ashley felt her eyes grow wide. "Is that what you think? That he wouldn't fit in? That he wouldn't . . . wouldn't feel accepted by us?"

"No." A still greater kindness shone in his

eyes. "Not at all." He hesitated. "But maybe that's what Dayne's thinking."

She breathed out long and slow. "Oh." Defeat danced across the waters of her heart. "I guess I can't believe he'd really think that." She looked at her lap, trying to imagine the possibility.

"Honey, your dad's waiting for us." He made a move toward the door. "Let's talk about it later."

She swallowed her sorrow and disappointment. If only Dayne would call. Even though it was almost the end of June, it wasn't too late. He could jump on a plane without notice, because he'd done it before. Whenever he needed to talk to Katy.

They helped the boys out of the car. She placed Devin in his stroller while Cole bolted for the front porch.

Before he reached it, Ashley's father stepped out. "Cole, my boy!" He held out his arms.

Cole ran, and the two came together in a swing-you-around-in-a-circle hug only her father could give.

Landon pushed the stroller and met them as they headed into the yard toward the pond. "Come on, Devin. Let's see if Cole can catch you a frog."

Ashley moved slowly toward the porch

and sat in the swing, the one her parents had always shared. The place where she'd come late at night when the trauma of being a teenager was more than she could take. She set the swing in motion and watched the action near the pond.

She thought about Katy and how she knew the truth now. They'd gone walking a few days ago, and Ashley had told Katy about her talk with Dayne. Ashley closed her eyes, and the moment returned. They'd walked around the track at Clear Creek High School, Ashley pushing Devin in the stroller. At first she'd only hinted, wondering if Katy would pick up on where the conversation was headed.

Finally Ashley figured it was better to be straightforward. When there was a break in the conversation, she drew a deep breath. "There's something I have to tell you."

They kept walking, but Katy looked at her, probably surprised by her tone. "Okay."

Ashley took a few more steps, then stopped. "I know Dayne's my brother."

The moment she said it, Katy came to a halt. She swayed, and for a moment it looked as if she might fall to the ground. But then Katy swallowed hard and blinked. "How . . . did you find out?"

"Jenny." Ashley smiled and explained the

situation.

When she was finished, Katy looked dizzy. "I thought you were acting strange that day."

"I could barely breathe." Ashley pushed the stroller, and the two of them started walking again. "Once I knew Dayne was adopted and that his birth parents lived in Bloomington, I remembered the phone call."

"Phone call?" Katy still looked a shade paler than before.

"During the trial. Dayne called my dad's cell, and when I answered he made something up, something about calling to pass on a message from Luke." Ashley tossed up one hand. "I saved his number, of course. Because you never know when you might need Dayne Matthews' cell-phone number."

Katy giggled. "You didn't!"

Ashley explained about her call to Dayne and how it felt to finally know the identity of her brother.

Katy apologized for not saying anything, but Dayne had asked her not to. "Besides, I only found out who his family was the week of the trial."

They spent the rest of their walk talking about Dayne and the way his lifestyle had trapped him. Ashley didn't mention her invitation to Dayne for the Fourth of July or the fact that he seemed determined — for Katy's safety and privacy — to walk away from her as well as from all of them. Those issues needed to be worked out between the two of them.

Ashley opened her eyes, and the memory lifted. She gave the swing a light push with her feet and found her guys by the pond. Her father looked twenty years younger than he had a year ago, and Ashley wondered. He knew that she'd talked to Dayne. An hour after she hung up the phone with her older brother, she finally got ahold of her father and told him about the call.

He wasn't surprised. Relieved, maybe. But not surprised. But then he said something that had rankled her conscience every day since. "Elaine told me it was time to tell you." Something about the way he said her name made him sound a little too peppy. "She said I should call Dayne and tell him we all needed to face the facts — whether all of you ever spent time together or not."

At that point Ashley almost forgot the reason she'd called. All she could think about, the only part of the conversation she walked away with was this: her father was getting advice from another woman, from Elaine Denning, the friend of her mother's. Which was wrong when her mother hadn't even been gone quite two years.

Ashley pursed her lips and blew out. There was too much on her mind to worry about Elaine. At least until after the Fourth. Her father wouldn't be interested in the woman, anyway, would he? She was too quiet, at least from what Ashley remembered.

No, the references to Elaine couldn't account for the gnawing in Ashley's stomach, the way she couldn't quite feel at ease lately. That was because their lakeside picnic was in just a few days, and Dayne still hadn't called. And according to her last talk with Katy, he hadn't contacted her either. Which was really the only explanation for how she'd been feeling lately.

She looked up at the sky and let the expanse of it loosen her tension. *God . . . where is he, and what's he thinking? He wants to meet us; he told me that. So why's he so worried about us? We'll be okay, right? And what about Katy? Nothing's working out, so we need Your help, okay? Please.*

The Lord's comfort was always with her, especially when she talked to Him. But now there was something else too. Not so much an audible answer or even a Scripture came to mind but more of a knowing. As if God was trying to warn her of something she already knew deep within her. The knowing that Dayne wasn't going to call or come to Bloomington.

And that despite everything Ashley had hoped for in the next few days, the sad reality was that they were all about to lose.

CHAPTER
TWENTY-SIX

Dayne grabbed his bags from the limo driver and stood in line at curbside check-in. He wore the baseball cap with the blond hair for this trip too, and so far the paparazzi hadn't figured out that he was on the move again. LAX was crowded, teaming with people heading out for tomorrow's big Independence Day celebration.

It was time to put his list into action. But the things he needed to say and do couldn't be done over the phone, so when the director gave them another three days off for the Fourth, Dayne was convinced. There could be no better time than now.

His disguise worked, and he boarded the plane without being recognized. The next six hours, during the change of planes in Denver and on into Indianapolis, he rehearsed exactly what he wanted to say.

God . . . give me the words. Nothing will be the same after today.

Verses from Ecclesiastes filled his heart, bits of wisdom about happiness and meaning and the transience of life. God would be with him; Dayne could feel His presence already. Whatever he needed to say, the words would be handed to him from the Holy Spirit. He was convinced of that much.

The conversations he needed to hold were private, nothing he wanted the press aware of. Like before, he rented an SUV using the name on his driver's license — Allen Matthews. He couldn't have asked for a nicer day, blue skies and a few puffy white clouds. The humidity was creeping up, but nothing could slow him down. Not with what he had to do.

After all the soul-searching and time on the beach, after his conversations with God and Bob Asher, and even after far too much time had passed, he was about to do the one thing he'd been dying to do: spend an afternoon with Katy Hart.

Missing her had become as common as breathing, a painful part of who he was these days. He wasn't sure how he was going to walk back into her life — even for a day — and tell her the things on his heart. But he had to. Because he wasn't living life for himself anymore. He was living life according to what mattered most. The aspects of his life that God had made clear that day on the Cancun beach were worth going after with every morning he was given from here on.

At three o'clock on July 3 Dayne pulled into the Flanigans' driveway. He could hear his pounding heart. What if Katy didn't want to see him? His surprising her this way would catch her off guard. Maybe she'd disagree with the things he wanted to say. He parked his SUV along the circle leading to the front door. The baseball cap was off, lying on the seat beside him. He took a quick breath, then climbed out and walked to the front door. He knocked, took a step back, and waited.

Whatever her response, he had to do this.

Jenny Flanigan opened the door and stifled a gasp.

Dayne Matthews was standing on her porch, looking like a terrified high school kid. "Hi."

"Hi." Jenny wiped her hands on her shorts. Jim and the kids were out back clearing weeds from the perimeter of their property, and she was making potato salad for tomorrow's swim party at their house. "Is . . . is Katy expecting you?"

"No." His expression was open and sincere. "There's something I have to talk to her about, something I have to ask her."

"Dayne." Jenny laughed and caught her breath at the same time. She opened the door wider and motioned for him to come in. "You amaze me, flying in from Los Angeles to ask Katy a question."

He stepped into the entryway and looked past Jenny, down the hall. "You don't think she'll be mad, do you?"

"Mad?" Jenny's mind was racing. Katy had talked about Dayne and missed him every day since she'd returned from California. No matter how impossible a relationship with him seemed, no matter what the tabloids said or how difficult the last few weeks had been, Katy still couldn't imagine having feelings for anyone else. Jenny kept all of that to herself and smiled at Dayne. "No, she wouldn't be mad. But she's not here."

"She isn't?"

"No." Jenny tucked her hair behind her ears and felt a bit of potato salad on her cheek. Great. Dayne Matthews stops by, and she has food on her face. She wiped at both cheeks, just in case. "Katy's at the theater. Going through props and costumes, taking stock for the fall season."

A shadow of disappointment fell over

Dayne's expression but only for a moment. "Is she by herself?"

"I think so." Jenny motioned to the kitchen. "Want me to call her cell?"

"No." His answer was quick. "I . . . I wanted to surprise her."

"Well, Dayne —" she grinned — "if you walk into the Bloomington Community Theater I have no doubt she'll be surprised. Beyond surprised even."

Dayne laughed and nodded to her. "Tell Jim and the kids I said hi." He moved toward the door. "Maybe I'll see you later today."

"Okay." Jenny was about to ask where Dayne was staying and how long he was in town, but Dayne was already halfway to his SUV.

"Thanks!" He waved once more, got into the driver's seat, and drove off.

As Jenny stepped out on the porch, she smiled. The guy was crazy about Katy; anyone could see that. Now all they had to do was figure out a practical way to act on their feelings. If only he'd take a —

Her thoughts stopped cold. She watched his SUV drive out of sight. What had he said? There was something he had to ask her? Jenny's lips parted, and she tried to imagine what kind of question Dayne might need to ask that would cause him to fly in from Los Angeles.

Chills ran down her arms and legs. A question? The two of them hadn't been together since early May, and they'd had very few phone conversations since. He couldn't be coming here — without warning — to ask her . . . to ask her *that* sort of question, could he?

Jenny's enthusiasm faded. No, that couldn't be it. They hadn't figured out how to date, let alone how they could even consider taking that sort of major step. She bit her lip, disappointed. He probably wanted to ask her to come see him or to attend a movie premiere with him. Something like that.

A scene came to her mind, something from an old movie *An Officer and a Gentleman.* The guy — Richard Gere — is finishing officer's training, and the woman — Debra Winger — is working in a factory, same as her mother and grandmother before her. Every year officers would fall for women who worked at the factory, and every year those women had their hearts broken when the officers graduated and moved on. Always the guys said the same thing. No bridge could span the different lives.

But in the final scene, Gere graduates and heads straight for the factory. Wearing his white officer's uniform, he marches through the rows of women hunched over dreary workstations, sweeps Debra Winger into his arms, and rides off with her on his motorcycle.

Jenny sighed. She walked back into the house and closed the door behind her. For a moment it had been nice to picture Katy in that kind of scene. Being swept off her feet by a guy whose world was so different from hers but who no longer cared. Because love really was enough. She smiled at herself, a sad sort of smile. Nah, that wasn't why Dayne had come; it wasn't why he was so eager to find Katy and ask her a question.

Scenes like that only happened in the movies.

The theater hadn't been used for almost a month, so the first thing Katy did this afternoon was prop open the doors and slide up the windows. Warm, fresh air and sunshine streamed in, touching even the coldest places in her heart.

She had two months before the fall session with CKT and no real plans for the summer. She would visit other CKT offices around the country, of course, and work on next season's lineup. They'd be doing *Joseph, Cinderella,* and *Godspell,* three shows that thrilled her creative team. None of them could wait for fall.

But what was she supposed to do until then?

One week she'd go back to Chicago and visit her parents, and another would be spent leading the kids in the overnight teen camp near Lake Michigan. But otherwise she would probably do what she'd been doing every day since she returned from California.

Missing Dayne Matthews.

He hadn't called recently, so she had to assume he was sticking by his determination. Not only were their worlds too different for anything to come of their feelings for each other, but it was too dangerous. That had been the tipping point. Katy had spent enough time thinking through the situation to understand now. As long as it was only her privacy at stake, both of them had been willing to take chances.

But with the near accident that day as they left Pepperdine, the dangers of his life had become painfully clear. Between knife-wielding fans and paparazzi, Dayne probably couldn't bear the thought of her getting hurt. Finishing things off were the weeks of abuse she'd taken in the tabloids. A few CKT parents still gave her distrusting looks or whispered when she passed by.

Of course he hadn't called.

She walked up the stairs and off to the right of the stage, toward the prop room. It was a huge oversized closet, musty from years of use, and inside were the props they'd used for every show since they first began a few years ago. CKT rented the space for practically nothing, and Katy was glad. This way the props were readily available, and with a little imagination and lots of hard work, they could be transformed for just about any production.

Blocking the way as she opened the door was an eight-foot prelit Christmas tree, dusty and sagging on one side. It had been donated from the Shaffers and had been used in CKT's production of *Annie.* She couldn't look through the props unless she moved it. Katy sized it up. Another person would make the job much easier, but she had come alone. Now she had no choice.

"Okay," she muttered, "here goes." She heaved it from its place and dragged it out through the wings and onto the stage. It wasn't as heavy as it looked, but the cobwebbed branches towered over her, and twice she nearly lost her balance. She was still dragging it when she heard footsteps near the back of the theater.

As she turned toward the noise, her foot slipped and all at once she fell backward and the tree came down squarely on top of her. Laying flat on her back, buried in Christmas tree branches, Katy couldn't find her breath.

"Katy!" The voice was familiar, a man's voice. Almost at the same time there was the sound of running footsteps.

Help . . . Katy tried to cry out, but she had no wind, nothing in her lungs. Panic surged inside her, but then she felt someone moving the tree off her. Whoever the man was, he was strong. In one single motion he lifted the tree and heaved it to the side.

That's when Katy realized she had something in her eyes. Pine needles, maybe. Or dust or cobwebs. Even though the tree was off her, she couldn't see. And she still could barely breathe, but she realized why. The fall had knocked the wind from her.

"Katy . . . are you okay?" The man's voice was urgent, but still it was familiar. He almost sounded like . . . no, that wasn't possible. The man took hold of her arm. "Katy, talk to me."

"I'm . . ." She took small breaths through

her mouth. "I'm okay." The panic subsided, and she exhaled through pinched lips, forcing her lungs to work again. This time she drew a full breath, and she rubbed her eyes with her fists.

The man helped her to a sitting position, and finally she was able to blink her eyes open. Her vision was blurry at first, but then — over a few seconds — it cleared and, like a dream, she was looking into the handsome, terrified face of Dayne Matthews. She squinted, and for the first time she wondered if maybe she was hallucinating. Maybe she'd hit her head harder than she thought. She blinked twice more. "Dayne?"

He was crouched down, holding her arms so she wouldn't fall back. "Did you black out?"

"No." She felt something gritty in her mouth. More cobwebs, no doubt. "I'm fine, I just . . ." How must that have looked? Dayne walks into the theater, and there she is, dragging a Christmas tree across the stage in the heat of July, then falling hard onto her back while the tree literally swallows her whole. A series of giggles built in her, and she began to laugh. If only the paparazzi could've seen that. Her laughter grew stronger.

He stood and allowed a partial smile. "I'll

take that as a good sign."

Between laughs she nodded. "I'm fine. Really." She held out her hand, and he helped her to her feet. Only then did she notice how she looked. The falling tree had covered her with dirt. She dusted off her legs and her shorts, but she had to keep stopping. She was laughing too hard.

Her laughter must've been contagious, because he started to chuckle. "That's what I like about you, Katy." He moved closer, dusting off her arms and picking pine needles from her hair. "Never a dull moment."

"I was pulling the . . ." She found a quick breath between bursts of laughter. "I must've looked ridiculous and then you were there and . . ." Her laughter faded.

Slowly, as if they could both hear the soundtrack switch to violins, the atmosphere changed and the moment felt magical.

Katy's breath caught in her throat, and she searched his eyes. "Dayne —" she sounded breathless — "you . . . you came?"

His arm circled her waist, and he pulled her close. The thudding in their chests was so loud, so strong, in that instant it felt as if they shared the same heart. He brought his hand to her face and dusted a cobweb off her cheek. "I couldn't stay away from you another minute." His voice was a whisper, full of passion and fear and promise and hope.

Tears clouded her eyes and spilled onto her cheeks. She let her forehead fall against him, and her hands encircled his neck. "You're really here." She was still catching her breath from laughing so hard, but now — with Dayne here, with his arms around her, she felt like weeping. She lifted her chin, and her eyes met his. Like every time before, it was easy for her to see past what the world saw, as if she alone had been given access to the private inroads of his heart.

Dayne moved his hands to the small of her back and slid one up between her shoulder blades. The laughter was gone for him too. "How did I ever let you go?" He pressed his cheek to her hair, breathing the words against her ear.

Katy knew what was coming, and she was helpless to stop it. Not that she wanted to, but what was the point? Why had he come at all? Yes, he was wonderful, and yes, she longed to be in this place, lost in his embrace, taken by his voice and his touch. But what sort of person was she to allow herself these feelings when he was only passing through town? The way he always only passed through her life?

Even so, being together like this they needed no words. The feelings between them were more consuming than any dose of common sense. And they only grew as he moved his lips to hers and kissed her. It wasn't the kiss of reckless abandon, of passion without limits. Rather, it was tame and tentative, and it somehow held a promise that surprised her.

He eased back, lost in the moment. "I told you once before, but —" he smiled — "with a dozen cameras snapping pictures it didn't come out like I wanted."

Again she could hardly believe he was here, how good it felt to be in his arms. Why was he doing this? Why had he even come, when moments like this would only prolong her heartache? She could no longer meet his eyes, no longer look into them without losing the battle to her tears. "Dayne . . . don't."

"Katy." He lifted her chin. "Look at me . . . please."

A long breath left her lips, a breath that seemed to come from the deepest parts of her soul. "It feels so right having you here." Her chin quivered, but she managed to find her voice. "But, Dayne, why?" Frustration rang in her tone. "Why, when it'll only be even harder when you go?"

"Ah, Katy." He gave her a sad smile. "I'm so sorry I didn't figure it out sooner."

Figure it out sooner? What was he talking about? She swallowed the lump in her throat and tried to understand. "I don't . . . what do you mean?"

Dayne took a half step backward and worked his fingers between hers. "My buddy Bob Asher asked me to make a list." He gave her a slow smile. "A list of what mattered most to me. Then he told me to spend the rest of my life going after those things."

"A list?" Her heartbeat doubled. Where was he going with this? She reminded herself to breathe.

"First on the list is God. I might've figured it out late, but I have no doubts now." His voice grew softer. "Life is nothing without Him."

Katy nodded. What was he saying? Had he come to tell her more about his faith? Her knees felt weak, but she found a smile. "I'm glad."

"And number two . . ." His eyes grew shiny. When he brushed his lips against hers again, there was no denying his emotion. "Number two is you." His lips parted, and determination added to the mix of feelings in his eyes. "I love you." He kissed her once more. "I couldn't wait another day to tell you."

Katy forgot where she was and who she was and everything except the way she was feeling, the joy dawning on the horizon of her soul. She was no longer on an old stage in the Bloomington Community Theater, no longer on a mission to sort through props and make plans for the fall. There was Dayne and only Dayne.

Then, before she could respond, before she could ask why he would come and tell her this when they'd already agreed nothing could possibly come from it, something happened.

With his eyes locked on hers, Dayne lowered himself to one knee. "Katy . . . I have something to ask you."

What? What was he doing? She moved one hand to her mouth, and a layer of tears clouded her eyes. She must've passed out and fallen into a dream state when the tree hit her. She couldn't possibly be okay. Because she couldn't be watching Dayne Matthews on one knee before her, his eyes lost in hers. "Dayne . . ."

"You know something?"

Katy was shaking. Was this really happening? "What?"

"This." He looked around. "This stage is the first place I ever saw you." He grinned even as tears filled his eyes. "And I haven't stopped thinking about you since." He looked long and deep into her eyes, stripping away all sense of doubt. "I can't promise I have all the answers." He was still holding one of her hands, and now with the other he reached into his pocket and pulled out a small velvet box. "But I want to live here in Bloomington with you, Katy. So that together . . . together we can figure out the answers."

Katy sucked in a quick breath. She blinked back tears and whispered, "Tell me . . . I'm not dreaming."

He released her hand but only long enough to open the box. Inside was a brilliant white-gold solitaire diamond ring. Carefully, he took the ring from the box, set the box on the floor beside him, and reached for her hand again. "You're not dreaming." He cupped his hand around hers and held the ring with his other hand. "God brought you into my life, and I've promised Him that as long as I live —" he smiled softly — "as long as you'll let me, I'll never let you go again." He moved in closer.

Katy could feel it then, the way he, too, was trembling. It was really happening. She wasn't dreaming, imagining this scene. The feel of his hand around hers, the look in his eyes, were far more than a figment of her imagination. She waited, memorizing the expression on his face.

"With you, I'm someone no one else sees, no one else knows." Dayne lifted the ring and held it out to her. "Marry me, Katy. Share your life with me, every tomorrow God gives us. Please . . ."

There was nothing she could do to stop her tears. They came unbidden, reminders that she wasn't dreaming. Then she had a picture in her mind again. Herself, hauling the old Christmas tree onto the stage and falling hard beneath it, being breathless and blinded and covered with cobwebs. And now minutes later Dayne Matthews was asking her to marry him, and suddenly she wasn't sure if she was laughing or crying.

She closed her eyes, allowing the tears and laughter to come at the same time. And that was life, wasn't it? The most brilliant minutes were laced with sorrow, and the saddest ones could still bring a smile. She breathed in sharply through her nose. This time when she opened her eyes, she could feel the joy pouring from them. Maybe her heart would explode from feeling this good. "I can't believe this!" She laughed, and the sound of it danced in the air between them.

Slowly, Dayne rose. He had laughter and

elation and forever in his eyes and something else. A certainty, a resolve, a sense of protection that told her he'd never leave, never want more than what they had together, right here. The ring dangled between two of his fingers, and he held it up. "Does that mean yes?"

"Oh, Dayne." She brought her fingertips to the ring. It was perfect, like the way she always felt when she was with him. When she spoke, she did so straight to his heart, his soul. "Yes. A million times yes."

He slipped the ring onto her finger and over her knuckle. It fit perfectly. "Good." He pressed her hand to his heart and kissed her longer than before. When they both needed a breath, his eyes held the familiar teasing. He nodded toward the Christmas tree. "Because it looks like you have a position open for a props guy."

"Mmm." She put her arms around his neck. "And a sets painter, someone to help your sister."

"Right." He kissed her again, working his hands around her waist. Together they swayed on the stage. "You know what you said a minute ago?"

"About props?"

"No." He gave her a slow smile. "About not believing it?"

"Yes." Of course she remembered. She still felt that way, even with his ring on her finger and his arms around her.

"Well —" he nuzzled his cheek against hers, his voice low — "I can't believe it either." He pulled back just enough to see her. "I looked at that list and realized that it didn't matter. If I had to move to the North Pole or the moon, I'd do it if it meant being with you."

"So Bob told you that, huh? About making the list?" The thought was more than she could imagine. Dayne, who not long ago considered God an enemy, had talked to his missionary friend first when he needed to find his faith and again when he needed to find her.

"Yep." He angled his head. "I figured if God was first and you were second, then I better get out here and let you know what I was feeling."

She was no longer trembling. Instead, in his arms, with the summer breeze and sunlight streaming into the theater, she was surrounded by warmth and love and a certainty that God was here with them. "So what was third?"

"On the list?"

"Mmm-hmm."

Some of the easy joy in his expression was

replaced by a more serious determination. "The third thing was family."

A dozen thoughts hit her at once. Of course family would come next. What had he said before? That he wanted to live in Bloomington. Which meant that he'd be in the same town, shopping at the same stores, and maybe even attending the same church as the Baxters. Katy could still see the look on Ashley's face, hear the way she'd sounded when she talked about her older brother and how badly she wanted to connect with him. But how hopeless the situation seemed. She ran her thumb along his brow. "I'm glad. The Baxters want to meet you so badly."

"I know." A hint of anxiety darkened his expression. "We have to pray about the tabloids, where it all goes."

"We will."

"Speaking of family . . ." Dayne relaxed, and the joy returned. "Do you have plans for tomorrow?"

"Swim party with the Flanigans. But I can get out of it." She loved everything about how she felt. The ring on her finger was from the man she had longed for every day they were apart. He was here now and he was offering her forever, and all the world was bright sunshine and rainbows. "Why?"

"Because —" he kissed her hand, the one with the ring — "I want to take you to a picnic."

CHAPTER
TWENTY-SEVEN

The early afternoon was cool under a sky of mixed clouds and sunny patches of blue, and the sounds indicated that another Baxter picnic was well under way. Ashley sat on a blanket at the top of the hill, little Devin asleep in the baby seat beside her.

Obviously Dayne wasn't coming. She'd resigned herself to that yesterday morning. Instead of being angry or hurt, she had spent half an hour praying for him, asking God to give them another chance, another day, when they might all come together. If Dayne wasn't ready now, then there was nothing she could do to change his mind.

Ashley watched her family playing hard along the shore of Lake Monroe. Kari and Ryan were sculpting a sea turtle in the sand, with the help of Jessie and Hayley and Maddie and Cole — all in life jackets. Nearby, little Ryan watched from his playpen. Ten yards away, Brooke and Peter sat on a towel, their arms around each other, staring out at the water. They were closer than ever, the faith they shared testimony to everything both sets of their parents held dear.

Landon was fishing on a grassy bank next to her father. Ashley smiled as she watched them. Long ago, her precious old friend Irvel had talked about her beloved Hank and how he loved to fish. Maybe, if Ashley was very lucky, God would let her have the same sort of memories about Landon one day.

Ashley recalled their conversation from earlier. They'd been packing the Durango, and Landon headed out with his fishing gear.

"Fishing?" She gave him a puzzled look. "It's a picnic, honey."

"I know." He winked at Cole, who fell in beside him carrying the tackle box. "But nothing tastes better on the barbecue than fresh-caught fish."

Ashley wrinkled her nose. "Fresh-caught —"

"Hey, Daddy —" Cole looked up at him — "aren't you gonna tell her about the bet?"

The pieces started coming together. "Bet?"

"Yeah." Cole grinned at her. "Papa and Daddy have a bet. Whoever catches the biggest fish, the other guy has to jump in the lake with his clothes on!"

She put her hands on her hips and tried not to laugh. "Oh, sure, Landon. Forget hamburgers and hot dogs. Nothing like fresh-caught fish on the Fourth of July."

"Okay, so I wanna beat him." Landon raised his pole in the air. "I, for one, can't wait to see your dad jump in the water with his clothes on."

Ashley laughed at the memory. Her dad and Landon had gotten closer since her mother's death. They shared something easy and genuine and a common love for helping people.

As she watched them, Landon's pole jerked, and he jumped to his feet. "Here it is!" His voice carried up the hillside. "The winning catch!"

"You took my fish!" John stood. His laughter sounded wonderful.

Landon reeled as hard as he could. "*My* fish, Dad . . . it's my fish." He braced himself, and the pole in his hand bent over beneath the weight of whatever he'd caught.

Kari and Ryan and the kids scrambled over to see, and Brooke and Peter watched from their place on the towel. Just then a clump of sticks and water plants broke through the surface at the end of Landon's line, splashing him and causing him to fall to the ground.

Ashley snickered and sat up straighter so she could see.

Cole was first to Landon's catch. "Daddy, where's the fish?"

"Yeah." Her dad helped Landon to his feet, then patted his back. "Nice catch."

"Wait!" Cole pointed at the twist of wood and greens. "There *is* a fish! Deep inside there. Look!"

Landon set his pole on the bank and joined Cole. "He's right . . . there is!" Landon tore away the wood and pulled back the tangled water plants, and after a minute of struggling he removed a fish. A fish so small, Ashley could barely make it out from her place on the hillside.

"Nice." Her father started laughing again.

Landon joined him. "But does the stick count? It's longer than anything you've caught."

The silliness grew, and the others chimed in. The sounds blended and became as familiar as a song. The Baxters laughing together. Ashley was giggling quietly under her breath when she heard something behind her, footsteps and hushed voices.

She turned around and tried to look, but the sun was in her eyes. She held her hand over her brow and saw that it was two people, a couple. Then her heart skipped a beat. Katy Hart was one of them, and the other . . .

Was she seeing things? Could he really have come after all? Goose bumps broke out along her bare arms and legs. In as much time as it took for her to stand, she had no doubt. The other person was Dayne Matthews. He was here! In time for the Baxter picnic!

Katy was smiling, looking straight at her. She and Dayne stopped, and he whispered something to her. She nodded and ran lightly down the hill toward the others. As she passed, she grinned at Ashley and pointed toward heaven. The sign was understandable. A miracle was taking place. There could be no other answer.

Ashley turned back toward Dayne. He hadn't moved, and he was watching her. He glanced toward the others, then crooked his finger and motioned for her to come. From the place where he was standing, the rest of the family couldn't see him.

He didn't have to ask her twice. She brushed the grass off her shorts and walked toward him. The closer she came, the less she saw Dayne Matthews, the movie star and celebrity. Here — standing before her

— was her parents' firstborn son. A brother who was every bit as related to her as Luke.

When she reached him, she stopped and searched his face. "You came." Her words were pinched with emotion, and tears stung her eyes.

"Sorry I didn't call."

"That's okay." Ashley was winded, her heart too full to draw a breath. "What . . . what changed your mind?"

Dayne stuck his hands in his pockets and shrugged. "All my life —" he bit his lip, as if he was struggling with his own feelings — "I've wanted a family."

"And all our lives," she said, taking a step closer, "we've missed having our brother." She let loose a single cry. "Even if we didn't know about you."

He held out his arms and pulled her into a hug, one that erased any trace of awkwardness between them. "I can't believe I'm here."

Ashley stepped back, but she took Dayne's hand. She looked over her shoulder. "You and Katy?" Her eyes met his. Last time she'd talked to Katy, her friend had figured she might never see Dayne again.

Dayne's eyes shone. "I asked her to marry me." He looked out at the lake and then back at her. "I want to live here and raise a family, and somehow — with God making it possible — I want to be part of this too. A part of the Baxters."

A ripple of laughter came from her heart and across her lips. Ashley tilted her head back. "I can't believe this. Thank You, God!" She gave him another quick hug. "I didn't think it would happen! My mother . . . Mom loved you so much, Dayne. I can feel her smiling down on us."

"Me too." He looked down the hill in the direction Katy had gone. A nervousness crept into his tone. "Is . . . is everyone here?"

"Not Luke or Erin or their families but everyone else. Yes." She laughed, and it held the sound of victory. Everything was going to work out after all. How amazing was God to give them this, after all the pain and heartache her parents had been through giving away their firstborn son, after all the years of longing and wondering. How great that God would bring Dayne into their family now, that he would marry Katy Hart and want to live in Bloomington. It was more than Ashley could take in.

She led Dayne down the hill. "Come on." There was a catch in her voice. "Dad's been waiting for this moment all his life."

So far John was winning. He had a ten-inch

trout in his bucket, and everything Landon had caught was either not a fish or too small to keep. The others, including Katy, had gone back to sculpting their sea turtle, and the banter between him and Landon was easy.

With Luke gone, he felt closest to Landon. Maybe because they both understood hospital work — John as a doctor and Landon as a firefighter. Or maybe because of the time when Landon had been critically injured saving the life of a small boy in a house fire. John had stayed by his side, carefully administering the right balance of oxygen and moisture and medication to Landon's damaged lungs.

Or maybe because God had used Landon to answer his prayers for his precious Ashley. Where would she be if it weren't for this young man sitting beside him? The way he'd loved her little Cole, the way he'd waited for her and sought her and understood her — even when she hated herself. Landon's patience and love could have only come from God.

Whatever it was, he enjoyed his son-in-law, and sometime later today he was going to enjoy watching him jump in the lake with his clothes on. Because John couldn't let the next generation beat him at a fishing contest. He rested his arms on his knees, his fishing pole balanced in one hand, and glanced at Landon. "Maybe it's your bait."

Landon had just finished putting a lure on his hook. "My bait?" He cast out thirty feet. There was laughter in his voice. "What about it?"

"Well —" John pointed to the tackle box — "I hear driftwood's crazy about those sorts of lures."

"Yes. Very funny." Landon raised his eyes. "Listen, it's not every fisherman who can snag the big driftwood. I want you to know that."

John was about to say something about Landon's lures scaring the fish in his direction when he heard Ashley's voice. "Dad . . . Dad, come here."

He looked over his shoulder, and what he saw made the blood leave his face. Ashley was walking toward him, a grin spread across her face, her arm linked through the arm of . . . Dayne. Without looking away, John set down his pole, stood, and faced the two of them. His children.

The others were watching, puzzled as to what was happening. Kari and Ryan stood and brushed the sand from their hands and legs; then Brooke and Peter rose. Katy Hart took a step back, giving them this moment.

The grandchildren glanced at the newcomer but then returned to their sea turtle.

Landon set down his pole and anchored himself next to John. "Ashley invited him."

"I . . . I see that." John's eyes blurred, and he struggled to keep from breaking down. Dayne, his firstborn son, was here. Here where he belonged. Was this really when everything would come together, here on the beach at one of the Baxter picnics? The moment Elizabeth had longed for all their married lives? He took a step closer, his eyes glued to Dayne's.

Kari and Ryan, Peter and Brooke moved in closer, looking from Dayne to their father. John saw Kari shoot a silent question at Ashley, and Ashley nodded.

Dayne looked at them, each of them one at a time; then he found John again. He pressed his wrist to one eye and then the other, and suddenly John understood why he wasn't talking. He couldn't.

But John couldn't either. How was he supposed to explain the situation now that Dayne was here? Would the others understand? Would they even believe it was possible that Dayne Matthews was their brother? He opened his mouth, but nothing came out, so instead of talking he closed the gap between him and his firstborn. Ashley stepped aside, and he hugged Dayne hard and sure. "Thank you . . . for coming." John could barely get out the words.

"I had to." Dayne whispered the words, so only John could hear them. "My sister invited me." When they pulled back, the emotions left them both speechless again.

Ashley looked at Kari and then at Brooke. "Everyone . . . I'd like you to meet our brother."

Understanding seemed to dawn on Kari and Brooke at the same time.

Kari gasped and looked from Dayne to John. "He's our . . . ?"

John still couldn't find his voice. He only nodded and wiped at the tears on his cheeks.

Brooke stepped up first. She went to Dayne and started to hold out her hand. Then she changed her mind and threw her arms around his neck. "Welcome, brother." She held on several seconds, and when she let go her face was wet too. "I've been praying we might meet you."

The shock faded from Kari's face, and it was her turn. She, too, hugged Dayne. "Now we know —" she searched his face — "why you and Luke look so much alike."

"Yes." He smiled, but John could see the loss in his eyes. The years they'd missed would always be a source of sorrow. Dayne looked from Ashley to Kari to Brooke. "I never thought this day would come."

Multiple conversations broke out, and in the background little Ryan started crying for his mother. Ashley's baby was still asleep in his car seat a few feet up the hill, but the other children seemed to sense something big was taking place. They joined the circle as the men shook Dayne's hand, welcoming him and making small talk.

"Hey!" Landon broke free from the group and scrambled for his fishing rod. "I've got it! Look, for real this time!" His pole had been sitting against a log, his hook and bait in the water, same as John's. As he reached the rod, he jerked it back, and like before, he dug in his heels and began cranking his reel at a record pace. Just as he pulled up another clump of driftwood, John's rod began to move.

"Here I come!" John held up his hand and began jogging toward his pole. All the grandkids followed him, like an impromptu Fourth of July parade. Even though John walked on the treadmill every day, he was breathless when he reached his pole and grabbed it, careful to keep the tension in the line. He reeled and reeled, while beside him his grandkids cheered.

"Papa!" Hayley, who was walking better every day, clapped. "Big fishie!"

"There's no way you've got a fish on that line!" Landon tossed his rod on the ground and moved in closer.

Behind them, John heard Dayne ask what was at stake, and Kari explained the contest. The tension built as John turned the reel again and again.

"Wow!" Cole jumped four times in place. "Papa, you beat my daddy good this time."

John started to bring the fish in. It had to be eighteen inches long — more than twice the size of anything Landon had caught.

Cole rushed up to help him unhook it and slip it into the bucket. "Fish tonight!" Cole raised his fist in the air. Then almost as quickly, his smile faded and he looked at Landon. "Sorry, Daddy."

Landon held his hands up in mock surrender. "Fine." He kicked off his shoes, cleared a path through the children, ran down the shore and into the water.

The kids cheered and danced along the sandy beach, pointing at Landon and laughing.

When Landon was waist deep, he flopped backward and disappeared underwater. A few seconds later he burst back through the surface, his face taken up by a huge smile.

He cupped his hands around his mouth. "There," he shouted, "I hope you're all happy!"

"Come get me, Daddy!" Cole stripped down to his bathing suit and scurried toward the water.

John watched all the activity quietly. A long time ago, when he and Elizabeth first married, they took a trip to Fort Myers Beach. Not far from their hotel was a flower garden, and one day on their walk to the water Elizabeth picked a bright red rose. She stopped, the ocean spread out behind her, placed the rose between her teeth, and faced him. "Take it," she mumbled through her clenched teeth.

John remembered how his heart had melted. "What am I going to do with you?" He took the rose and held it close. "I fall more in love with you every day, Elizabeth Baxter."

"Then take a picture." Her tone had been playful. She took the rose back from him. "That way you'll never forget."

He'd laughed and raised his eyebrows at her. "One problem. I don't have my camera."

"I know." She made a silly face and put the flower between her teeth again. With her jaw clenched she managed to say, "Take a mental picture."

Take a mental picture.

It was something the two of them had said to each other often through the years, raising their children and living everyday life. Whenever something happened that they wanted to remember forever.

Now John looked at his older son — the child he never thought he'd meet — talking and laughing as if he'd always been a part of their family. They had a lot to work through. Erin and Sam and Luke and Reagan needed to know the news, and one day — hopefully one day soon — everyone would find a way to be together. But for now, he could hardly believe the scene playing out bigger than life before him.

As the afternoon wore on and boats zigzagged across Lake Monroe in the distance, John studied Dayne and he could see the resemblance, the way he moved like Luke and laughed like Ashley. Everything else faded as he watched Kari put her hand on Dayne's shoulder and whisper something close to his ear and Dayne chuckle as if whatever she'd told him was the funniest thing he'd ever heard. He watched Ashley chatting with Katy, and that's when he saw it. The ring on her finger. And he knew — he just knew — that Dayne had asked her to marry him.

He watched Brooke and Peter chasing Hayley and Maddie along the damp sand and Brooke take hold of Dayne's arm as she ran by, looping around him and using him as a decoy, and Dayne laughing hard as he joined in the chase.

As John watched his family at play, his heart hurt for missing Elizabeth. She would've loved this moment. *God, please let her see that it's happening. Dayne's really becoming a part of our family.*

He smiled because he could feel the Lord's hand on his family, their relationships, and everything about the moment. There would always be trials — Jesus promised that much. But with his family together, they could get through anything. Then, his eyes never leaving the happy scene, he captured it in his heart and did what Elizabeth would do.

He took a mental picture. One that would last until he drew his final breath.

The picnic was over, and Dayne hadn't had so much fun in all his life. Not at movie premieres or nightclubs or on location — not ever. Katy sat beside him as they drove out of the parking lot. They were headed to the Baxter house, where Landon had asked him to help light the kids' sparklers.

They rode in silence, not because Dayne didn't have anything to say. More because Katy understood him, understood that this was something he needed to savor — the feeling he had after spending a few hours with the Baxters.

He held Katy's hand and couldn't get the smile off his face. "It's amazing."

"Yes." She didn't have to ask what he meant.

Every time they'd had a minute alone, Dayne had gushed about how wonderful they were, how funny and well connected.

She would laugh at him because she'd known them first. "Of course they're wonderful." She'd give him a kiss. "They're related to you."

There was a slight sorrow to the feeling of joy, because this was what he'd missed. All those years alone, living in LA, he'd missed watching his siblings grow up and get married and have babies. He'd missed birthdays and Christmas mornings and graduations. He'd missed more than he could even comprehend.

But he wouldn't dwell on that. God had given him this day, and somehow God would give him tomorrow with the Baxters as well. He and Katy, living in Bloomington, spending summer afternoons here at the lake with Ashley and Landon, Kari and Ryan, Brooke and Peter. And their wonderful kids.

Dayne still wasn't sure how it would come together, how he would create a life with Katy and the Baxters and still fulfill his contracts with the studio, or how he would ever live a normal life — the way he'd lived it this afternoon. But he didn't need all the answers. God would take care of that part too.

Because being with his family had given him a feeling he'd never known before. He could hardly wait for the evening, setting off sparklers in the Baxters' driveway, catching fireflies with the little girls, and sitting around getting to know his sisters and their husbands. The emotion was more than he could put into words.

He was following Ashley and Landon's Durango, and he wondered if maybe the sensation was one of freedom. Appropriate for an Independence Day celebration. Because he'd escaped the paparazzi for a few days. But as the Durango slowed, as it turned into a long driveway that cut through a vast grassy field and headed toward a beautiful country house, complete with a wrap-around porch, he suddenly realized what the feeling was.

It didn't come from the freedom he was experiencing. The emotion came because for the first time he felt the sense of belonging, of being connected to people who cared about him, not because of what he'd done but because of who he was. The feeling of love and laughter and acceptance and encouragement — completely unscripted.

Dayne smiled as he parked his rented SUV, as he squeezed Katy's hand and looked through the windshield at the Baxter house.

The feeling became more obvious with every heartbeat because it was something he'd longed for a lifetime.

The feeling of family.

A WORD FROM
KAREN KINGSBURY

DEAR FRIENDS,

It gets harder and harder to write these books, because I know each one takes me closer to the last book — the last time I'll write about the Baxters and Katy and Dayne and the Flanigans. I still have a while, of course. One more book in the Firstborn series, then four books in the Sunrise series — which will focus on the Flanigans but will include constant involvement with the Baxters and Katy and Dayne.

The other day I was at a book event in Pennsylvania, meeting many of my reader friends, when one woman put it perfectly. "I love these books because the Baxters are family to me."

I guess I realized it then. The reason these series will be hard to wrap up is because the characters feel like family to me too. They sort of live in the recesses of my mind, and even when I'm not writing about them I can check in with them and see how they're doing.

I know . . . that sounds a little crazy. My husband always teases me about my close connection with these fictional people. He often says that when I'm old and forgetful, I'll probably get our kids and my characters mixed up. "I can just hear you," he says, "saying, 'That Ashley! She never calls, never writes!' "

We share a good laugh over it, but there's a deeper truth that always stands out when we talk about these series — the importance of family.

One of the key things I felt God wanted me to illustrate with the Firstborn series was that nothing compares to having a family. Not fame or success or wealth or popularity, not having the right job or the right car or the right clothes. All of that can get us by, and to the world we can look like we're doing pretty well. But without family, it's a lonely life we come home to.

Now I know some of you reading this are thinking you'd give anything to have a family. Your lonely life has not come by your choosing. For you, I can only say hold on. God wants you involved with people. If your biological family has died or moved away, He wants you teaching a Sunday school class or attending a small group, joining an outreach ministry, or volunteering at the church library. Churches are supposed to be families, and whether you have one waiting for you at home or not, becoming part of a church family will make your life rich.

That said, most of you do have a biological family — a group of ragtag people who don't always say and do the right things but who gather around the dinner table with you each night or show up at birthdays and Christmastime. Think about those people. That's something I did as I wrote this book; I spent a lot of time thinking about my family.

God has put your family members in your life for a reason. They may not all be lovable, but they all need loving. Sometimes getting past the hurts and strained relationships that can come up in families is as simple as making a choice to love.

And so I thought I'd share three things that our families need from us — whether children, siblings, parents, or distant relatives. These are things I've noticed while raising a family these past seventeen years. They need our time, our touch, and our testimony.

Time is fleeting, no question. Around our house we smile and say, "Time is a thief!"

and it's true. I like telling how one spring day my husband and I dragged our kids from a quaint play area at Sea World and hurried them across the park to the sea lion show.

Out of breath and a few minutes late, we hurried to the top of the stairs and searched for a seat. There was one row still open, about two-thirds of the way down. I pointed at it and took off, but there was a problem. The steps alternated in width — big, small, big, small — and while my foot fit nicely on the first step, I completely missed the second one.

The tumble down those stairs caught the attention of the entire stadium — including the sea lions, who were already onstage. Many people turned their video cameras toward me thinking I was part of the show. To make matters worse, I had on a backpack full of our kids' belongings, so as I rolled and fell and sputtered, things were preceding me down the stairs. Water bottles, combs, ChapStick, apples. I was truly a sight.

As it turned out, I stopped rolling and falling right at the empty row. I stood up, waved off the crowd, and motioned for my husband — still standing shell-shocked at the top of the stairs — to bring the children and join me.

Later, when I was certain I had no broken bones, I took stock of the fiasco and realized something. What was my hurry? It was supposed to be a day with the kids, time to make memories together and appreciate the sights at the park. Why didn't I stay at the quaint play area and push my kids on the swings? Couldn't we have caught a later viewing of the sea lion show?

The ordeal reminded me that our families need time. National statistics say that most parents spend only three minutes each day having one-on-one time with their kids. Let's make sure we spend more time than that with the people we love.

Our families also need our touch. A pat on the back, a hand hold, a hug — these are very real ways to communicate love. A study on the power of touch was conducted at a Korean orphanage. Babies were split into two groups. The first received only nominal, standard care as was the practice at the facility. The second group was given fifteen minutes additional time in the arms of the workers. During that period, the babies were cradled and cooed at, their tiny arms and legs stroked by the workers.

The results of the study were mind-boggling. The babies in the second group thrived beyond anyone's imagination. They gained weight and height and head circumference and suffered 90 percent fewer illnesses. Though the study lasted just six weeks, the benefits could be seen in the babies until their first birthdays.

Please . . . hug the people in your life. Let them know you care. My brother who died this past October was an amazing hugger. He couldn't always say the words, but I knew he loved me because of his hugs.

Finally, the people you love need your testimony, your story. Every one of you reading this has a story, something you've overcome or a lesson you've learned. A journey of faith. Take time to work your history into the conversations you have with your families.

My husband was one of those few young men who — when I met him — made it clear that he wanted to be sexually pure. His dedication to God turned my head and made me take a long look at faith. Eventually I gave my life to the Lord because of what I saw in him. Now it's up to us to share that story with our children so they'll understand purity in a very personal way.

In some ways I see all of you as part of my extended family. If you've read these books, then you already know a great deal about my heart. When we connect on my Web site (www.KarenKingsbury.com) through the pages dedicated to discussion or prayer requests and through my weekly journal of happenings or at one of my events, I truly feel like I'm meeting a friend. I pray for you daily, that God would use the power of story to deepen your faith and change your relationships. How awesome is our God that He gives us these fictional people to teach us truths that can help us every day. They help me; I know that.

By the way, I'm starting a new and ongoing contest. Each spring I will pick one winner and fly that person and a friend out to the Pacific Northwest for a summer day with me and my family. We'll see the sights and share meals and laughter and make memories we won't forget. In addition, you will go on a forever list to receive a free, signed Karen Kingsbury book for every new release I have from here on out. As long as I'm writing books!

Here's how you enter.

Share a Book — Spend a Day with Karen Contest

1. Lend one of my novels to someone you know, someone who hasn't read one

before. This person can be a friend, a neighbor, a cashier at your local grocer, someone at church, or a family member. Even a stranger. Anyone who hasn't read a Karen Kingsbury book. Life-Changing Fiction isn't life-changing unless it's being read.

2. Next, contact me at my Web site, www .KarenKingsbury.com. E-mail me with the subject line: *Shared a Book.* In the body of the e-mail, tell me the first name of the person you shared my book with and why you felt compelled to share it. Also include your contact information. This will enter you into the drawing.

What you win:

1. A trip to the Pacific Northwest, where you and a friend will spend a day with me and my family.

2. One copy of a signed Karen Kingsbury book for every release I have thereafter.

By doing these two simple steps, you will automatically be entered into a drawing. If you share one of my books with more than one person, please feel free to enter each time. The first drawing will be held at the end of March 2007, and the winner will be selected at random. The first prize-winning trip will take place the following summer. After that, I will choose a winner each March until further notice. You can check www.KarenKingsbury.com to make sure this contest is still ongoing.

I pray this finds you healthy and happy and drawing closer to the families you're a part of. As for me, I'm taking time to play some Frisbee with my kids today. I'm sure I'll get a chance to hug them a little in the process.

Until next time, in His light and love,
Karen Kingsbury

DISCUSSION QUESTIONS

Use these questions for individual reflection or for discussion with a book club or other small group. They will help you not only understand some of the issues in *Family* but also integrate some of the book's messages into your own life.

1. Fear was something that marked Katy's time with Dayne from the beginning. Explain a few of the things Katy was afraid of.
2. Explain when fear was part of one of your relationships. Discuss how your situation was similar to Katy's and Dayne's or how it was different.
3. What were Dayne's concerns as the trial began? What were his hopes?
4. Fear also played a role in John Baxter's decision to keep information from his children. What did you think about this?
5. Was there a time when you withheld

information from your children? Share the details and how they are similar to John's situation.

6. Have you ever wanted to be a celebrity? Why or why not?

7. What do you feel is right or wrong with our society's fascination with celebrities?

8. What was the turning point that caused Dayne to believe his blossoming relationship with Katy was over? What was his motivation for this?

9. Which of the Baxter kids are you most like? Brooke, Kari, Ashley, Erin, or Luke? Explain why.

10. Talk about the different personalities in your family or a family you're connected with and how they work together.

11. Can you see comparisons between some of your family members and the Baxter family? Who and why?

12. Why was Ashley so adamant about meeting her older brother?

13. What advice did Dayne's missionary friend Bob Asher give him?

14. Has there ever been a time in your life when you needed that sort of advice? Discuss this.

15. If you listed what was important to you, what would the first five things be? Evaluate whether you are living your life accord-

ing to that list.

16. What role does Jenny Flanigan play in Katy Hart's life? Do you have a similar relationship with your mother or father or with an older, respected friend?

17. What is the importance of having someone you can call for advice? Think about whom you call when you're struggling. Share your thoughts on this.

18. How did Ashley see Dayne the first time they met? As a movie star or as her older brother? Explain this.

19. The Baxters frequently get together for picnics and dinners. Talk about how often you spend time with your family. What is the importance of such gatherings?

20. Define the word *family.* What does it mean to you? How can you improve the relationships you have with yours?

ABOUT THE AUTHOR

Karen Kingsbury is the bestselling author of eighteen books, with a total of more than 1.3 million copies in print. She is also a recognized author with the Women of Faith Fiction Club. One of her books was made into a CBS *Movie of the Week*. Karen lives in Washington state with her husband and six children.